Praise for *Path of Fate*

"What's better than a story about a stubborn, likable hero-
ine thrust into events fraught with danger, wizards, and
gods? Well, all of the above, plus a goshawk. . . . I thoroughly enjoyed *Path of Fate* by the talented Diana Pharaoh
Francis and look forward to more of the adventures of
Reisil and her goshawk, Saljane."
            —Kristen Britain, bestselling author of *Green Rider*

"This is an entertaining book—at times compelling—from
one of fantasy's promising new voices."
                    —David B. Coe, award-winning
                        author of *Seeds of Betrayal*

"In this delightful debut, Diana Pharaoh Francis caught me
with a compelling story, intrigued me with the magic of her
ahalad-kaaslane, and swept me away with her masterful feel
for the natural world."   —Carol Berg, critically acclaimed
                        author of *Guardians of the Keep*

"Plausible, engrossing characters, a well-designed world,
and a well-realized plot."   —*Booklist*

Path of Honor

Diana Pharaoh Francis

A ROC BOOK

ROC

Published by New American Library, a division of
Penguin Group (USA) Inc., 375 Hudson Street,
New York, New York 10014, USA
Penguin Group (Canada), 10 Alcorn Avenue, Toronto,
Ontario M4V 3B2, Canada (a division of Pearson Penguin Canada Inc.)
Penguin Books Ltd., 80 Strand, London WC2R 0RL, England
Penguin Ireland, 25 St. Stephen's Green, Dublin 2,
Ireland (a division of Penguin Books Ltd.)
Penguin Group (Australia), 250 Camberwell Road, Camberwell, Victoria 3124,
Australia (a division of Pearson Australia Group Pty. Ltd.)
Penguin Books India Pvt. Ltd., 11 Community Centre, Panchsheel Park,
New Delhi - 110 017, India
Penguin Group (NZ), Cnr Airborne and Rosedale Roads, Albany,
Auckland 1310, New Zealand (a division of Pearson New Zealand Ltd.)
Penguin Books (South Africa) (Pty.) Ltd., 24 Sturdee Avenue,
Rosebank, Johannesburg 2196, South Africa

Penguin Books Ltd., Registered Offices:
80 Strand, London WC2R 0RL, England

First published by Roc, an imprint of New American Library,
a division of Penguin Group (USA) Inc.

First Printing, December 2004
10 9 8 7 6 5 4 3 2 1

Copyright © Diana Pharaoh Francis, 2004
All rights reserved

Cover art by Alan Pollack

ROC REGISTERED TRADEMARK—MARCA REGISTRADA

Printed in the United States of America

For Tony

Acknowledgments

Thanks go to Tony for all his support, for giving me time, and for making me laugh. To my mother and father for trumpeting the word to the planet about *Path of Fate*. To the Roundtable Writers, especially Fighter Guy. To Alan Pollack for yet another fabulous cover. And to my readers who spend their time and money to let me keep doing what I love. Thank you all.

Prologue

Rain drove the wind through the canopy and washed down the mountain in fierce torrents. Nicxira bent crablike and struggled up the path. Water ran over her bare feet and hands as she grasped tiny outcroppings. Her fingernails tore, and her long hair clung to her arms and back. At last she came to the lip of the sacred road girdling the top of the mountain. She hauled herself over the edge and started running, her bare feet splashing in the swift river of rainwater. She came to the south basin, skirting it carefully. At the south basin, she paused at the shrine to offer a handful of kalmut grain from the pouch at her waist. She ran on, pain stitching beneath her ribs. She passed the east and north basins, repeating her offering, stopping at last at the west. She piled the kalmut offering in the shrine and stripped, leaving only the tiny, chipped-obsidian knife dangling on a leather thong between her breasts. She slid into the water, comfortably warm with the mix of rainwater cooling its heated depths. The bottom was curved like two cupped hands, making it impossible for her to stand. Nicxira bathed quickly. Somewhere ahead on the path was Kinatl.

She hoisted herself out of the basin and returned to the path, leaving behind her clothing. She found the stair upward and started climbing, her limbs warming. More than once Nicxira thought to rest, but though her legs burned and her lungs ached, she dared not. If Kinatl succeeded . . . She groaned. It was her fault. Taunting Kinatl, making such a show of having greater powers. Now Kinatl was going to ask the gods for more, for greater magic. As if the gods were so easily prevailed upon.

At last the stairs ended. Nicxira stepped out onto the

mountaintop, the rain and wind battering at her, driving
her back. She struggled forward, feeling the ridges in the
stone beneath her feet. Long ago, the Monequi had been
the sacred gathering place of the Teotl, the fifty-two gods.
The top of the mountain had been sheared off as if sliced
by a knife, and the names and faces of each of the gods
had been etched in the stone.

Nicxira hunched her shoulders, cold making her flesh
prickle like a plucked bird's. She could not see Kinatl, but
that meant nothing. Nicxira could hardly see her own outstretched hands through the streaming rain. She started
toward the middle of the sacred circle toward the image of
Ilhuicatl. Father of the gods and creator of the nahuallis,
he was the one Nicxira would choose if she was seeking
favor. She pushed slowly into the pummeling wind, hoping
she'd be in time.

Of all the Teotl, only Ilhuicatl was represented in his
entirety. Man-shaped, his body stretched more than a hundred paces. Serpents wrapped themselves around his legs
and arms. His penis stretched in a great staff, sprinkling
rain and life from its spearpoint head. In his hands he held
a sun and a moon. On his head he wore a feathered head-
dress, and around his neck was a string of skulls. His mouth
gaped open. A trick of the mountain drained it so that the
rainwater did not collect inside. Nicxira made her way
around the god's likeness, searching for Kinatl. But there
was no sign of the other woman. Her stomach tightened,
and she knew what she must do.

Nicxira paused beside Ilhuicatl's gaping mouth. She
dropped down inside. The flat, moist bottom was warm
against her bare feet. Without hesitation, she lifted the ob-
sidian knife from around her neck and sliced across her
wrists. Blood ran from the wounds, mixing with the rain.
Nicxira sank to the hot floor. She closed her eyes and began
to pray, using the old words, those Ilhuicatl had given to
the nahualli before the scattering.

Time passed. The heat intensified. If not for the rain, she
thought she might have burst into flame. Her blood continued to trickle. Dizziness crept over her, and her words
slurred. She felt her heart slowing and struggled to breathe.

"You have sought me. You have given me your blood.
Your life. Tell me your need."

The words rumbled through her like an earthquake. Nicxira blinked. She found herself sitting on a vast gold plain. Above there was blackness, and coiled in front of her was a tiny snake. Its head was triangular, and it was the color of fresh grass, its stomach as red as her blood. It stared at her with brilliant yellow eyes, the tip of its tail twitching.

Nicxira licked her lips, sitting up straight. What to say? She'd been prideful and foolish, and now Kinatl had risked herself, perhaps thrown herself away. There was no asking forgiveness, only help in restoring balance to the tribe. There were too few nahuallis now to chase even one away, and with her actions, she might have lost the tribe two. How could she balance that?

"I seek aid for my sister. She sought greater powers because I goaded her. If she has been punished for overstepping, then I ask to take her place so that she may return home."

"Ah." The snake's bright yellow tongue flicked out. "She did not come to me. I have nothing to give you."

Nicxira stiffened. Kinatl had not gone to Ilhuicatl? But surely she knew how capricious the others were, and how little they cared for the nahuallis. Nicxira swallowed, under the snake's unwavering gaze.

"I fear for her," she said. "How can I help her?"

There was the faintest pause.

"She has made her choices. She will become what she is meant to be. But what about you? Have you nothing else to ask?"

Nicxira shook her head. She'd been proud and greedy. She would not be so again.

"Nothing for all the blood you spend? Even now your body dies." The voice was cold and reproving.

"I would serve," Nicxira said. "I would ask you for a task. For balance."

"Ah. And what if that task required great sacrifice?"

"I am nahualli."

"Then you shall have your wish. There comes that which even the Teotl may not stop. Does that frighten you? Good. Because it will remake everything, including the gods. There may be no hope. I cannot see so far. But the Teotl takes what steps it may to salvage what we can. Go now to she who waits; serve her well. For in serving her, you serve us all."

The snake's mouth opened, tiny teeth shining. It struck her wrist where blood continued to spill. Nicxira screamed, pain sluicing over her in rising waves.

She woke again, this time in a glade. Pillars of silver and gold circled around her, hanging heavy with flowering vines. The grass was thick and soft. She dug her fingers into it. Never in all her wanderings had she seen a place like this.

"You are welcome here."

Nicxira startled, yanking her head up. Standing before her was the most beautiful woman she had ever seen. Her honey-colored hair spilled down her back to her feet, and was twined about with flowers and leaves. A silver crown made of leaves circled her forehead. Her pale face was austere as she examined Nicxira. Her eyes were an unworldly green from corner to corner, and her fingers were tipped with talons of shining crystal. Beautiful as she was, she looked every inch the warrior, and around her the air was heavy and thick with power.

Nicxira trembled and bowed her head. "I am to serve you."

"Are you? So says the one who sent you, but you must choose. I require your heart and your mind. If you cannot give me both, you are useless."

Nicxira nodded, her mouth dry.

"You came here a powerful witch. You are no longer."

Nicxira's stomach clenched, and her teeth closed on the agonized protest that rose in her throat.

"Only farsight remains to you. Even this close to me, the talent sparks in you. It will not be so strong as before, for in my lands magic is forbidden. You shall go among my people and live as one of them. When your visions come, you will tell me all you see, down to the smallest detail. When it is necessary, you shall act as my hands."

She paused, stepping closer.

"You will never see your homeland again. You will live amongst strangers, in an unfamiliar land. You must do this willingly, without reservation. For what is coming is dangerous, and my weapons must be strong and true. They must not break in the heat of battle."

Nicxira didn't have to think.

"I am yours."

The god nodded, a smile softening her severe expression.

"I will give you my language, and I will send you to the town called Kallas. There you will live and wait for what comes next. Henceforth you will be known as Nurema. Call on me, and I will answer."

Then she extended a hand. The crystal claws curved around Nicxira's head. Darkness swirled around Nicxira, and she felt herself falling down a great hole. As she fell, a name came to her. Amiya. The Blessed Lady.

Chapter 1

"I don't understand." The sharp complaint in Reisil's voice made Indigo's velvet ears twitch. The dun gelding tossed his head reprovingly as he clopped up the slope.

"Give it time. They will come around." Sodur reached over and patted her knee. Reisil frowned. It certainly wasn't the first time she'd brought up the subject in the last year, but Sodur never seemed worried, always giving her the same answer. The longer it went on, the more stale his reassurances became.

"It's been a year. How long does it take to welcome a new *ahalad-kaaslane*? Besides, they were fine when I first arrived. And like that"—she snapped her fingers—"things changed. Now I might as well be a ghost for all they look right through me. I can't stand even going to the Lady's Temple anymore. It would be different if Reikon and the others were still around. Or the *magilanes*."

Sodur shrugged, his thin, drooping face shadowed beneath the brim of his floppy hat. "Reikon, Bethorn, and Fehra were all there when you destroyed the wizards. They saw your bravery and what it cost to challenge the wizards. They felt the Lady inside you. How could they doubt you? As for the *magilanes*—" He broke off, shrugging again. "They're a breed apart. No one rules them; no one frightens them. It was enough that Saljane made you one of them."

And it was true. The *magilanes*, those *ahalad-kaaslane* who shared a bond with predator birds, had sought her out. But being among them was like being a single bird in a silent flock. They spoke seldom, conveying much by a flick of the fingers, a turn of the wrist, a tip of the head. Reisil hadn't had time to learn this silent language of spies and explorers. So she sat mute, watching, listening, alone but for Saljane. If there had been time—

"You have to be reasonable, Reisil. The stories of what you did in Patverseme *are* frightening. After Upsakes's betrayal, it's no wonder the rest of the *ahalad-kaaslane* fear you. Think about it. They thought they knew him. Not one of us doubted him, not even me—and I was his closest friend. And all the while he was plotting with the wizards. How he could imagine killing another *ahalad-kaaslane* . . ." His lips pinched together. "All this from a man we trusted without question. And then you come along and incinerate a hundred wizards without batting a lash. . . ." Sodur sighed. "I was there, and it still curls my hair to remember. The story only grows in the telling. Can you really wonder that you frighten them?"

He glanced over at her. Reisil glared back.

"Because I killed our enemy, I cannot be trusted. Should I have just let the wizards attack us?"

"Of course not. You did exactly what was required." Sodur scratched his jaw. "Try looking at it from their point of view. The wizards were our greatest enemy in the war. There was nothing we could do to defeat them. We had no magic of our own, and they were merciless. The only thing that kept us safe was the Blessed Amiya's prohibition of magic within our borders. And even then, look what they did at Mysane Kosk. The *magilanes* had managed to kill wizards before, but usually at the cost of their birds. Here you kill a hundred in one blow. You *must* know how frightening such power is. But then you came to Koduteel and—" He gestured meaningfully.

But Reisil was determined to say the words aloud. "The Lady disappears, and my power drains away. Do they think I chased Her off? That I'm *pretending* I lost my power?"

"Before you came, the Blessed Amiya was always present, offering guidance, answering prayers, giving us new *ahalad-kaaslane*. Since your arrival, there have been no new *ahalad-kaaslane,* and our prayers go unanswered. Is it any wonder they blame you? No," he said, forestalling her reply with a raised hand. "I'm not saying you're responsible. She gave you power, and I think there can be no doubt that She's withdrawn so you could learn to use it. Her very presence suppresses magic; you could not do what She wants you to do if She remained. But the result has been devastating. The other *ahalad-kaaslane* have become powerless. Those amongst the nobility who have long resented our power in Kodu Riik have begun to move against us, and we have no means to stop them. And all wonder if you have plans of your own. . . ."

"Like Upsakes," Reisil said, her lips twisting.

"Yes. And no one would—or could—challenge you after your annihilation of the wizard circle. And what if you really are the Lady's Chosen? The *ahalad-kaaslane* dare not go against you either way. So instead they hold their distance. It is unfair, but not unreasonable given all that's happened." Sodur brushed away a deerfly. "Maybe if destroying the wizards had been the end of it, everyone could start healing. But with the loss of the Lady, the plague and the *nokulas*, not to mention the Mesilasema's death and the Iisand's withdrawal from rule, no one feels safe. They have to blame someone. The main thing to do now is to learn how to control your magic and heal the plague. That will prove your loyalty like nothing else could."

Reisil gritted her teeth. Her chest was tight, and her stomach felt hard as a stone. Even the relief of being out of Koduteel and in the mountains couldn't melt away her bitterness. In those early days when she'd returned to her hometown of Kallas, she'd been able to do so much. She'd spent long days just healing, her instincts guiding her. But now her magic rarely came to her call, and when it did, she didn't know if she would accidentally light the whole world on fire. How would she ever control it enough to heal the plague? Nor did it help that many blamed her for the Mesilasema's death and the Iisand's self-imposed isolation. But that *wasn't* her fault. The Mesilasema had refused even to let Reisil be in the same room during that awful childbirth.

Reisil thrust the thought away. She was not going to start pitying herself. She drew a deep breath, turning her face up to the afternoon sun and pushing back her hat. The cloudless sky arced like a brilliant ocean above. The morning had dawned cold and frosty, but the autumn day had warmed nicely. The air was redolent with the smell of evergreens and aspen, meadowgrass and damp earth.

Sodur's explanation made sense, but the relentless snubbing from the other *ahalad-kaaslane* was a wound that never stopped bleeding. Between her own failures and their constant suspicion, she had begun to feel as welcome in Kodu Riik as a Patversemese wizard. Except a wizard would be able to *do* something with his magic. But this trip was to change all that, she reminded herself. And outside of Koduteel, with Sodur's unfailing, stalwart support, surely she'd find a way to tap into her power and heal the plague.

She pulled her hat back on and straightened her spine. Whether the other *ahalad-kaaslane* trusted her or not, she still had her duty to do, and whining wasn't going to help.

"Has anyone heard from any of them?" she asked as she pulled the cork on her water bag and drank the sun-warmed water. "Reikon? Fehra? Bethorn?"

Sodur frowned, nudging his liver chestnut with his heels as the gelding dropped his head to snatch a mouthful of grass. A flurry of gnats swirled up around his head, and the beast shook his head vigorously, rubbing his head against his forelegs.

"Not for a while now. Not since late spring. But most *ahalad-kaaslane* don't send word except in an emergency."

"How long do *ahalad-kaaslane* usually ride circuit?" Reisil startled herself with the question. It seemed she ought to know after more than a year in Koduteel. But then, how would she have found out? Except for Sodur, none of the *ahalad-kaaslane* would even speak to her, and Sodur spent most of his time in the palace these days, trying to keep the nobles from revolting against the failing power of the *ahalad-kaaslane*.

"There's no set length of time. No set place to go. Each *ahalad-kaaslane* comes and goes as he is called and travels wherever the Lady guides him."

"Juhrnus wasn't called."

"No. But then it is customary for new *ahalad-kaaslane* to spend time learning about Kodu Riik by traveling its length and breadth. I suggested Juhrnus make such a journey, listening to what calls guided him as he went."

But there wouldn't be any calls. Not since the Lady had withdrawn from Kodu Riik. Reisil didn't say it. "How do you know what to do then? What the Lady wants you to do?"

"For me, being at the palace is the best way I know how to serve Kodu Riik. Without the Iisand on the throne, the Verit Aare jostles for the regency. It would devastate the land. He's hungry for war, and he hates the power of the *ahalad-kaaslane* more than the other nobles do. He's already developed a substantial network of supporters. If he became regent, the Arkeinik would soon bend to his will—and then we'd be in much worse trouble than we are in now. If the Lady *was* to speak to me, I believe this is the path She'd choose for me."

"How can you be sure?"

Sodur grimaced. "Who is sure? But what does it matter? We know we must protect Kodu Riik. Even without the Lady to guide us, we must answer our oath to Her. Certainly we cannot sit on our hands, doing nothing. Your path is to find a way to use your power, and mine is to give you the time to do so while keeping the court from tearing itself apart."

Reisil nodded, thinking of her experiences with the court nobles. Most didn't like her any better than the *ahalad-kaaslane* did, only they didn't mind telling her so. Or they cultivated her for what they thought she could do. On those rare occasions she'd accompanied Sodur to the palace, she couldn't escape a feeling that she was prey and that lions and wolves stalked in the shadows. Sodur had shouldered a staggering task. She slanted a look at him. He looked much as he had when she first met him: clothing patched and threadbare, now covered with the dust and dirt of nearly two weeks' travel. His shoulders were slouched, his thin figure unprepossessing. He felt her eyes on him and glanced up, a smile illuminating his haggard features, his eyes twinkling.

"Not the most impressive-looking diplomat, am I?"

Reisil grinned back, shaking her head. "But I've seen you. You know how to manage people. And you don't make them angry when you do it."

"That's because they don't realize what I'm doing. That's the key, Reisil," he said, sobering. "They are a prickly bunch. They're born to lead, and they know it. They don't take interference well, even well-intentioned efforts. Some would rather burn in the Demonlord's third circle. Better to herd them slowly in the direction you want and teach them to see reason—but never let them know what you're up to."

Reisil fell silent, thinking. Then she asked, "You didn't say—have you heard from Juhrnus?"

"No."

"You're not worried anything's happened to him? To any of them?"

Sodur turned his head to look for Lume, his *ahalad-kaaslane*. The silver lynx wound through the shady grasses along the tree line, leaping after grasshoppers and tree lizards.

"Of course I am," he said at last. "Things have changed in Kodu Riik. People do not welcome the *ahalad-kaaslane* as they used to. They still haven't recovered from the war, and the drought hasn't helped. Bandits and thieves prowl the land. *Nokulas* are everywhere, slaughtering entire villages. And then there's the plague." He drew a breath. "As I said, no news is probably good news, but yes, I worry."

There didn't seem to be an answer to that, and so Reisil settled back in her saddle, thinking about the two weeks since they'd departed Koduteel. The people they'd encountered thus far had welcomed them, offering food from their meager stores. They did not seem to blame the *ahalad-kaaslane*. Not yet. But that didn't mean everyone felt the same. Reisil closed her eyes, sending a prayer to the absent Lady to protect her friends.

She tipped her head back, making an effort to push aside her worries and enjoy the breeze on her face and the smell of the summer grasses. Saljane had disappeared several hours before, and now Reisil could feel the goshawk's happy satiation.

~Fat girl. Are you going to eat all the squirrels in the forest?

~Marmots. Two, came Saljane's smug reply.

~Two? How are you going to fly?

Before Saljane could answer, a sudden prickling ran up Reisil's arms. The hair on her neck stood on end. She jerked around, eyes darting to the trees swathing the hills to the left and the right. Behind and before, the long grassy channel they'd been following snaked away between the rising foothills, the tall, heavy seedheads waving in the breeze. She could see nothing. Dread closed a hard fist around her throat.

"What's that?" she whispered. The birds and insects had ceased their chatter. The only sounds were the creak of the saddles, the thud of the horses' hooves, and the rustle of the wind. Sweat slicked Reisil's palms and she tightened her hands on her reins. Indigo pranced and tossed his head, snorting. "Do you feel it?"

"There's something . . . ," came Sodur's hushed answer as he slid his sword free. Reisil grimaced. Would that she had any ability to fight, but there'd been no one to teach her in Koduteel. Sodur was the first to admit his own paltry skills. Which left them nearly defenseless now. *Stupid, stupid arrogance . . .* Her hand fell to the hilt of her dagger. It was sharp enough, but in her hand would do little damage against—*what?*

A fierce yowl sounded from the trees. Lume bounded through the grasses, tufted ears pricked, teeth bared. At the same moment, Sodur's horse squalled, eyes rimmed white. He spun around, crushing Reisil's leg between the two horses. Fire spiked up to her hip as Indigo staggered, his bray echoing through the trees. Reisil lurched against the pommel of her saddle. Pain bit into her stomach, the air gusting from her lungs.

"Run! By the Lady, Reisil, run!"

Sodur's hand cracked down on Indigo's rump. The terrified horse leaped, and Reisil clutched her reins, her left leg dangling loose from its stirrup. Indigo flattened into a thundering gallop. Reisil clutched his mane for balance, wobbling in the saddle. Sodur shouted behind and she twisted to look. Like her, he hunched flat over his gelding's neck, the horse stretched long in panicked flight. Behind them Reisil could see nothing.

They raced up the fold in the hills, slowed by the high, thick grasses. Foam lathered on Indigo's neck, and his ribs bellowed with effort. By the time they crested the hill, Sodur's long-legged chestnut had pulled even. Blood ran from a long slash in the animal's neck and freckled Sodur's pale face.

They plunged down the swell, leaping a trickling creek at the bottom. A narrow game track opened on the other side, and Indigo slotted himself into it, racing up the slope. Sodur fell in behind.

Fury. Fear. Purpose.

Kek-kek-kek-kek!

~Saljane!

The goshawk dropped from the sky, skimming past the galloping duo with another shriek. Reisil twisted around, but could see nothing except Sodur's bloodstained face.

"Go!" he yelled, waving, his sword still clutched in his hand. Reisil faced back around, patting Indigo's sweat-slicked shoulder. Neither horse could keep up this pace much longer. The gelding's breath came in rasping gasps, and his gait was becoming more choppy as exhaustion shortened his stride. Sodur's taller chestnut thumped against Indigo's haunches, and the smaller horse bounded forward only to slow again.

But their pursuers had not given up. Reisil could feel them closing in. Her skin prickled warning, and her blood went cold with sudden certainty.

Nokulas.

~Saljane! What do you see?

Reisil's head whirled as she found herself looking out through Saljane's eyes. They were close above the grass, flying behind the fleeing horses, the ground a sweeping blur. Glinting shapes fanned out behind the horses, their bodies alternately silvered and transparent like moonlit water. Saljane winged upward, circling and returning to dive at the foremost of the beasts. It reared up, eerily silent, swiping at the goshawk with ruthless talons longer than Reisil's fingers. Its nose was blunt and full of needle-like teeth, its eyes an uncanny opaque silver.

Even as Saljane twisted away, Reisil snarled, yanking on Indigo's reins. The gelding swerved and stumbled. Sodur's chestnut veered away into the tall grass. Too late, Reisil realized her mistake. The *nokulas* swarmed through the grasses, surrounding each rider in a ring of gnashing teeth and knife-edged claws.

It was hard to know how many there were. Their shapes flickered and shifted like shadows on water. Reisil caught a glimpse of a head, a paw, a haunch. There a curve of shining starlight, here a distortion in the grass. They sniffed and circled, silent as hunting cats. Reisil's stomach churned, her breath thick in her throat. Beneath her, Indigo tensed. She held him still. Any movement would invite an attack.

As the beasts circled, she began to pick out details. They were graceful, muscular things, all teeth and armor, with sharp spines spiking down their necks and backs. Long, snaking tails whipped from side to side. None looked alike, except for their coloring, if the patchwork translucence could be called coloring. They prodded in closer and seemed to gloat at Indigo's stricken moan.

High above, Reisil felt Saljane's fear and anger as the goshawk circled.

~*No. Wait,* she said as she felt Saljane preparing to dive in for another attack. *It's too soon to move.*

Reisil glanced over at Sodur. He held his sword out to the side, still as marble. His mount pawed at the ground, sawing his head against Sodur's taut hold. *No!* Reisil cried silently. *Stay still!*

Suddenly the horse gave a braying neigh and reared. He spun to the side and bolted through the ring of *nokulas.* The beasts whirled and dashed after, flowing through the grass like floodwaters down a steep mountainside. They romped after the desperate pair, teasing them, driving them. The *nokulas* herded the frothing horse first one way, then another, then round in a circle. Reisil was left to watch or run.

Frantic, she reached for her power, praying it would answer. Nothing happened. She tried again, demanding, pleading. Still nothing. Like calling for help in an empty room. Tears ran down her cheeks, and she sat helpless.

Sodur's gelding slowed and staggered to a halt, head dangling, his breath coming in great, echoing pants. Sodur whirled his sword about himself, driving the *nokulas* back. But as one dodged aside on the left, three more rose snapping and snarling on the right. The chestnut sagged to the ground. Sodur lunged clear, sweeping around himself with his blade until one of the *nokulas* snatched it scornfully and flung it aside.

Reisil's nails dug gouges in her palms. Sodur backed away, falling back to lie prostrate over his collapsed horse. A *nokula* pounced up on top of him. Horror swept Reisil, and her mouth dropped open in a silent cry. Gone was the shimmering watery transparency. The creature crouching over Sodur was molten silver. It had a long, narrow head. Tusks protruded from its mouth and curved like scythes along its jaw. Spiked horns sprouted from behind a bony knob on the top of its head. There was a rough texture to its hide, with odd lumps and bumps running down the length of its body, ending in a stubby tail. Ridges rose like serrated mountain peaks down its spine.

It crouched over the fallen man, a snakelike tongue slithering out to taste its victim. Sodur lay still, eyes wide, his neck soft and pale and white. The *nokula*'s lips pulled back in a sinister smile. The beast drew back its powerful foreleg, claws shining in the afternoon sun, and tongue sliding over its muzzle as if revelling in Sodur's moan of terror.

For a long moment it did not move. Reisil's legs clamped tight around Indigo, and he stuttered forward a few steps then stopped, digging in stubbornly. The other *nokulas* closed in until Reisil could see nothing of the fallen horse and only glimpses of Sodur's clothing. She dashed at the tears on her cheeks and kicked at Indigo. The gelding refused to move.

A shape flickered past her. Lume. The lynx burrowed through the grass, a low growl sounding in his throat. Reisil jumped to the ground to follow, ignoring the pain raveling up her leg. She yanked her dagger free and dropped down to scurry after, watching the scene through Saljane's eyes.

The *nokula* on top of Sodur remained motionless as ice, muscular foreleg levered back. It would take only one swipe to tear out the terrified man's throat. Seconds ticked past. Still the blow did not come. Reisil edged closer, hunching down as Lume fell silent. Saljane swooped lower. Not far ahead in the grass, Reisil could hear the sound of the *nokula* pack sliding through the grass, and the shuddering breaths of the chestnut gelding.

Suddenly the beast on top of Sodur moved. Reisil bit her lips to stop her scream as its foreleg dropped. But it didn't strike. Instead it pinched Sodur's face in its claws, bending forward, snout a bare inch from Sodur's crooked nose. Saljane shrieked and dropped until she was barely ten feet above the tableau. Reisil clenched her fist around the dagger and squirmed forward.

Then inexplicably the *nokula* leaped from Sodur, landing silently amongst its companions, leading them away through the grass. Straight toward Reisil. She stiffened, crouching ready, but they parted around her. In moments they were gone.

Reisil stared after them, her mouth agape. She lurched to her feet, legs shaking. Sodur had slid to the ground, one arm looped tightly around Lume, who nuzzled at him furiously. Sodur turned his head and began to retch. Reisil dropped to her knees beside him, instinctively lifting her fist to catch Saljane.

"Are you all right?"

Sodur nodded, wiping his mouth with his sleeve. Beneath the spatter of his horse's blood, his face was white. There were four bleeding holes on his jaws where the *nokula* had held him.

"Horse is worse off than I am. Got to get him up or he'll founder for certain. Hate to have to walk the rest of the way."

Reisil paused a bare moment and then stood, allowing him his privacy. She heard him retching again as she coaxed the exhausted animal to stand. She loosened the saddle and dropped it to the ground and then led the animal in looping circles. Slowly the big chestnut's breathing steadied, the sweat dried and the trembling stopped. He walked with his head down, his hooves dragging and catching in the grass. The slash on his neck continued to seep, but Reisil was pleased to see the wound was shallow.

By the time the horse was cool and out of danger, Sodur had regained his composure. He'd washed his face and hands in a little rill and recovered his sword.

"We'll camp up in the trees," he said.

"What if they come back?"

He looked off into the distance, expression remote. "They had their chance." He sounded quite certain, and Reisil wasn't sure how much farther they could manage anyway.

They built a roaring fire and picketed the horses close by. Reisil cleaned the chestnut's neck and applied a salve, not bothering to use her magic for a healing. She turned, feeling Sodur watching her. She felt herself flush hotly and averted her face.

Saljane brought back a fat grouse and retreated to a low branch to preen herself. Reisil plucked the bird and set it over the coals in a pot with water and rice. Afterwards she gathered more wood, piling it in a small mountain near the fire.

When there was nothing left to do, she sat down opposite to Sodur, who hunkered back against a tree, whittling at a piece of pale birch, Lume flopped over his outstretched legs. The sun had slid down behind the mountains, and the moon rose like a sickle blade, reminding Reisil of the *nokulas*, of their eyes, the sly, cruel knowingness behind them.

The silence stretched thin, Reisil looking alternately at the fire, at the horses, at Sodur.

"I thought they were going to kill you," she said finally, twisting a stick between her fingers. Even saying it made her skin turn cold. Sodur had mentored her since they'd left Kallas. But he was more than that. He was her friend, as well. Aside from Juhrnus, he was the only one she had left. Tears trickled down her cheeks, and she swiped at them in annoyance.

"I thought they were too." He never looked up, scraping the wood gently with his knife.

"Why didn't they? Why didn't they kill us?"

"They didn't want to, I expect," came the unhelpful answer.

Reisil stared, unnerved by his diffidence. "But why?"

He shrugged, finally looking up. "Isn't it enough, the Lady sent them running?"

Reisil stiffened, taken aback by the reproof in his tone. She opened her mouth and then closed it. *The Lady is gone. The* nokulas *left for some reason of their own.* "No one has ever escaped a *nokula* pack before."

"Not that we know of. I just thank the Lady for Her aid."

Reisil squirmed. Though his tone was even, she thought she heard a cold reproach in his words.

When the meal was ready, they ate in silence. Hungry as she was, Reisil could barely keep her food down.

"Tomorrow we should get to Veneston. They'll have word on where the plague might have struck recently," Sodur announced, wiping his fingers on his thighs. "Might get a cup of kohv there too."

He sounded more like his usual self, and Reisil looked

up at him, startled. He smiled at her, eyes twinkling once again. "Good food. I don't remember being so hungry."

She frowned. It was as if he'd donned a mask. Or put one aside. He wanted to be strong for her, she knew. But pretending the attack hadn't happened— She wasn't going to forget it. Still, she didn't want to force him to relive what he chose to put aside.

They said little else to one another, tying the horses close and curling up to sleep on opposite sides of the fire, counting on Lume and Saljane to keep watch. That night Reisil dreamed of a hovering black presence, a green snake with yellow eyes and a bloodred belly, and invisible beasts that gnawed the flesh from her bones.

Chapter 2

Reisil woke before dawn, her left leg aching. She sat up, biting back a groan. Sodur was already awake, feeding twigs to the coals. He glanced up with a smile, but said nothing. The flames flickered, reflecting in the shadows and hollows of his craggy face and making him look sinister.

Reisil stood slowly, breathing a sigh, her breath pluming in the chilly air. Snatching up her pack, she retreated into the underbrush to have a look at the damage. Her skin was a mottled tapestry of black, purple and blue from midthigh to ankle. Luckily the shaft of her boot was a soft, slouching leather, with crisscrossing straps to hold it in place. The swelling around her ankle wouldn't prevent her from putting it on again. With gentle fingers, Reisil rubbed a salve over her ankle to reduce the swelling. There wasn't much she could do for the bruises.

By the time she returned to the fire, Sodur was stirring a porridge. Reisil checked the horses, pleased that the wound on the neck of Sodur's gelding was cool to the touch. Indigo shoved his head into her belly and pushed her playfully. Reisil staggered.

"Itchy? All right, come on, then." She scratched his forehead and behind his ears. He groaned, stretching and tilting his head. Sodur's horse looked on enviously, and Reisil obliged him with a chuckle.

Sodur and Reisil ate their breakfast in silence. Reisil couldn't help twitching every time something scurried through the underbrush or the wind rattled the trees.

"They're gone. They won't be back," Sodur said, scraping his bowl.

Reisil cast him a dubious look. "Met a lot of them, have you? Or maybe they whispered it in your ear?"

He flushed. "They're gone. That's all." He rose and strode off to rinse his dishes in the rill.

When he returned, he began packing up their camp, and Reisil quickly finished her porridge and joined him. Most of the last two weeks had been a meandering journey, a chance for her to see Kodu Riik, meet more of its people and, perhaps most important, relax after months of winter confinement in Koduteel. But now she felt all the tension come flooding back. They were here for a purpose. Her stomach tightened, the porridge balling thickly in her stomach. She thought about the previous day, her inability to call up even a trickle of power. They were here to find plague victims. But what she was going to do with them, she didn't know.

The morning quickly warmed, though high clouds made wearing a hat unnecessary. They ranged higher into the foothills, Sodur pushing their pace as fast as the exhausted horses would go. Lume trotted close beside him while Saljane flittered and twisted through the trees.

As they crowned a high ridge, Reisil couldn't resist twisting in her saddle to gaze behind at the Karnane Valley stretching out below them. Far across the vast valley she could see a purple smudge where the Melyhir Mountains hemmed in the eastern expanse of the Karnane. They had traveled through the southern end of the valley after leaving Koduteel, taking a wide, circuitous route from the city. Drought continued to hound the valley dwellers, with the rivers providing the only source of water. Even deep wells had run dry. Fields were stunted and withered, except in those small green patches where farmers had devised ways to draw water from the rivers.

Reisil sighed and turned back around. The irony of the mountain greenness did not escape her. But with the *nokula* packs, who from the valley would brave the mountains to hunt or forage? She glanced at Sodur. She ought to tell him about her failure to draw her power yesterday. The words withered on her tongue. He stared ahead, his gaze distant and brooding. She'd never seen him like this. Not even after Upsakes's betrayal. Until now he'd always shown infinite patience and unshakable tranquillity.

Reisil turned away, touching her bond with Saljane for reassurance. The isolation was creeping up again: the feeling that she was always on her own, even in a crowd. Sodur didn't mean to do it. He had no idea how much she had come to rely on him. And it wasn't fair to burden him. But the sudden wall between them was like a slap in the face, and she felt lost.

~Times like these, I even miss Juhrnus.

~Juhrnus is a friend.

~Juhrnus is a bully and boil on my backside.

~You like him.

~Don't tell him.

~He knows.

~And takes advantage of it every chance he gets. I wonder when he'll get back.

~Before winter. Esper does not like the cold.

Reisil's lips quirked. Juhrnus's *ahalad-kaaslane* was a sisalik. The enormous lizard hated anything resembling cold and would revolt against another winter riding circuit. As completely besotted with Esper as Juhrnus was, she didn't doubt that the two wanderers *would* be back before winter took hold. She smiled. As much as he'd bullied her through her childhood, she never would have imagined Juhrnus could care about anything as much as he cared for Esper. But nearly losing his *ahalad-kaaslane* when Upsakes had tried to murder them had made Juhrnus grow up.

"Nearly there. Over that ridge." Sodur pointed to a heavily wooded slope. The sun broke through clouds, spangling the trees with light.

Reisil yawned, her jaws cracking. "Hope they have kohv on the fire. And hot bread."

"Best not dawdle, then. Don't want to be late for lunch or there won't be anything left. Not in a town this small."

Veneston was situated in a rich valley, the drought having had little impact on the thriving town. It perched on the edge of a narrow, quick-running river that sparkled in the sun, reminding Reisil uncomfortably of the *nokulas*.

At the top end of the valley was a mine shaft where the villagers quarried copper and silver. A waterwheel poured water into pipes that ran down to the fields and filled cisterns in the town. The air smelled of blue spruce, hemlock and birch. It was an idyllic spot, with tidy, half-timbered houses, green meadows dotted with black sheep and spotted goats.

There was no stockade to discourage visitors, and Reisil wondered if the town had been troubled by *nokulas*. But she saw no signs of violence. They rode down the main street, eager to break their midday fast, charmed by the quaint tidiness of the town.

But as they passed between the boat shed, cartwright and smithy, the wind turned, and the stench of death rose about them in an invisible fog. Reisil covered her mouth and pinched her nose, gorge rising in her throat. Down on the ground, Lume whined, his hackles rising. The two horses snorted and shifted uneasily.

Now Reisil noticed that the town was eerily quiet, except for the low musical sound of wooden pipe chimes ringing from the gable of the nearby tavern, the swishing rush of river, and the sough of the wind through the trees.

"I guess we found what we were looking for," Sodur said grimly, pulling his gelding up and dismounting. He tied the animal to the hitching post. As Reisil swung to the ground, she called Saljane. The goshawk arrowed from the trees and landed on Reisil's gauntleted fist, her slate wings making a popping sound as she spread them to halt her descent. Reisil lifted Saljane to her shoulder, glad of the goshawk's fierce strength in her mind.

"Where is everybody? They can't all be dead—can they?" Her voice quivered. The reports spoke of entire villages killed, but she hadn't believed that. She couldn't even conceive of such death.

"Not all, not yet," came a harsh voice from within the

tavern. Sodur and Reisil jerked in surprise. "Soon enough. Best get back on those beasts and ride like demons was chasing you."

"We came to help." Sodur stepped up onto the wide, skirting porch.

"Nothing you can do, *ahalad-kaaslane*. Nothing anyone can do. Justice from the Lady, I reckon. Built our fires, made our prayers, did our rites. No answers but for more dying. Maybe that was the Lady's answer."

"Maybe we're the answer." Reisil sent a silent prayer to the Lady that this was true.

"Likely not," came the unimpressed reply. "But if you're so eager to die, go down to the shearing sheds at the end of the street. Go on, then, and don't come back here after."

Sodur and Reisil looked at one another and proceeded down the street, leading their horses. On all sides, the houses turned grim faces on the *ahalad-kaaslane*. One had been burnt to the ground, leaving a gaping hole filled with ash and charred timbers. Several others had been sealed shut from the outside and archaic symbols painted on the shutters and doors. Reisil gasped and angled toward the closest of those boarded up. Sodur caught her arm, his face harsh.

"Don't bother," he said. "Whoever's inside is probably long since dead, from thirst or hunger, if not the plague. Better to see what we can do for the people in the sheds. They might still be alive."

Reisil nodded jerkily. Saljane dipped her head and rubbed Reisil's cheek.

~It will be well.

Trust. Faith. Solace.

Reisil returned the caress, stroking Saljane's black-and-white breast, savoring her *ahalad-kaaslane*'s confidence.

~If I can't call my magic . . .

~As the Lady wills it, came Saljane's impassive reply.

Reisil's lips pinched together. Everything she had been taught said that the Lady protected Kodu Riik from ill, and would do so as long as its people remained faithful. But then why permit the war with Patverseme? Why send a drought? And what about the plague and the *nokulas*? Kodu Riik and its people were dying, which pointed to an obvious conclusion. The Lady no longer cared. Or worse, were all these horrors punishment? Was Saljane right? Did the Lady *will* this?

A chill ran down Reisil's spine, and her toes curled inside her boots. "I hope not," she muttered.

As they walked by the boarded-up houses, Sodur swore, eyeing the symbols painted garishly on the walls.

"What?" Reisil asked.

"You don't recognize them? No, of course not. You shouldn't. These villagers shouldn't either. These are ancient hexmarks and curses, wards against evil. They have no business here." His voice was clipped, his chin jutting like a hatchet blade.

Reisil glanced at the crude, stark symbols. They had been drawn with charcoal and a paint that looked unnervingly like dried blood. "I've never seen anything like them."

"Stupidity," Sodur spat. "They look for salvation and ask for worse than what they've got. These symbols belong to the old gods and those evil times before the Lady saved us." He shook his head again, lip curling. "The price was faith in Her. Absolute faith. All the old gods were to be left behind forever. And we wonder why She does not answer our prayers. The people have proved themselves faithless."

"Did the people lose faith and the Blessed Lady stop answering? Or did She stop answering and so the people lost faith?"

Sodur jerked to a halt, rounding on Reisil and grasping her arms in a bruising grip. "Don't *you* question the Lady! *You*, of all people!"

Startled, Reisil couldn't find the words to defend herself.

He dragged her forward, his lips pulled thin and pinched face flushed. "Look there, that first one. The mouth in the circle with the eye inside? That one represents Betinue. God of secrets and lies, of seeming and tales. He's an eater of souls. They say that those unfortunate enough to grace his palate scream their torment forever in the black depths of his stomach. You curse your neighbor with that one and hope Betinue doesn't turn on you.

"And there, the hand with the waves below and the lightning above? That one is Elwaak. She swims silent beneath the water, yanking the unsuspecting under like a hungry crocodile. She is blind, righteous vengeance, and *chodha* anyone who gets in her way. And there's another. Suthmanya, the spoiler. A spider's body, hands like talons, the long tongue. Do its bidding, and you will reap blood and power. But the spoiler is fickle and not even its disciples are safe from it."

Sodur faced Reisil again, his eyes glittering, flecks of spit speckling his lips and chin. His expression was so twisted that Reisil hardly recognized him.

"Can you imagine what would happen to Kodu Riik if we went back to following them or the dozen other gods we put aside when we embraced the Lady? There's not one that doesn't revel in blood and carnage and suffering. There would be war again, like nothing we saw with Patverseme. And blood sacrifice. These gods must be fed, never forget. And I imagine they would want a bit of revenge for our faithlessness. Their power has faded in the years since the Lady's held us in Her hands, but feed them, and they would ravage this land. Kodu Riik would dissolve into a horror of rape and pillage and brutality. Believe me, this plague is nothing, *nothing*, compared with what these monsters would visit on us if we turned from the Lady."

Sodur stopped, breathing hard, glancing back along the streets at the symbols repeated across so many of the houses. He held up his hands, looking up at the sky. "How can they even remember? We have worked so hard for so many years to erase such knowledge."

Reisil rubbed her fingers over her arm, wincing, frowning as his words sank in. "I didn't know that. *Why didn't I know that?*"

Sodur turned a look of aggravated impatience on her, sliding his fingers roughly through his hair. "Demonballs, Reisil! Because you don't look. You don't pay attention to what's right in front of you. Sometimes I wonder if you can really be that naïve. One wonders how you've survived this long."

Reisil stiffened at the contempt in his voice. He was looking at her like she was something smelly he'd stepped in. Her teeth clamped together and she faced him, her expression tight. "*Am* I naïve, then?"

"Like a child hiding in her mother's skirts."

Reisil recoiled. She'd been abandoned as a child, raised

by charity. There had never in her life been anyone to
protect her. She'd never had the choice to hide in her mother's skirts or anywhere else.

"Maybe you should educate me," she said, biting off
each word as she folded her arms across her stomach.

"Would that you could see it for yourself," he returned.
"Open your eyes! You are never going to survive if you
can't see what there is to be seen. Being *ahalad-kaaslane*
means standing on your own, making your own decisions."

At Reisil's continued look of hostility, Sodur flung out a
hand and explained grudgingly.

"The Iisand has been a supporter of the *ahalad-kaaslane*
all his reign, but he's unusual. Many Iisands have rebelled
against our authority. The *ahalad-kaaslane* have the power
to gainsay the nobility. The Iisand and the Arkeinik rule
Kodu Riik, but only so far as we allow them. It sticks in
their craw. Since the founding of Kodu Riik, there has been
a constant push to limit the influence of the *ahalad-
kaaslane*." He snorted and shook his head. "All they
needed was an excuse. Upsakes gave them one. Now our
heads are truly on the block. Our warnings fall on deaf
ears; our protests are dismissed as self-serving, greedy or
treasonous. The nobles begin to move openly against us.
Even to murder. They no longer believe the Lady watches
and judges."

"And you think She does?" Reisil said.

His lip curled. "She always watches. But they forget, just
like you." He gestured at the scrawled curses and hexmarks. "Seeing that filth, can you doubt what I say? Why
do you think I spend so much time in the palace? Why do
you think—?"

Sodur broke off abruptly, his cheeks red. Reisil stood
very still. A quiver began deep in her chest. Her mouth
went dry. She felt as if she were standing on the edge of a
precipice, a vast darkness looming before her.

There was something— Something she should *see*.

And then it came to her.

For a moment she couldn't breathe. Everything inside
her turned sere and cold and hard. The pain was like a
needle through her brain. Her knees sagged. With great
effort she caught herself, standing firm. No. Not in front of
him. Never, ever again. Naïve? Not anymore. Nor trusting.

She took a step back, her voice uninflected, giving no hint of the storm raging inside. "It was you all the time. You sent anyone away who might be my friend, who might tell me what's going on. And the rest of the *ahalad-kaaslane*—you told them to avoid me. Convinced them they couldn't trust me." It wasn't really a question, but she hoped with all her heart that he would protest.

Sodur said nothing, his lips pursing.

Pain tightened around her throat like hot copper wire. It was all she could do not to spit at him. "All the time you said not to worry, they'd come around, and all the time you were sabotaging me. Why?" Reisil bit the tip of her tongue, welcoming the pain.

Reisil's voice cracked, and she spun away. She paced down the street, her gait stiff and graceless. She managed a dozen feet before Sodur strode past and stepped in front of her, blocking her path.

His face was haggard and unrepentant. "I'm sorry Rei-siltark," he said, deliberately using the more formal term of address. Empty words. He was trying to manipulate her, to get her to focus on the plague and not on his lies. That way his plan, whatever it was, wouldn't be ruined. Her palm itched to slap him. She balled her hands into fists and shoved them in her pockets.

"It isn't so simple. With the Iisand as he is—"

Sodur broke off, a spasm rippling across his thin face. Unwilling sympathy bloomed in Reisil's chest. Sodur and the Iisand had been close friends before the death of the Mesilasema. But since then, the devastated Iisand had become a recluse, refusing even the company of old friends. The Iisand's unofficial abdication had hurt Sodur deeply. It had left Kodu Riik drifting and vulnerable. Now his eldest son, the Verit Aare, maneuvered for the regency, while the bickering Arkeinik attempted to lead the land, presided over by Lord Marshal Vare. Little was accomplished. The only thing they all seemed to have in common was that they despised Reisil.

Her lips tightened, her sympathy evaporating. He had made them hate her. "Why?" she repeated.

Sodur didn't answer right away, rubbing his hand over his face and pinching his lower lip.

Fury crackled up inside Reisil. "Don't bother. You can

keep your lies. You want me to see for myself, act for myself? Then that's what I will do."

"You want to know why? The *ahalad-kaaslane* are in terrible danger. If we want to serve the Lady, if we want to protect Kodu Riik, then the *ahalad-kaaslane* have to find a way to resurrect the nobles' allegiance. I am one of the few *ahalad-kaaslane* that certain powerful nobles yet trust. They have included me in their discussions, allowing me to offer counsel. If only to appease the Lady. But they do not like you, Reisil. They fear you, and they think you are playing coy with your powers."

"Whose fault is that?" she demanded. He ignored her.

"Worse, given the rift that already exists and their own eagerness to be out from under the *ahalad-kaaslane* thumb, here you are with the magic to force their cooperation. But if it is believed that you are not welcomed among us, if it is believed that you will not become the banner for the *ahalad-kaaslane*, the court relaxes. It buys us time for you to do what you need to do. That is why."

Sodur paused, wiping his forehead.

"Believe it or not, your isolation protects you. If they thought you were an immediate threat, they would kill you tomorrow. It's the only way to keep you healthy and whole until you can solve the problem of your magic. And that, Reisiltark, is my duty to the Lady."

Reisil shook her head in disbelief. "Do you hear yourself? What happens when I do manage to conquer my magic? You've made me their enemy. They'll be so afraid of me, they'll treat me like a Patversemese wizard. No matter what I do now, they'll always see me as a vicious dog they can't turn their backs on."

"You're wrong. You'll cure the plague. They'll have to trust you. The *ahalad-kaaslane* will stand beside you."

"Now who's being naïve? Thanks to you, the *ahalad-kaaslane* think of me as another Upsakes. No one will believe I haven't withheld my power on purpose. You've painted me a traitor, and nothing is going to wash it away. You should have told me. If you had—" If he had, what? Reisil didn't know. "I'm not going to be your puppet anymore."

"You aren't my puppet. Trust me—this was *necessary*."

"Necessary?" She shook her head sharply. "That's just

what Upsakes thought when he kidnapped Ceriba and had her raped and tortured. He thought he had all the right answers too."

Sodur had stiffened, his face turning pale. "You're too innocent, too green an *ahalad-kaaslane*, to understand. You don't know the court as I do. You don't know how these things work. But believe me, this is for the best. You will see."

"I already see. You're right about one thing. I have been too trusting. You couldn't have taught me that better if you'd wanted to." The quaking inside was spreading outward. However pure Sodur's motives might have been, an enduring chasm had opened between them, and she felt like she might shatter from the loss. "I guess this is why the *ahalad-kaaslane* aren't supposed to get too close to anyone, not even each other," Reisil said bitterly. "It makes it much easier to betray your friends. But what if you *are* wrong? Have you thought about that? What if you've only made things worse?"

She didn't wait to hear any more, but turned and strode up the street, the bobbing weight of Saljane heavy on her shoulder. She reached out again to touch the bond between them. Despite her fury at being manipulated, deep down, Reisil couldn't help but wonder if Sodur really was right.

~He thinks if I gain control of my magic, then everything will be fine. But it won't bring the Lady back. It won't make the nobles any less greedy for power. It won't protect the ahalad-kaaslane.

But that wasn't really the problem. It wasn't the source of the pain screwing through her in slow turns.

~He told them to shun me, all the time smiling and holding my hand and telling me they'd come around. He watched to be sure his plan worked, fanning the flames whenever someone might have reached out to me. It's Kaval all over again. I was so in love with him, I couldn't see that he was a traitor, that he'd even think of raping and torturing a woman. How can I still be so gullible? Sodur's right: If I were a proper ahalad-kaaslane, *I would have known better. I never would have depended on him so much. All along he's been playing his game and I've been too blind to even notice it was a game.*

~He does as he believes necessary.

But Saljane's mindvoice was flat, chill and unforgiving. Her talons tightened on Reisil's shoulder.

~Is he right?

Saljane was silent so long that Reisil didn't think she was going to answer. When she did, it seemed as if she'd changed the subject.

~Blessed Amiya does not require such sacrifice of the ahalad-kaaslane. *The tradition is human.*

~What?

~It is simpler to have no ties than to have to choose the Lady over someone you care about, as sooner or later every ahalad-kaaslane *must. But it is not the Lady's law to be alone.*

Reisil's head reeled, and she stumbled, glancing up incredulously to meet Saljane's carnelian eye.

~How can that be? Everyone knows it. All the ahalad-kaaslane *believe it.*

~Everyone knows many things that are not true, was Saljane's terse answer. *Just because it is what you do does not mean the Lady decrees it.*

~Who does?

~You do. The human ahalad-kaaslane.

~But the animals know better? Why not tell us?

Reisil got the sense of a mental shrug, not dismissive, but frustrated. *~I did not think it would help.*

Reisil didn't reply, her thoughts chasing one another. She didn't have to guard herself against friendship, against taking lovers. Not that she had any prospects of either, except perhaps Juhrnus. He would have her in his bed, she knew, but the idea only made her want to giggle like an eight-year-old. But she wasn't *prohibited.* It wasn't the Lady's law. And no one else knew it.

She hugged the knowledge to herself. A secret of her own. Not earth-rending. It wasn't going to save or destroy anybody's life. Still it made her feel independent, as if she'd taken her first step out of Sodur's shadow.

~Sodur isn't right, she said slowly to Saljane, answering her own question. *This isn't going to work. It won't stop with being suspicious of me. The* ahalad-kaaslane *will stop trusting one another, and the court will take advantage of our weakness. Sodur wants to make it look like I'm no threat, like the* ahalad-kaaslane *are no threat, but it's more*

than just show. We're going to become what we appear to be.

And she winced as she remembered the advice from her mentor Elutark, the advice that had carried her through becoming *ahalad-kaaslane*: *You are who you pretend to be.* She thought of the way Sodur seemed to put on and remove masks in the last day. Maybe Elutark was wrong. Maybe you weren't who you pretended to be.

She was wrenched back to Veneston as the stench wafting from the shearing sheds overwhelmed her. She coughed, pressing her hand to her lips.

No time for self-pity, she scolded herself. *People are dying.*

She stopped outside the latched door of the main shed. Stacked beside the wall were charred logs. The side of the building was scorched. Someone had tried to burn the place with the sick inside.

"If you can't cure them, burn them. After all, they're only friends and family," she said acidly. Sodur came to stand beside her, saying nothing.

Reisil reached for the latch, a twist of wire securing it from the outside. She paused, her eyes streaming at the unrelenting smell. After a moment, she motioned Sodur to follow her around behind the sheds. A row of kitchen gardens stretched the length of the row, taking advantage of the ready fertilizer and sunny southern exposure. Now, however, most of the neat patches were withered and brown.

Reisil walked along the row until she found a patch of lavender and rosemary growing in a green clump amidst the ruin of vegetables. She collected a handful of each and retreated to the cistern at the end of the garden row. She untied her scarf from her neck and dipped it in the tepid water before rubbing it thoroughly with the two herbs. The resulting odor was pungent and did much to cover the stench when she tied the scarf across her nose and mouth. Sodur followed suit.

"Are you ready?" he asked, and the doubt in his voice made Reisil's spine snap straight, glad now that she had not admitted her failure to summon her magic when the *nokulas* attacked.

"I am a tark," she replied, sidestepping him. She returned to the doorway, unfastening the wire and latch. An angled chute led up a ramp into the wide shearing area. The dimly lit oval stretched a hundred feet in length and was dominated by rows of shearing tables. The interior wall around the oval was lined with slatted wooden bins for the wool. Gates leading into the holding pens between the inner and outer wall interspersed the bins every ten feet. Each of these small enclosures was designed to hold a dozen sheep. No doubt the place doubled in winter as both a barn and a village gathering area for meetings and celebrations. A dusty red ribbon dangled limply from an overhead beam. No one was celebrating now.

The dead and the sick littered the tables and dirt floors. It looked as if many had collapsed in their tracks while tending others. The miasma of death, putrefaction and feces made Reisil's eyes burn and her stomach buck despite the masking scent of lavender and rosemary. Ignoring her discomfort, she marched resolutely to the closest table.

The man was dead. He wore only a filthy loincloth around his hips. His arms and legs were black up to nearly the shoulders and hips and swollen to five times their normal size. Black scabs pocked the surface between yellow blisters. His legs and the table were thick with dried, bloody feces. His face was smeared with the blood that had trickled from his eyes, nose and mouth. His tongue protruded from between his lips. His skin, where it wasn't black and swollen, was yellowed and covered with a purple rash. Flies crawled over him and clustered in his eyes and mouth.

Reisil moved to the next table and the next, her jaw clenching tighter and tighter with every death until she thought her teeth would crack. She paused to kneel and check those lying on the floor. In some, the blackened arms and legs had ruptured from the pressure of the escaping gases within, the putrid inner flesh crawling with maggots and flies. Reisil swallowed, her tongue dry and feeling too large for her mouth. How could she hope to defeat this devastation with crippled magic?

Reisil remembered the wizard circle, the tremendous surge of power, of knowing she could call lightning. The blistering power that had filled her then, the glorious, rich fullness when she had grown back Reimon's arm in that little grass hut on the Vorshtar plain. *That* power could pinch out the plague like a blown candle.

But she didn't have it anymore. Maybe she never did. Then the Lady's hand had guided her. That hand was gone now. Reisil stopped, staring around her at the bodies scattered like tortured dolls. Most people, the ones who didn't blame her, said the wizards had done this. And she knew, down to the soles of her feet, that it was true. The plague suited the wizards' style perfectly. It did their dirty work for them, efficiently, with no wasted energy.

They will pay, Reisil promised herself. *I will make them pay.*

Halfway down the line of tables, Reisil found a girl still alive. She lay sprawled half on one side as if she'd tried to curl into a ball. Her hands were black halfway to her elbows, and her feet were black where they protruded from her skirts. Her breath came in wheezing gasps, and she jerked and twitched in agony. Reisil could hear a soft, crackling sound, like crumpling paper, and realized that it came from the blackened limbs, the gases within bubbling and popping. The girl gave a little groan, her mouth moving, her eyes closed.

"Here," Reisil called to Sodur, who dropped down beside her.

"By the Lady," he whispered.

"I'm going to try to heal her."

Reisil reached down inside herself. To her astonishment, the magic answered immediately, roaring up ferociously to engulf her with volcanic heat. Power crackled over her skin and snapped in the air around her. Reisil snatched her hands up to her chest. Sodur grunted and scuttled aside as the searing heat licked at him.

Reisil struggled against the rising power. *Either it came too fast and hard or it came not at all. What use was magic if she couldn't control it?* Long moments passed, her mouth growing parched, her skin feeling stretched and tight as the heat grew more intense.

At last she managed to contain the magic, but it pulled at her like a chained animal, snapping and growling.

She laid tentative fingers on the girl's chest, her light touch making the girl twitch and moan. Reisil closed her

eyes, concentrating, moving inside. The girl's body was as
bloated and rotten as a corpse floating in a river. Reisil
shuddered as she explored the damage. Collapsed blood-
ways; pulpy, bruised organs; putrid, decaying flesh. Reisil
couldn't imagine how the girl still clung to life.

She slid inside on a thick tendril of magic, wincing at the
girl's pained cry of protest, the way her body twitched and
flinched. Reisil tried to thin the magic, but to no avail. She
pushed further along, determined to do what she had to do
quickly. Elation rolled through her as she went deeper. It
was working!

How long she sat over the girl, she didn't know. Over
and over again she repaired tattered nets of veins and arter-
ies, restored putrid flesh, swallowed poisons and corrosion.
But corruption returned, sliding unabashedly in behind her
as she moved on to the next repair. She was besieged on
all sides. Over and over she sought the epicenter of the
body's disaster, the source of the spreading horror. Over
and over.

The girl died.

Reisil reeled back, feeling the child's life fleeing away,
trying to catch it with spectral hands. But the girl was gone,
her body a patchwork of healed flesh and voracious rot.
Reisil sobbed, the heels of her hands pressed hard against
her eyes, her fingers curling hard into her scalp. She felt
Sodur's hands on her shoulders, pulling her against him in
a rough embrace. Dry, racking sobs shook her like a sapling
in a rough wind.

"Next time, next time," Sodur soothed. The words
worked their way into Reisil's brain, and at last she pushed
herself away from him, scrubbing away her tears.

"Then let's try again."

There were a dozen others still living in the shearing
sheds. Reisil tried again with each of them, to no avail. At
last Sodur dragged her drenched and shaking body away
from the corpses.

"You cannot do this anymore. Not yet. You still have
more to learn. And Kodu Riik cannot afford to lose you.
We'll have no hope then. You must survive and learn to
use your power."

She resisted his commands, pulling away. She owed these
people. She was supposed to save them. That's what her

magic was for; that's what the Lady had told her to do. *Heal my land. Heal my children.* If she couldn't do as the Lady bade, she didn't have a right to walk away. And who else would care for these pitiful creatures in their last days? Certainly not those hiding in the tavern.

In the end, Sodur promised to send back *ahalad-kaaslane* to help. Even then Reisil would have waited for them, but Saljane agreed with Sodur and urged Reisil to leave. Reisil allowed herself to be drawn away, though she couldn't help but wonder if Sodur would do as promised. He saw her skepticism and there was an answering flare of pain in his expression, but Reisil wasn't sure she believed it. He wore too many masks, too well.

Before they left, she insisted on making the dozen still-living plague victims as comfortable as possible on pallets, moving them to a vacant home nearby. Then Reisil incinerated the sheds with the bodies inside, her magic still flaming bright inside her.

As with the wizard circle, it seemed she could always destroy. It gave her no satisfaction.

Chapter 3

The snow began to fall again as Juhrnus rode into Koduteel through the Lady's Gate. He waved at the guards in the gatehouse, pulling his cloak tight as a chill burrowed into his skin. Snow whirled in his face and melted down his collar, driven by the briny wind off the ocean. The banners along the walls snapped welcome, and Juhrnus gusted a happy sigh, looking forward to a hot kohv, a hot meal and a hot bath. And tonight there would be no rocks or branches or lumps of uneven dirt prodding his backside as he slept.

Esper humped in an uncomfortable-looking pile between

Juhrnus and the pommel of the saddle, protected from the
snow and cold by a curly sheepskin. The sisalik's tail, too
long to fit in the narrow space, hooked around Juhrnus's
waist, the tip twitching.

~*We're here,* Juhrnus announced.

~*Cold. Hungry.*

~*You've been saying that for weeks. Tonight we'll have a
fire at the Temple, a warm bed and plenty to eat. And tomorrow we'll have more of the same. No more traveling for
awhile.*

~*Good.* Esper's tail twitched again, and Juhrnus chuckled.

They turned north inside the city, Juhrnus resisting the
urge to push his tired mount faster. The cobbled streets
were treacherously slick. He gave the mare her head,
allowing her to pick her way, glancing up at the sober lines
of the banking and merchant buildings of the passing brown
district. Few people were about this late in the afternoon.
A group of four men walked hurriedly down the middle of
the street ahead, talking rapidly and waving their hands
emphatically. They bustled inside a forbidding edifice, gargoyles snarling from above the lintel. A carriage rolled
down the street in the opposite direction, drawn by matching gray hacks. Juhrnus didn't recognize the crest embla-
zoned on the door, but he admired the high-stepping horses
as they trotted past with their silver bells jingling. Woodsmoke twined with the smell of the sea, overlaid with the
lighter smells of cooking meat. Juhrnus drew an apprecia-
tive breath.

A vendor closing up his cart caught sight of the travel-
worn *ahalad-kaaslane*. "Bright evening. Come far?"

"Lately from Kallas."

"Through Karnane or past Mysane Kosk?"

Juhrnus rubbed a gloved hand over his beard, frowning.
"Mysane Kosk."

The other man nodded his silvered head, taking two
sticks of roasted pork from his cart and passing them up
to Juhrnus, who took them with a thankful grin. "Bad as
they say?"

"Like nothing I've seen."

The other man nodded again, absently stroking the decorative green stitching adorning the collar of his cloak. "Was
a pretty city once. Brother's wife's family was there. Glass-

makers. Haven't heard from them since . . ." He paused. "Seen any of those *nokulas*? The plague?"

Juhrnus swallowed and wiped his mouth. "Saw where they'd been. Bad way to die."

"They say they're coming here."

Juhrnus shrugged a shoulder, taking another bite. "Most *nokulas* seem to stay up in the western mountains. Not that many down low. Not yet anyway."

"They'll come, though, won't they?" The vendor didn't seem to need an answer, looking up at the sky and shaking the snow from his head. "Won't keep you. Appreciate the news." He staggered forward as his mule shoved against his back. He muttered and cuffed the beast lightly on the neck. The mule brayed a protest. "Winter's going to be long and hard. Don't think you won't end up on the pointy end of a stick," he said in the tone of a threat oft made.

Juhrnus thanked the vendor again and continued on. The Lady's Temple sat inside the brown district, a stone's throw from the road separating brown from orange, where the nobility played. Across that road expensive dining rooms, luxurious hotels, posh theaters and music halls abounded, as well as gambling dens, drug parlors and elite brothels that catered to every whim.

The Lady's Temple was an ancient four-story building made of polished green stone ranging from shades of early spring green to brilliant sea moss to shadowy evergreen darkness. Two sweeping wings circled around a spacious courtyard, large enough to fit a dozen merchant caravans with room left over for a herd of a hundred cattle. It was roofed over by a lattice of vines looped around spreading tree limbs. In the warm months, it was a shady glen of cool comfort and retreat. Now the lattice was bare, and leaf litter collected in fountains, in piles against the walls, in ice-scummed pools and in thick blankets beneath the trees.

Nothing moved in the courtyard as Juhrnus rode in, his beard thick with snow. He crossed to the archway leading into the mews, where he found a crew of the orphan stable boys dicing in an empty stall. The stable master was at dinner, and the boys started guiltily when he poked his head over the door. He didn't recognize any of them.

"Sir!" one of them said, scrambling to his feet.

Juhrnus held up his hand. "None of that. See to my mare.

She needs a hot mash and a good rubdown. Don't stint her or I'll be having a word with your master."

They swarmed out of the stall, watching as he pulled his cloak aside and lifted Esper to his shoulders before removing his saddlebags.

"Where'd you come in from?" one of the boys dared.

"West."

There was an audible gasp and Juhrnus couldn't help but grin. A dangerous trip, riding through the western mountains. The boys were suitably impressed by the journey.

"Did you see Mysane Kosk?" one asked breathlessly.

Juhrnus felt his face harden. "Hurry up the mare. Don't want her getting stiff or colicky. And don't forget—a hot mash and plenty of straw in her stall."

With that he returned to the expansive courtyard, turning left from the archway and up the cloistered walk to the main entrance. He pushed open the doors and was greeted by a cacaphony. A swarm of orphan girls was rallying in a nearby classroom, singing loudly off-key, much to the annoyance of their long-suffering teacher. A group of both boys and girls slid raucously down banisters and played a boisterous game of tag in the sprawling foyer.

Juhrnus entered quietly, adroitly avoiding the careening bodies as he proceeded up the stairs, aware that a certain silence targeted him as the children first noticed him, evaluated him and then carelessly returned to their play. Reaching the top of the stairs, he turned first into the large common room, the corners of his mouth turning up at Esper's grunt of pleasure. Heat permeated the room from the two enormous hearths on either side of it. A horde of chairs, couches and tables filled the space, illuminated by the fires and a host of oil lamps and wall sconces. A few human *ahalad-kaaslane* snored in chairs. Brilliant disks of shining green, amber and red peered at Juhrnus as the animal *ahalad-kaaslane* blinked sleepily from their own beds on laps and couches.

On the other side of the heavy doors blocking the far end of the commons came the muted sounds of laughter, clinking dishes and rumbling discussions. More important were · the mouthwatering smells of fresh-brewed kohv, roasted meats, yeasty breads and spiced vegetables. Juhrnus's stomach growled, and he sped· across the room.

There was a hush, and then he was surrounded by welcoming voices and thumping backslaps.

"Juhrnus! We'd thought you'd fallen into a swamp!"

"Should have known you'd arrive in time for dinner. Your timing is always perfect."

"Did you run into anyone? Meriis? Olvaane?"

Other names were volleyed at him, and Juhrnus nodded or shook his head at each, finding himself pushed to one of the long tables, his saddlebags taken from his hands, his cloak whipped away. He sat down before a trencher piled high with roasted potatoes, thick roast pork, gravy, baked apples and fried onions. A mug of ale sloshed down in front of him followed by a basket of crusty rosemary bread and a crock of honey butter. Juhrnus helped Esper onto the table and set to with gusto as Esper began his own feast of greenhouse-grown lettuces. Later Juhrnus would grab a couple of fat mice or a rat from the rodent cages to fill the sisalik properly.

He talked around his food, answering questions, finding no entry to ask any of his own. Yes, he'd seen signs of the *nokulas*. No, he hadn't seen any himself. Yes, he'd seen where the plague had hit, but long before his arrival. Yes, the drought had made for a bad harvest in the Karnane Valley. No, the people didn't seem to blame the *ahalad-kaaslane*, feeding, housing and clothing him as usual. Yes, there were bandits prowling everywhere. No, he hadn't been attacked. He was *ahalad-kaaslane*, after all. Untouchable. The questions went on, skipping from town to town, topic to topic. He answered as best he could, beginning to feel the weight of his long ride as the food and ale filled him warmly.

"Where's Reisiltark? And Sodur?" he asked when the din around him lulled. His question was met with a peculiar silence.

"Sodur spends a lot of time in the palace these days. Trying to keep a cork on the court, specially the young Verit Aare. The Verit and the Lord Marshal are snapping at each other like dogs over a bone. Won't be long before they dig in for a real fight. Sodur'll want to know you're back, though. We'll send someone." This was from a short, thin man—Vesil was his name. His *ahalad-kaaslane* was a red squirrel.

The conversation soon picked up again, this time centered on the Iisand and his strange withdrawal from the court after his wife's death.

"Man of feeling. He'll be back. Wait and see. He still sees Sodur, and that's something. He's still loyal to the *ahalad-kaaslane*."

"Not like that whelp of his. Had his way we'd all be thrown to the sharks. Iisand better come to his senses soon or the young Verit will have his throne."

"Lord Marshal isn't much better. Have you seen the way he looks at us? Like ants in his sugar. The eyebrow, the sneer. You know what I'm saying. He's more cautious about showing it is all. The court takes its cue from them. If it weren't for that *ganyik* Upsakes. . . ."

"If the Mesilasema could have been saved, you mean. The Iisand wouldn't have buried himself alive and left his nobles to run amok."

Juhrnus frowned, rubbing a hand over his bulging belly. "What happened to the Mesilasema?"

"You don't know?" It was Vesil again. "When did you go on circuit?"

"Over a year ago. At the harvest."

Vesil's expression had turned dark, and a shiver ran down Juhrnus's spine. "Happened less than a month after that. The Mesilasema died in childbirth. No one could save her."

But there was a peculiar twist to Vesil's voice, a twitch in his jaw, a flick of eyes. Something he wasn't saying. Fear clutched Juhrnus's throat, and Esper lifted his head, gouging his heavy talons into the tabletop.

"Didn't Reisiltark try to help?"

Vesil's shrug said nothing.

"Where is she?"

The other man stroked his squirrel and then pushed away from the table. "Couldn't say. I'd best be going."

Juhrnus glanced at the others gathered at the table, but they too had begun to mutter about work and business and rose from the table with sudden alacrity. He watched them go and scowled.

~Sorry Esper. We're going to have to go out again.

It was late when he returned, empty-handed and more

than a little disturbed. He knew the meaning of the green stitching on the vendor's cloak now. And the lack of interest among his fellow *ahalad-kaaslane* for Reisil. Only it wasn't lack of interest. It was suspicion.

He built a fire in his room and stripped, stretching out on the bed, his jaw knotting. No one knew where to find her. She certainly wasn't staying in the Temple, and the *ahalad-kaaslane* he asked answered with only shrugs and blank stares. Reisil's green-wearing supporters were of no help either. Many had seen her recently, but none could— or would—say where to find her. Clearly they wanted to protect her. Juhrnus didn't much care for the way they looked at him—wary and hard, as if he wanted to hurt her. He'd had about as much luck finding Sodur.

He yawned. Tomorrow. A bath in the morning, and then he'd find them.

~Warm enough? he asked Esper, who was curled against his side.

His question was met with drowsy contentment, and Juhrnus pulled the bedclothes over himself and fell into a heavy sleep.

Juhrnus found Reisil just before noon the next day. He ambled into the stableyard of a cloth merchant. Tirpalema was cousin to Veritsema, mayor of Kallas where both Reisil and Juhrnus had grown up. After searching unsuccessfully, he'd finally remembered when she'd first come to Koduteel, Tirpalema had agreed to stable Indigo. In return, she'd made a point of checking the health of his animals regularly, a fact that brought Juhrnus down to the pink district against the chance she'd be there. He'd been gone so long, he didn't know her usual haunts—not that she'd had much time to develop any before he left. He'd asked again in the Temple, but the blank stares and shrugs were only repeated.

The stableyard gate was pulled invitingly wide. A sign showing bolts of colorful cloth and a spool of thread and needle swung from the crossbar. He saw Reisil within fastening bulging saddlebags onto Indigo's saddle, her green cloak vibrant against the snow.

"Leaving town just when I get here? Could make a man

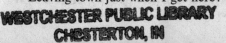

worry about his welcome," he said, sauntering close. She started and spun around. A smile bloomed on her lips, and she ran across the yard, throwing her arms around him.

"Juhrnus! When did you get back?"

He returned the embrace. "Yesterday evening. Thought I'd see you at the Temple."

She stiffened and pulled away, her hood falling back. She continued to smile, but lines of strain bracketed her lips as if the expression was difficult to maintain. Her pale skin wrapped her skull tautly. Feathers of silky black hair escaped her braid, doing little to soften the angles of her face. They lent her face a severe quality emphasized by the dark circles around her eyes. The golden ivy that was a blessing from the Lady ran over her left cheek and down into her collar and glittered stark and garish against her pallid skin. Beneath his hands her body felt gaunt—bones and wire.

"You look like *skraa,*" he said. "Don't you eat, little sister?" The diminutive had made her cringe growing up, a way to pretend kindness while insulting her. Now her grin grew more natural.

"Not as much as you do, little brother." She poked his stomach. "You look fat enough, though someone might mistake you for a bear wandering into Koduteel."

Juhrnus rubbed his beard. "Good for the trail. Keeps the wind and snow from peeling away my face. Besides, Esper likes it."

"Where is he?"

"Curled up by a roaring fire. Where I should be. But you're going somewhere," he said, gesturing at her loaded gelding.

"Not far."

"Oh?" He lifted his brows and she flushed.

"I'm tired of sleeping in a stall. The straw is itchy. And Tirpalema is too kind to tell me he's tired of feeding me. So I've found a new place to stay."

"What about the Temple?"

Her look was sharp and hard as a jade knife. "No."

"What's going on?" Juhrnus demanded. "Tell me. I've had enough evasions from everyone else."

Reisil looked away, chewing her upper lip. Then she gave a little shake of her head and looked back at him. "The nobles and the *ahalad-kaaslane* have come to believe that I'm a threat—like Upsakes. I've been able to use my power only sporadically and have had no luck curing the plague. They think I'm doing it on purpose. That I'm just letting people die for some plan of my own."

"That's . . ." He searched for adequate words. "That's stupid! How did they get such a *skraa*-for-brains idea? How could they believe it?"

Reisil grinned, bitterness coiling through her voice. "I wish I could tell you." Juhrnus hooked his thumbs on his belt. She obviously wasn't telling him all of it. But she wasn't ready to talk, and he knew better than to try to force her.

"Where's Saljane?" he asked, following after her as she returned to Indigo and tightened his cinch.

"Hunting. She doesn't much care for the city." Again there was a sense of something she wasn't saying, and Juhrnus clenched his jaw. Reisil had never been one to talk about herself or depend on anyone else. Abandoned by her parents at birth and raised on the charity of Kallas, she'd always been too aware of being a nuisance, an added expense. She was always afraid of making herself more of a burden. As a boy, he'd hated her obsequiousness, her self-effacement. For a long time he thought it was sucking up. Then he figured out it was stiff-necked pride and shame. Nothing he did made her stop—though in the way of boys, he'd not been kind. He winced. That didn't begin to cover what a *ganyik* he'd been. He couldn't seem to stop attacking her, as if sooner or later she'd have to defend herself and quit sulking around. Not then, and not later, not until he'd almost lost Esper.

He shied away from the memory. He'd never forget Esper's limp, broken body; he'd never forget the way Reisil had nearly sacrificed herself and Saljane to save Esper. Unthinkingly he reached out and touched his bond with Esper. The sleeping sisalik radiated contentment. Juhrnus smiled. He owed Reisil everything.

The last straw for Reisil was discovering that Kaval was a traitor—finding him in that room, Ceriba battered and raped. Juhrnus didn't know if Reisil would ever trust anyone with her feelings again. He rubbed the back of his neck. Maybe Sodur knew something.

"I thought I'd go looking for Sodur later. We could all have dinner and I could tell you about my circuit."

For a bare moment Reisil's hands froze in the middle of untying Indigo. Then she tugged the reins free and guided the horse out the gate. "Not tonight."

"Tomorrow, then."

She strode quickly down the street in the direction of the Sea Gate, Indigo clopping behind. Juhrnus swung along beside her. "I don't think so."

"Don't tell me he agrees with those *skraa*-headed imbeciles."

"No. He definitely doesn't agree with them." Her voice was grim.

Juhrnus scowled, tired of the puzzle. "Then what?"

"Ask him."

"I'm asking you."

She shook her head, her face white as alabaster, her jaw jutting. "Let's just say I was a fool. Again."

Jurhnus ground his teeth. "Could you be more specific?"

She pulled up short. "I could. But there are some things that I'd just as soon stay buried in the dark where no one can find them. You want to know any more, you ask Sodur."

She glared at him until he nodded and they set off again.

They passed out of the pink district with its fancy shops into the green trader district and then out the walls through the Sea Gate. The pink district had made a great many repairs since the Patversemese siege years before, but the walls and streets of the green district still showed the damage caused by trebuchet and ballista fire, as well the scorch marks from barrages of burning oil. There were great fissures in the cobbles of the streets and cracks in many of the buildings yet standing. Even the snow could not mask the decay and ruin. It grew worse the farther east they went. In the poorer quarters beyond the Sea Gate, whole blocks were decimated. The palace had funded many rebuilding projects, but the gray, white and red districts composing the southeastern quadrant of the city had not yet seen much help. Juhrnus eyed the passing destruction, hoping that Reisil's destination was among these ruins.

"So where are we going?" Juhrnus asked, relieved when they at last passed out of the gate and out onto the bluffs.

The wind off the ocean buffetted them, picking up the snow and swirling it in the air. The clouds hung heavy and leaden, signaling another storm to come. The cliff boomed as whitecaps rolled across the bay and crashed into the harbor cavern below. Deep and high enough for even the tall ships, the harbor cavern resonated like an inverted drum with the thrust of the waves and the rush of the wind. The sound vibrated along the cliff wall, making the ground feel like a living thing.

Reisil said nothing, but pointed ahead to the abandoned lighthouse perched out along the edge of the cliff.

"There? You're going to live there?" He'd have preferred the ruins inside the city. The lighthouse was far more unstable and dangerous. "Have you a death wish? That place will tumble down around your head in the middle of the night. Probably tonight."

"Don't worry about me. It's perfect."

There was something hard edged and bitter in her voice, and again Juhrnus wondered what she wasn't telling him.

He gazed up at the scarred tower as Reisil unloaded Indigo. During the Patverseme siege, the tower and its outbuildings had taken substantial damage to the keepers quarters, storage sheds, and the stairway twisting up its exterior. After the siege, a new lighthouse had been built out along the headland, one that boasted a taller tower with an interior stairway and a greater beacon range.

"You're going to get snowed on this winter," he observed, looking at the gaping holes in the slate roofs of the outbuildings and the white-crusted droppings of the seabirds that nested inside. "Or you'll have to share with the birds."

"It's not that bad. Besides, I'm not going to live down here. I'm going to live up in the tower. There's a perfectly good watch room just below the lantern deck. No damage to it at all. Even the windows are in good shape. If any birds want to bother me, they can talk to Saljane."

With that she proceeded up the winding stairs, ignoring his scornful exclamations at the missing railing and decaying steps. Rubble from chipped walls and broken stairs crunched and rolled beneath his feet, tiny drifts of snow along the risers making the footing more treacherous. He eased each foot down carefully, pressing against the lighthouse wall to avoid looking down at the frothing harbor below. Reisil had no such anxieties and climbed the steps easily, nimbly skipping over the gaps in the stairway.

They stopped at the gallery deck, where a scarred wooden door led into the watchroom. Juhrnus grudgingly had to admit that Reisil was right. The room was sound. Though the wind moaned and gusted, the mullioned windows remained impervious, despite the many cracks in the panes. Reisil had already cleaned the room and piled wood next to the hearth, but the rest of the round space was bare.

"You need some furniture. A bed, a table and chair at least. I don't want to sit on the floor when I'm here."

"Who says you're invited?"

"I'm *ahalad-kaaslane*. I don't have to be invited," he said loftily.

He watched as Reisil unpacked her few possessions, folding her clothes and situating them on a shelf, setting out a plate, a spoon and a fork and a cup on the mantel as well as two candles. Her few toiletries she put next to her clothing and then spread her bedroll on the floor, bits of straw from Tirpalema's stable still clinging to it.

Juhrnus made a face. "That's something I won't miss about riding circuit."

"Don't tell me you had trouble finding a soft bed every night? And some willing woman to warm it for you?"

Juhrnus averted his face from her amused stare. "Not often enough," he muttered. "Apparently you've had the same trouble." Her blush was as hot as his, and he grinned. "So you need a bed, and a chair and a table."

Juhrnus walked back to Tirpalema's with Reisil, wringing from her a promise to meet him for dinner. Not in the Temple, but at a kohv-house in the yellow district.

"The Four Bells," she repeated obediently. "An hour after sundown."

Satisfied, he returned to the Temple to retrieve Esper and hunt for Sodur. He snatched a cold meal in the dining commons and then departed for the palace.

He came to the main gate of the palace grounds. It was situated beneath a towering stone barbican riddled with arrow loops and crowned with toothy crenellations. Flanking towers at intervals along the thick walls gave testimony that the castle had once been expected to defend Koduteel against invaders. It served now as its last bastion. The city had long since grown too large for its population to cram inside the palace walls. A massive curtain wall had been erected ninety years ago to protect the populace, but even that had grown too small to hold everyone. Those who could not afford to live inside were relegated to a chancy life in the Fringes, a hodge-podge of tents and ramshackle lean-tos huddled against the north wall of the city.

The guards scanned him over and then waved him inside. Juhrnus nodded his thanks, wandering across the broad expanse of the bailey where skeletal copses of trees and mulched flower beds dotted the winter-killed lawns. He followed the long, spiraling driveway around the hill and toward the palace at the top. More guards passed him, dressed in midnight blue and gold livery over chain mail, red-eyed gryphons splayed on their chests, shining halberds carried stiffly above their heads. Juhrnus smiled greeting to them, suddenly conscious of his scruffy beard and travel-stained cloak.

"Juhrnus! Bright day! Vesil said you'd come. I've been expecting you for more than a month. Did you have a good journey?"

Sodur had come over the crest of the hill with several other men. He waved them on, stopping to hail Juhrnus with a welcoming smile and slap on the shoulder. His silver lynx trailed at his side, tufted ears flicking back and forth.

"You look a sight. You got in yesterday?"

"In time for dinner."

"Are you here for me?" At Juhrnus's nod, Sodur turned them back down the hill. "Let's walk. I was going to the Temple. Have to get away from all the stiff-necked posturing."

As they walked, Sodur questioned Juhrnus closely about his journey. Juhrnus dredged through his memory for the details that Sodur seemed to want, part of his mind worrying the question of Reisil like a dog with a rabbit. But there didn't seem to be an opening to ask about her.

At the Temple, Sodur yawned and rubbed his stomach. "I've not eaten since breakfast. I'll have someone send something for us to my quarters."

Soon Juhrnus found himself ensconced in an overstuffed

chair, booted feet propped on the andirons, Esper sprawled along his legs. He cradled a mug of mulled wine in one hand, a flaky meat pie in the other, idly noting the cracks and holes in his boots. The fire crackled, and his eyes grew heavy.

"Did you go by Mysane Kosk after Kallas as I suggested?" Sodur asked, wiping his mouth with a napkin.

Juhrnus blinked and shook his head to clear it. "I did. How did the wizards do that? What did they do?"

Sodur gave a little shrug. "What did you see? It's been more than a year since I've been there. Does it continue to expand?"

"That's what they say. The *ahalad-kaaslane* watching over the place showed me the markers where the borders had moved. They say it's expanding faster now. Almost fifty yards this year."

Sodur sat back, tapping the side of his cup as he sipped his wine, watching Juhrnus carefully. "You didn't try to go inside?"

A frisson ran down Juhrnus's spine, all hint of sleepiness evaporating. "It's a foul place. Even without the warning of the *ahalad-kaaslane* guarding it, I wouldn't have gone near the place." He paused, licking his lips, tasting cloves and cinnamon and orange. "It's like there's something inside watching, waiting. You can feel it. And the place itself . . . I've never seen anything like it. It's beautiful in a terrible way and so very, very *alien*." Sodur waited as Juhrnus crushed his meat pie in his fist, dropping it onto his plate and wiping his hand on his napkin. "You've seen it. You know how it is."

"It's been a long time. I'm sure a lot has changed. I'd like to know what it's like now."

"Like the Demonlord's fourth hell, if there was one." Juhrnus swigged the rest of his wine, setting the cup on the table with a clatter.

Sodur nodded, waiting.

Juhrnus glared at the other man. "All right. Have it your way. There's no color. Not the grass, not the rocks, not the trees, nothing. And yet everything sparkles like glass in the sun. It all looks sculpted, twisted, cursed." Juhrnus splayed his hands. He didn't have the words. "There's a sound to it, like the wind blowing through a field of knives. A sharp, eerie sound that scrapes along your bones and puckers your ass. And the smell—like something rotten, only you can't place where exactly it's coming from, because there's this sweetness to the air, like syrup. It clogs in your throat and makes you want to turn your stomach inside out to be rid of it. Down where the city used to be is a mist. It's the most beautiful thing you'll ever see. Sparkles like a sea of gemstones. You can't see anything inside it. The *ahalad-kaaslane* there say it's growing too, expanding with the borders. Whatever the wizards did there, it's still thriving. It's evil, and I don't know when it will stop."

Juhrnus filled his cup again and drank deeply. Just laying eyes on the place had frightened him in ways he didn't want to admit. Nightmares pursued him down from the mountains, and only the thought of Reisil and her magic staved them off. She'd destroyed a hundred wizards in one blow; all the way back to Koduteel he'd imagined how she would wipe Mysane Kosk clean. But now her magic wasn't working. And something else was going on. . . .

"I saw Reisil today," he said abruptly, fixing his gaze on Sodur.

"Did you?" Sodur began to eat again.

"She's found a new place to live."

Sodur glanced up. "Oh?"

"The old lighthouse. It's a death trap. We can't let her stay out there."

"We can't force her not to," Sodur said, a quiet look of satisfaction sliding over his features.

Juhrnus scowled.

"She's had a hard time of it recently. I don't know if she told you—"

"Some. That the nobles and other *ahalad-kaaslane* think she's a traitor like Upsakes because her power isn't working well. But the townspeople think she's the Lady's Chosen. That's why they wear green tokens on their clothes. They support her and no one is going to change their minds."

"She told you *that*?"

Juhrnus shook his head. "Not about the green. But it isn't much of a secret."

"And the nobles aren't happy about it either. Supports their theory. I've been trying to smooth feathers and give

Reisil time to find her power again. It'll help that she's out of the city. Out of sight, out of mind."

Juhrnus frowned. "I don't think so. She's hurting. You don't know her. She'll wall herself off and lick her wounds alone. Or shrivel up and die."

"Well, we just won't let that happen, will we?" Sodur returned with a dismissive wave of his cup.

"We? I don't get the impression she wants you around."

"A minor disagreement. She'll come around."

"What's it about?"

Sodur shook his head, leaning back in his chair and shoving away his tray. "Not good form to discuss it with you. I'd rather keep it between Reisil and me. Least said, soonest mended."

Despite Sodur's airy words, Juhrnus sensed an underlying current of worry, even grief. As if he were mourning a death. This was no mere disagreement. Reisil wasn't one to hold a grudge. But whatever had happened between them, Juhrnus got the impression that it burned more unbearably with every passing moment. For both of them.

"Don't worry. We'll go see her tomorrow. She'll need some furniture up in the lighthouse, no doubt. What else? Shall we help her fill her larder?" Sodur's tone was jovial and unconcerned; he would say no more than he already had.

The conversation soon slipped into Juhrnus's disgusted evaluation of the lighthouse tower and what the two of them could do to make it safer. They didn't know how long Reisil would be living there. Juhrnus had a feeling it would be a long time. Longer than Sodur pretended.

Chapter 4

Reisil stood on the lantern deck, Saljane clutching her fist. The sky was a murky blue—a break between storms. To the right, the city hunched under a frozen blanket, and to the left, the steel surf rose and fell with a roar.

~I don't want to argue anymore. This is for me as much as for you, Reisil said, her face rigid. She was determined not to cry.

~You need me, Saljane said, an edge of unfamiliar fear rimming her voice.

Traitor tears slipped down Reisil's cheeks, the wind turning them to ice. She brushed them away, pulling Saljane close.

~Of course I need you. That's the point. You're suffering here. You're too thin, your feathers are ragged, you don't sleep, you hardly eat. You have to leave. You have to go and get healthy. For me. I can't watch you fall apart and know I'm the cause. As long as I know you're safe and thriving, I'll be able to keep going. But I can't watch you die right in front of me.

Reisil's throat burned. It was true. Saljane had become a wraith of herself. And it *was* Reisil's fault. She wondered if Sodur had meant it to go this far. She'd thought it was bad before, but now she wasn't welcome in the Temple at all, and more often than not, crossing paths with another *ahalad-kaaslane* meant insults and recriminations rather than mere snubbing silence. Every day their disgust grew harder to bear, and she couldn't keep the hurt and anger to herself. She hoped if Saljane left, she'd be able to keep the spreading venom of her thoughts and emotions from further poisoning the goshawk.

Reisil drew a breath, staring into Saljane's carnelian eyes. *~I need you. I love you. But I'm killing you. No, don't*

*argue. You know it's true. If you go, you'll have a chance
to get strong again. Strong for me. And maybe you can find
the wizards. Whatever Juhrnus says, I'm going to have to
go to them for help. They have the answers we need. I need
you strong for that.* What she'd do when she found them,
she had no idea. Somehow she'd have to make them tell
her what she needed to know. But that bridge could be
crossed later. Until then—

~*It won't be long. A few months. By then spring will have
set in. If I haven't learned some control by then, it'll be time
to look for the wizards.* Reisil paused, waiting for more
protests, but Saljane only dipped her head and rubbed Reisil's cheek with her beak. More tears welled, but Reisil
blinked them away. Suddenly there was nothing left to do
but swing Saljane up into the air and send her away. For
a moment Reisil went rigid, everything in her resisting. She
stroked Saljane's head and back, trying to capture the feel
of the bird's crisp feathers, her musty smell, the shine of
her eyes. Saljane nipped her fingers.

"Be well. Fly strong," Reisil whispered, her voice
breaking.

Reisil drew her arm back and flung Saljane up. The goshawk leaped from her gauntleted fist and winged upward,
flying west toward the Suune Vaale Mountains. Reisil could
feel Saljane's joy in being aloft and in escaping the city.
She watched until Saljane disappeared, jagged-edged sobs
bunching in her throat. When she could no longer see her
ahalad-kaaslane, she went inside, latching the door and
leaning against it. Her knees gave way, and she slid down
the wood, giving in to her racking grief.

The torrent did not last long. Reisil could feel Saljane
beginning to falter with growing uncertainty and concern.
Viciously she repressed her wild misery, for the first time
in their bonding building a mental barrier between them.
Methodically she set it in place, willing herself to be
strong.

Standing, she took her cloak off, shaking it out and
hanging it on a peg. Then she cleaned the small room,
sweeping and dusting invisible dirt. She washed her already clean breakfast dishes and put them away, made
her unwrinkled bed and added a log to the roaring fire.

True to his word, Juhrnus had provided furniture for her. Jurhnus *and* Sodur.

Reisil snarled, hauling her washbucket out to the stone balustrade and emptying the water over the side. Sodur had moved out of the Temple and into the palace and spent most of his days there. Except when he accompanied Juhrnus to see her, at least once a week. Always she had the feeling he was watching her like a spider eyes a fly: measuring, hungry, impatient. He'd made no effort to counter the ongoing rumors, and Reisil had a dreadful feeling that he was weaving more plans—plans that she wasn't going to like any better than the last. And like that fly, she would find herself tangled helplessly in his schemes before she knew what she was getting into.

She slammed her palm against the table, kicking a chair. There was nothing to do about it but wait. She tried finding her magic, every day she tried. She never told Sodur of her failures, but he knew. He could read it on her face, and that made her more livid, knowing she was doing what he wanted her to do. She was his tool, his weapon, and she was powerless to be anything else. The Lady had given her the power, and if she wanted to help Kodu Riik, Reisil had to find the key to her magic, even if it played right into Sodur's plots. Nor would avoiding their visits do any good. Juhrnus was content for now to wait until she was ready to explain what had happened between her and Sodur, but that patience would evaporate quickly if she tried to hide.

Why didn't she just tell him?

Everything in her revolted at the thought. He'd side with her. He'd be as angry with Sodur as she was. But there was little comfort in knowing that. Sodur could just as easily turn the *ahalad-kaaslane* against Juhrnus as he had her. He would too, if it suited his plans. It would devastate Juhrnus. She knew how much. She lived it every day. And it wasn't as if there were anything Juhrnus could do for her; there was no point in jeopardizing his entire life because her misery wanted a little company.

Reisil straightened the chair and drew a deep breath. If she couldn't make her magic work, she was still a tark and could help the people of Koduteel with traditional healing. She went to her wardrobe and pulled out her pack, dropping it on the table and sorting through her medicines. The apothecary shops had been generous in giving her supplies. It always astonished her how willing they were to acknowledge her as *ahalad-kaaslane*, giving her the deference and respect she never got from her brethren. But the wearing of the green bothered her. More and more Koduteelians had begun to wear it, as if they too thought she was plotting something and were signaling their favor.

She could imagine what Sodur would say: *You've the support of the people. Once you find your magic, the nobles won't dare challenge you or they'll face a rebellion.* And it was true. But the other side of the coin was that she was a growing threat to the nobles and the court, especially since they already thought she was hatching some treasonous plan of her own.

She glanced somberly at her green cloak hanging by the door. Elutark had given it to Reisil when she'd become a tark. *You are who you pretend to be.* But what was she now that someone else was pretending she was something she wasn't?

A knock at the door made her start. Juhrnus leaned in the jamb, his beard long since shorn. Esper made an odd hump over his shoulders beneath his cloak. Her chest ached to see him, to think of Saljane. *It's necessary,* she reminded herself. *And not forever.*

"Going out?" He glanced at the table as she motioned him inside.

"To the Fringes." She paused. "Where's Sodur?"

Juhrnus shrugged. "He'll be along. If we leave now, we'll likely miss him." His eyes danced, and Reisil warmed at his conspiratorial tone.

"Then by all means, let us leave now." She shouldered her pack, and pulled the door wide.

"It's cold. You'll want your cloak."

Reisil shook her head. "Not that one. I think it's time for another. Not so obvious. Something gray maybe."

"You women, always thinking of your fripperies."

"And you don't," Reisil said. "What's that scent you're wearing?"

Juhrnus leered. "Not *my* scent, little sister."

Reisil only shook her head and went out the door. "Try to be careful. I'd hate to have your bits rot off from the pox. Nothing could hide that smell."

Juhrnus pulled the door shut behind them and slid his arm around her shoulders. "But that is what you're for, my favorite tark. You'd never let me suffer that way."

Reisil chuckled as he expected, tasting bile on her tongue. *There are worse ways to suffer*. And she knew that not telling him about Sodur was the right choice.

The gray-haired woman sat naked in front of a blazing fire, eyes closed, sweat making her bronze skin shine in the firelight. Her hands were cupped around something, elbows braced on her knees. She hadn't eaten or drunk for two days, but she held herself firmly upright, straining forward against some invisible force. The cottage was thick with blue smoke and the heavy scent of burning herbs.

Suddenly the fire died, the flames falling into themselves as if doused by water. Nurema slumped, opening her hands. Inside coiled a tiny green snake, its belly crimson, its eyes a brilliant yellow to match its forked tongue. Shining faintly in the darkness was a gold sigil on her palm. A gryphon ringed around by ivy.

"It's time. We don't have much time, not going on foot." Nurema waited, staring down at the snake. It rose up on its tail, hardly taller than the width of her hand. Then it leaped upward and down, burrowing into her arm until it disappeared inside her flesh.

"I'll take that as agreement, then," she said dryly, crawling stiffly to her feet. She sluiced herself off with a bucket of frigid water, drinking a few sips and chewing on some almonds. She dressed and filled her pack. It didn't take much. Most everything was ready. Then she went to the door and opened it. Outside the sun had just risen. The sky was a panorama of pink and gold and white. Nurema drew a deep breath.

Outside the door a man stood guard. She didn't doubt he'd been there since she'd closed the door in his face. A rush of love filled her for this slow-speaking giant of a son. She didn't think she'd see him again.

"I'm going to Koduteel," she announced.

He glanced up at her, his felt hat rolled in his hands. "Alone?"

She nodded.

"When?"

"Now."

He stood, towering over her, and she couldn't help but smile at his frowning sorrow. "I want you to get married soon, Teemart. It's long past time, and I know you've got an eye out for young Nivi. Don't wait any longer. Bring her here and have children."

"You ain't comin' back."

"If I can. Doubt it, though. There's things I've got to do. But I will if I can, and I expect grandchildren."

She stuffed a withered apple and some dried meat in her cloak pocket to eat on the path, and drank some tea with plenty of sugar. She wouldn't get far this day, not after her fast and farseeing, but there was no time to waste. Teemart wrapped her in his big arms, and she hugged him.

"Tell your brothers not to worry," she said roughly, pushing herself free. "And mind what I say. You marry Nivi. Cottage is yours now. She'll be a good wife for you."

And then she snatched up her pack and went off through the copse, heading south. Before she went to Koduteel, she was going to Mysane Kosk.

Chapter 5

Reisil staggered off the path as a sudden pressure fastened around her scalp. Tears streamed down her cheeks at the unbearable ache. Black mist circled her vision. She tottered, grasping at the air for something to steady herself. She heard the ocean roar. Where was the edge of the cliff? Wind battered her, and she dropped to all fours. Pain sheared through her skull, and she grabbed the sides of her head with both hands, moaning.

Then as suddenly as it came, it was gone.

Reisil lingered, panting, and then slowly pushed herself up onto her heels. Her head felt tender and swollen. She brushed her gloved fingers over her brow. Was she getting sick? A cold dagger thrust through her gut. Was this the first symptom of the plague? She swallowed. No. It didn't begin like this. This was different. Maybe her magic? She'd come to the bluffs to try to reach it again. It hadn't worked. Or had it? Hope flowered in her chest.

She remained sitting for several minutes, breathing slowly and waiting to see if it would come again. But her head remained clear, and there was no surge of magic. At last she sighed and clambered to her feet, hope withering. She was just hungry. She'd forgotten to eat lunch, and breakfast had been a cold boiled potato left over from the night before.

She drew a deep breath of the chill, salt air and resumed picking her way down the slick path. Far below, the tide rolled higher on the shingle.

After nearly two years in Koduteel, she still marveled at the deep water's ever-changing moods, its coy secrecy, its paradoxical threat and promise. Spray bathed her face and she made up her mind. Reisil strode to the cliff's rim, peering down into the steel waters. Her toes jutted out over the sickening drop. She flexed them, grinning. Once she would have remained a safe twenty or thirty paces from the edge, standing on tiptoe, never seeing the stark shore, the brilliant green moss growing in the crevices, the seals sliding through the waves. Even the stench of the cormorants was welcome, the humping shapes of their nesting rocks glowing white with droppings in the twilight noon.

There was a notch in the white spume below where the waves rushed into the harbor cavern. In the bay, a few fishing trawlers tossed on the whitecaps as fishermen returned home. Above the bay, cormorants and seagulls hung still against the looming sky, their wings beating furiously against the wind. One by one they plumeted into the water, where they bobbed like corks. Liver-colored seals splashed and rolled among them, undaunted by the battering surf.

Reisil blinked and wiped at her eyes, squinting to shield them from the lash of the wind. She scanned the waves beyond the headland spurs, but the gathering fog blocked the horizon in a ghostly wall.

Since last evening, there had been a painful burning in her stomach. Now it churned hotter. Knowing what she did, shouldn't she tell Sodur? What could he do? Report to

Lord Marshal Vare? As if he would believe her. As if anyone did.

But Scallacian sorcerers. Scallas had been chewing at
Patverseme for years, and only the might of their wizards
had held the sorcerers at bay. How could Kodu Riik defend
against them? But if she said nothing, they would sail into
Koduteel without warning.

She had to tell Sodur. It *was* possible that he could make
the Lord Marshal listen.

If he chose to do so.

Lady, but she was tired of not knowing what to do or
how to do it!

She needed Saljane. Her *ahalad-kaaslane* had a way of
cutting to the heart of a problem.

But—

For four lonely months since she'd sent Saljane away,
they had shared only limited contact, once every few days
or more, and then it had been glancing, shallow. A necessary choice, Reisil thought, sure of this, if nothing else. It
had saved Saljane's life.

Reisil's chilled lips twisted. If Saljane's health had improved, hers had not. With Saljane's sudden disappearance
came dozens of rumors. That the Lady had revoked Her
trust in Reisil and seized Saljane. That Reisil was no longer
ahalad-kaaslane. Others claimed that Saljane's vanishment
was part of her ongoing plot to destroy Kodu Riik. Or
overthrow the throne. She hadn't figured out exactly what
they thought she was up to.

Reisil sat down, poking at a pocket of wolf's-claw moss
wedged in a crease of stone. She ached to have Saljane
with her again, to fly with her, to open herself to that blend-
ing, like two streams running together, flavoring each other's thoughts, at once distinct and entwined.

But winter storms continued to bluster through the
spring. Returning to Koduteel would only mean a relapse
for the goshawk, and both the healer and *ahalad-kaaslane*
in Reisil refused to allow it. Saljane still needed the recu-
perative freedom of the wild. But every contact made the
separation harder.

She sat for long moments, contemplating the moss. There
was no choice. She needed Saljane's wisdom.

Reisil knotted her fingers in her lap, pulling her thoughts to order, even as her heart danced anticipation.

~Saljane, where are you? Are they still there?

The answer to Reisil's silent query was immediate and wrenching. Her vision shifted. She grabbed the ground on either side of her thighs and shut her own eyes against the disorienting double vision of looking out of two sets of eyes at once.

They were high in the air, circling above an inlet set in a thin bezel of rocky white sand and surrounded by steep, tree-covered ridges. They dipped and rose on the gusting wind. Saljane's fierce pleasure wrapped around Reisil.

~I have missed you!

And the words came with an eager wash of sharing: memories of hunting, soaring, eating, loneliness. Back on the cliff, Reisil savored the communication, soaking it up like water on cracked mud.

~I have missed you as well. But there was little time for communion. *What about the ship? What about the sorcerers?*

Saljane tipped on her wing, dropping in a long spiral.

~They wait.

Far below, a ship lay at anchor in the mouth of the inlet. Farther out, along the coastline, Reisil could see dark shapes rising out of the fog. This was the Strait of Piiton, where the spiny tail of the Dume Griste Mountains plunged into the sea. The emerald peaks of the submerged mountains made beautiful if inhospitable islands, while the ridges beneath made a treacherous and difficult passage. The strait guarded Kodu Riik from invading armadas. Passable to ships only at high tide, even then the navigable channel was narrow. It was easy to be blown off course or lose one's way in a sudden fog and end up shattered on the rocks.

~Tide's almost in. If the fog holds off, they'll make a run for it. There's plenty of wind.

Saljane responded with silent agreement.

~Let's go closer.

Saljane obeyed, jolting and skidding along the buffeting winds.

The sleek body of the ship was painted brilliant emerald and trimmed in gold. Three tall masts pricked from its decks, each strung with a complicated network of ropes. Above the crow's nest at the top of the swaying mainmast flew two banners. One was the green Scallacian flag with a gold, eight-pointed star contained in a white circle in the upper left corner. Below it flew the yellow flag of the Scallacian sorcerers. Centered on the brilliant dandelion field was a drop of crimson from which rotated five rippling arms, each darkening to black as they turned on the cloth. As Saljane circled, Reisil saw sailors scurrying like a hill of angry ants over the deck and up the rigging.

~*Sorcerers,* Saljane pointed out.

The three of them stood motionless on the forecastle. All around them sailors in green uniforms scuttled, shouting, singing, swearing. The ship leaped and tossed, struggling against its anchor. The flags cracked, the wind whistled through the shrouds and ratlines, and the ocean grumbled and roared. The sorcerers remained oblivious of it all.

Saljane circled the prow of the ship. With the aid of her *ahalad-kaaslane*'s keen vision, Reisil had no difficulty making out the details of the sorcerers' faces and clothing. The two men, perhaps thirty-five years old, wore robes skillfully painted to look like flames. Crimson tongues rose from the hems, hues of burning orange traced with blue and fading into sunset yellow at the shoulders. The sleeves were caught tightly at the wrists and billowed up over the arms. Their collars were high and straight, and on the corners of each were the same swirling vortex as appeared on their flag. Deep-set dark eyes were framed by darkly tanned, smooth-shaven skin. Their cap of ghostly white hair contrasted sharply with their swarthy darkness. They both wore their hair in a blunt, unforgiving style, cut straight just above the high collar of their robes, making their jutting features more austere.

Their companion was a woman. And though she shared their general coloring and appearance, there was something different about her. It wasn't only the color of her robe, in shades of green mottled together to look like a forest canopy. Nor was her expression any less remote than those of her companions. But something in the set of her jaw, the line of her lips, the brilliance of her eyes, spoke of hardreined emotion.

Suddenly there came a creaking of the capstan and the

groaning rattle of the anchor chain drawn up through the hawsehole. The captain shouted rapid-fire orders, and the sailors swarmed faster. Sails were unfurled, bulging full and taut as the wind thrust into them. As the ship departed, Reisil noticed for the first time that the full robes of the sorcerers showed no effect of the wind or ocean spray spurting over the prow. Rather it was as if they stood in the calm eye of a hurricane.

Back on the cliff outside of Koduteel, Reisil shuddered at their ready show of power. It was followed immediately by a corrosive burst of envy. To be able to mold her own magic so effortlessly, so purposefully! Maybe *they* could teach her—

But the thought withered like a frost-touched vine.

Even if they would teach her, even if they weren't here to attack Koduteel, she couldn't reveal her weakness to them. Reisil was all that stood between the renegade Patversemese wizards and Kodu Riik. If anyone learned how little control of her magic she had, they would descend like starving wolves. The wizards and Scallas both. In that one respect, Sodur's rumors kept the hounds at bay. No one knew she was unable to use her power.

~*Why would the Lady give me this gift and then not show me how to use it?*

~*The Blessed Lady believes in you. You will find a way.*

Reisil felt a faint stir of hope at Saljane's conviction. After all, she *had* destroyed the wizards' circle. She *had* returned Ceriba from the brink of death, and healed many others. She knew it *could* work. She didn't have any sense of *how* she succeeded, or why it went wrong, as it so often did. But with the plague spreading and the arrival of the Scallacian sorcerers, she was running out of time to learn.

~*Then why bother at all?*

~*Perhaps the path to discovery is important.*

~*Well. Unless I figure out something soon, it may be too late.*

An updraft caught Saljane, and she shot high in the air. The Scallacian ship was receding quickly along the strait. Already Reisil could no longer make out individual people. Again she wondered if there was any point in telling Sodur.

~*He will know what to do*, was Saljane's reply. *There is no other choice.*

Reisil felt herself nodding. ~*I'd better go*, she said reluctantly.

There was a moment of snatching, grappling emotion, each trying to absorb a little bit more of the other to carry her through to the next time. Then the thread between them severed.

Reisil drew a jagged breath. Urgency kindled in her blood, and she levered herself up, shivering. Little had changed in the landscape of the bay below. Though it felt like she'd been with Saljane for hours, only fifteen or twenty minutes had passed. She rubbed her hands over her arms and turned toward the path.

She was halted in midstep, her head twisting to the side as that grasping pressure snatched at her again. It clamped around her head like a fist. More tears rolled down her cheeks, the bones of her head compressing. She pushed back at the force with all the strength of her mind. To no avail. Suddenly she felt something digging into her head. *Inside her head!* Reisil felt it groping, unformed and wild edged, like desperate, scrabbling fingers.

Saljane? But no, this wasn't her *ahalad-kaaslane*. Saljane's touch was unmistakable, sharp and clean. This was uncertain, faltering, yet . . . There was a power to it, a rich consciousness, complex and—*angry*. More than angry. Murderous. Reisil's mouth went dry, and she gave a mental wrench, slamming shut the walls of her mind.

The crushing pressure vanished. Her head reeled, and Reisil crouched down, her head bent between her knees, rubbing the back of her neck with shaking hands.

It was an attack. She had no doubt of that. But what? Who? She thought of the sorcerers, and fear scuttled down her back. But how would they know her? How would they find her? Not the sorcerers. *Wizards*. Who else had reason to hate her that way? She glanced over her shoulder with a sudden sense of someone watching, fumbling inside for her elusive power, a weapon to defend herself.

Nothing. Just as when the *nokulas* had attacked on the way to Veneston.

"*Chodha!*" she swore, pushing to her feet. Fear pimpled her skin as she scrambled back onto the path, turning toward Koduteel, fleeing like a rat with a cat fast on its heels.

Chapter 6

Reisil slipped and skidded along the path, coming dangerously close to the cliff's edge. Still she did not slow down, depending on the march of ancient jack pine, white spruce, junipers, and bare-twigged tamarack to keep her from falling into the bay. She flung herself through a narrow notch between a rock shelf and a flourishing cluster of bittersweet, still wearing its deadly wealth of scarlet berries. On the other side, she ducked beneath a low-slung limb, sliding on the slippery stone as she straightened, losing her balance. She cried out and twisted, arms flailing. She caught one arm around the low limb, hanging there as she scrabbled for purchase on the path below.

It was this accident that saved her.

Even as she clutched the limb, an arrow pierced her cloak and stuck fast in the wood beside her forearm. Reisil stared at the vibrating black-and-white fletching for a bemused moment, too surprised to realize she was being attacked. She screwed her head around to look over her shoulder.

Her pursuers swarmed silently down the path, their faces hidden beneath closefitting gray scarves wound tightly around their heads. So quickly did they move, so well matched to the storm-gloom was their apparel, that Reisil couldn't count how many of them there were. At least four. She saw the glint of knives and the curve of bows. In only seconds they would reach her.

Reisil fought for footing, kicking and sliding on the rock. Her grip slipped, and she fell, ripping her cloak free and landing hard. Instantly she rolled under the limb and scuttled on her hands and knees down the path. She reached the narrow notch and lunged to her feet, shielded by the

rock shelf. She wasted no time checking how closely they
followed. Heart caught in her throat, her lungs constricted
and she careened along the path, grabbing branches and
brush for balance. With every step, she expected to feel an
arrow driving through her chest.

She raced past the point where she'd sat communing with
Saljane. She might lose them if she could make it to the
Fringes, but it was still half a league away, and she had to
cross an open slope in between. They would have no difficulty shooting her then. She didn't dare trust her magic
against them.

Her legs felt sluggish. Her lungs screamed agony, and
her throat was an icy ache. Behind her she thought she
could hear footsteps closing in. She sobbed, yanking her
cloak free from where it had caught on a wind-twisted bush.
An animal whine escaped her chest as she struggled up a
steep rise. Her feet slid from beneath her, and she caught
herself on a juniper branch, crab-crawling upward on her
hands and feet.

Lady help me! she cried silently as she topped the rise.

The Lady did not answer. But something did.

It swept over her in an appalling maelstrom of black
rage. Aimed at her, for her. Single-minded, unswerving,
fanatical.

The attacker from the cliff's edge.

It crashed over her mind, smothering in its boiling fury,
dragging her under and under.

Reisil screamed.

She choked, struggling against the frenzied tide. Only the
long months of unremitting diligence in segregating her
mind from Saljane's made it possible to sever this alien
connection.

But she could not so easily rid herself of her body's
spasming reaction. She gagged. She vomited, bitter juices
spattering her cheeks and running over her chin to stain
her cloak. She kept running, instinct goading her. But that
rage stayed with her—like clots of worms twisting and
sliding beneath her skin. Her legs began to shake, and
she slowed, everything inside her shrieking to run faster.
Faster!

Reisil stumbled down the fork leading from the bluff and
around the eastern wall of Koduteel into the Fringes. Not

far now the open greensward where she could not hide, where her only hope lay in crossing far in advance of her pursuers. And still she slowed, her entire body beginning to quake.

But deep within, she felt something kindle, something that responded to the brutality and rage, something that was feral and cruel. It flickered and swelled, hot and greedy. It streaked along her bones, heat licking her nerves with scorching strokes. Her hair rose on her arms and neck, and unformed, unbounded energy crackled around her fingers. A red fog blurred her vision. Her tongue grew parched and she could not even blink, so dry were her eyes. She felt her skin burning, felt her lips splitting, smelled the acrid stench of burning hair.

Ruled by the thing growing inside her, Reisil lurched to a halt. A savage joy blossomed in her chest. Her magic had answered her need at last.

Reisil turned, licking her lips. Her chin dropped, and she hunched her shoulders. She swiveled her head back and forth slowly, scanning the path behind from beneath lowered brows. Her nostrils flared. Her fingers flexed and curled.

Movement. She jerked her head up. Blurry shapes moved on the path, where she thought the path ought to be, for she could no longer see it through the veil of red sweeping across her vision. Her lips peeled from her teeth. She brought her hands forward fingers spread, holding them straight before her. The magic flew from her like a bolt of lightning, blood scarlet.

There were no flames or crash of thunder, no screams. Silence congealed. Crickets and birds alike froze in place, camouflaging themselves in stillness. Even the booming of the harbor cavern muted.

Reisil swayed. For a single, exquisite moment she felt unalloyed jubilation.

Then the veil dropped away, and she came to herself. She smelled the sour odor of vomit staining her cloak. She felt a breeze on her cheek, icy, like the whispering kiss of a soul-shattered *rashani*. A chill swept her, prickling the hairs on her legs.

Dear Lady, what had she done?

Reisil retraced her steps. She reached the foremost of

her attackers. All that was left was a mound of ash, vaguely human shaped, like a gray shadow cast upon the ground. Already the wind was eroding it. There was another one a few paces back and to the left, and one more to the right.

Reisil crouched to the ground, elbows on her knees, laced knuckles pressed hard against her lips. She wanted to cry, to shout and to beat the ground with her fists.

The wind picked at the ashes. For the second time since the Blessed Lady had gifted Reisil magic, Reisil had used it to kill. More than that. To annihilate. And both times it had been like riding the storm winds with Saljane. A wild, dreadful ecstasy. She ground her knuckles against her teeth. What was she that she should savor killing so?

Another thought struck her like a blow from an executioner's ax.

Was it her own fault that she could not use her magic to heal the plague victims? Deep inside, would she rather kill than heal? She had never felt much remorse for destroying the wizard circle. She had believed it was the only way to protect Kodu Riik. But was it? Couldn't she have disabled them somehow and left them alive? And these men—certainly they had wanted to kill her. But was that reason enough for a healer to kill?

She could argue that she had no choice. That the power had taken her, that she had no control over its use. And that would be true, Reisil acknowledged scornfully. She had feeble control at best. It was no justification. It was an indictment.

A memory tickled in the back of her mind and pushed upward, flowering like a thornbush in her mind. *The damage you could do . . .* The Demonlord's words had accused her, and she had defended herself, certain she would always serve the Lady faithfully. But now she was not so certain.

Her gaze swept over the three dissolving shapes. She had erased all evidence of who and what they were. And she had *laughed*. She could go and chase the other one, for certainly there had been at least four. Had the other twisted an ankle in his chase and been left behind, saved by luck? Or did he even now train his arrow on her exposed throat? Reisil lifted her head, chin elevated, inviting the unseen hand to loose its arrow. Nothing happened.

She stood, staring up the path. If she went to Sodur now,

she might meet that last assassin. Everything in her revolted from the sudden eagerness at the thought. Disgust curled her lip.

But there was something worse. If she went to Sodur, she would have to tell him what had happened. He would congratulate her, proud that she had brought her magic to bear on her enemies at need. He would see it as a triumph, a ray of hope, a justification for his plotting. She couldn't hear that. She glanced down at the smudge of gray beside her. It wouldn't be true.

She turned and hurried down toward the Fringes, her throat tight with a strangling sense of failure, of fraud. Healing someone, even to mend a cold or start hair on a bald pate—that would be a ray of hope for Kodu Riik. Not this butchery.

Clinging like fungus to the curve of Koduteel's northern wall, the Fringes was comprised of sprawling neighborhoods made of ramshackle buildings and squalid tents built from jumbles of patchworked and broken materials. They were arranged in twisty, clustered knots, each neighborhood split by narrow, zigzagging crevices that served as walkways and streets. The neighborhoods shifted constantly like the shore dunes east of the city, so that no road was ever in the same place it had been, and houses and people disappeared with alarming ease.

Reisil descended the rocky switchback along the lee side of the bluff, following the curve of the towering east wall. She pulled up her hood and huddled deep inside the folds of her cloak.

The track jerked and meandered down the steep pitch, stitching in and around strips of scree and low hummocks of rock seamed with moss and grass. There were no trees or shrubs for a quarter of a league around the walls, providing a field of fire for archers. The wall itself was pocked and blackened in places where the Patversemese had laid seige. As the trail brought her close to the wall again, Reisil patted the rough stone. Battered and pounded, the walls had held.

The Fringes smelled oppressively of manure, human waste, lye, fish guts, and acrid smoke. Children and dogs scurried through the fetid maze like ants, each as flea-ridden and filthy as the other. Their fathers worked paltry crafts, many without arms, or legs, or hands—scars of the war. Their women were equally scarred. Many in ways no one could see. Each day, sometimes twice a day, the women hiked a half a league over a steep, snow-covered ridge to the river. To discourage vagrancy, the Fringes were not permitted a well. Starvation and disease ran rampant there, and every day one or two rag-wrapped bodies were carried to the lych-ground northeast of the city.

For a while, Reisil was content to wander through the sprawl, winding around fires, dodging thin, bleating goats, carefully stepping over uncovered midden trenches. As always, she found herself both saddened and inspired by the strength of the Fringes' denizens, the joys they wrenched from their sere lives. Tattered children, feet wrapped in rags, chased each other in a game of tag, laughing, cheeks blushing red as ripe apples. A cluster of women chatted and giggled and tied limp red ribbons in the hair of a young bride. A father taught his son the art of tying knots, the son beaming at his father's praise. A young man presented his beloved with a wooden pendant in the shape of a dove.

The towers along the wall marked Reisil's passage as she worked her way through the sprawl: Sunrise Tower, *Ahalad-kaaslane* Tower, Horn Tower. Far down the wall, past the Iisand Gate, she could see the blue cone-shape topping Talis Tower. There was a family camped below there that she had promised to visit again when time permitted. She turned her footsteps in that direction.

As she walked, she nodded absently to those who greeted the stranger in their midst, noting with dismay the ragtag bits of green affixed to a great variety of shacks and tents. Knobs of painted wood, ribbons, rags, even grass and moss. How could they keep wearing it when the nobles and the other *ahalad-kaaslane* hated her so?

She stopped at the edge of the Iisand's road to wait for a midden wagon to pass. The teamster slouched on the box, his hands stained yellow by his cargo. Inside the wagon, Reisil heard a thick sloshing sound, and then the wind shifted and she caught the stench full in her face. She gagged and pressed her hand to her mouth. The teamster smiled a black-gapped smile and snickered.

"Never mind," said a thick, scratchy voice beside her.

"Happens that way sometimes. Remember to hold your breath is all. Makes a body grateful to have a head full of cotton."

Reisil smiled at the snub-nosed, squinty-eyed man who crossed the road beside her. His nose was dripping. He swiped at it with his sleeve, shaking his head.

"Sure wish the Lady would invite spring to Her table," he said. "Been passing this cold back and forth among the whole family. Third time I've had it. Can't get any sleep for all the snoring. And my wife—" He shook his head and coughed, spitting a gob of greenish phlegm onto the rutted road. "She got a nursling. Poor itty-bitty is so stuffed up she can hardly suckle. Wife's pulling out her hair."

Reisil didn't hesitate. "I've some things here that might help. If you'd like," she said, showing him her pack.

He stopped, examining her shadowed features within her hood. "Can't pay," he said, his fleshy face flushing.

Reisil gave a faint, emphatic shake of her head. "There's no need."

Finally he nodded. "All right. Anything to get some sleep. Name's Tillen," he offered over his shoulder as they walked. "Right there." He directed her between two sagging tents. Better than many, his home had two wooden sides. A patchwork blanket of wool was supported by the walls and a framework of gnarled branches, creating a space high enough to stand inside. Tillen waved at Reisil to follow after as he ducked through the low opening.

Inside was gloomy and thick with smoke. Three children huddled under blankets close to the low flames of the fire, arms and feet wrapped in strips of cloth. Their mother sat opposite on a square of wool, cradling a wailing baby. She raised red, swollen eyes at their entrance. Seeing Reisil, she hastily jerked up on the shoulder of her lowered tunic to cover her pale, milk-heavy breast.

A dog barked in the corner where he was tied. The younger of the two boys, eight years old, Reisil guessed, scurried from beneath the blanket and went to crouch beside the thin, flop-eared animal. The boy stroked the dog's bristly black head to quiet him, watching Reisil, his nose and upper lip red and chapped.

Tillen went to his wife, grasping her shoulder with a gentle hand. "Suli, I brought some help."

He glanced meaningfully at Reisil, who unslung her pack as she circled the fire and knelt beside the exhausted woman, noting her hair, dry as straw, her concave cheeks, thick breathing and dry, rasping cough.

"I'll need some water—boiled," Reisil said to Tillen.

"Kes and Mara aren't back yet," piped a hoarse young voice from the folds of the blanket. Then before her father could respond, the girl, all angles and bones, unfolded herself. She was about twelve, with a wide forehead and pointed chin and lank hair. Like her brother and father, her nose was running, her upper lip chapped red. "All we have left is for washing. I'll see if Mer Wilka has any."

She snatched up a pot from a makeshift sideboard and ducked out of the tent.

"May I?" Reisil asked, stretching her hands out to take the baby. Suli cast a fearful glance at her husband and then reluctantly passed the infant to Reisil.

Reisil bent and pressed her ear to the tiny boy's chest, and then turned him over and did the same on his back. Though his breathing was stertorous, his lungs did not have the liquid, bubbling sound Reisil feared. As she examined him further, Reisil was pleased to discover that the patch-work swaddling was free of fleas and dirt.

The girl returned, setting a pot of water over the fire. Reisil set about ministering to the family, providing loz-enges for sore throats, an unguent for congestion, a thick infusion of meadowsweet, wormseed, and willow bark to ease pain and congestion, and a chamomile ointment for the chapping. She worked quietly and without any attempt to use her magic. The ashes of the dead assassins swirled in her mind, and she feared what she might do.

At last she settled the woman on a pallet beside the fire, the baby nestled close and suckling at last. The other chil-dren snuggled against her at Reisil's orders, warming each other and their mother beneath shared blankets.

"I'll come back in a day or so," Reisil told Tillen, step-ping out of the tent more than an hour later. "But you need to find some good food. Bread, fish, something." The look she gave him was apologetic. Certainly if he had food, or the means to get it, he would have. She did not want to be the one that suggested he butcher the dog, though its

protected station inside their home meant he knew someone else *would*, if he were not careful.

"Fish are running far from shore these days, and a body
has to go a far piece for crabs anymore. But I've got the
dog. Good tracker." Tillen shrugged. "Since Suli's been
sick, haven't wanted to leave her alone—things get bad
here sometimes. But she'll be easier now. I'll head out in
the morning. See what game there is. Wapati are still forag-
ing low, since it's been cold. With the dog, I usually bring
something back."

Reisil nodded, understanding now how the man could
keep his family in such comparative splendor. She inwardly
winced at the irony. But it was true. They had clothes and
blankets, wood and a substantial shelter. More than many.

"Anything I can do for you? Where you headed?"

"I'm looking for a young couple with a son. Liitsun is
the husband's name."

Tillen nodded. "Know 'em. Came last fall from Poldmari
in the Dume Griste spur. Lot of blight fallen on that family.
You going to see the boy?"

Reisil nodded.

"I'll show you the way. Least I can do."

Reisil didn't recognize the field of waist-high tents that
proved to be their destination. The smell here was worse,
wetter, with a clinging miasma of body waste and decay.
She frowned at Tillen.

"This is not where Liitsun and Nisek had their tent."

"Is now. There was a *wave*, couple of nights ago. Happens. Folks get restless, mob together, overrun their neighbors. Best of it is that Liitsun and Nisek managed to keep
hold of a little bit—tent, some bits and pieces—and they
didn't get hurt. They're wanting pretty bad for supplies. If
I bring something back tomorrow, I'll give them some of
the meat. They found a patch there, up near the Gryphon
Tower." He pointed. "Gets some wind, but mostly in the
lee of the wall. Low though, stays wet.

"Lots of folks from Poldmari here. Those who lived. And
a lot of the other mountain villages. No place else to go.
They'd rather die here than be bait for *nokulas*."

Reisil scanned the long hollow and shivered. This was
not a good place. It was a killing field, a dying field. She

sucked in a quiet breath, hardening herself against what she couldn't change.

"Ready, Reisiltark?"

Reisil jerked around, her hood falling back. "How did you know?"

Tillen flipped back his cloak to reveal his vest beneath. Green stitches zigzagged along the collar, brilliant and festive.

"Isn't one of us down here that doesn't know you and the Lady's mark." He pointed to the unfurling pattern of golden ivy.

Reisil looked away. Their trust only made her guilt worse. They, of anyone, should hate her the way the nobles and *ahalad-kaaslane* did.

Tillen squeezed her arm in his thick-fingered grip. "You're the only healer what cares to come to the Fringes. Only *ahalad-kaaslane* I seen in a while either. None of us have to see your face to know you."

Reisil felt her face convulse. *Table scraps. I ought to do more.* Tillen's hand dropped away, expression sympathetic as he turned to gaze over the spread of tents, waiting while Reisil recovered her composure.

"Ready, then?" he asked gruffly after a few moments.

Reisil nodded, drawing up her hood and pulling her cloak tightly around herself, following after. The last hours had been more than she could comprehend. She felt a numbness creeping through her, and she welcomed it, welcomed the balm on her endlessly gnawing questions, her self-doubts and the loneliness that followed her like a shadow.

But the day was not over yet.

Chapter 7

Four rough-hewn steps, a long sloping curve, a switchback, twenty narrow steps, another long curve, another switchback, more steps. Down and down into the stone roots of the castle.

The drumming of the harbor cavern echoed through the maze of passages, intensifying as Sodur and Lume descended, covering any sounds they made. The smell of brine and damp earth leached from the walls. The darkness was stygian. An iron cage of red coals dangled from Sodur's left hand, a wicker basket from his right. The coals gave sufficient light for Lume to see, with no telltale glare to mark their coming. Sodur borrowed the lynx's vision, though in truth, he hardly needed to. They'd trod this path at least once a day for over a year.

From the basket rose mouthwatering smells. Food fit for an Iisand. Sodur's lips clamped together against the pain of a wound that would not heal. Not *an* Iisand. *The* Iisand, Geran Samir. Who was a secret prisoner in his own castle. Whom Sodur loved like a brother, even as he snapped the locks on the door, even as he kept careful watch against Geran's escape.

The man and lynx came to a wide area where several corridors broke away like spokes on a broken wheel, some going up, others deeper into the stone. The pair turned into the leftmost passage. After several steps, it dropped in a sudden angle, the rock floor smooth and slippery with moss and damp. Sodur edged his way slowly along, pressing his back against the undressed wall. Once, many centuries before, this tunnel had been used as a waste chute, to dump the castle's refuse into the ocean. Now it was unused. Briefly he considered dropping the contents of the basket down the shaft and into the salt waters below. But no.

There must be nothing to invite the curious to investigate. And it *was* possible that Geran might eat something this time.

Despair closed stone hands around Sodur's throat, strangling the vague hope. It wasn't likely. No, once again Sodur would choke down the delicacies so that everyone would continue to believe the lie that Geran remained locked in his apartments, clinging to solitude after the loss of his beloved wife. For a man must eat to survive, to get better, to return to his throne and rule his people.

But the Iisand Geran Samir hadn't eaten in six months. Any ordinary man would have died long since. But then, the Iisand was no longer a man.

Sodur stopped, pain snagging in his thin chest. He teetered and then inched himself around the serpentine wall-niche that disguised the entrance to the prison. He set his feet sideways on the narrow steps of the stairway that dropped away abruptly on the other side of the niche. When he reached the safety of the bottom, he paused, wheezing as Lume pressed against his shins and then stood on hind legs to rub against his thigh. Sodur sank down to sit on the bottom step, hugging Lume.

~I don't know how much longer I can do this.

Lume's reply came in a rapid-fire collage of images. Normally they would be too much to assimilate. Yet this time Sodur saw each in surreal slowness and clarity.

~dusty booted feet . . . perfume and the throne . . . sweet ice wine . . . tobacco and mint . . . the Mesilasema . . . clear gray eyes . . . fish and leather and bergamot . . . a scrape across the wrist . . . musty odor of sex . . . pungent ink and dusty maps . . . armor and oil . . . salt and blood . . . booming laughter . . . cedar and raspberries . . . jaggedness . . . tang of difference . . . ice and metal and clouds and . . . difference.

Image after image rolled by. Twenty years' worth. Circling, coiling, returning to that *difference* again and again. Sodur felt Lume's animal emotions like a river of blood through the memories. They whispered over his skin, danced along his nerves. His limbs began to shake as he tried to hold it all. It was too much.

His head jerked back, and he yowled. The cry echoed

down the stone burrow. When it came back, other sounds rode it, high-pitched, almost beyond human hearing.

Laughter. Voices—gabbling, swarming.

The deluge of images sheered off as quickly as they'd begun. Lume blinked at Sodur with shining green eyes, tufted ears perked up, head tilted.

Sodur panted. Suddenly he groaned, gouging the knuckles of his thumbs against his closed eyes. He pressed, digging hard, trying to squash the wordless sounds that still scuttled in his head on hooked beetle-feet.

Lume whined and licked his rough tongue over Sodur's fisted hands.

~*I am here.*

The words burst into Sodur's brain like a beacon in the darkness. Before its illuminating strength, the teeming sound fled. Sodur sat up and breathed deeply, fear winding his nerves taut. He swallowed, tasting bile. He stroked Lume's head with a shaky hand.

"Let's get on, shall we?" He did not dare mindspeak. Did not dare invite a return of the onslaught. Never had he felt Lume so closely, so intimately. And the crawling in his head after—

He shivered. He'd thought he'd escaped unscathed. But more and more he wondered. The memory of the *nokula* perched on top of him flashed through his mind. Geran had been struck within months. Why so long for it to affect him? And if it had, then—

It changed everything.

He ignored the tremor in his hands as he collected himself and stood. He took a torch from the wall sconce above his left shoulder and lit it from the coals. The serpentine niche above would prevent any telltale light from escaping. Leaving the lantern, Sodur picked up the basket and strode down the corridor.

The ancient stone passage had room for three men to walk shoulder to shoulder. The stone walls had been chiseled to give the appearance of mortar and brick. Long unused lucernes hung from chains every fifteen feet. Many of the bronze lamps remained upright and steady, as if impatient to be lit, despite the green of corrosion dulling their metal curves. Others dangled drunkenly from broken chains or had vanished altogether.

Sodur paused at the entrance to the prison ward. Fluted pilasters topped by snarling gargoyle heads framed the doorway. He glanced up at the bestial faces. There was a cunning malevolence to their expressions, as if they knew his fears—and enjoyed them.

He dragged his gaze away and passed inside. The chamber opened into a wide teardrop shape lined by prison cells. The doorways of these were framed by more gargoyle-topped pilasters. At the center of the space was a great hearth fully eight feet across, set upon a round pedestal of stone. Surrounding the hearth was an assortment of stone tables, benches, chairs. Many had metal pins where leather straps had once been fastened. The debris piled on the floor contained bits of bone and teeth, rusted tools, hair and shards of glass. Beneath it, the stone floor was stained black from centuries-old blood.

Sodur circled the torture chamber, swallowing uneasily at the shapes looming in the flickering darkness, like *rashani*s bound for vengeance.

The Iisand's cell was the farthest from the door and down another passage, this too narrow and low for Sodur to do much more than slide sideways, chin hunched into his neck. It was almost as if the builders had never meant for it to be used. Or perhaps it was that they did not want it remembered.

At the end, it widened into a cul-de-sac containing one cell. The gargoyles here had bulbous, red glass eyes that seemed alive in the torchlight. They were half again as large as those standing watch in the outer chambers, as if whatever was kept here needed more powerful warding. Almost they might have been brethren to the Blessed Amiya's griffins, but these disturbing creatures seemed more likely to have been spawned in the realm of the Demonlord. The light flickered over their beast-faces, and Sodur steeled himself against the reflex to startle at their seeming movement.

Inset into the iron-bound oak slab covering the Iisand's cell was a window. Through its grille, Sodur could see the vertical bars of the interior door. He inserted his torch into a sconce on the wall and set his basket on the floor. He gazed broodingly at the heavy door. Three bars set at shoulder, waist and knee heights secured the outer door, each fastened in place by a different lock. Each bar was inscribed with ancient symbols scrolling across the flat metal surface in now meaningless beauty. Those same symbols were etched across the interior of the cell, as well as the bars of the inner door. Prayers, Sodur supposed, or incantations robbed of power by age and disuse.

Vare would join him soon. He should wait. After a moment he dug in his pocket for a ring of keys. He never liked sharing this moment. Sodur never liked exposing Geran. Especially to Vare.

He began at the bottom, removing each lock and bar in turn, his ears straining for noise on the other side of the door. There was only silence. He grasped the iron handle with his left hand, his right hand falling on the hilt of his sword. The well-oiled hinges made no sound. Sodur swallowed, hesitating before borrowing Lume's sight in an effort to pierce the gloom within. Their connection wrenched Sodur out of himself. He felt the cold floor gritty beneath his paws and flexed his claws uneasily. His skin prickled with a sense of wrongness, of danger, and the hackles on his back and neck pricked up in stiff points. He growled low in his throat, nostrils flaring at the smell within, like lightning after a strike. He crouched nearer to his *ahalad-kaaslane*'s tall legs, glad of the bars that separated them from what lay within. His stumpy tail twitched back and forth, and he growled.

Sodur fought against the sensations, struggling to separate himself from Lume, to share the lynx's mind without losing himself. At last he found a precarious balance. But it was like standing hip-deep in a rushing river. If he shifted wrong, if his foot slipped, he would be pulled under by the current, to be lost in its powerful embrace.

The interior of the cell appeared empty but for the bed, the mattress long since shredded to bits, the heavy pedestal scarred and gnawed. On the floor were scattered bits of the splintered washstand, shards from the basin and pitcher, and the dented, overturned chamber pot. There was nothing else to be seen.

Sodur pulled himself from Lume's mind, feeling an odd prickling behind his eyes as he did so.

"Geran?" he called, his voice gentle and cajoling. "Come now, it's only me. I've brought some food. Aren't you hungry? Don't you remember Lemmuel's seedcakes? They are still warm from the oven."

There was movement within, a tapping and a scraping in staccato succession.

Sodur squinted and inched closer.

Light flickered and gleamed in the cell, running like molten silver to outline a shape—too close. Sodur gasped and stiffened.

Geran, what had once been Geran, rippled into sight, one moment invisible, the next a shape made of moonlight and water. *Nokula.*

Translucent hairs sprouted along his head, back and arms. They moved separately and deliberately as if tasting the air. Daggerlike talons tipped his six-jointed fingers, and Geran's mouth had become a maw of shining fangs. His tongue had grown long, prehensile, and was tipped with a gleaming tooth, like one of Lume's brilliant fangs. He stood stooped, sometimes walking on all fours, as graceful as a hunting cat, his body powerful and thick. But worst of all were his eyes. Set wide apart above ridged cheekbones and a pointed snout, they were as hard and curved as the bowl of a silver spoon. They appraised Sodur with keen intelligence. But there was something deeply alien about them, as though the mind behind that intelligence was entirely different from the man Sodur had once called friend. Different and malevolent.

For a moment Sodur was back in the foothills near Veneston. He was lying on top his horse, the *nokula* straddling him, the same alien knowingness in its silver eyes, in the cold, dank touch of its mind against his.

Sodur drew a harsh breath and yanked himself out of that memory. Geran—the *nokula*—had moved closer. His eyes gleamed beyond the bars. Sodur's eyes fastened on the barb tipping the creature's long tongue as it swayed just beyond his nose. Milky poison pearled on its tip, looming large as the moon. As he followed the hypnotic movement, Sodur's stomach twisted and his throat jerked. He forced himself to remain still.

And so they stood. Minutes ticked past, and Lume growled low in his throat, an angry, forlorn sound.

Suddenly there came a clatter and the sound of something rolling from the main chamber. The *nokula* jerked his head and snarled, a high, windy sound. Sodur took advantage of his distraction to lurch out of reach.

Quick, determined footsteps and a nimbus of yellow light in the darkness of the passage signified the arrival of Lord Marshal Vare. Sodur straightened, drawing a calming breath, cold sweat making his undertunic cling to his back and ribs.

"Ah, so there you are. Everything secure?"

The Lord Marshal glanced into the cell, brighter now with the added luminosity of his torch. Once again the Iisand had faded from sight.

"Not showing himself today, eh? Well, our guests from Scallas should be running the Piiton any time now. Won't be long before we'll know if they can save Geran."

"You really think they'll help?"

Lord Marshal Vare glanced sharply at Sodur, his walnut gaze quick and discerning. A slender man, he stood a bare inch over six feet. His face was clean shaved, sporting a thin, crooked nose and wide, sensual lips. His short brown curls were threaded with silver. Over his shoulders he wore the collar of his office, a heavy chain made of flat squares of blue and black enamel embossed on yellow gold. His reputation for tactics and strategy was well earned, and his intensity and charisma made men and women alike flock to his side, hanging on every word, every nuance of expression. He was notorious for his passionate devotion to the Iisand and Kodu Riik, and was not to be diverted from his duty for anyone. His only vice was women. He kept multiple mistresses, leaving his wife of twenty-five years to molder at their country estate.

"Don't tell me you've changed your mind?" he asked, brows winging up.

Sodur shook his head. "I don't know. The closer they come . . . I think, can they help? Maybe. Will they? It's a desperate game, and the scheme could easily turn on us. Except for Reisil, we're defenseless against them." He paused. "And even if they *will* help us, it won't come cheap."

"What price is too high if we get Geran back and keep that puppy of his off the throne? Aare's got a taste for Patverseme blood and an eye for glory. He'll have us back at war within a month of being crowned."

"He's not going to take it well. Are you ready for that?"

"He's not regent yet. I head the Arkeinik at the moment and have no obligation to consult him on my decisions."

"Still, we should have let Reisiltark have a try—" Sodur broke off. Vare was already shaking his head, his lips pulled tight in an expression of distaste.

"I know you think highly of her, Sodur. But I cannot share your faith. Besides, the *ahalad-kaaslane* are in bad odor right now. If it weren't for your discretion about this," he waved his hand toward the Iisand's cell, "you wouldn't even have been included in the discussions."

"Lucky the Iisand came to me first, then," Sodur said, bristling at the other man's condescension. "But she is one of *us*. We shouldn't expose ourselves to the Scallacians without at least giving her a try."

"Is she really one of us?" Repugnance curled his patrician lip. "Even the *ahalad-kaaslane* don't claim her. And if, as she claims, her powers really aren't as strong as they were in Patverseme, she's useless for this. I've been to Scallas. I've seen what the sorcerers can do. With enough money, they will be reliable."

Sodur rubbed his hand over the stubble on his cheeks and chin, pinching his upper lip between his thumb and forefinger. After a moment, he nodded reluctantly.

"I hope you're right. If not, we'll soon be on our knees to their Kilmet. And lucky to be alive to do so."

"I'm counting on Reisiltark's reputation to keep them in line. Her powers may truly be erratic, but they don't know that. And they will know what she did to the wizards in Patverseme. I'll make sure of it. The Scallacians have never defeated the wizards themselves, so they'll be sufficiently cowed into behaving themselves. She will need to be very visible. You will see to it?"

Sodur bit back the urge to spit. He looked up at the ceiling and then back, meeting Vare's demanding gaze. "I'll see to it. It's time for her to come back down out of the lighthouse and show her face in Koduteel anyhow. I'll put Juhrnus on them too. The more eyes watching them, the better."

Vare paused as if about to say something and then gave a little shrug. "How is Geran today? Did you manage to see him?" he asked, changing the subject.

"You might say that."

"Still not eating?" Vare nudged the basket of food with his foot.

"No, and you'd better have a bit of it. I've about had a stomach full."

The Lord Marshall turned a narrowed gaze on Sodur, hearing the doubled meaning. "You're *ahalad-kaaslane,* and I can't require you to follow my orders, but I'll do whatever it takes to bring Geran back and protect Kodu Riik. Don't ever forget that."

Sodur crossed his arms and watched as Vare retreated up the passage. "So will I," he murmured. "So will I."

After a moment he closed the outer door of the cell and refastened the three bars. As he gathered up the basket and the torch, he glanced down at Lume, the Lord Marshal's none-too-subtle threat scraping on him like sandpaper on soft flesh.

~Do you feel it, my friend? Inside and out, there's a storm brewing.

That alien prickling arced over his brain again, scurrying beneath his skull. Sodur gave his head a sharp shake, gritting his teeth together. Lume leaned against his knees and whined.

~You feel it too.

Agreement. Unease.

Sodur stroked a soothing hand over Lume's head.

~Then it's time to make our choice. If we don't tell Reisil soon, we may lose the opportunity. Derros is right about one thing. He cannot order the ahalad-kaaslane. *We must protect Kodu Riik the best way we know how. And Reisil is the only real solution. The Lady chose her. How can we not trust the Lady's judgment?*

Even as he settled on his decision, a chill of foreboding swept over him. He was running out of time. Would she listen to him?

Chapter 8

"Don't toy with him, Metyein. It's much too cold, and I'm hungry besides. I want hot wine, a groaning table, and a lapful of woman."

Metyein flashed a thin-lipped smile at his second. There was no other man his father wanted less as a companion for his eldest son, and no other that Metyein trusted so well. His father's disapprobation merely served to spice their friendship.

"You have no heart, Soka. How can I prick Kaselm's pride that way? How will he consider himself a man if I merely swat him like a child?"

Soka eyed Metyein's smiling countenance banefully. "He can plump up a woman or six like any other civilized man. I swear, Metyein, all winter long you've had us out here freezing our balls off. I tell you now, you're going to have to find yourself a new second if you can't wait for a more mild season for your little wrangles."

At Soka's first words, Metyein's face shuttered, his fine-drawn features turning to chiseled marble. "Some of us don't find studwork as manly an enterprise as others," he said.

"Oh, for the love of the Demonlord's warty, purple horn, Metyein, I didn't mean your father," Soka said impatiently. "You appreciate a warm, wet, willing woman as much as the next man, and none of us have wives—which, I might add, will salve your conscience when you poke a hole in Kaselm. So why shouldn't we enjoy ourselves? Having a noble's byblow gets a doxy a bit of status, some extra money for her old age, and lets a man be certain she's a good breeder before he makes her his wife. We're doing a service."

Metyein couldn't help but chuckle as he unpinned his cloak, short brown curls tossing in the wind.

"All right," he said, giving the promise to Soka that his Lord Marshal father had not managed to bribe, blackmail or reason from him. "This will be the last time—at least until the demon-blighted spring arrives. So long as no one gives me cause."

"Kaselm *was* foolish to mention your mother so. It should be quite obvious to anyone that you have taken charge of your mother's reputation, and that you are by far the most superior swordsman in Koduteel. The man has offal for brains. His father must despair for the future of his House."

"His father may thank me, then." Metyein said, rolling his shoulders and tugging his cuffs down over his wrists. His clothing fit impeccably as always, and yet, as always, he fussed with it restlessly before proceeding with the duel. Not that he expected to lose. Still his blood roared in his veins, and his muscles tensed with anticipation.

"Likely he wouldn't mind a different choice of heir," Soka agreed. "But I'm not sure there is a better choice available. He was so deep in his cups that he doubtless can't even remember his offense."

"Then before I stop his heart, I shall refresh his memory."

"Don't be such an ass. Killing Kaselm will do nothing to mend your father's habits. Let Kaselm off with a scratch. His pride will suffer with the story that you defeated him almost before he drew his sword. That he won't soon forget, thanks to Nedek's flapping tongue. You can hardly inflict a worse punishment. And then you and I can find someplace to get warm." He grinned lasciviously and waggled his brows.

Metyein chuckled and clapped Soka on the shoulder. "All right, all right. You win. A scratch. But on his cheek. Every time he looks in the mirror, he'll have cause to remember."

"It could be worse," said Soka, pulling a flask from a cloak pocket and taking a quick swig. The folds of his hood fell away from his face. He had a straight nose with prominent cheekbones, his chestnut hair forming a dramatic widow's peak on his high brow. But his strikingly handsome features were marred by the brilliant patch covering one eye, the other glittering like blue topaz.

"Better hurry before he piddles himself or the watch interrupts your fun. They patrol the gardens more avidly now that you've made it such a fashionable site for dueling."

"Certainly the gangs of thieves and assorted vagabonds who have taken up residence here aren't reason enough to step up patrols," Metyein replied sardonically.

The two men paced up the Lovers' Walk toward Kaselm and Nedek. The Jarrah Gardens formed the hub of the social season's entertainment. They consisted mostly of shady woods spreading over low knolls and clustering in grassy hollows. Paved walks crosshatched the gardens at intervals, providing seclusion and privacy for amorous assignations and other, less savory activities. The Lovers' Walk ran along the western edge, a cloistered tunnel beneath the trees. South and east lay the orchestra pavilion and the rotunda. Supperbox wings braced the orchestra pavilion on either side.

The Lovers' Walk was often Metyein's choice for duels, and not only because of the privacy it offered. It was also his way of rebuking his father for his ever-growing catalog of mistresses. The current favorite wore a scent of star flowers and sweet bren resin. The cloying fragrance had clung to his father's skin and hair the last three days, staining the air around him and turning Metyein's stomach with every tainted breath he took.

Metyein found his father's romantic exploits intolerable. His mother, too shamed to sit passively by and watch her husband's sexual sport, remained sequestered in Doneviik, the Vare ancestral home. A quiet, dignified woman, she rarely ever spoke of the man who had begun straying within months of their marriage. Though he'd warmed her bed sufficiently often to produce three sons and two daughters, theirs was a sterile relationship. To Metyein, he had been little more than a low voice, a scent of tobacco and a pair of polished boots. But on Metyein's twentieth birthday, the Lord Marshal had sent for him in preparation to become the next Kijal Vare. That had been two years and more than twenty duels ago.

Metyein sucked his teeth and spat in an ungentlemanly fashion. He had had years of intensive tutelage in all those things necessary to prepare him to inherit the title—social graces, languages, mathematics, history, swordplay, and tactics. His mother had been scrupulous in making sure he learned his lessons. But he was like a child learning to read compared with his father's brilliance. Over the last two years he'd learned more than he would have believed possible on every facet of the court, politics, the war, and even his father. It rankled almost beyond bearing that he was forced to respect this man who'd had so little care for his wife's reputation. But if he'd come to respect the Lord Marshal's mental agility, he continued to be infuriated by his father's casual rutting. Those who admired his sire made Dajal Vare the brunt of their merrymaking, publicly speculating about the woman who would drive a man to such heights of excess.

Metyein ground his teeth. If winning duels against those bucks was proof of her virtue, then his mother was perfect indeed. He never lost. Even his father's swordsmaster had been startled at his skill, and their training sessions soon became full-scale contests, driving both to new levels of ability. The lewd speculations about his mother had dwindled sharply as Metyein's reputation had spread amongst the Lord Marshal's toadies and they began to fear for their lives. More than a few of his father's allies had complained about his transgressions. His father's admonitions only spurred him on.

"You're quiet. Not having second thoughts?" asked Soka.

"Not at all. I'm merely wondering which cheek Kaselm would prefer marked."

"Either will make an improvement. But perhaps you should ask."

The wind whined through the bare trees, and ice crunched beneath their boots. Kaselm and Nedek waited beside a small fountain, its marble basin cluttered with winter debris and snow. Kaselm was several years older than Metyein. He had narrow, piggy eyes and a bulking chest that appeared entirely out of proportion to his bandy legs. His doublet was stained with wine and vomit from the previous night, and his sleeves revealed all that he'd eaten since donning it. Nedek was equally broad shouldered, but his gut jutted above his waistband, and his fine features disappeared in the fleshy folds of his face.

"Gentlemen," Metyein said with a nod. "Are you ready to begin? It seems my friend Kaj Soka longs for indoor amusements."

Nedek scowled at Soka, stepping away with a sour expression. Metyein's gaze sharpened, but Soka gave a faint shake of his head and rolled his good eye.

Metyein swallowed his resentment. Soka had resided in Koduteel as a hostage to the court for twelve years, more than half his life. In that time, he'd never once been allowed outside its walls. The price he paid for the crimes of his father. That and a constant barrage of insolence from the other nobility for which Soka had no recourse: he was forbidden to fight by the terms of the hostage compact. He'd been permitted to carry a weapon only after Patverseme had attacked Koduteel, and since then no one had thought to revoke the privilege. He would not soon forgive the humiliation of having Metyein defend his honor from the likes of Nedek. Still, if it was Nedek he was dueling and not Kaselm, Metyein wouldn't hesitate to separate the man's idiot soul from his body.

"Shall we?" Metyein asked, gesturing toward the walkway and pulling off his gloves. Kaselm and Nedek glanced at one another, and then Kaselm mumbled miserably as he removed his cloak. Metyein retreated along the walk, leaving Soka standing beside the fountain with Nedek. Kaselm shuffled out to a point opposite Metyein, fumbling at the hilt of his sword.

Both men drew, the metal of their swords chiming brightly in the frigid air. Kaselm's sword was a court-sword. Metyein eyed it with derision. Kaselm's limp, awkward grip indicated it was more decorative than functional.

As both men settled into guard positions, Metyein paused. "It should comfort you to learn, Kaselm, that I've decided to take my satisfaction in first blood rather than heart's blood. But that leaves me with something of a dilemma. Would you prefer to wear my mark on your right or left cheek?"

Kaselm's jaw dropped and then closed, then opened

and closed again. Metyein remained poised and ready. Kaselm bellowed and galloped forward. Metyein ducked under his wild slashing blow, and Kaselm stumbled past, unable to stop. If this had been battle and Metyein had been using a sword with a cutting edge, he might have ended things right there with a quick slash at Kaselm's exposed hamstrings. But instead he spun around, weight forward on the balls of his feet, waiting for Kaselm to charge again.

Kaselm lumbered about, looking faintly baffled. He clutched his hilt with white-knuckled fingers. Already he was panting, his breaths bursting forth in feathery plumes. His stance was too wide, Metyein noted, and he held his sword too high. His dagger drooped uselessly in his other hand.

Even without Soka's admonition to hurry, Metyein doubted he could have toyed long with this buffoon. He slid his tongue around his teeth. He could not allow Kaselm's comments to pass unchallenged, and yet how could he consider this a fair duel? How could any idiot be allowed to strap on a sword if he was this incompetent?

Disgusted with them both, Metyein didn't wait for Kaselm to formulate another attack. Shifting his feet quickly, he brought himself in under Kaselm's guard, caught the other man's bobbling sword with his dagger and flipped it easily out of his hand. A moment later, he flicked the point of his rapier across Kaselm's florid right cheek. Blood welled along the line of the cut and trickled down his flummoxed face.

"I declare myself satisfied," Metyein said with a cold salute of his sword. "I would caution you against further insults to my mother, however." With that, Metyein gave a stiff bow and backed out of reach.

"Well done," Soka murmured, handing Metyein his cloak.

"He won't think so. But I'll be damned if I'll protect his pride by playing a gull to his abysmal skills."

"Basham Odelm will be grateful that you didn't carve his son's heart out. And I am grateful to be on my way. Shall we?"

"I want a drink."

Soka flashed a feral grin. "Delightful idea. Cantra's got that new black-eyed wench. Wild thing. She will be just the thing to warm my bones, one in particular."

They had hardly gone a dozen steps when an eerie, high-pitched squeal shrilled from behind. Metyein and Soka whirled about, yanking their swords free.

Kaselm sprawled open-eyed on the ground, an arrow holing his throat, blood spreading from him in a steaming puddle. Nedek toppled forward, mouth wide, thudding lifelessly over Kaselm's legs. A bouquet of arrows sprouted from his back. Before either Metyein or Soka could react, an arrow thudded into Metyein's thigh, and two more bit into Soka, one through his shoulder, the other just below his ribs.

Pain ripped through Metyein, his leg buckling with the force of the impact. Beside him, Soka made a whining sound, like a hound caught in a trap. He staggered back, lurching into Metyein and ramming his knee against the arrow in Metyein's thigh. Metyein coughed and swallowed, a gray haze blurring his vision. He grappled Soka around the shoulders, pivoting on his good leg and thrusting Soka ahead of him into the trees. Arrows clattered on the pavement behind and lodged, vibrating, into the tree trunks.

"They shoot too well to be common bandits," Soka gasped, his right arm dangling uselessly from his wounded shoulder.

"Can you make it to the horses?" Metyein asked, grasping Soka and dragging him through the trees. Farther up the Lovers' Walk he heard the thuds of booted feet.

"Not and keep breathing," Soka said, slumping against a tree. "You'll have to pull the arrows and tie off the wounds. Don't argue! I know how stupid it is, but I'm going to bleed to death anyway."

Metyein sheathed his sword and braced his hand against Soka's chest, grasping the arrow's shaft in his other hand. Sending a prayer to the Lady, he pulled the arrow from Soka's shoulder, trying to follow the same track out as the arrow had made going in. It slid out easily, and Metyein stared at the tip in surprise. It lacked barbs, looking more like the square head of a crossbow bolt or a practice arrow.

"Stop mooning, and get the other before I bleed dry," Soka said through white lips.

Metyein bent and repeated the procedure for the arrow

protuding from Soka's ribs. Blood flowed rapidly from both wounds. He heard only silence from the Lovers' Walk now, and his skin crawled, knowing they were hunted. He tore strips from his cloak with the aid of his dagger and tied bandages around both wounds.

"What about your leg?" Soka gasped as Metyein pulled him up, slinging Soka's good arm over his shoulder.

"They're too close. I'll survive for now."

"Long enough to get shot again? Let's go before you drop me."

They stumbled through the trees, Soka's sword serving as a crutch. Metyein's thigh screamed, the protruding arrow brushing trees and bushes. He gritted his teeth against the agony and lurched on, feeling his strength withering as blood trickled down his leg. Behind, he heard voices calling and the crackle of twigs and leaves. Their pursuers had given up any pretense of stealth.

"They're gaining," Soka muttered.

"They can't use their bows in the trees unless they get closer. We need to go faster."

"By all means, let us do that," Soka said, and he managed to move a little more quickly, biting bloody dents into his lips.

They staggered up a long rise, leaving a crimson trail in the snow. Metyein guided them around a thick stand of trees, expecting every moment to feel an arrow piercing his back. They blundered through a thicket of skeletal bushes and vines. The shaft of the arrow in his leg caught in the tangle, and pain unraveled along every nerve. Metyein moaned and lurched forward out of the bushes. But his leg had gone limp. His head spun and his body shook. He staggered another step. Soka said something, but Metyein couldn't hear it through the rush of wind in his ears. Then the ground beneath his foot vanished and he was falling.

Agony snapped him in its jaws as he thudded against the frozen ground, and then everything went black.

Ice and fire. Metyein tried to open his eyes, but they were too heavy. Frigid water trickled down his neck, and he shook his head feebly. His legs flared white hot at the movement. Metyein groaned.

"Well, it's a change from faking dead, though I don't think you want to be so loud," came Soka's strained whisper. "No, don't go passing out again."

The cold came again and more water trickling. Metyein forced his eyes open and glared at Soka, who was pressing a handful of snow against his cheek. His face was scraped, and his eyepatch had been pushed askew.

Metyein batted weakly at Soka's hand. "Stop that."

"Ah, so you're done with your nap? We can move along now? Brilliant tactics, by the way. Cover under a foot-bridge, and not so far from the horses, unless I'm turned around, which is entirely possible." Soka tossed aside the snow and helped Metyein sit up. At Metyein's clipped-off whine, Soka frowned, his eyes traveling down to Metyein's ugly thigh wound. "Got the arrow out, but the fall stirred it about in your muscle. I've tied it off best I can with one wing, but it doesn't look good."

Soka had made a makeshift tourniquet using a strip of cloth from his cloak and a stick, twisting the fabric tight around Metyein's thigh. Blood continued to seep from the ragged hole. Metyein tore a strip from his own cloak and wrapped it around the wound, sweat beading on his brow, his breath coming in wheezing gasps as he knotted the bandage in place.

When he was through, he looked around. They had fallen down a hill and onto a frozen stream. The hillside was bare of snow, and the dried grasses showed little evidence of their precipitous passing. Above his head arced a stone footbridge. Soka had managed to drag him along the ice into hiding beneath it. Cold seeped through his cloak. His head swam, and he eyed Soka blearily. "The horses?"

"Downstream and over a hill. The bushes on the banks give fair cover. We might make it."

"Care to lay odds on who they are?"

Soka shook his head. "Too many possibilities to count, what with our fathers' politics and your duels. Of course Kaselm or Nedek could have been the primary targets and we're just the sweeping up."

"You don't believe that."

"No, but can we discuss it later when we've stopped bleeding?"

Metyein's smile was little more than a grimace, but he levered himself up, clutching the span of the footbridge until the shadows clouding his vision receded. This time Soka aided him to walk, grasping him around the waist.

Metyein's hand brushed Soka's empty scabbard. "Where's your sword?"

"On top of the hill."

"Silly place to leave it." Metyein swung about as if to fetch it. His leg buckled, and the two men hugged one another for balance on the ice.

"I'll get it later," Soka gritted. "Hostage compact says I shouldn't have one anyway, and besides, don't know what I'd do with it just at the moment."

"Let's hope we get to the horses before they do, then."

"Hag willing."

They shuffled along the ice, making little sound. They heard the calls of the searching men and the crackle of their passing. The sounds of the attackers seemed to come from every direction; there was no way to tell where they might be.

Finally Soka turned up the bank and up over a low hill. There were a few scattered trees and bushes on the slope, but mostly they were exposed as they staggered upward. Metyein couldn't find his equilibrium. He would have fallen more than once without Soka to hold him steady. As they crested the hill, shouts erupted behind them, and two arrows whizzed by in quick succession. A third buried itself in Metyein's gut beneath his ribs as he swung to the side. He grunted and jerked back against Soka, whose footing gave way. Once again they tumbled forward down the hill, pain netting Metyein in an unceasing, fiery tangle.

Blessedly, he kept his wits this time.

A burly groom wearing the navy and yellow colors of the House of Vare ran to Metyein and helped him up. "Milord! What has happened? Oh, my Lady," he said as his hand came away sticky with blood.

"Help Kaj Raakin. Get him on his horse. Quickly. Where's Pelodra?"

"Here, sir," the other groom answered, leading Soka's and Metyein's mounts from the trees.

"Go with Kaj Raakin. See that he gets to safety," Metyein ordered in a pinched voice.

"But sir, your father commanded me to stay with you always." The stocky groom scowled and slapped the hilt of his sword. He wasn't so much a groom as a bodyguard. Which was why Metyein wanted him with Soka.

"Go. He's unarmed. I want him protected. Stop arguing and . . . go!" he said, hissing as Urviik, the other groom, bound the wound in his stomach, leaving the arrow in place. Without looking at it, Metyein knew that the arrow had bit deep.

Pelodra hesitated. Shouts from the other side of the hill spurred him to action. He spun to hoist Soka into the saddle. Soka clutched the pommel, listing sideways, his face ashen beneath the crimson slash of his eye patch. Pelodra helped Urviik shove Metyein into his saddle, grappling him, as he would have tumbled over the other side.

"Ride with him," Pelodra said to Urviik. "He's going to pass out."

Urviik nodded and swung up behind Metyein. Metyein moaned when the groom brushed the arrow.

"Get him to the residence as fast as you can," Pelodra ordered, then slapped the blue-roan gelding on the haunches. The gelding lunged into the trees with a startled neigh. Urviik guided him onto a winding footpath. The bare tree branches whipped across Metyein's face, raising welts and opening cuts.

"Almost to the gate, sir," Urviik said against his ear. The groom guided them onto the South Walk between the orchestra pavilion and the west supper boxes. The gelding's hooves hit the cobbles with sharp, staccato sounds that echoed in the frigid air.

The gate loomed before them, a square opening at the center of the palazzo's first floor. The blocky structure housed an extensive conservatory, elaborate ballrooms, cavernous banquet rooms, museum galleries, guest accomodations, kitchens, and servants' quarters. Its windows glittered in the frosty light, and the gates hung open as they had when Metyein and Soka had arrived, their locks picked daily by thieves.

Urviik urged the gelding through the square opening without slowing. Metyein felt the impacts of the arrows as they shuddered through Urviik. One. Two. Three. Four in all.

Urviik exhaled wetly against his ear, gurgled, and then canted sideways. The horse neighed shrilly and crow-hopped. Metyein clung to the pommel as Urviik's weight pulled like an anchor. Then the groom's body thudded to the ground, and the horse bolted. Metyein doubled over, clinging desperately to the saddle. The panicked gelding turned and turned again, clattering down a long, winding avenue seaming between blocky warehouses and tall, cramped houses.

A jump, a jolting landing, another turn.

The animal skidded on the cobbles and fell heavily, sliding on his haunches into a midden cart. Metyein tumbled out of the saddle, instinctively rolling away from the animal's deadly hooves.

Chapter 9

Tillen led Reisil between tents piled together like mounds of dirty rags and decrepit shacks that sighed and swayed with the wind. The soft ground squelched and sucked at her boots, and there was a stink of decay and human waste. It was barely past noon, but the temperature was already dropping. Wind whistled around the wall towers with a forlorn sound.

Cookfires guttered and steamed from damp wood. Children huddled close by, feet tucked beneath them to keep warm, faces ruddy. Nearby a toddler whimpered, bending and clutching his stomach. Reisil halted, seeing at once that he was very ill. She went to kneel beside the boy, Tillen trailing after.

"Hello," Reisil said. The boy flinched and scuttled backwards, tripping and falling hard on his bottom. Reisil made no move to follow, but pushed her hood back and gave a reassuring smile. "I'm a tark," she said. "Does your stomach hurt?"

He nodded and peered over her shoulder. Reisil followed his gaze and saw a gaunt young woman glance up from where she was sewing a few tents away.

She leaped to her feet and hurried toward them. "Who

are you? What do you want?" she demanded in a shrill voice as she snatched up her son and hugged him to her chest. He whimpered. "We don't have anything. They already took it all. So go on. Go!"

Now Reisil noticed that indeed the unlucky little family had not even a tent. Only a few soiled blankets, a pot and a bucket and a sackful of odds and ends.

"Where's your husband?" Tillen asked. "The rest of your family?"

The woman's lips pinched together, and she straightened, staring down her nose at her two visitors.

"That's none of your business."

Reisil stood. "Your son is ailing. I'm a tark. I'd like to help."

The woman hesitated, and her arms clutched tighter around her son, her eyes fastening on the ivy adorning Reisil's left cheek. The boy moaned and struggled against the pain of her grasp. The look she gave Reisil was full of fear tinged with skeptical hope.

"Stomach's been bothering him for days," she yielded, her voice tight. Then it turned hard, defensive. "He's hungry is all. We been hungry since—" She broke off and pressed her cheek to her son's head.

"Can I have a look at him?" Reisil asked gently.

The mother hesitated again and then nodded. She sat on the ground, holding her son in her lap. He watched Reisil fearfully as she knelt and looked him over. He was gaunt from lack of food, and his skin and eyes were tinted yellow. *Jaundice*, she thought, and for a moment her muscles seized in fear. Jaundice was an early sign of the plague. But no. He had no rash, no bleeding in his mouth. The jaundice came from hunger and his resulting inability to rid himself of his body's poisons. Relief made Reisil giddy for a moment. The plague would come to Koduteel, but not yet. Please the Lady, not yet.

She focused back on the boy, setting her hands against his stomach, pressing here and there. His belly was soft and gave beneath her fingers. As she moved lower, he whimpered again and squirmed, tears rolling down his cheeks. He pulled away and pressed his cheek against his mother's shoulder. Her arms curled around him as she glared at Reisil over the top of his head.

Reisil sat back on her heels. The boy's face was flushed beneath the grime. He had a fever and stomach pain, and he was yellow. She chewed the inside of her lower lip. Something inside him had gone wrong. Maybe the liver. Maybe the kidneys. Elutark had taught her how to cut into a body and remove infections and diseased flesh, but doing so was tricky in the best of conditions. Here . . . Reisil blew out a tight breath. She couldn't just leave the boy to die, and she knew he would, slowly and painfully. Which left only her last resort. She would have to try her power, and that might kill him anyway. She licked her lips, drawing a whistling breath between them.

"I need to hold him." Reisil held out her hands. The woman darted a fearful look at Tillen, who nodded reassuringly; then she whispered in the boy's ear, kissed his forehead and passed him to Reisil.

Reisil sat cross-legged on the ground and nestled the boy between her legs. He stared at her, wide eyes like polished wood. He scrubbed a fist at his tears and clenched his hands together, holding himself away from Reisil.

She smiled. "This won't hurt," she said. She hoped.

She put her hands around him, touching her fingertips lightly to his back. She thought of the drifting ash that had been the assassins and bit the insides of her cheeks, tasting blood.

Closing her eyes, Reisil felt tentatively for her power. For so long it had been elusive, like a constantly shifting stream, like cockroaches scuttling from the light. Now, since she'd obliterated the assassins, it coursed through her like a fast, deep river.

Too fast, too deep.

Would the magic take her again? Would it make her want to stop the boy's heart? Feel his life drain through her fingers?

Reisil's fingernails cut half-moons into her palms. The boy was dying. He was going to die whether she tried and failed or whether she did nothing. "Lady guide me," she murmured. But the words were hollow. The Lady was gone.

The boy remained rigid and unmoving. Taking a steadying breath, she reached for her power. It leaped up, gushing through her on a wave of heat and light. She heard Tillen and the boy's mother gasp, and Reisil knew that the ivy pattern on her face had begun to glow as it always did when she used magic. Power coiled around her hands, ready. But now that it had come so willingly to her hand, what to do?

The memories of Veneston haunted her: so many bodies, and nothing she could do.

But this wasn't Veneston. And it wasn't the plague. In Patverseme she'd given an armless man a new arm. In Kallas she'd healed bones, sprains and disease. She could heal this boy. She *could*.

She held her breath, concentrating, imagining a slow river current. Her magic responded, flowing readily down through her fingers, filling the boy with gentle heat, like sunlight and stars. With a fleeting smile, Reisil followed it, letting her consciousness flow through his body, seeking the damage that was killing him.

With nearly thoughtless ease she repaired scrapes and bruises as she searched. Under her ministrations, she felt the boy relax and lean into her. She sought her goal from the outside in, moving from his hands and arms to his legs and then into his torso. Finally she came to it. Deep inside him festered a place of feverish heat, of swelling and throbbing. Reisil's nose wrinkled. She could almost smell the stink of infection.

She hesitated a bare moment, then thrust herself forward. Working in a spiral, she mended the lesser-damaged outer tissues first, moving slowly inward over the pulpy flesh. Beneath her touch, it grew whole and pink. At first, the sickness resisted her, like thickly thatched weeds in a neglected garden. But her touch was insistent. She prodded open clogged bloodpaths, eliminated infection, and dammed seeping blood. As she proceeded, she felt the boy squirm.

"Easy now, not much longer."

She pushed harder. The boy made a keening sound and jerked in her hands. Reisil closed her arms, maintaining the channel between them.

"Almost there," she chanted. "Almost there."

The core of the disease was soft and dense, like a peat bog. It squashed aside when she pushed on it, then restored itself. Reisil knew instantly that it could not be repaired. But it could be contained. Gripping the boy firmly, she reached out and grasped the seed of the disease in a magical fist. The boy shrieked and spasmed. Reisil held tight.

She cocooned the last remnants of the disease inside a hard shell of magic, isolating the corrosion so that it would not contaminate his body again.

When she was through, she tried to withdraw slowly, not wanting to shock the boy's system. But her magic bucked beneath her restraint. Panic shrilled along Reisil's nerves. She yanked back. The power resisted and then gave way, snapping back inside her with scalding force. As it did, the boy moaned and went limp, his tunic damp with sweat. Reisil clutched him, feeling for life as she fought to bring her magic to heel.

It burned through her, fierce and white. It wormed through her muscles like lava and lifted her hair with crackling sparks. The pain of it was excruciating; the pleasure of it shook her to the roots of her soul. She wanted—*oh, how she wanted*—to loose it, to feel it rushing from her, to feel it incinerate and annihilate.

For an exquisite moment, Reisil let herself relax into the shuddering pleasure and pain. Her hands began to uncurl as she succumbed to that primitive *want*.

Then she caught herself, reining back with a panicked gasp. The confounded magic sizzled through her. She could do little more than bear it as it circled wildly, searching every avenue against escape. Her muscles knotted and her body heated until the sweat drenching her skin dried.

At last the power settled reluctantly back into its former channels. But now it ran higher, faster, like a flood-lattice of melt-swollen rivers. In the calm, as she realized what had happened. Reisil's joy rang through her like silver bells—she'd summoned her power and used it to heal!

But the boy still lay slack, his head dangling heavily over her forearm, mouth gaping. A chill drove to the marrow of her bones. *Had she killed him after all?*

Then the boy quivered and struggled feebly. She loosened her arms. His face was flushed, but the fever was gone. His eyes were no longer dull, though his lids hung heavy with exhaustion.

Reisil raised her head, grinning wearily at the mother. But surprise froze her tongue and her smile faded as she encountered the wheel of expressionless faces ringing her. The gathered denizens of the Fringes stared down at her. Their silence seemed condemning.

The woman inched forward, eyes flicking from Reisil to her son, lips trembling. She clasped her arms around her stomach, grasping her elbows with red rough hands, as if to prevent them from snatching her son away.

"Is he—? Fretiin? Come to mama, sweetling."

She reached out, and the boy struggled up. He stumbled to his mother and wrapped his legs around her waist as she lifted him up, pressing his head against her shoulder.

"Hungry, Mama."

The mother gave a choked laugh and stroked his back. "I'll find something. Do you hurt? Do you want to rest?"

He shook his head against her shoulder and hugged her tighter. "Fretiin wants carried, Mama. Hungry."

Tears rolled down the woman's face. She looked down at Reisil.

"He'll be fine," Reisil said.

"Praise the Lady," she sobbed, and clutched her son tighter.

"Praise the Lady," Reisil echoed. She'd done it! Her power didn't just come to kill. Was this it? The turning point? Had she broken through the barriers that kept her from healing? She had to try again. Her mind lit on Nitsun and Liisek. They were still waiting for her.

Stiff from sitting so long on the cold, damp ground, she struggled to stand. A half dozen hands reached out to help her. The faces surrounding her continued to remain mask-like, but now one man stood resolutely forward. "My girl's ailing too. Both of 'em." There were nods around the circle, and beyond Reisil saw other people beginning to drift closer as news spread and hope took root.

Reisil licked her lips. She could promise them nothing. If it wasn't true, if her power failed again— "There's a family I need to tend. Then I'll see what I can do."

The afternoon passed in a blur. Tillen led her to Nitsun and Liisek, their tent pitched in a swampy hollow where sewage and rain pooled. They rose and waited stoically as Reisil and Tillen approached at the head of a long, murmuring snake.

"Reisiltark, Tillen," Liisek said coolly, eyes flicking past to the trailing army. "What brings you?"

"Reisiltark came looking for you and happens as I knew where to find you," Tillen replied.

"What's all this?" Liisek jerked his chin at the hushed crowd that now began to wind around, circling the little group.

"Not to worry," said Tillen. "Folks interested in Reisiltark, is all. Came along to watch the goings-on. She thinks she can help your baby boy."

Nitsun stiffened. "You brought your special medicines? The ones you told us about?" The hope in her voice made it crack.

"Better than that," Tillen said before Reisil could answer. She gave him a sidelong look, then turned back to the young couple.

"I've brought medicines, but it may be that I can do better for him."

"Better? How?" Liisek's gaze darted uneasily over the surrounding crowd as he wrapped his arm around his wife and pulled her tightly against his side.

Reisil opened her mouth, but didn't know what to say. Magic? After all the damage the wizards had done in the war, the word *magic* was a curse in Kodu Riik.

"Can I hold him?" she asked instead.

Nitsun glanced at Liisek, hesitating, and then passed the limp bundle that was her son to Reisil. There had been little change in his condition. His dark eyes drifted from side to side, one pupil larger than the other. A spreading bruise on his head was turning mottled yellow and green. He'd fallen when Nitsun had laid him down on the bank of the river on her daily walk for water. He'd rolled from the bed she'd made him and slid down the rock bank, landing against a boulder.

Once again, Reisil sat cross-legged on the ground, setting the baby in the cradle of her legs. She grimaced as clammy wetness seeped up through her cloak and both layers of woolen hose. Ignoring her discomfort, she touched the baby with delicate fingertips in the same way she had touched Fretiin. She did not hesitate this time. Her power spurted through her in a wash of searing heat, then quickly settled. Releasing her breath, Reisil began the process of exploring and mending the baby's injuries. His skull was fractured, and the tissue beneath swollen and pulpy with excess blood. Reisil smoothed the swelling, redirected the blood and mended the bone. She did it quickly, knowing now what to

do, and when she withdrew, this time her magic came doc-
ilely to heel.

She looked up, her green eyes bright with triumph. The
baby began to squirm and opened his mouth in a mewling
cry. His pupils were the same size now and ranged over
her with a purpose. He didn't recognize her. His cries grew
louder, angry. Nitsun dropped to her knees beside Reisil
and snatched up the child, putting him instantly to her
breast. He began to suckle with loud slurping noises, and
all around the crowd began to laugh and clap. Liisek settled
a hand on his wife's shoulder and stared openmouthed at
Reisil, the fingers of his other hand rubbing the patch of
green sewn on his vest.

"He will be well," Reisil said. She stood, once again
aided by a thicket of helping hands.

Before Nitsun or Liisek could voice any more questions
or gratitude, the head of the snake whirled her off, led by
the man with two sick daughters. And so the afternoon
went. After each healing, someone new led the way. Word
spread to various other neighborhoods within the Fringes,
and people began to bring their sick to her. She was grateful to find herself settled on a pile of blankets as one after
another, the sick and the dying were guided to her.

Exhaustion soon began to take its toll, and neither water
nor the meager food pressed into her hands could assuage
it. Her arms had begun to tremble with her efforts, and her
head swam. But Reisil refused to stop. If she stopped now,
there was no guarantee her magic would answer again.

As she finished with a man who had lost his ability to
speak, the left side of his face slack and drooping, Tillen
bent down beside her, concern coloring his voice.

"Reisiltark, this is too much. There are too many of us.
You must rest."

Reisil didn't have the energy to shake her head or argue.
She merely held out her hands to the next in line.

Time flew past—minutes or hours, Reisil didn't know.
Her shoulders ached, and her entire body trembled. She
swayed, catching herself on the dirt with outstretched
hands.

"No more," Tillen announced loudly. "Reisiltark can do
no more today."

His pronouncement was met by silence. Nor could Reisil

summon the energy to protest. Tillen hooked her beneath her arm and helped her to stand. She staggered as circulation returned to her numb legs. Tillen steadied her. The crowds parted. Reisil heard sounds of crying, and then a murmuring rustle of *Thank you, Bless the Lady, Lady watch over you*, and more urgently, *Come again. Please come back.*

She gripped Tillen's arm tightly, her knees buckling every few steps. Her head felt heavy as lead. She yawned, her entire body feeling limp as rope. She thought of her bed and winced as she remembered the lighthouse stairs. But she had done it! Her magic had answered her need at last, and she'd done it! She would rest and come again tomorrow, and the next day, until she had served all who needed her. She must tell Juhrnus and Saljane and—

An ache curled around her heart. There wasn't anyone else to tell. Only Sodur, and she wasn't sure she wanted him to know. She wasn't sure what he might do with the knowledge, and she'd already discovered how powerless she was in the face of his manipulations.

She lifted her chin, putting aside the hurt, focusing on the triumphs of the day. She'd healed. She might be able to heal the plague now. She yawned again. But first she needed sleep.

Chapter 10

Metyein sprawled dazed on the cobbles, the pain throbbing through his body beyond nightmare. Blood trickled from his wounds, and he fought for breath, but the air seemed too thick. Footsteps approached. A hand reached down and pulled him over. He whined and flinched.

"By the Lady! What skived him?"

"Nipped by cloyes, looks like," came the rough answer.

"Must've been dangling too near the Gardens. Bilgerman don't like toffs chiseling in on his walk."

"Maybe Captain Sharpe as what got him. Gambling cattle, this lot. Skipjack is what I reckon. Too wet behind the ears to be out of knee britches. What say we should do with him?"

"Seen wounds like that in the war. Be dead afore long. Coin for the knackers, poor duffer."

"Yer cousin's a knacker, ain't he?"

"What of it? Man's gotta make his way in the world. This cove's done in, clear as glass. Why shouldn't Girfik make an easy muff-head? Got five mouths to feed, he do. He'll bone up the horse too, if yer not wanting it."

Metyein struggled to open his eyes, to contradict their judgment, but he couldn't. There was too much pain, too little blood; his body refused to respond to his commands.

"He's not dead yet."

A new voice, commanding and sardonic. Sudden relief drenched Metyein, and he sobbed out loud.

"No hope for him, mate," came the surly reply. "Oh, yer pardon. Dinna realize . . ."

"No need to worry. But his father won't be pleased if he dies. I'm going to have to get him some help. May I have your cart to move him?"

"Yes, *ahalad-kaaslane*. Of course."

The deference in the man's voice startled Metyein. When someone at court spoke to or about the *ahalad-kaaslane* these days, it was always with no little insolence. But more, that the man would agree to give up his livelihood without question—the trust stunned Metyein so that for a single moment of astonishment, he forgot his wounds.

"And I'll need something to stop the bleeding."

There were ruffling sounds and then tearing cloth.

"Yer pardon for saying so, *ahalad-kaaslane*. But never saw a man survive wounds the likes of his. Arrow's in his gut up to the fletching."

Hearing that, Metyein's slack muscles tensed as if he would physically force the man to recant. But he could not elude the truth, and he collapsed in on himself. The man was right. Metyein cas Vare was dead. His body just didn't know it yet. Metyein's mind flashed to his mother, and he felt tears slipping into his hair. *Ah, mother, I have failed*

*you, just like father. And now he'll steal another of your
sons from your side to take my place. What a fool I've been!*

"I don't know that I'd like to bet on his chances either,"
the *ahalad-kaaslane* said, interrupting Metyein's agonized
thoughts. "But I will take him to Reisiltark anyhow."

Reisiltark? The name drifted through the red fog in Metyein's mind. Reisiltark? The *ahalad-kaaslane* his father dis-
trusted so much? Then the thread of his thought snapped
as pain lanced through him. He felt himself lifted up and
laid on a wood surface. It smelled of fish. There was a
keening sound, and Metyein realized it came from him.
Then whimpering cries shook his frame as he was bandaged. He felt his bladder release and warmth puddle beneath his thighs.

"Easy, now. It'll be over soon," came the voice of the
ahalad-kaaslane.

"One way or t'other," one of his other rescuers
muttered.

Someone spread a blanket over Metyein, careful not to
prod the arrow in his side. "Where do I return the cart?"
the *ahalad-kaaslane* asked as he climbed up on the wagon
seat.

"Yidral Street in the salt quarter," the man replied.
"Name's Pechic. Not far from the tower. Most folks can
point you right."

"I thank you, and I shall return it before morning."

Then the *ahalad-kaaslane* made a clicking noise with his
tongue, and the wagon rumbled over the cobbles. Pain
skewered Metyein like hammered nails. He screamed and
then succumbed to blackness, grateful for the release from
his agony.

Chapter 11

Reisil bumped into Tillen, who had stopped abruptly in front of her. She shook her head, dimly aware that she'd been following behind him like a docile milk cow. But walking took all her concentration. Even breathing was an effort. She tugged on her cloak, feeling cold biting through the wool as the brewing storm settled over Koduteel. The wind blustered and slapped her face with a stinging hand.

"What is it?" she asked Tillen, realizing suddenly she'd let her mind wander.

"Reisiltark's done enough today," Tillen declared gruffly to someone she couldn't see. "She must rest. Would you work her to the bone?"

The woman responded in a low, ratcheting voice.

Tillen shook his head. "No help for it," he declared. But suddenly he rocked forward and then lunged. Reisil heard him swearing as a hand grasped her arm.

"*Ahalad-kaaslane*, Reisiltark, we need you!" the stout, middle-aged woman cried out as Tillen grappled her around the waist. She clung to Reisil's cloak, knotting the wool in her fists. The neck pulled sharply at Reisil's throat and wrenched her sideways.

"Please! You must come!" The woman writhed against Tillen's grip. She kicked at him, fingernails gouging his arms, the whites of her eyes gleaming in the falling darkness. "There is no time! You must come now!"

Her obvious desperation sent chills racing along Reisil's bones. Twisting fear made her exhaustion evaporate as she came painfully alert. Only one thing she could think of would give birth to such razor-edged terror. Reisil's body gave an involuntary shudder.

Not yet, not yet, not yet. I'm not ready!

"Tillen." Her voice was nearly inaudible. She cleared her throat. "Tillen, stop. Let her go." Her voice cut across the woman's pleadings and the curious chatter of the gathering crowd. Silence descended like a knife thrust. Tillen's hands dropped away from the agitated woman, and his florid, snub-nosed face turned somber at Reisil's expression.

"Show me," Reisil said harshly, and then hurried after as the woman darted away, looking over her shoulder every few steps. Reisil could hear Tillen's panting breaths behind her and the shuffling thump of dozens of feet as curious watchers joined their hurried procession.

The woman led them away from the walls, toward the northeast edge of the Fringes between the Horn Tower and the *Ahalad-kaaslane* Tower, where the dwellings became sturdier and less squalid. There was an air of jealously guarded permanence to this neighborhood, where cooking pits were lined with stone and garden patches had been tilled in preparation for spring.

The woman came to a breathless halt between two shacks on the edge of a community circle. Looking back at Reisil, she flung out her hand, pointing toward the interior of the circle. "There."

A beaten-dirt ring surrounded a central cooking pit. Doorways opened up onto the cul-de-sac, and Reisil could imagine that this was a cornerstone of joy and kinship for this community. Inside, near the firepit, she could see a heaped shape wrapped in a cloak.

"Who is it?"

"Nobody knows." The woman pressed a hand to her mouth, shook her head and stood back, refusing to go any nearer. In the spaces between the ramshackle houses, Reisil could see others hovering. Their terror was palpable; she could taste it in the air, sharp and bitter as brewed bloodroot.

Reisil stepped into the circle and approached the collapsed figure. She heard familiar wet, rattling gasps as whoever it was struggled to breathe. Reisil squatted down and pulled the woman onto her back. Seeing her, Reisil scuttled back and sprawled onto her back. For a moment she was

back in Veneston, surrounded by rotting bodies, mouth and
nose clogged with the stink of rotting flesh, hearing nothing
but the sounds of agony and death.

Reisil took a shaking breath, swallowing hard and wiping
her lips with the back of her hand. The stench of the woman's illness rose like a barrelful of rotten eggs and forgotten
entrails. Reisil scanned down the wasted body, one hand
pressed over her mouth, her nose pinched between her
forefinger and thumb. *Where did she come from? How had
no one noticed her?* Her stomach lurched and she bit her
tongue. By the Lady's hand, did it really matter where the
pitiful thing had come from? She was here now. The conta-
gion was *here*.

The woman's eyes were closed against the firelight, the
disease making even dull light painful. The silvered hair
at her temples was the only clue to her age, for the rest
of her had not waited for death before beginning to
decay.

Reisil cataloged the symptoms, her mind moving ponder-
ously. It was exactly the same as Veneston. Blood trickled
from the closed eyes, nose and lips, turning the woman's
face into a demonic mask. Her bodice and full skirts were
stiff with feces, blood and vomit. A pebbly purple rash
spread across her skin, pocked by spreading yellow blisters,
many of which had burst, leaving behind black scabs the
size of Reisil's thumb. Mottled blue black to the elbows
and knees and swollen like sausages, her infected limbs
stank like spoiled meat.

For a long minute Reisil stared helplessly, the memory
of Veneston stark in her mind. Her magic had slid away
from the disease like a snake escaping down a hole. A
sword that wilted in her hand with every thrust.

She squared her shoulders and set her jaw. But today
her magic had healed.

"Blessed Amiya guide me," she whispered to the absent
goddess. And then she set her hands gently on the woman's
shoulders. The wide shoulder-collar of the dress was crusty
beneath Reisil's fingers. Heat radiated through the broad-
cloth like banked coals.

"Easy now," she murmured, whether to soothe herself
or her twitching patient Reisil wasn't sure. She reached for
her power, half-fearing it wouldn't come. But it rose to her

call as it had all afternoon. Breathing a sigh of relief, Reisil
began to probe the damage to the woman's body, quailing
beneath the severity of the destruction. It was a miracle
she was still alive. The dead tissues in her arms and legs
had poisoned her blood. Her liver and kidneys were pulpy
masses within the cavity of her body. Many of her bloodpaths had collapsed or constricted, and her blood was turgid from dehydration.

Where to start? The heart, Reisil decided. Move out
from there, for it was still pumping, having the least appar-
ent damage. Reisil mended the tissues. But soon it became
obvious that her efforts were having as little effect as they
had in Veneston. Each repair collapsed behind her, an illusion of healing. Desperately Reisil backtracked, recon-
structing the rotted tissue and cleansing the poisons from
the woman's blood.

To no avail.

Again and again, but the disease was like a horde of
ants, peeling away from her assault and swarming around
her flanks to attack again. Reisil poured more magic into
the woman, straining against her own exhaustion, feeling
the power leaking up her arms. She smelled burnt hair and
cloth—her own, but she refused to stop.

An idea struck her. She grappled at her neck for the
Lady's talisman. It was a circular disc showing a red-eyed
gryphon in full flight, a moon and sun gripped in its talons,
a streamer of ivy in its beak. Nurema had given it to her
the night before Ceriba's kidnapping. Shortly thereafter she
had used it to gain the Lady's aid to save Juhrnus's *ahalad-
kaaslane,* Esper. And with any luck, she could do the same
for this woman.

Reisil slid a slim knife from the sheath in her boot, not
pausing as she sliced it across the pad of her thumb. She
dripped blood onto the silver, and the metal flared with
brilliant light.

~Saljane!

Instantly her *ahalad-kaaslane* joined minds with Reisil.
Reisil got an impression of whistling wind and a storm-
tossed tree branch. Neither Saljane nor Reisil spoke. The
goshawk read instantly what Reisil was attempting and lent
her strength to Reisil's efforts.

But it was like reparing a dam with mud, despite Saljane's strength and the sudden influx of power from the talisman. With every fixed leak, another exploded a few feet away. Move to fix that one, and another leak sprang up where she'd already made repairs. Again and again her patches gave way and she was forced to rebuild them. The stench of burnt hair and cloth grew stronger, and Reisil began to feel the heat reddening her skin. She gritted her teeth. She *would not* give up, would not give in.

Then the choice was taken from her. The woman's body spasmed, her chest and stomach arching off the ground, her mouth open in a silent rictus. She remained so for a few fleeting seconds, and then she splayed back to the ground, her body slack beneath Reisil's fingers.

"No!" Reisil cried hoarsely, her voice cracking. She scrabbled inside the woman, but there was no bringing life back to the body. The woman was dead.

Reisil's head fell forward. She couldn't breathe. Jagged sobs lodged in her throat. Reisil clamped her teeth tight against them. Her magic began to ebb, and she struggled to her feet, legs aching. There was one other task to do, one other task she was *certain* she could do.

She backed away from the corpse, her feet dragging the ground. Ten paces away, she summoned her power again, thinking of the incinerating fire she'd used against the assassins. She let the fire build inside her, relishing the pain of it. Finally, she brought her fists forward, opening her hands and letting go of the flames. They engulfed the dead woman, and in seconds the body turned to ash.

Reisil withdrew her power and let it drain back to where it came from. Saljane remained silent, a font of strength and comfort as Reisil turned and crossed to the edge of the circle where the people of the Fringes still watched. Their faces were tight with expressions of horror and fear. When she came to Tillen, she paused, her gaze fixed straight ahead.

"It's the plague. There's nothing I can do." With that she strode away.

As she walked, she began to shake. Tears rolled down her cheeks. She wanted to scream, she wanted to pound her fists until they bled. She'd failed again. And now what had happened to Veneston was going to happen to Koduteel.

She felt Saljane stirring in her mind and sent a silent plea not to speak. Not yet. She wasn't ready. She was too raw. Reisil felt something akin to a mental hug as Saljane gathered her close in her mind. Then the goshawk released Reisil, allowing her *ahalad-kaaslane* the privacy to come to terms with her emotions on her own.

"Reisiltark." Tillen's gruff voice caught her as she began to climb back up the hill to the ocean bluffs. She stopped, then slowly turned around, looking down as he gazed up at her, his square face pale in the early evening, his cloak pulled tight against the wind. Her own flapped loosely on the wind, but she didn't feel the cold. She didn't feel anything. She thought of the wizards. They would wait like vultures until Kodu Riik was dead and then eat their fill of its remains.

"Reisiltark, you did your best. You healed many people today. You did more than anyone else has been willing to do."

"I failed." The words were flinty and bitter as salt.

"Yes. But many people fail."

Reisil eyed him narrowly. "She died."

"We all die, sooner or later."

"It will be sooner. And it will be hideous and painful. The Blessed Lady gave me this power so that I could save Kodu Riik. *Why can't I heal with it?*"

Tillen stepped forward, grasping her hand. "No one learns overnight how to build a house or make a boat. And we must have patience until you do."

"There is no time."

"There is always time. Not for all of us, certainly. Maybe not even for most of us. But we will pray to the Lady, and you will seek to learn. We must have faith that it will all turn out as it is supposed to."

Reisil stared incredulously, remembering the burning sheep sheds, the smell of charred flesh. He didn't know. If he did, he would not be so unruffled.

"I don't know that I will ever be able to cure the plague."

"I am certain you will."

"How can you be? How can you believe in me?"

"You are mistaken. I don't believe in you. I believe in Amiya." A smile flashed across his lips and then faded. He gazed at Reisil soberly. "You must have faith too, Reisil-tark. I don't know why you can't heal the plague yet. But I know the Blessed Lady loves us. We may not understand Her plan, but certainly She has one.

"Go home now. Rest. Tomorrow is time enough to begin again. We thank you for today. You are always welcome here."

Tillen let go of her hand and touched his forehead. Reisil watched him walk away and then turned to climb up the path. Frigid rain pecked her face, turning to ice on her cloak. Through the soles of her feet she felt the throbbing of the harbor cavern as waves surged high. Suddenly Reisil stopped, staring up into the sky, the charcoal clouds churning.

"I will not give up," she said, voice as hard as the rock she stood on. "I will not let you beat me. I will find a way." Whether she spoke to the Lady or to the plague or to the wizards, she didn't know.

Chapter 12

Juhrnus reined the wagon in beside the lighthouse. "*Skraa*. This is a stupid way to die." The wind blew the words back in his face.

With a gusty sigh, he set the brake and went to look at the injured man. Metyein cas Vare. The *skraa*-for-brains idiot had really done it to himself this time. Blood pooled on the wagon boards. "Duel didn't go so well, did it?" he asked the unconscious man, pulling him to the end of the wagon bed. "Now this next part is going to hurt, so best not to wake up for it. And if you do, don't look down. Don't want your puke running down into my boots."

He hoisted the other man over his shoulder, positioning Metyein so that the arrow protruding from his gut stuck out to the side. Esper wriggled out of the wagon and clumsily began up the stairs, gripping the stone with his claws, his green and yellow stripes dulled with the chill.

~*Cold.*

~*And going to get colder. Better hurry. Reisil will have a fire going.*

Esper scurried upward. Juhrnus followed, setting each foot carefully on the slick steps and leaning close against the tower. Between the icy spray from below and the freezing rain from above, the footing was more treacherous than usual.

"Watch your head, then," Juhrnus muttered when his food slid sideways and he fell heavily against the wall. Pain shot up his elbow, and Metyein's head knocked against the stone. "Well, at least you won't be waking up soon," he grunted. "Good planning. Sleep until Reisil has her way with you. Now don't get your hopes up, little lordling. She's not that way. Have to work harder than that to get between her legs, you do. It'll take more than bleeding all over her to do that."

Juhrnus fell silent as they circled upward. He panted with exertion, resting on the lee of the tower and laboring against the wind's pounding fists as he rounded the windward side. When he arrived on the gallery walk, he found Esper curled up against the closed door. The windows in the watch room were ominously dark.

"She's not here?"

~*No. Cold.*

"It'll be warmer inside."

It wasn't much warmer, though the cessation of wind and rain was a relief. Juhrnus laid Metyein on Reisil's bed, covering him with her heavy wool blankets.

~*Our lordling hasn't got a lot of time left. We'd better go find her. Come on—you can ride in your sling.* Juhrnus lifted Esper into the leather sling he wore around his waist beneath his cloak. The sisalik snuggled in with relief.

~*Come on. No time to fix him a fire. Reisil's let the coals go out. His best chance is for us to find Reisil soon.* Juhrnus pulled up his hood and slipped out the door. "Lady watch over him," he added in an undertone as he went.

The frigid wind made Reisil's eyes ache. She clutched her cloak around her nose and mouth as she shuffled along the ice-slicked road. It had taken her an hour to walk from the Fringes. Rain whipped across the road in sheets freezing wherever it touched. Ice glazed the rocks, bushes, trees and grasses. There would be a lot of toppled trees and collapsed roofs in Koduteel, wagons frozen solid to the street, doors and windows iced shut.

The lighthouse loomed out of the darkness, and Reisil angled up the gravel path, ducking between the ramshackle keeper's quarters and oil storage shed. She began up the steps, digging her fingers between the cracks in the stone and bracing against the wind. Below the ocean roared, and along the headland, the new lighthouse flashed a warning through the driving rain.

She reached the gallery deck at last, her heart pounding. She paused beside the crumbling parapet, ice crusted in her hair and cloak. She panted, inhaling the tumultuous darkness, feeling inside herself for an answering blackness.

The wind gusted and shoved her back a step. Reisil grappled at her billowing cloak and retreated to the door. Ice glazed its surface and formed seams along the bottom and sides. She shoved against the wood, until it gave, and she lurched inside. Instantly the roar of the wind and rain dimmed, and she became aware of the sound of breathing. Her scalp prickled.

"Who's here?"

No one answered. Reisil untied her cloak, dropping it to the floor with a rattling swish before reaching for the fire poker dangling next to the hearth.

"What do you want?"

Again, no answer. Reisil turned her head, straining to hear. The breathing was shallow and quick. It came from her bed. Realization struck her, and she dropped the poker with a clang. She groped along the mantel until her fingers knocked against a flint and a basket of sawdust and splinters. Quickly she struck a light and touched a burning splinter to the tall candle waiting beside the tinder basket. Grasping it, she went to examine her guest.

Reisil recognized his handsome face immediately.

"And what is the Lord Marshal's son doing in my bed?" She frowned, setting the candle on the washstand. He was too pale, and his teeth rattled. Sweat gleamed on his skin.

Crimson stains spread across her blankets. She pulled the
blankets back, finding the protruding arrow and the ugly
wound in his thigh. His stomach was distended and hard,
and even unconscious he jerked away from Reisil's touch.
"By the Lady, what happened to you?"

Sudden fury sparked inside her. Had someone left him
here so that she could be blamed? To give the Lord Marshal a real reason to come after her? She sighed. It didn't
matter. He was here, and he was just half a step away
from death.

Reisil knelt beside the bed, her muscles twinging protest.
Exhaustion gnawed at her nerves, and her eyes felt leaden.
She stared at the dying man a long moment, hands closing
upon the bedclothes. This was not the plague. This was the
sort of thing she'd done successfully all this day. She had
to do it only one more time tonight. Just one more time.

She reached for her magic. It felt sharp edged and brittle.
She strained against it. It rose sluggishly, spreading like
crushed glass through channels raw from the day's work. Reisil jerked, catching her breath against the fiery pain. There
was no time to waste. She couldn't keep this up. Forcing
her clenched fists open, she set them against Metyein, one
on his chest, the other on his hip.

She began with the arrow in his abdomen. Blood and
waste pooled in his stomach. The arrow had sliced a furrow
across his liver and punctured his intestines. Toxins had
leaked from the wounds and begun poisoning the rest of
his body. Reisil chewed her lip. She could clean the toxins,
she could repair the wounds. But she didn't know how to
replace lost blood. He could still die.

But she had to try.

When she finished, Reisil left Metyein pale and panting
beneath the bloodstained blankets. She pulled a straight-
backed chair from the table in the center of the room and
dragged it to one of the windows. She collapsed onto the seat
and propped her feet on the wide stone windowsill, letting
her head dangle back over the headrest. Sometime since she'd
started working on him, the wind and the rain had paused.
In the silence she listened to Metyein's quick breatuhing.

She woke with a start, her legs and lower back stiff, her
neck cramping. She yawned and sat up, rubbing her neck.

Metyein's breathing had slowed, though it remained shallow, and he no longer sweated. But his skin had a dreadful pallor. Too soon to tell if he'd live.

Her stomach growled. Reisil lit two more candles on the mantel and took a piece of hard bread from the larder, dipping herself a cup of water from the bucket near the door. Too tired to build a fire, she grabbed a blanket from the foot of the bed and returned to her seat. Wrapping the blanket about herself, Reisil propped her feet against the window ledge and hugged her knees.

Outside, a sheet of hail swept across the bluffs with a sizzling sound. The pellets ratcheted against the walls, rattling as they rolled across the deck and tumbled down the stairs. Her heart felt as tiny and frozen as the hailstones. Her chest ached, but there were no tears. They were as frozen as her heart, as her blood.

A skittering sound came from along the stone walk outside. Reisil heard a thump and a loud yelp. After a few moments, the door rattled and was flung inward with a crash. Reisil pulled her attention reluctantly from the cracked, filmy planes of the mullioned window, watching Juhrnus limp inside. He cursed, dabbing at the blood running from his cheek. He cradled his right elbow in his left hand, and a bruise spread along his forehead.

"So you made it back. I've been looking everywhere for you. And you perching up here on the top of the world. Might as well be in Scallas, as hard as it is to get up those miserable steps in this weather."

"Only fools and monsters walk those stairs," Reisil murmured. "Is Esper all right?"

"Well, nice to see you care about one of us. He's fine. I have all the damage. Why don't you have a fire? It's like a tomb up here. And speaking of which, did our friend die?" Juhrnus crossed to Reisil's bed and looked down at Metyein.

"You brought him up here? What if he dies? Do you know what his father will do?"

Juhrnus shrugged, untying his cloak with his uninjured hand and dropping it near hers. Esper hung in the sling around Juhrnus's chest, his tail dangling listlessly, his bright colors a torpid gray. "We'd heave him over the wall into the ocean and let him wash up on a shingle somewhere. With all those duels, he's enemies enough to murder him."

Reisil raised her brows. "You've certainly thought it through."

Juhrnus brushed aside her sarcasm. "*I* didn't poke holes in him. At least this way he has a chance. So which is it?"

Reisil shrugged. "I've done what I can."

It was Juhrnus's turn to raise his brows. "Really?"

"Really," she said, her expression shuttered. She wasn't ready to talk about what had happened that day: about the assassins, about her healing in the Fringes, about the plague. Juhrnus opened his mouth and then shut it, going instead to kneel beside the fireplace. Reisil almost chuckled. Tact. Not a trait that came easily to him.

He sank stiffly to his knees beside the wood box and tossed a handful of sawdust and splinters into the grate. He wrestled the flint and steel out of the pouch at his waist. Putting the fingers of his injured arm through the steel, he struck the flint. Sparks flew and he yelped, clutching his arm against his chest.

"Big brother, you are a pitiful sight."

He called her a crude name and sat back on his heels. "You could help me."

"Mmmm. But I don't need a fire."

He scoffed. "That's the least of what you need, little sister. Let's see"—he ticked off items on his good hand— "a fire, a month of good meals—enough to gain back some of that weight you've lost—and oh yes, above all things, a tumble in bed with a good, stiff man."

Reisil could not help grinning. The muscles of her face gave in to the expression grudgingly. "Not you, I hope. I really don't want a case of the pox."

Juhrnus sniffed. "At least I don't hide myself away like a monk."

"At least until your favorite bits fall off. Get out of the way."

She didn't have to use magic. But a recklessness smoldered in her, driving her to push.

She stacked a pile of seasoned oak in the grate and touched her finger to the wood. It exploded into flame. Sparks showered the room, and Juhrnus swore as he pat-

ted at his hair, and then he leaped to stamp out his cloak.
"A little showy, don't you think?"

"At least it's good for something." Bitterness laced Reisil's voice like twisting eels.

"I don't know. Gave him a chance he didn't have," Juhrnus jerked his thumb at the unconscious Metyein. "But
Esper is grateful." Juhrnus pulled his *ahalad-kaaslane* from
the sling, and Esper stretched full length along the rapidly
warming hearth. He touched the back of Juhrnus's hand
with his fleshy black tongue, then closed his eyes to bask
in the fire's spreading heat. Reisil's heart jerked. To have
touched Saljane that way . . . Her fingers clenched around
the memory of the goshawk's soft feathers.

"Tell me about it," he said, gesturing at Metyein and
pulling a chair close to the heat. "Before Sodur gets here."

"Sodur?" Of all the people she didn't want to see
tonight— "In this weather?"

"You weren't at all concerned for me."

"Your head is much harder. A lot of people would
miss him."

"Including you?"

Reisil stiffened. "Of course."

He looked at her in silence. She retrieved both their
cloaks from the floor and shook them out, hanging them
from the wooden pegs beside the door. Once again he re-
frained from pursuing the subject. Instead he stretched out
his arm, rotating the wrist and elbow, wincing.

"Don't suppose you want to have a go at this."

Reisil hesitated. "I can try."

"You don't have to."

"Afraid?"

He grinned, sitting back in his chair. "Well if you're
going to put it that way, I'm at your service."

Reisil stood behind him, breathing slowly, flexing her
fingers. She flattened her palms against the warmth of Juhrnus's chest, and the power within her roared to life. Gasping, she jerked her hands up.

"Don't worry. I can take it any way you give it." His
voice was soft and reassuring, but Reisil heard the ragged
edge of fear he couldn't hide.

Reisil looked at her hands. They trembled. What was she
doing? She was so tired, she could hardly see straight. Her

magic had long ago lost that rich fluid feeling, and now it struggled against her. But she couldn't stop. Not yet. Just once more, something so minor . . . She touched her fingertips back to his chest. Once again she loosed her power, willing it to cooperate.

"Gently, gently, gently," she chanted. Within her, the torrent of magic subsided, though it remained knife-edged and corrosive.

The healing took longer than it should have. When at last Reisil pulled away, her legs shook and darkness clouded the edges of her vision. But tired as she was, restless energy consumed her and she paced aimlessly in the small space.

Juhrnus stretched out his arm again, sweat beading his flushed forehead and cheeks. "Good as new. If I don't slide off the stairs into the bay."

"You're a good swimmer. You could probably make the docks—if you didn't shatter your head on the rocks first."

Reisil took up a broom and began sweeping up the melting ice.

"A tragedy you would no doubt feel deeply. After all, who would remind you of where you came from? Keep your feet on the ground and your swelled head out of the clouds?"

"That doesn't appear to be a problem these days," Reisil returned sardonically.

"Could change at any moment. Healing his son might bring the Lord Marshal around."

Reisil shook her head. "No. The Lord Marshal would take it as proof that I use my powers selectively to further my own secret cause." She paused. "Anyway, it won't matter soon. I'm leaving Koduteel. It's time to track down the wizards."

Juhrnus lunged to his feet, the chair clattering across the floor. "No. That's suicide."

"It's worse than suicide to stay. Look around. The plague—" She broke off. "How long am I supposed to wait? Until everyone dies?"

"They'll kill you as soon as look at you. Besides, what makes you think they have the answers, even if you can make them talk to you?"

"They started this plague. I know it. And I can handle them," Reisil said, remembering the way the power had sung through her when she had killed the assassins.

Juhrnus laughed—a harsh, barking sound. He threw his hands into the air and turned around, addressing the air above. "Bright Lady! Do you hear this hen-witted arrogance? Rescue me from fools!"

He swung back around, crossing his arms over his chest and glaring at her. "You can handle them. Do tell. Your magic is crippled—you could barely heal my shoulder. So tell me. Just *how* will you *handle* them, little sister?"

His words struck her like a blow. She knew well enough how to kill. Her mouth opened and then closed. A needle of cold stitched through her spine. She was a healer. That was no point of pride.

Juhrnus picked up the chair and rammed it back down on the floor. "I thought so. No idea, have you?"

Reisil stood a moment longer. Then with a strangled sound, she snatched up her cloak and fled, shoving past a heavily laden Sodur and vanishing up the decrepit stairs. Behind her, Juhrnus swore furiously, kicking the chair he'd just righted, sending it careening across the lighthouse chamber to crash against the opposite wall.

Chapter 13

Metyein woke to angry voices. A hammering sound jolted him. Then more irate voices and a loud clattering as something banged against a wall. Metyein winced as pain speared through his throbbing head. *Where am I? What happened?*

A sense of danger swallowed him, clenching around his bladder, squeezing his lungs. He twisted his head to the side. Two men stood talking in the flickering candlelight. He blinked, trying to clear his vision, but his gritty eyes refused to focus. *I went to the Gardens. A duel.* Metyein scowled, the movement sending streaks of pain over his scalp. He remembered . . . *Nedek and Kaselm, blood pool-*

ing on the ice, Soka, the attackers, the chase, pain . . . Metyein's throat spasmed. He closed his eyes, groaning.

"What's this?" The candlelight darkened as the two men came to stand over him. "By the Lady! Metyein cas Vare! What in the Lady's name is he doing here?"

"Found him in the street. Ambushed, by the looks of it." Metyein recognized the voice instantly. The *ahalad-kaaslane*. Some of the tension drained out of him. His attackers hadn't caught him. "Leaking like a sprung cask of ale and closer to dead than not. I thought Reisil might have a go at him. Give us a marker against the Lord Marshal."

"And if she failed?"

"Dump the body off the bluffs. No harm to us, and for him, better a slim chance than no chance."

"Was Reisil successful?"

"Can't say."

Metyein went rigid as the bedclothes were pulled away.

"He's stopped bleeding, anyhow. What's this?" Movement along his side, the rustle of cloth, the brush of a hand.

"Hmph. No barbs. Odd choice for murder. And there's the hole where it went through his clothes." Metyein felt a tugging on his doublet and the tunic beneath, then a rush of cold air against his skin. Neither of the two men spoke for a moment.

"Guess we won't be dropping him off the bluffs," came the younger man's dry comment.

For a moment the words made no sense to Metyein. Then a flood of icy shock ran through his system. What were they saying? He was going to die. A gut wound was a seal of death. The blankets were pulled back farther, and the chill made Metyein shiver.

"Thigh's healed too. Ugly scar, but he can live with it."

"Yes, but can we? Can Reisil?"

"What do you mean?" The younger man sounded belligerent. Metyein recognized the tone. It was the tone he usually took with his father.

"Think, Juhrnus. Reisil can't heal anyone, and then suddenly she heals the Lord Marshal's son? What would you think?" The blankets were pulled and the two men drew away, their voices falling. But Metyein didn't need to hear the explanation. He knew exactly how his father would react. This would only confirm his worst suspicions: she withheld her magic for political influence. That she was another traitor *ahalad-kaaslane* like Upsakes.

Under the blankets, Metyein slid tentative fingers up over his stomach, his arm feeling wooden. He touched the stiffening blood on his clothing, pushing aside the heavy material of the doublet and the lighter tunic beneath.

There wasn't even a scar. Just a single point of tenderness where the arrow had gone in. He didn't have to touch it to know it. He could still feel the wood burrowing through his flesh.

His hand worked lower, reaching down to touch his thigh. His hose were torn, the edges of the material stiff with blood. Underneath, his skin was rippled like spilled wax. The scarring was about the size of his palm, and where he touched, he felt nothing. A scrap of death like a patchwork square on a quilt. Metyein slumped, his head reeling. He wasn't going to die. Reisiltark *had* healed him. Political influence? He didn't know. It didn't matter. If his father didn't owe her, he did.

Metyein's senses swam, and tears ran from the corners of his eyes to dampen the hair at his temples. By the grace of the Lady, he was going to live.

"So even now when Reisil's magic actually works and she does a miracle like that," Juhrnus pointed to the bed against the wall, "she is still going to get pilloried. For doing the Lady's work."

Sodur sighed. "Yes, but it isn't that simple."

"Seems simple. And stupid."

Sodur rubbed his eyes, a hollow feeling blooming in his chest. The healing was a good sign. This was what she was supposed do to, what he'd been hoping she'd do. How could he complain? But it wasn't going to help. The fire he'd started had grown far beyond his control and saving Metyein cas Vare was only throwing oil on it. But how could he tell either of them it would have been better to let the boy die?

"That's because you don't know everything." Then quickly, before Juhrnus could push the issue, he waved toward the door. "What's that about?"

Juhrnus hesitated. "Wizards."

"Ah." Sodur took a wrinkled handkerchief from his breast pocket and blew his nose.

Juhrnus scowled at the door. "I should go after her."

"Better give her some time."

Juhrnus paced across the room. "Damned stupid fool."

"We do need answers."

Juhrnus whirled. "What? By the Demonlord's shriveled balls, she can't light a fire without blowing up the room!"

Sodur shook his head, the sense of vanishing time pressing harder on him. His mind felt muzzy. "She healed the boy well enough. And we're running out of options." The Scallacian sorcerers only exacerbated the problem. He couldn't help but think Kodu Riik would deeply regret their coming. At least going to the wizards didn't involve stupidly inviting them into the front parlor. Juhrnus was eyeing him balefully. Sodur gestured placatingly with his hand. "We need answers. Finding the wizards may be our best chance, before things get really bad."

"You think they'll help? Just like that?" Juhrnus's voice shifted to a falsetto, pretending to be Reisil. "Excuse me. Sorry about killing so many of you last time we met. But I just dropped in to ask if you would explain how to cure the plague that you probably started in the first place. And while I'm here and still breathing, might I borrow some flour?"

Sodur's lips quirked, but he didn't answer. Instead he squatted down beside his pack and rifled through it.

"Grab that pot over there, would you? I've got a bit of mutton I filched from the kitchens, and some vegetables from the winter bins—they're a bit wrinkled, but they'll do."

He continued to paw through his pack, ignoring Juhrnus's withering disbelief. After several long moments, Juhrnus snorted and went to grab the pot. Sodur expelled a quiet sigh and closed his eyes. A weight sat on his heart, and his breath rumbled in his chest like rocks down a hillside.

Lume bumbled his cheek against Sodur's knuckles, scraping his *ahalad-kaaslane*'s skin lightly with his teeth.

Concern.

Sodur rubbed behind the silver lynx's tufted ears. The

cat's emotions were becoming tangible, like heady wine or
hallucinatory herbs. Words no long seemed necessary between them. Sometimes they seemed nearly impossible.
Frighteningly so.

He drew a deep breath and opened his eyes, gazing at
the pile of foodstuffs from his pack. It was time to put his
trust in these two striplings and pray to the Blessed Amiya
that they could survive the burden.

Several minutes went by before he realized that Juhrnus
had fallen silent.

The younger *ahalad-kaaslane* contemplated Sodur over
folded arms, scowling. "So. Don't you think it's about time
you told me what's going on? Reisil never will."

Sodur hesitated, carefully slicing through the white flesh
of the turnip he held. "After we have some food in our
stomachs."

Juhrnus nodded. "Fine." He retreated to the table while
Sodur set the pot over the fire, stirring in a handful of
barley grains and a pinch of salt. Sodur already knew how
Reisil was going to take his revelations. If Juhrnus was
molten, she was glacial. Since Veneston she'd frozen him
out of her life.

Familiar sorrow made his shoulders slump. Between one
moment and the next, Reisil had stopped confiding in him,
stopped asking questions, stopped looking at him. If she
could have, she'd have avoided him altogether. *Thank the
Lady severing our tie isn't so easy!* He rubbed his eyes,
pinching the bridge of his nose. He missed her. After Upsakes, there had opened such a great hole in his life. Reisil
had filled it generously. She'd been a friend, a daughter, a
student and a teacher. And now that hole was back again,
larger, more raw than before.

The stew bubbled and soon filled the room with hearty
fragrance. The storm outside continued to blow. Juhrnus
sat at the pitted plank table, weaving intricate braids from
strips of finely cut leather he carried in his belt pouch.
Sodur sat in the chair Reisil had vacated, his feet propped
on the windowsill, whittling a piece of fine-grained chestnut
into the shape of a gryphon.

Minutes ticked past. Each man looked to the door whenever the wind rattled the latch. At last it slid silently up.

Reisil eased herself inside, her cloak stiff with ice, her

cheeks brilliant, her lips pale. Purple shadows filled the hollows around her eyes. For a fraction of a second she met Sodur's glance. She flinched and looked away, hanging her cloak on its peg. Wordlessly she took a kettle from the mantel shelf and filled it with water, adding lemons, dried apricots and currants, and several spoonfuls of honey from a cracked green crock that sat on the end of the shelf. She bent and situated the kettle firmly in the coals before sinking down beside Esper, her hunched back to the fire's heat.

And so they sat, the stew bubbling, the fruit brew steeping, the snick of Sodur's knife on the wood, the gentle rapping of Juhrnus's knuckles on the table. Outside the ice became snow, driving horizontally through the black night. Inside, the fire collapsed with a rush of sparks and glowing coals.

Sodur sat up, dropping his feet to the floor. "Should be ready."

Juhrnus laid more wood on the fire while Reisil brought out a loaf of rosemary flatbread. She set a pitcher of water in the center of the table as Sodur spooned the savory stew into bowls. Soon they were sitting around the table in less than companionable silence.

As he ate, Sodur felt the weight of his confession press heavier. And even heavier was what he still couldn't reveal. He glanced at Reisil's gray cloak, the melting crust of ice and snow making a puddle on the floor beneath it.

"Did you need a new cloak?"

"I like this one."

"The green one was nice. Didn't Elutark give it to you? Hardly worn, really."

Reisil glared at him and bit off a hunk of bread. His eyes traced the pattern of golden ivy unfurling along her neck and left jaw. A sign of the Lady's blessing. Or curse. He wasn't sure anymore. The burden of the Lady's gift was proving very difficult indeed. And it was about to get harder.

"It won't change anything, you know. They won't stop wearing the green just because you have."

"No?" Her gaze cut into him. For months she'd refused to look at him. Now she skewered him with feral intensity.

Sodur nodded, the hairs on his neck lifting. He'd been expecting ice, but the glacial mask she'd worn for months was nothing but a thin sheath now. *How do I handle this?*

"You can't hide from what you are," he said carefully.

"Tell me, just what do you think I am?"

"You—," Sodur began and then stopped as she bent forward, her green eyes too brilliant, her jaw jutting like an ax-blade. There wasn't an ounce of fat anywhere on her. All that had ever been soft or young or unfinished about her had vanished, stripped away in the last year. "Hope," he said. "You are our hope."

Her nostrils flared, and she laughed, a short, guttural sound that echoed from the curving stone walls. "And you are not only a liar, but a fool as well," she said. "Or is it an act? Another mask?"

There was something waiting beneath her words. A trap. Sodur's tongue slid between his teeth and his lips. She wanted a fight. She wanted blood. His especially. "I am what I am, Reisiltark," Sodur said mildly, trying to shake her from this mood. "And you are what you are, no matter what color cloak you wear."

"And you think that I am hope. Which leaves us wondering—what are you?" She smiled, a humorless stretching of her lips. "Shall I tell you?"

She waited. Sodur nodded, uneasiness twisting in his bowels.

Reisil leaned forward until she was a scant six inches away. The wind blustered, and the chimney moaned.

"Dead. You are dead."

Chapter 14

Sodur sat back, face stony. "Is that supposed to be funny?"

"No."

Sodur's mouth thinned. "A threat, then?"

"Hurt an *ahalad-kaaslane*? Oh, no. Possible rumors to the opposite, I am loyal to the Blessed Lady and Kodu

Riik. No, what I said is merely unvarnished fact. Truth. *You* may have difficulty recognizing it, of course. But it remains. You are dead."

Several turgid moments passed. The tension inside Reisil knotted. Her boiling frustration and fury were unbearable. Sitting still, doing nothing, holding it in—she couldn't do it anymore.

"Perhaps you would explain it to me," Sodur said, his hand dropping to Lume's head. The lynx had come to stand at his knee, a low growl rumbling deep in his throat. "I have a sniffle, and my joints hurt. Nothing fatal, I should think. But then, I suppose I ought to be surprised to be feeling anything at all, dead as you say I am."

Reisil's lips curved reluctantly. Damn but she *liked* him. But even as she thought it, her smile faded. He held the keys to the locks that shackled her. They were not friends. "I went down to the Fringes today," she said abruptly.

Sodur frowned. "Is that wise?"

Reisil lifted a shoulder. "I had been on my way to see you, actually."

"Oh?"

"Yes." She didn't elaborate. "But to answer your question, the *ahalad-kaaslane* serve all of Kodu Riik, not just those who smell good. And I have done some good for the people of the Fringes on occasion."

"Of course you have, but to go there alone . . . You must be careful. The *ahalad-kaaslane* don't enjoy the respect they once did. And you're not a favorite of many."

"I wonder why." She watched the color rise in his cheeks and felt a certain satisfaction at his discomfort. "What kind of *ahalad-kaaslane* would I be if I refused to do the Blessed Lady's work because I was afraid of getting hurt? What kind of *ahalad-kaaslane* would that make any of us?"

"You're talking about going to the wizards again," Juhrnus said accusingly.

"Whatever it takes," Reisil said. "And it is *my* decision."

Before Juhrnus could retort, Sodur interceded. "That is an argument for later. I'd like for Reisil to get back to my being dead."

Reisil gave a short nod. "All right. But know that I've decided. I'm going to find the wizards." She chopped her hand in the air as Juhrnus began to bluster. "Yes, they might kill me. But at least it's a chance, and staying here won't change anything."

"Surely you will find a way to heal the plague before then," Sodur said. "You healed the stripling Vare tonight. You're coming into your own at last. Even now you might be able to heal the plague and just don't realize it."

Reisil turned. She spoke slowly, as if to an addled child. "The plague is here. I cannot heal it. We're out of time. And we are *all* dead."

The two men sat transfixed. Reisil paused for a moment, gathering herself, and then plunged into the story, starting after the assassins attacked her. She wasn't ready to tell them about that, or about the Scallacian sorcerers either.

As she described the woman's condition, Reisil covered her eyes, pressing her knuckles against her closed lids as if to gouge out the memory.

"Incontinence, weeping blisters, bleeding in the eyes and ears and mouth, the purple rash, her arms and legs black and swollen. The smell—"

"No," Sodur said, gripping the edge of the table. "Not so soon!"

Juhrnus said nothing, but Reisil felt him like a hungry black shadow. She hunched her shoulders and dropped her hands from her face.

"She had a broken wrist. I could fix that."

"You'd have been able to heal her if the Lady had willed it," Sodur said, but his words lacked conviction.

She laughed, a mocking sound that tore at her throat. "She gave me magic to heal Kodu Riik." *Heal my land. Heal my children—human and animal.* Reisil heard the words again and felt herself cringe. "So there you are. The plague is here. You, Juhrnus, me—we're all going to die. It's only a matter of time. I certainly cannot save you. Unless the wizards can teach me how."

A thick silence descended. At last Reisil slapped the table. "Why give me the power if it does no good? Why doesn't *She* do something?"

"That may not be the worst of it," Sodur said, letting the words go reluctantly. Reisil jerked around, and Juhrnus grunted.

"All right then. We've eaten. Get on with it."

Reisil's gaze flicked back and forth between the men,

her brow furrowed. Juhrnus ignored her, settling a heavy, belligerent gaze on Sodur.

Sodur rubbed his hand over his mouth, staring into his empty bowl as if scrying in the drippings. "One of the *nokulas* came to Koduteel about a year ago."

He waited, head down, his scalp shining like an egg through his thinning hair. The meaning of his words first sidled past his two listeners, made benign by their quiet tone and Sodur's blunt telling. Then it circled back, biting from behind like a starving dog. Juhrnus leaped to his feet.

"Here? How? Where is it?" When Sodur didn't move, Juhrnus sank back down in his chair. "A year. It's been here a year. Why didn't you tell us?" His voice was dull with anger.

Or was it fear? Reisil couldn't tell.

"It's not as simple as that."

Reisil glowered. That was just what he'd said in Veneston. And he was right. It wasn't simple. But he'd never given them a chance.

"The creature was here before we knew it for what it was. As for why we said nothing—after Upsakes, we dared not trust anyone. With the peace so new and delicate, we feared what could happen."

Sadness washed his voice and pulled down the corners of his eyes and mouth.

Didn't trust even us, Reisil added silently.

"And you've seen fit to enlighten us at long last." Juhrnus's voice had turned ugly. Not just from fear or anger, Reisil decided. It was helplessness.

Juhrnus began to hammer Sodur with questions. Reisil let the sounds flow around her, a wrongness slowly taking shape out of her swirling emotions and torrential thoughts. At length Juhrnus rumbled to a halt.

She spoke in the sudden silence, her voice uninflected. "What else?"

Sodur cast her a sharp look and drew a deep breath. "There's a lot you don't know about the *nokulas*. We hadn't even heard of them until three years ago. Then *ahalad-kaaslane* on circuit started disappearing, mostly in the mountains between here and Patverseme. We thought it was the war—it seemed obvious. But then there began to be sightings. One here, another here. Then more often.

Nothing definitive. The reports described ghostly beasts that could chase a mounted man down at full gallop. They had teeth like daggers, slaughtering whoever they encountered. It was hard to credit the stories. Village superstitions. But we sent *ahalad-kaaslane* to have a look anyhow. They confirmed the villagers' accounts. But you know how things are. Few at court listened to us.

"Then the war heated up, and we needed everyone to fight, so we curtailed our investigation. Meanwhile, the *no-kulas* spread through the mountains. Some thought it would keep our borders safe from the Patversemese."

"That's worse than stupid," Juhrnus said, shoving up from the table to stalk restlessly across the room.

"Sure, and that's what we told the Arkeinik. They didn't want to hear it."

"But the *ahalad-kaaslane* don't answer to anyone. We do what needs to be done, no matter what anyone else says."

Sodur laughed hollowly. "You've been here long enough to know better, Juhrnus. With the Lady's leaving, the *ahalad-kaaslane* no longer have the means to enforce what we say. And the nobility know it only too well. We have had to change the way we work in order to protect Kodu Riik. We have organized a council to correlate information, to send *ahalad-kaaslane* where they are most needed, to organize ourselves efficiently and to greatest effect. If the Lady won't tell us what to do, we must plan for ourselves."

Juhrnus stopped his pacing and turned to stare, hands dangling at his side. "What? Since when?"

"For a while." When Juhrnus only continued to stare, Sodur said, "since we returned from Patverseme."

"And you never told us." Juhrnus glanced at Reisil. She shook her head. "Are we the only ones?"

"Yes."

Reisil slumped in her seat. Said out loud and so baldly, it was like a fist in her gut. It shouldn't have been shocking. It was only reasonable after Sodur had gone to so much trouble to make everyone despise and distrust her. Of course they wouldn't want her to know anything that would help her plot against Kodu Riik. And Juhrnus, he was her friend. He wouldn't have kept secrets from her. But knowing it and hearing it were two different things.

"Why?" Juhrnus pressed.

Sodur glanced at Reisil. "It was deemed prudent."

"They think I'm a traitor, after all. I'd be a worm in their apple, and you too. Bad judgment to be friends with a known traitor," Reisil said.

"So what changed? Why tell us now?" Juhrnus leaned over his chair, gripping the back with white-knuckled fingers.

"We all must make difficult choices. We all pick our allegiances. And I— I have come to wonder whether the decisions the *ahalad-kaaslane* council has made are the best for Kodu Riik. Call it hedging my bets if you'd like, but I have grave doubts that the path we have chosen is the correct one. Not if it excludes you and Reisil."

Reisil snorted. "*Now* you wonder?"

For long moments Sodur did not answer, did not look up from where his fingers smoothed over the rough grain of the table. The wind blustered, and the door and windows shuddered.

"So, the *nokulas* were allowed to spread and now have begun to move down from the mountains, thanks no doubt to the hard winter and the drought," Reisil said at last, returning them to the subject. "And what, one just wandered into Koduteel?"

"Would that it had. No, this *nokula* was . . . born . . . in Koduteel." He ignored Reisil's indrawn breath and Juhrnus's expletive. "He used to be human. He's—" Sodur's lips tightened. "I don't know him anymore. And it's not just his body—his mind is gone too."

Reisil's fingers traced a whorl on the table and Juhrnus came to sit, his face blank with shock. "The *nokulas* were men?" she said.

"And women, children, maybe animals too—I can't begin to guess."

"How?"

"Magic. Has to be."

Understanding arrived like a key clicking in a lock. The secrecy, the politics, the entire last year began to make sickening sense. "Iisand Samir," Reisil breathed.

Sodur's head jerked around, his gaze like a burning brand. He nodded reluctantly.

"So it's not grief over the Mesilasema's death that has kept him locked away. Is he the only one?"

Sodur shrugged. "So far."

Reisil's brows lifted skeptically.

Sodur flushed. "He's the only one *I* am aware of."

"And you've kept it from everyone. What about his family?"

"We moved the three youngest out of the city. They're too young to ask questions. But Aare and Emelovi refuse to go. We've kept them away from their father, but it's not been easy."

"We?"

He scratched behind one ear. "That's not something I can say. I'm breaking faith in telling you this now."

"Breaking faith? I'd think you were getting good at it by now. Why bother telling us at all?" Bitterness leached into her voice.

Sodur had picked up his spoon and was turning it over in his hands. He dropped it back into his bowl and shoved the dish away. "There are things that we need you to do. Our enemies have caught scent of our weaknesses and have begun to position themselves. Young Kebonsat's arrival to pay court to the Iisand's eldest daughter is certainly no coincidence."

Hearing Kebonsat's name, Reisil flinched. She jumped up and fetched crockery cups and the hot currant-and-lemon brew. Tears burned in her eyes, and she willed them away. She knew, had always known, that there was no future for her and Kebonsat.

"So what do you want from us?" Juhrnus asked at last.

"The Scallacians," Reisil answered for Sodur.

"You know?" Sodur looked worried, as if the knowledge might be common gossip. Reisil bit her tongue to keep from snapping at him. It wasn't up to her to keep *his* secrets after all. Finally she said in a brittle tone, "Saljane saw the ship coming through the Straits of Piiton. I couldn't imagine why they were coming. But you sent for them; you're going to ask the sorcerers for help."

"There's no doubt it's a risk. This may shatter any vestiges of trust we still have in the court. The sorcerers could very well turn on us and do to Koduteel what the wizards did to Mysane Kosk. Which is why we need you close by."

Reisil began to shake her head, and Sodur forestalled her. "I know you want to go find the wizards, but at the

moment, the Scallacian sorcerers are more dangerous to
Kodu Riik. Just knowing how you broke the wizards' circle
in Patverseme will make them cautious. Who knows—
maybe you can learn something about the plague from
them."

Reisil searched his face. "What else? You're still not telling us everything."

Sodur stroked Lume's head, the silver lynx leaning into
his leg. "If what we've learned is correct, then the plague
and the *nokulas* both are spawning in Mysane Kosk. And
that means the wizards aren't going to help. They want us
dead. And don't think they won't be ready for you this
time. If you put yourself in their hands, chances are you
won't come back."

Chapter 15

Reisil wrapped up the leftover bread, head aching, eyes
dry and burning. Her legs and arms felt unwieldy, as
if they belonged to someone else.

Juhrnus and Sodur stood over the unconscious Metyein,
Juhrnus standing stiffly apart from the older man. Reisil
knew exactly how he felt. So many times she had wanted
to claw at Sodur and kick and scream, just to make him
know how hard she felt his betrayal. Only physical distance
kept her from giving in to her rage.

"When do you want to move him?" Juhrnus asked.

Sodur's expression was somber. Reisil could read his intent as if he'd spoken it aloud.

"No," she said, coming to stand protectively at Metyein's
shoulder. "I won't let you undo what I have done. How
can you even think it?"

"And when he tells his father? Or worse—what if he
overheard us? Damned foolish—" He scrubbed his fingers
over his scalp. "We've got to be careful. This can't get out.

None of it. His life isn't worth the safety of Kodu Riik," Sodur said.

"It is to me."

"Need we even worry?" Jurhnus asked. "Is he even awake?"

Reisil stared at Sodur. He gave a quick nod, and she dropped her hand to Metyein's chest, calling up her magic. It flowed into him, and instantly she knew he *was* awake, though for how long, she couldn't guess. She pressed her hand down warningly, hoping he was coherent enough to understand his danger.

"You may be assured," she said. "He's lost a lot of blood. When he does come to, he's going to be confused, delirious even. I doubt he'll remember anything after he was wounded."

Sodur's shoulders dropped. "Good. Then Juhrnus and I will take him home now."

Reisil stood aside as they pulled back the blankets.

"Should we do something about the blood? Someone might ask questions," Juhrnus said.

"We'll scavenge something," Sodur said. He glanced up at the ceiling. "The wind's letting up. Better hurry."

Juhrnus hoisted the limp man over his shoulder, having already tucked Esper into his chest sling.

Sodur followed, pausing to look back at Reisil. "Tomorrow you should move into the palace. Before the sorcerers arrive. I've made the arrangements. And congratulations. Today you made great strides with your powers."

Reisil shut the door behind him harder than necessary. Her head swam, and she crossed to her bed, yanking off her boots as she went. She slid into the warm pocket made by the Lord Marshal's son, uncaring of the blood staining the blankets. In moments she fell asleep, her dreams haunted by snarling monsters with human faces and the desolate cries of plague victims.

Metyein forced his body to remain slack as he was up-ended over Juhrnus's shoulder. He hardly felt the cold as they stepped onto the parapet, snow kissing the back of his exposed neck.

"What idiot put steps on the outside of this thrice-damned place," Juhrnus grumbled. Sodur didn't answer, setting a steadying hand on Metyein's back. Metyein concentrated on remaining limp, though every muscle in his body fought to clench as Juhrnus skidded and slipped. At last they arrived safely at the bottom.

"How do you want to get him into town? I already returned the cart I borrowed," Juhrnus said.

"Can you get him to the gates? We'll find a horse or cart there."

"Let's go."

The road was no less slick than the lighthouse stairs, and twice Juhrnus fell to his knees, despite Sodur's steadying grip. At the gate, a guard opened the inset pedestrian entrance.

"He had a bit of a blow in the Fringes," Sodur explained in a disgusted voice. "Juiced himself. His father sent us to retrieve him." He made a show of spitting. "Lad ought to know better."

"Fringes is no place for a cup and a wench," the guard said. "Boy ought to take his urges to Rotten Row. Plenty willing women and good ale as well."

"Aye and that's the Lady's own truth. He's spoiled though, won't be told. Has to find out for himself. If not for the weather and his father, I'd let him wake up in the morning with his prick rotted off."

The guard chuckled. Juhrnus staggered through the gate after Sodur and up a narrow street. Sodur halted him outside a barbershop.

"Wait here. I'll see what I can find," Sodur said.

Metyein heard Sodur's footsteps scuffle away, and then Juhrnus dropped him onto a wooden bench. Metyein's breath left him in a gust, and he bit his tongue as his elbow banged against a wall. Cold and damp seeped up through his clothing as the snow on the seat began to melt.

"Sorry about that," Juhrnus muttered. "You still alive?"

Metyein held still, trying to keep his breathing even. Juhrnus pushed Metyein's head aside and perched on the arm of the bench.

"Give it up. You've been doing a pretty good job pretending to be a corpse, but you aren't fooling me. Don't worry. I won't tell Sodur." Metyein sympathized with the bitterness he heard in Juhrnus's voice. He felt the same harshness for his father.

"I'm alive," he answered, opening his eyes. "Barely. Thanks to your Reisiltark. She—" He broke off, his throat closing. "I don't understand how. . . ."

"Consider yourself lucky, and don't think too hard about it. Just thank the Lady, thank Reisil, and don't forget what she did for you."

"I won't. And I won't tell what I heard either."

Juhrnus looked up the street. There was a sound of rattling wheels. He looked back down at Metyein, his face set. "They aren't my secrets. You do what you want with them. Now shut your eyes."

Obediently Metyein closed his eyes and let himself go limp. The wheels rumbled up and stopped.

"Where did you find that?"

"Masonry warehouse. If it can carry stone, it can carry him."

"What about clothes?"

Metyein heard the rustle of cloth.

"Not up to his usual standards."

"These don't have a lot of laces or buttons. And I don't care what questions he has to answer about what he's wearing so long as no one links him to Reisil," Sodur said. "Let's load him up. We'll find a less exposed place to change him on the way. I found this too. Should keep anyone from asking questions."

Hands grasped Metyein, pulling him up by the shoulders and lifting him at the legs. He found himself heaped into a small cart—a wheelbarrow, he realized, his nose itching as he inhaled rock dust. He swallowed the sneeze, his eyes watering. Sodur and Juhrnus prodded at him, shoving him inside the rough box and then spread a foul-smelling blanket over him. It stank of cat piss, rancid meat and lamp oil.

"Whew! What midden did you pull that out of?" Juhrnus exclaimed.

"You don't want to know. But it'll serve."

With that they began trundling Metyein through the city. He peered out from beneath the filthy wool. Through the narrow opening, he could see a wedge of the gray stone buildings tilting inward over the narrow street. For the first time Metyein noticed Koduteel's ravaged beauty beneath the shining veil of ice and snow. Dirt and wretchedness clung to the buildings, filling the cracks in the cobbles and sneaking in through the shutters and doors. Even the more respectable houses seemed shaken and infirm. Groups of poor huddled together outside taverns and inns, hoping for a handout. Bright lights burned in the yellow district's bakeries, and ragged children climbed the roofs to curl up against the chimney pots.

Watching Koduteel wheel slowly by, a prescience settled over Metyein. Soon the streets would fill with the sick and the dying, and the nearby forests would be stripped for the pyres. His mind shied from thinking of his mother, brother and sisters. Even sequestered in Doneviik, sooner or later the plague would find them.

Beneath the blanket Metyein clenched his fists, a cold wire twisting around his innards. His father had to be neck-deep in covering up the Iisand's illness. Derros cas Vare despised the young Verit. It was one thing he and Metyein agreed on wholeheartedly. Aare was arrogant, cruel and ambitious, and he despised the *ahalad-kaaslane*. Metyein's father would do most anything to keep Aare off the throne. Being Aare's Lord Marshal would gall beyond reason, and Aare wouldn't be fool enough to appoint anyone else. But with the plague's arrival, it wouldn't be possible to keep the secret anymore. Which meant that Aare would be made regent, if not crowned Iisand. And either way, the *ahalad-kaaslane* would lose what little power they had left. Aare would kill them all rather than share his power. Reisiltark especially, unless he could make her serve him.

Beneath the blanket Metyein snarled, remembering the pressure of Reisiltark's hand on his shoulder warning him not to move. Twice tonight she'd saved his life, and not because his father was the Lord Marshal or because she was scheming for power. She'd never serve Aare. Never betray the Lady. Metyein clenched his fists. Whatever else happened, she wouldn't face Aare alone. He would give her his sword arm. Soka's too, once he told him—

Memory scorched through his brain. Soka. Had he escaped? Been caught? Or worse? He forced himself to remain still. His own danger was still real. And even if Soka wasn't all right, the *ahalad-kaaslane* were taking him home, where Soka would send word. And if not—

Though heir to the ancient house of Bro-heyek, Soka's peers treated him little better than a servant, thanks to his father's incessant border tussles and Soka's dubious position as hostage to the court. He gained little sympathy even when the Iisand ordered his eye put out after Thevul Raakin made yet another incursion against one of his neighbors.

Soka had been nine years old then, but the memory of his father's indifference and betrayal lurked constantly in his expression—in the hard twist of his lips and the sharp glint in his remaining eye. It was that expression that drew Metyein. Metyein understood it all too well. The two men had become instant brothers, kindred spirits. It was Metyein who secretly taught Soka swordplay, and in return Soka taught him to navigate the waters of the court, the thick undercurrents and lurking reefs.

If Soka still lived, Metyein would find him. If he was dead, Metyein would have vengeance for him.

He didn't remember ever feeling such pain, not even when they took his eye. His legs felt weighted by heaps of hot coals—so heavy he couldn't move them, and so raw with pain, he would gladly have cut them off to be free of it. Soka opened his eye, wondering where Pelodra had brought him.

He saw nothing.

Panic struck him like a bolt of lightning. He flipped his head back and forth, reaching up to rub at his eye, discovering that his hands were leashed to the boards on which he lay and that his eyes were blindfolded. He yanked his arms against the restraints and then cried out when pain flared in his body. He fell back, panting.

Where was he? How had they been captured? He couldn't think; his mind was sluggish and thick and his head pounded. Then he heard footsteps and muffled voices, the sound of a bolt sliding back and the creak of hinges followed by a wash of cool air, and the smell of an expensive musky perfume. His balls shrivelled. He knew that scent. . . .

"*This* is what you brought me?" came a haughty, austere voice. The hairs on Soka's arms prickled. Not *him*. Good Lady, not him.

"This one was *supposed* to be dead. Where, pray tell, is the Lord Marshal's son?"

"He ordered me off. Wanted me to take this piece of *skraa* instead. What could I do?" Pelodra's gravelly voice was high and whiny.

"Not enough, apparently."

"Wasn't time with your men closing in. And the master is a stubborn man, and Urviik was there besides," Pelodra defended. "Young Vare was gut-shot anyhow. One of your men put an arrow right through his middle. Wasn't gonna live long after that."

"So you brought me this instead." Soka felt a hand pushing on his shoulders and tensed.

"Ah, you're awake. Leave us. I'll deal with you later."

Soka heard Pelodra's heavy treads and the squeak and thump of the door shutting. He felt the Verit's hand on his head, stroking his hair. A shiver he couldn't suppress shook his body.

The Verit chuckled. "What am I going to do with you?" he murmured. "I am told you will heal." Soka felt the Verit move away, heard the sound of him pacing, the swish of his clothing, the soft *clink* of his sword. Soka's mouth went dry, and his heart pounded in his chest. He fought to remain still and not struggle against his ropes. Aare would enjoy that. It took everything Soka had to keep still, memories of an earlier time intruding. Then he'd been strapped down, his head wedged in place, straps biting into his forehead and chin. No blindfold then. But blindness was to come.

The room had been a card salon, with marble floors, bright red curtains and tasteful plush furniture. It had been just before breakfast. The Iisand had business elsewhere and had sent eighteen-year-old Aare in his stead. Because someone royal had to bear witness and take possession of the bloody token—the message to his father that the Iisand would tolerate no more defiance. Soka remembered drinking the draft the herbalist gave him and the feeling of paralyzing lassitude that descended. The drug prevented him from feeling the panic he knew he ought to feel as the young Verit stood over him and explained what he wanted done, his finger soft against Soka's skin.

"But Daz Aare!" protested the healer-turned-torturer. "These are not your father's commands."

"Am I not my father's voice in this room? Oppose me

and you oppose him." He paused. Soka could hear the
menace in the silence like a snake crawling up his leg. "Be
assured I will not fail to remember this day. Nor will
your family."

The healer made no answer but began to lay out his tools
with soft metallic sounds. Then there was the sound of flint
and steel and the smell of burning coals, the murmuring of
voices as the healer instructed his assistants. Tears rolled
from the corners of Soka's eyes as he lay helpless. Too
soon the cutting began.

"Be certain to leave the eye whole," Aare ordered. "His
are a distinctive color, and his father must see that the
message is genuine."

Soka remembered the shining curve of the blade. Dull-
edged and narrow, hammered smooth and wafer thin, its
elegant length filled his vision like a shining, curved tooth.
Cool fingers held his eyelids open. The smell of sage sausages and stale ale puffed hotly over Soka's cheeks. The
blade slid under his upper eyelid. It probed deeper, touching places too horrifying to think about.

Soka's mouth filled with vomit. There was nothing to do
but choke or swallow it down again. His throat jerked.
Then there was a tugging sensation, a levering. The shaft
of the tool pressed hard against the bridge of his nose and
the healer's knuckles ground against Soka's forehead. Soka
struggled to close his eyes against the tool's prying force,
but the fingers held his eyelids firmly open.

Suddenly the tension released and he cried out relief.
But it wasn't over.

"Help me up. Can't get enough strength on it from
down here."

Suddenly he found himself straddled, the healer's weight
settling heavily onto his chest. Quickly as it had stopped,
the pressure began again. The healer leaned against the
handle of the blade. Soka twisted against the confining
straps, straining his head away from the blade.

Suddenly his eye gave with a soft *plop*. The healer fell
forward at the abrupt release, knocking his elbow against
Soka's nose. At the same moment there was a sickening
squelching sound and dizziness swept Soka as his vision
shifted and split. Suddenly he was staring simultaneously
up at the ceiling and down at the legs and crotch of the

man lying across his chest. An unmerciful itching sensation assaulted his left eye, and there was a coolness where nothing cold should be.

"Put it back," his nine-year-old self sobbed. "Lady help me!"

"Next part is a bit tricky," rasped the healer, breathing heavily as he slid to the floor. "Got to cauterize the bleeders quick. Hold those needles in the coals. No, not that way. Like that. And have that ointment ready. Quicker we get it on the less chance it'll turn septic."

Then there was more tugging. Soka felt it deep in his skull. No one spoke to him. He was like meat on a butcher's table. He heard himself sniveling but could not make himself stop. At last the tugging halted. The nauseating smell of burning flesh filled the room. Soka retched again as he realized it was his flesh that was burning.

"That should do it. We ought to bandage his eye, let it heal. Sewing it up now could mean serious trouble."

"No. Finish it. Exactly as I ordered. Quickly now, the troops are waiting."

The answering silence was thick, but soon Soka felt the work begin again. First the stitching, then the cutting. A map of his father's lands. A permanent reminder so that neither he nor his father would forget their limits. Aare had brought something to rub into the cuts so that they would scar. After, Soka had been left in the care of the tutors hired by the Iisand and paid for out of his father's tithes. They said little, giving him more of the drug so that he would sleep.

"I won't kill you, of course." Aare's cultured voice brought Soka back to the present, to the hard table, to the blindfold and the ropes around his wrists. He was sweating, and his body was shaking. "I may yet find a way for you to be useful. I shall think on it. In the meantime, you shall enjoy my hospitality."

Soka started when Aare's fingers trailed over his face, lingering at his lips. "You might be amusing, one way or another."

Soka jerked his head away. "Blinded and tied? Your tastes have become plebian, Daz Aare."

"Who better to know than you? It's said your father got you on his favorite mare."

"It is a well-known fact that the men of my family have the equipment to satisfy even a horse, while yours . . ." Soka lifted his arm as high as it would go and twitched the pinkie finger back and forth. "I think perhaps you are more suited to mice and rats?"

"Do remember that you live only by my mercy," came Aare's clipped reply. He moved closer, bending over the table. "You are blindfolded now, but I could easily make the dark permanent. I trust you haven't forgotten."

Soka's mouth opened, but fear closed it again.

Aare chuckled. Then Soka felt the Verit's hand on his crotch. It rested there, cupping his balls. "Another thing you shouldn't forget—you could lose these and still remain useful to me."

Soka said nothing, the air fleeing his lungs.

Aare chuckled again. "I shall return soon. I will expect you to act then as befits your position."

The door opened and closed, and Soka remained in darkness. He cursed himself. *Why did I antagonize Aare?* He knew better. Now he must survive, heal his wounds and then plan an escape. He must find Metyein, warn him of his enemy. He didn't believe Pelodra's story that Metyein had been shot fatally. It was a self-serving lie, meant to protect the traitorous groom from the wrath of his master. Nor could he trust Aare to tell him the truth. No, Soka wouldn't believe it until he saw Metyein's body for himself.

Chapter 16

There was no way to know if the sun was shining or not. The world was drawn in shades of charcoal. Koduteel huddled within its walls, a beetling mass of snow-shrouded buildings. Clouds billowed on the horizon, and the wind keened through the streets. Reisil braced her hands against the stone parapet, staring up at the pewter sky.

Today Saljane was coming home.

Reisil's right arm was sheathed from knuckles to throat in a supple leather gauntlet. Fire-hardened oak slats had been fitted into pockets on the underside of the leather sleeve, running in flat spokes around her forearm and horizontally over her shoulder. The glove, forearm and shoulder had been reinforced with plates of boiled leather and showed both the scars of hard use and the polished sheen of recent care.

Reisil ached to hold Saljane, to scratch her fingers through the goshawk's crisp feathers and feel the caress of Saljane's beak against her cheek. "Come on! Come home to me!" She called, startling herself when her voice echoed in the stony courtyard.

~*The wind blows strongly. I am almost there.*

Reisil grinned and waved, though Saljane was in no danger of not seeing her. Bound heart and soul as they were, she could find Reisil in a tule fog with her eyes closed.

Reisil held up her fist. The black speck grew with agonizing slowness. Saljane circled, her wings bright against the dark clouds. She plunged out of the sky like a bolt from a crossbow. Her wings flared, and her talons clamped around Reisil's raised fist. Reisil drew her in, pressing her cheek to Saljane's sleek feathers, smelling the goshawk's familiar warm, musty smell mixed with the scent of evergreens and mountains.

~*I missed you so much.*

Joy. Belonging. Satisfaction. Hunger.

Reisil sniffed and laughed, tears sliding down her cheeks. "Right," she said, carrying Saljane inside. The luxurious palace room held a four-post canopy bed on a broad pedestal, a hearth large enough to stand inside, a wardrobe, a closet for bathing and dressing, a divan, a handful of chairs, a table, a writing desk and a dresser. A wine-colored carpet patterned with gold leaves and fruit covered the slate floor, and tapestries of hunting scenes adorned the walls.

Reisil lifted Saljane up onto a tall perch made of red cedar standing at the foot of the bed.

~*Either you have been stuffing yourself this winter, or I have become a weakling in your absence.*

~*I hunt with skill.*

Reisil smiled at Saljane's smug satisfaction.

Saljane mantled, shaking her feathers like a dog. She
flicked a glance at Reisil and then at the tray of meat sitting
on the table.

~*Hungry*.

Reisil's smile widened. "Go ahead. Stuff yourself. You've
had a long journey."

Saljane leaped from her perch with alacrity and glided
to the table, where she snatched at the meat.

"We have a gala tonight," Reisil said, retreating to her
wardrobe. "For the Scallacians. The city is buzzing. Hopefully
with everyone gawking at them, no one will notice me."

She paused to look at herself in the mirror before dressing. Giving in to Sodur's nagging about her appearance,
she had turned herself over to a tailor and a brace of maids
to renovate her from the ragged-nailed, haggard-faced
drudge she'd become. The thin, broken ends of her hair
had been trimmed, washed, and plied with a variety of
emollients and herbal rinses. It now shone like a raven's
wing. It was caught up on the crown of her head with silver
clasps and tumbled down her back in a smooth fall. No
number of curling devices could convince it to do otherwise
than hang straight.

Reisil grudgingly acknowledged she did look a lot better.
Nor had her wait on the gusty balcony done more than
loosen a few strands of hair and heighten the color in her
cheeks.

Reisil smoothed her hands down her sides. She had not
worn anything so fine or feminine since Kallas, since that
fateful night of Ceriba's abduction. The memory rose
jagged-edged and fierce. The person she had been forced
to become since then needed the armor of leather and
coarse cloth, severe hair, rough skin and the gray cloak
Sodur complained about.

Her outfit was of simple lines, though elegantly cut. It
was sewn of a soft heavy fabric that draped with a pleasing
voluptuousness. The arms were closely fitted so that her
sleeve wouldn't bunch beneath the gauntlet. The tailor had
sniffed sourly at her insistence that she *would* wear it, sub-
mitting to Reisil's demands with ill grace. A sharp contrast
to her treatment in the Fringes.

"Because they don't understand!" she exclaimed, striking
the air with her fist. Saljane jerked her head up, a strip of

meat dangling from her beak. "They think I will save them. If they only knew. If only the Lady would show me how to cure the plague . . ."

~She would have if she thought there was need.

"What more need could there be?"

~You will find a way.

"Except that I can't. The power is finally answering, but nothing I do affects the plague. So what good am I really?"

~You will learn.

"I don't know. The wizards—" Resil stopped. Even if she knew where to find them, the wizards weren't interested in a cure. She could try to force them. . . . A tremor shook her, pimpling her arms and legs with gooseflesh. Sometimes in the night she could still smell the charred bodies of the hundred wizards she'd killed in Patverseme.

She stared down at her feet. "I don't know what to do, and doing nothing is going to get everybody killed."

Saljane's answer, when it came, was gentle.

~We aren't alone.

"Aren't we?" Reisil lifted her head to look into Saljane's ember eyes. "The Lady has gone. The only ones who can help us would rather kill us. And the sorcerers aren't any better than the wizards. Maybe worse. At least we know where we stand with the wizards."

~The Lady weaves her pattern carefully. Only she can see all, Saljane said obliquely.

Reisil stared at the goshawk for a long moment. Did Saljane know more than she said? Or was it a reflection of her faith in the Lady? Reisil rubbed her forehead, feeling a headache hatching in her skull. So many questions. But there wasn't any point worrying about it anymore tonight. She would need all her wits to get through the party unscathed.

Reisil turned back to the mirror, tugging on the long beaded belt that cinched her flowing tunic. The tunic hung to her knees over full, loose-fitting trousers. A pattern of ivy matching that on her face was embroidered onto the midnight material in silky, dark-blue thread. A subtle effect, and one that Reisil appreciated. Her silver gryphon necklace peeked out from between the folds of the deeply slashed neckline. She looked—exotic. Even as much as the sorcerers in their brilliant robes, dark skin and pale hair.

No longer wilting and safe, her appearance proclaimed her a woman of power and danger, like the elegant beauty of a finely wrought sword. They wouldn't know what to think. It would make them nervous. She smiled at herself. Good.

Behind her, Saljane resumed her perch. A happy satiety radiated from her.

"Have you done stuffing yourself? Then let's be on our way. We don't want to add tardiness to our crimes against the court."

A sharp knock on the door made Reisil start. Three raps, a bare pause, and again. Whoever it was was impatient. Had Sodur come to fetch her? Did he think she needed a shepherd? She scowled and crossed to the door, opening it a handsbreadth. Her breath caught.

"Kebonsat," she said, her voice hardly loud enough to be heard above the pounding of her heart.

He put his hand flat against the door, his lips taut, his jaw knotting. His dark hair was ruffled as if he'd run his fingers through it, and his eyes blazed. A surge of longing rushed through her. Reisil tightened her hands on the door handle and jamb. It had been more than a year since she'd seen him. It wasn't long enough.

"Are you going to let me in?"

Reisil's eyes flicked to the corridor behind him, seeking escape. She wasn't ready to see him. Not yet.

He followed her gaze. "No one's watching, if that's what you're—"

There were sparks and a clattering *thunk* of something hitting the stonework just above Kebonsat's head.

He jerked and thrust himself forward with a grunt, shoving Reisil back inside. She floundered backwards, lost her footing and thudded onto the floor as Saljane screeched and leaped into the air. Reisil's head bounced on the carpet. Black and red erupted across her vision. A split second later, Kebonsat pounded down on top of her, driving the air from her lungs. She coughed, struggling for breath, even as he rolled away, kicking the door shut and dropping the latch.

He crouched by the door, listening, his breath coming hard between his lips, his lohar in his hand. It looked like a miniature pick, the handle inlaid with a complex pattern of silver and brass, the slightly hooked blade glinting. Some might mistake the Patversemese habit of wearing the weapon an affectation. It looked like a child's toy. But Reisil was not fooled. In skilled hands, the blade could scythe away limbs, block sword thrusts and disarm swordsmen. It never ceased to amaze her that the Kodu Riikian court so blithely permitted the Patversemese to carry the weapons.

After a moment, Kebonsat turned back to Reisil, who had regained her feet. He frowned, scanning her up and down. "Don't you even have a knife? What if they got in here?"

Reisil flushed. "I was going to the reception for the Scallas sorcerers."

A look of disgust flittered across his face and then disappeared as his expression settled into lines of wrath. Whether aimed at her or the Scallacians, Reisil didn't know. "You cannot go about unarmed. Especially among Scallacians." He looked at her expectantly.

Reisil felt herself flush hotter and crossed her arms over her chest. "I don't have anything that will go with my outfit," she said, her chin jutting.

He reached into his boot, yanking out a stiletto in a plain black sheath. He tossed it to her. "Carry that."

Reisil caught it, turning the slender knife in her hands. She gave a little shake of her head and tossed the blade back to him. "I can't."

"You are not going to feed me pap about being a tark and not taking lives, are you? I know better. I saw what you did to the wizards. Besides, as *ahalad-kaaslane,* you at least have to be able to defend yourself. And don't natter to me about magic. You won't always have a chance to use it."

Reisil winced, feeling the lump on the back of her head with delicate fingers. *Why can't he just leave it alone?* She sighed. But inside, there was a growing warmth that he still cared, enough at least to harangue her.

"It isn't that. But your knife wouldn't do me any good except to cut bread. Or myself."

Kebonsat snarled. "What in Ellini's name have you been doing this last year and a half? Is there no one with enough sense to teach you to defend yourself? Or are you trying to get yourself killed? Reisil?"

The concern in Kebonsat's voice undid her. Tears rolled

down her thin, pallid cheeks. He reached a hand to brush them away, his own face contorting. Kebonsat slid the lohar back into its sheath and then pulled her into his arms. His body pressed hard and warm against hers, radiating reassuring heat and healing.

"Gods, I am a jackass," he growled against her neck. "This is not what I had in mind for us."

Reisil gave a choked laugh. "There's a lot I didn't have in mind."

"You've been avoiding me."

Reisil didn't reply. There was no need, and he knew why as well as she did. Still she could not bring herself to pull away as she ought to. He sighed, his chest fluttering beneath her cheek. He rubbed his hands over her back, and she felt herself relaxing into his embrace, desire dancing over her skin.

"I cannot deny the reason that I have come to Koduteel," he said, his breath whispering across her skin like butterfly wings.

She tensed.

"I have come to pay court to Vertina Emelovi."

Reisil flinched. Her hands dropped to her sides.

"Yes, so I've heard. Making any progress?"

Kebonsat pushed back on her shoulders and captured her cheeks between his palms. He waited. At last she looked up—his face was so close, so impossibly far. He wore a haggard expression, his lips stiff and white beneath his aquiline nose. Longing to match her own pooled in his dark eyes, like liquid jet. Reisil's hands crept up to cover his.

"This is my choice," he said in a hard voice that denied his want. "This is my honor to do for my family and for my Karalis."

Reisil nodded again. He was a man of honor, a man of courage and pride, and he had a duty to his house and his Karalis. Kebonsat had been sent to strengthen the alliance between Patverseme and Kodu Riik. He would no more chance ruining his mission with an illicit romantic liaison than he would torture a child. And he valued truth too much to pretend otherwise.

Reisil closed her eyes and took a breath, fighting the tears that continued in a slow, gelid trickle down her

cheeks. She stepped back and went to Saljane. The goshawk jumped to Reisil's fist. In those moments with her
back turned, Reisil grappled to gain a semblance of control.
After long moments, soothing cold rose to frost her heart,
settling over her in a longed-for numbing glaze.

She swung back around, the corners of her mouth turning
up in an offhand smile she did not feel. "I never thought
we were meant for one another." Before he could pursue
the topic further, she changed the subject. "But apparently
someone thinks to be certain of that."

Kebonsat glanced at the door, frowning. "I had not
thought I was followed here."

Unthinking, Reisil said, "Perhaps you weren't."

His head jerked around. "You think they were waiting?
But no one knew— No, that isn't it. You think they were
after you." His expression, already hard, turned feral. "And
you don't even carry a weapon? What in Ellini's name is
wrong with you?"

Reisil gave an inward sigh, kicking herself for opening
up that subject again. "What do you want to do now? Both
of us are late. I'm sure the Vertina is wondering at your
absence."

His expression darkened, and Reisil could tell he wanted
to say something caustic, probably something about wringing her neck. Instead he took a quick glance around the
room, assessing the furniture, the doors leading to the balcony, and returning at last to the door through which
he'd entered.

"Really only one way out," he said. "And as you say,
we *are* late."

With that he went to the vanity table beside her wardrobe. It was about three feet long and a foot and a half
wide, made of bird's-eye walnut with slender, rolled legs.
Nodding to himself, Kebonsat set it on its back and kicked
off its legs.

"Open the door, and keep out of sight. Latch it as soon
as I pass." He drew his lohar and held the table before
him like a shield. Reisil slid back the latch. Kebonsat eased
out into the corridor. Reisil hesitated, then shut the door.
There wasn't much else she could do. After a moment, she
reached for one of the sundered legs and held it like a club.

Should she have told him about the assassins' attack?

She shook her head. Nothing she could have told him
would have made any difference. Her fingers tightened on
the table leg.

Please Lady, keep him safe.

Chapter 17

Several minutes passed. Sweat trickled down Reisil's back
and slicked the hand holding the table leg. Saljane was
heavy on her shoulder. Just when she thought she couldn't
wait any longer, she heard a tapping and Kebonsat's low
voice. Relief swamped her. She opened the door, and he
squeezed back in.

"Whoever it was is gone. I found this outside." He held
up a crossbolt, the tip glistening. "Poisoned. Should have
had me dead to rights." He looked at Reisil. "Unless you're
right and it was you they were after. You could have healed
any poison in me." The last was pitched like a question,
and Reisil nodded. "So why did he shoot at all? There was
no hope of hitting you and no point to hitting me."

Reisil shrugged. "I might have missed tonight's gala if
you were injured," she suggested. Strangely, the idea of
someone shooting at her didn't frighten her much. Quite
the opposite, in fact. She felt angry. The emotion rolled
through her like thunder, powerful and cleansing. Saljane
caught that anger, raising her wings and snapping her beak.
Kebonsat flicked a glance at the bird and back to Reisil.

"Distraction? But why?"

"Any number of reasons. Let's see." Reisil ticked them
off on her fingers. "I sat in someone's favorite chair. I
sneezed at just the wrong moment. I forgot to smile at
someone. I blinked. I breathed." When Kebonsat flushed
and opened his mouth, Reisil held up her hand. "No, I
promise, I'm taking this seriously. But I am not popular in
court. You must know that already. Plenty of people would

like to see me embarrassed or worse. Most are like rats.
They work from the dark behind walls, and I don't know
their names or their faces."

She paused, thinking. "Not that you *couldn't* have been
the target. Even if I neutralized the poison, you might not
have been in any shape to go. It might have undercut your
position with the Vertina. Perhaps you have become a
threat to someone."

Kebonsat rubbed his hand over his jaw, scowling as he
began to shake his head. "He shouldn't have missed."

"Maybe he was hurried. A maid might have come along,
or anyone."

He lifted his brows. "Very pragmatic. Taking this all in
stride, are you?"

Reisil's mouth twisted at his unexpected thrust, and she
felt pain erupt from the wound as if he'd actually struck
her. Taking it in stride? Knowing that someone was hunting
her? That someone wanted her dead? It could be anyone,
even Sodur, if he thought it would help Kodu Riik. That
realization sawed at her anchoring ties to Kodu Riik, to
the *ahalad-kaaslane,* to everything she was.

Reassurance. Pride. Devotion.

Reisil felt Saljane's fierce strength runnel into her, wrapping around her like a heat from a fire. There was one
anchor still firmly intact, strong as steel and stone and
ocean waves.

~*How have I managed without you, dear heart?*
~*You have managed. But I am here now.*

Bolstered, Reisil returned her attention to Kebonsat,
aware that he was waiting for a response.

"Pragmatism seems like a good choice right now," she
said, pleased with the steadiness of her voice. "However,
if you'd like, I can attempt hysterics." Not that she'd have
to try very hard.

Kebonsat crossed his arms, shifting back on his heels to
scrutinize her. Reisil flushed. She glanced down, realizing
she still held the table leg. Jerkily she retreated to the fireplace and set it on the coals. Kebonsat's next words took
her off guard.

"You look . . . ," Kebonsat began and then paused, sighing. He collected himself. "Nice. Striking." He paused
again, as if considering saying more, but then changed sub-

jects again, his tone shifting suddenly to courtly formality. "We are both overdue, though I need a shave and a change of clothes. All the same, I shall walk you down before I return to my chambers."

Reisil nodded, relief and disappointment washing through her.

They proceeded down through the corridors of smooth stone and dark paneling, their footsteps silent on the woven rugs. Reisil had been assigned rooms in the north tower of the western wing. The Scallacian sorcerers were housed in the south tower—within easy reach, yet far enough away to lend Reisil privacy and seclusion.

Kebonsat paced in silence. He radiated tension, his eyes darting down cross-passages and up stairways.

"Have you heard from Ceriba?" Reisil asked, feeling the silence straining.

His answering smile was unfettered. "She is well. I visited her on my way here. She tells me Elutark is a hard taskmaster, but she has regained her color and her spark." He paused. "She'll never forget what they did to her—" He broke off, looking as if he wanted to spit. After a moment he continued, his voice like gravel. "But she has purpose now, and she is thriving. I am glad she did not remain home. I think that might have killed her."

Reisil nodded, remembering the future Ceriba had described for herself. A life of snubbing and ostracization, of being the family scandal—a permanent, immutable disgrace. Another kind of rape to add to the first. Ceriba would certainly not have survived, and her family would have suffered greatly to watch their once vibrant daughter dwindling, her former friends avoiding her, her former haunts barred from her. And they would have been able to do nothing for her against the might of social judgment.

Reisil had learned firsthand what gossip and intrigue could do—how snubbing and whispers could humiliate and degrade, and make a person want to hide in shame. Ceriba had expected it, had expected to withdraw into seclusion, to become a ghost in her own home until she died in fact. Had Reisil not done the same? Retreating into the lighthouse, scurrying around in the shadows, snatching scraps of food when no one was looking, running at the slightest hint of discovery? Rats in the walls indeed.

~They aren't going to like this. Are you ready?

Kek-kek-kek-kek! Saljane's cry echoed down the corridor, accompanied by a flash of fierce pride.

"What's that about?" Kebonsat asked, brows arched.

"Fair warning."

The look he cast her was as sharp as his lohar.

The corridor they followed emptied into a gallery overlooking the Grand Foyer. Reisil and Kebonsat gazed down at the brilliant spectacle. The floor was a vividly colored mural of inlaid stone, polished to a high sheen. It depicted the Blessed Amiya in her glade, surrounded by gryphons and a host of animal *ahalad-kaaslane*. In one crystal-taloned hand she held a crimson pomegranate. In the other, the hereditary crown of the Iisands. Her face wore a smile, but her unworldly eyes, filled from corner to corner with polished opals, spoke a solemn warning. A wide skirt of trees and vines bordered the oval, and from its edges sprouted an imposing white marble staircase ascending into the Great Hall, and several smaller flights of steps leading into various salons and galleries. Seven crystal chandeliers dangled in a descending circle over the Foyer.

"Magnificent," Kebonsat said in a low voice that held none of the awe Reisil felt. But then, he was used to such sights. He pulled back, gesturing for her to accompany him.

"I must return to my rooms to dress. However, before we part, I must ask a boon of you." His tone was once again formal. Reisil gave a hesitant nod for him to continue. "I count you as a friend, and as such, I cannot accept that you have no weapons skills, especially given tonight's attack. I ask that you meet me in the morning, every morning, at first light in the copse behind the barracks. I shall instruct you."

"Is that wise? There will be rumors; it could make things difficult for you."

"I'll worry about that."

Reisil hesitated another moment. She could not argue that she didn't need instruction, and more, she did not want to. She had felt entirely silly and useless holding the table leg. She nodded. "I will."

A pleased grin lit his face, and he bowed with a fluid, courtly flourish. "Your whim is my fondest wish, Dajam Reisiltark."

The answering merriment bled from Reisil's face, and she stepped back. "Don't mock me. That's what *they* do."

Kebonsat scowled. "I cannot imagine how my words could be considered mocking. Nor how you could have so little opinion of me that you accuse me of doing so."

Reisil looked away. He was right to be insulted. He wasn't one of the lords like those gathered downstairs. They called her Dajam and bowed to her, all the while hating her, even plotting her death.

But even though he was nothing like them, he was nonetheless one of them. She looked at him as if seeing him for the first time. Everything about him—his carriage, his expression, his clothing—spoke of gentility and breeding. Though he called her friend, he was not. He could never truly be one, for his interests and those of his country did not coincide with hers as *ahalad-kaaslane*.

This is not news, she told herself, her fists clenched until her knuckles whitened.

"Reisil?" Kebonsat reached out his hand. She flinched. If she let him touch her, she wouldn't be able to keep herself together. She drew a deep breath.

"I hadn't realized until just now."

"What?"

"Who you are."

"And who am I?"

"You're—" How to say it? How to put it into words? "You're the next Dure Vadonis."

He thrust out an impatient hand, waving her words away. "It's hardly a revelation. That cannot be what has made you goggle at me."

"You always seemed so . . . ordinary." That wasn't true. He'd never been *ordinary*. He'd been generous and courageous and kind. "I had forgotten you were in line to become Karalis."

"A very long line, and one that I don't anticipate ever reaching the head of," he said dismissively. "Is that what is suddenly troubling you?"

"Here, those who use such language with me are most certainly *not* my friends. But then . . . neither are you. It isn't possible."

Fury kindled in his expression. He stalked to the balustrade, staring down into the milling crowd, his fingers tapping the buttery marble.

Almost too low for Reisil to hear, he muttered, "In prosperity our friends know us; in adversity we know our friends." After a long moment, he spun around and stalked back, standing so close, she could feel his breath on her cheeks.

"You must understand this, Reisil. Courts are battlegrounds. One makes alliances; one advances and retreats, ambushes and sacrifices. Rules of manners have to be obeyed—otherwise, it would be madness and slaughter. That is the first lesson my father taught me. To believe a court is merely a place of social congregation is suicide." To emphasize his warning, Kebonsat grasped her upper arms and gave her a little shake. Saljane hissed at him, swaying on Reisil's shoulder as her talons gouged the leather of the gauntlet. Kebonsat gentled his grip but did not let go.

"It is a hard fact, never to be forgotten without fatal consequences. One cannot afford friendships at court. One cannot count on them to survive in this toxic atmosphere." He paused, his brown eyes grave as he stared down at her. "But hear me well. I vow this on my honor: You may count me among your true friends. I will never betray you."

Reisil's heart stopped and her breath froze in her chest. She put up her hand as if to block the words. "Don't say that. You can't. What about Vertina Emelovi?"

He captured her hand in his. "That's not your concern."

Reisil's hand tightened on his, urgency coloring her voice. "It is an astounding gesture, and I thank you. It means more than I can say. But surely you must see that you cannot do this. It will endanger all you have come here to do."

"It is done. I will hear no more about it," he said, withdrawing his hand. Reisil caught his arm.

"At least sleep on it. I won't think anything less of you for changing your mind."

Kebonsat hesitated, and then gave a short nod. "I will not change my mind. But if it will please you, I will obey." With that he bowed again, kissing her hand as he would that of any noblewoman. "I must go. If I do not see you downstairs, I shall see you at first light. Do not be late."

Then he spun on his heel and was gone. Reisil gaped after him. What had just happened? Even if he changed his mind, she would cherish that gesture forever.

Reisil reached up and scratched Saljane's chest.

~We aren't alone after all. Are you ready? The sharks await.

Saljane's answer was to raise her head with a piercing cry, hot with pride and defiance.

Kek-kek-kek-kek!

Every head below shot up like a herd of startled deer. Reisil's face settled into a chiseled mask, green eyes glittering. She had Saljane and Kebonsat and Juhrnus. Whatever happened next, she need not face it alone.

"If it's a fight they want, then it's a fight they'll get. I'm done sitting on my hands."

With that, Reisil began her descent onto the battleground.

Chapter 18

Kebonsat stalked through the corridors to his quarters in the east wing, his mind tracing methodically over his encounter with Reisil. She was too thin by far, like a dagger honed too fine and equally brittle.

He paused at the turning to his apartments, stopping in the shadows. He leaned against the wall, closing his eyes. *What have I done, making such an oath?*

With a groan, Kebonsat scraped his fingers along his scalp, yanking his hair clasp free and several strands of hair with it. She'd opened her door, and desire had slammed into him like a battering ram. Had it blinded him? To commit himself that way—had he fatally damaged his suit to marry the Vertina before he even entered the running? Kebonsat had been here hardly a day before he discovered the depth of hostility, jealousy and distrust Reisil generated in nearly every soul at court. The Verit and Lord Marshal would likely see him thrown out of Kodu Riik for having anything to do with her.

And yet, would he do it differently? There was something about Reisil—and it was more than his desire, more than an urge to protect her from her enemies. Events were about to transpire. The plague was already moving into Patverseme, and those demon beasts the Kodu Riikians called *nokulas*. They were harbingers of something worse, something that would destroy his country. Kebonsat could feel the danger swelling like a summer storm. At the heart of it would be Reisil. And he was certain she would stand on the side of right and honor. Not even his innate wariness and cynicism raised a single doubt about that. By her side is where she would need him, and where he would need to be if he was to protect Patverseme and his family.

He straightened, giving himself a shake. His decision was made. He didn't need to sleep on it. When she needed him, he would support her. He sighed. But that didn't mean abandoning his mission to win the hand of the Vertina. Not yet, anyhow. And he was late, an unacceptable quality in a lover.

He set off up the corridor in a brisk walk, unable to stifle his groan upon seeing his steward hovering outside the entry.

"My lord, I do say, you are quite late! Punctuality, sir, is a virtue not to be carelessly disregarded."

"Yes, Quillers. I had an appointment."

Quillers followed him inside, wringing his hands, his pursed lips too small beneath his softly formed nose and jiggling white cheeks. Kebonsat retreated into his dressing room, where Palig, his whipcord-lean valet, added steaming water to that cooling in the copper tub. Kebonsat stripped off his clothing and settled into the bath, relaxing under Palig's deft ministrations. Quillers paced outside, flashing back and forth in the doorway.

"Sir, I would be quite pleased to keep your calendar updated so that you did not run late, if you would just make me aware of your appointments. I should not wish to inconvenience you with a conflict." His voice was breathy and high-pitched. Kebonsat hunched forward, dangling his head and letting Palig massage his neck and shoulder muscles with sweet-almond oil.

A sudden memory made him smile. The Dume Griste Mountains. Reisil, sitting by a fire, combing tangles from her wet hair, teasing him about his life of leisure with valets and housekeepers. A sharp ache flared in his chest and his smile faded. That had been the night Upsakes and Glevs had sprung their ambush. Glevs. Maybe that was why he had felt so driven to make his oath to Reisil. Glevs had been closer than a brother, and he had betrayed Ceriba, betrayed Kebonsat, betrayed Patverseme.

Kebonsat scooped water in his hands and splashed it over his face. He and Reisil had learned together how little professed friendship meant. His vow to her had been as much for his sake as hers. He had needed for her to believe in him: to be certain his friendship was solid, irrevocable and immutable.

He leaned back, letting Palig sponge his face with lather. He felt a surge of irony as the razor smoothed over his cheek and jaw. There was an attitude of great trust involved in letting this little man anywhere near his throat with such an instrument. But it wasn't trust at all. It was calculation. He needed his diplomatic contingent to work well under him, to believe in his confidence and judgement. If he refused to let them do their jobs, they would perceive it as a sign of weakness. One that he could ill afford. Let it get around that he didn't even have confidence in his own valet and he would become a laughingstock. But it was a difficult façade to maintain. Glevs' betrayal had tainted him, coloring every relationship he had, excepting only his family, excepting only Reisil.

Palig finished attending him, and Kebonsat stepped out of the tub. Palig impatiently allowed his master to aid in his own dressing, not yet resigned to Kebonsat's sad lack of decorum. Like a nervous hen, Palig smoothed and tucked, buttoned and laced, twitching every last wrinkle out of the tailored cobalt jacket over the black, hip-length vest, tugging the elegantly tied cravat about Kebonsat's neck *just so*, adjusting the white cuffs of his lawn shirt, buffing his boots and flicking nonexistent lint from his black trousers. Palig lastly settled the heavy chain of office around his master's neck before securing Kebonsat's hair with a clip made of silver knotwork.

Glancing in the mirror, Kebonsat had to commend the valet's efforts. On the battleground of intrigue, appearance was but another weapon, a means of distraction, diversion and disguise. It was never to be overlooked, but always planned carefully.

"Very nicely done, Palig. I shall turn heads."

But would he turn the right one? Would he even be allowed close enough to the Vertina for her to notice him? In the few weeks he'd been in Koduteel, he'd seen the Vertina a bare handful of times, and in each one he'd spoken fewer than ten words to her. Hardly an auspicious beginning. He spared a grim smile. Battles were never won in a single engagement, and he was prepared for a long siege.

"Really, sir, you are *most* late. The Vertina will be curious at your tardiness," Quillers called from the other room. Palig had forbidden the nervous steward entrance into his domain, for which Kebonsat was grateful. "Evral Ogal and Evral Eyan are expecting you in the drawing room to accompany you down."

"Thank you, Quillers. Please inform them that I shall join them shortly. And send Rocis to my study."

"But sir, the time!"

Kebonsat cast his fussy steward a mild look.

Quillers paused, his mouth open, recognizing the warning. He snapped it shut, looking as if he'd just eaten a handful of chokecherries, and nodded. "Very well, sir. I shall be quick."

Kebonsat made his way to his study, leaving the door open. It was a dark-paneled turret room, its angled windows offering a view of the steel-gray ocean and the lighthouse standing watch over the deepwater harbor.

He settled himself behind the ornately carved chestnut desk, its corners and edges finished with hammered silver. From a drawer, he withdrew a lockbox banded with iron and sealed with three locks. He turned a key in the first and murmured a word, and then repeated the procedure with the next two locks. As he turned the last key, the box sprang open. Inside were several sheaves of papers. He withdrew a thick packet and began to flip through the pages of closely written information.

"Sir?"

Kebonsat glanced up and motioned Rocis forward. The

other man stepped up to the other side of the desk, his
eyes fixed on the empty shelves behind Kebonsat's head.
He stood halberd-straight, his uniform unwrinkled and un-
stained, his brown beard closely trimmed, his hair neatly
caught behind his head. He wore his lohar secured to his
belt, the simple hilt inlaid with brass.

"I have an additional assignment for you."

"Yes, sir." Rocis shifted his gaze to Kebonsat, his almond
eyes sharp and discerning.

"I have become aware that some of the court politics
have taken a rather more fatal turn for some. I need to
know more specifics than are here." Kebonsat tapped the
packet in his lap. "It is essential that this information be
obtained quickly and quietly. I want to know the factions,
the players and their recent activities. Particularly the less
savory ones. This is all very good as far as it goes, but
lacks depth and detail." He tossed the packet back into
the lockbox.

"Do you have any questions?"

Rocis considered a moment and then shook his head.
"No, sir."

"You shall report to me twice a day, more often as necessary. I shall expect your first report before breakfast."

"Yes, sir." Dismissed, Rocis spun and moved fluidly out
the door. Kebonsat frowned after him, drumming his fingers on the desk. Then he closed the lockbox, securing the
locks and resetting the magical wards. He returned the box
to the drawer and stood, turning to face the bank of
windows.

There was someone after Reisil. He was certain of it. He
couldn't imagine that he was sufficient a threat to anyone
to merit the attempt. Not yet anyhow. A marriage between
him and the Vertina was far from likely. And assassinating
him, the Patversemese ambassador, would likely provoke a
war that Kodu Riik could ill afford.

But why such a blunder? Any assassin worth his salt
would have aborted an attempt with such little chance of
success. Why put her on her guard? Why involve him? And
what was the purpose of the poison?

The rattling of the windows brought him back to himself.
When would the next attempt come? He could teach Reisil

to defend herself from sword and knife attack, but he couldn't do a damned thing to help her against a crossbolt, short of locking her in a closet. Silent and deadly and impossible to counter, even with plate armor, they were ideal for the determined, patient, shadow work of a proficient assassin.

Kebonsat jammed his hands into his pockets. He couldn't protect Reisil. No more than he could protect any of his soldiers when they took the field for battle. And on this battleground, far from home and with little authority, there was even less he could do to protect her. The only thing he could do was give her the benefit of his experience and training. Which meant anticipating her enemy, seeking out and exploiting his weaknesses. And that required information.

His last thoughts as he departed his study to join his waiting companions were of Reisil in the moist heat of summer, her flower-scented hair tangled around his fingers, her pale, naked body urgent beneath his.

Chapter 19

"**M**ust you go?"
"I'm late already."
"I could come with you."

Juhrnus bent to kiss Karina's inviting lips, slipping his hands inside her robe to stroke her breasts. His body quickened as she squirmed closer. He lifted his head, breathing heavily.

"I would not be able to spend any time with you. This is *ahalad-kaaslane* business."

Desire evaporated with the words. He pulled away. *Ahalad-kaaslane* business. As if he had any business with them. As if they hadn't turned the same cold shoulder to him that they had to Reisil. How did she stand it? The feeling of helplessness and abandonment? He lifted Esper into his sling and pulled his cloak on.

"I'll try to visit again soon."

"Don't be too long," she said, sitting back down on the bed, reclining to reveal her long, pale legs and the tuft of red hair at their apex. "Father will be sailing home soon. I'll be less . . . available . . . then."

Curiosity stayed him. "I will admit that I'm surprised your mother and uncle allow my visits. I cannot marry. Our play taints you for the kind of husband that might answer their ambitions."

Juhrnus disliked Karina's fawning uncle Halvasti, a useless fop who dangled around the fringes of the court licking boots—a ring-pigeon for anyone's plucking. Her mother was little better. She craved the power her wealthy merchant husband spurned and didn't mind using her four daughters to gain it. Juhrnus couldn't regret that they turned a blind eye to his frolics with Karina, but it did not earn them his respect.

Karina smiled and stretched, her robe falling open to expose her curved body, her full breasts above a narrow waist, and the pattern of finger bruises and bites Juhrnus had left on her skin.

"I wouldn't worry for me. I shall get the husband I want. But to answer your question, someone might have told my uncle and mother that you were highly placed among the *ahalad-kaaslane* and at court—that you have the ear of even the Iisand himself."

Juhrnus's mouth fell open. "You didn't?"

Karina smiled wider, running her fingers through her long auburn hair and then suggestively down her body. "I couldn't help myself, could I? And they have been so grateful for my help. They have so little time until Daddy comes home. He dotes on mother, really, but he won't put up with her machinations. Are you sure you won't stay a while longer?"

Juhrnus shook his head. He'd spent much of the last couple of days in bed with Karina, trying to forget. He found a few moments of oblivion in her arms, but he couldn't avoid the truth forever. He was a token *ahalad-kaaslane*. Even more so than Reisil. At least she still had a calling; she wore the Lady's blessing on her face and carried Her power in her hands. The Lady did not call to him. Nor did his *ahalad-kaaslane* brethren accept him into their circle. They spoke to him, welcomed him back to Koduteel, ate and drank with him, but shut him out from their secrets. They asked him for nothing, expected nothing of him. Useless as tits on a boar.

His assignment to play nanny to the Scallacians was hardly more than a bone, but it was all he had, and he meant to do it.

"I'll come again soon," he promised again.

Karina yawned delicately, pulling a sheet over herself and settling back on her pillows. "You can see yourself out, can't you?"

Juhrnus skittered as fast as he could along the twisting roadway, its cobbles slick with ice. Wind rattled the shutters on the upper stories of the buildings, dipping down to swipe at him as he made his way along. His cloak belled like a sail, tugging him sidewise, and he lurched to a knee, cursing as he fell, pain shooting up to his hip. Esper squirmed in his sling, his tongue flicking uneasily at the rough ride.

~Sit still, Esper. I can't keep my balance as it is.

~Cold. Esper's mindvoice was as cool and dry as a salt cave.

~I know. Another ice storm. Don't complain. Reisil says it's a blessing that winter hangs on. Keeps the plague from spreading as quick. Better to thank the Lady and hope winter never ends.

Juhrnus lurched to his feet, holding his arm against Esper's sling to steady him. He took a step, and pain exploded up from his knee. He bent to examine it. His breeches were torn, and blood trickled down his calf to where his pant leg tucked into his boot, staining the buff-colored material a red brown. He scowled. This wouldn't get him to the palace any faster. A gust of wind shoved at his back and sent him stumbling forward. Cursing, he caught himself on the corner of a building. Juhrnus paused a moment to lace his hood more tightly before setting out again.

He paused at the palace entrance, rubbing his gloved knuckles over his eyes, knocking away the ice crystals clinging to his lashes and brows. The guard examined him and

then passed him in with a wave. Inside, the trees were
sheathed in a thin casing of ice, and their branches groaned
heavily as the wind rushed through them.

He wound up the hill toward the palace, skidding backwards a step for every two he eked forward. At last he
topped the crown and paused, gazing over the spectacle.
Lights danced like fireflies in every window he could see.
The dome of the rotunda glowed. Glossy carriages with
heavily blanketed horses filled the east ward and spilled
out onto the entry avenue. Long snaking banners strung
from the towers struggled against their moorings, and
midnight-blue and gold pennants bearing red-eyed gryphons cracked and snapped in the wind. The wide, columned
portico of the main entrance glowed with colored lights of
violet, cornflower blue and alfalfa green. The columns were
wound with blue and gold ribbons decorated with silver
and copper leaves and trimmed with tinkling bells. Liveried
guards stood at attention, stoically unmindful of the bitter
wind. The bells in the campanile clanged together softly,
the sound mournful.

Juhrnus angled for a side entrance, stopping several times
to identify himself at the hail of patrolling guards. At last
he managed to scurry inside a servants' entrance. He pulled
off his gloves with his teeth, shook out his cloak and
stamped his feet. A shower of ice pattered onto the slate
floor. He stroked Esper with chill fingers.

~*Time to go grovel for our saviors.* Juhrnus's mindvoice
was as bitter as the wind.

~*They may help.*

~*And they may wipe us out.*

~*Not all who have magic are bad. You trust Reisiltark.*
For a moment, an image of Reisil appeared in Juhrnus's
mind. A halo of green limned her, radiating a glowing
warmth that was echoed in Esper's mindvoice.

Juhrnus glanced down at his *ahalad-kaaslane*, his throat
knotting. He'd always accepted Reisil's magic without a
second thought. Because she had given him back his soul
in saving Esper? Yes. But that wasn't all. He had known
her since they were children. As much as he'd despised
her then, he knew she would never use her magic against
Kodu Riik.

~*You never hated her. You liked her.*

Juhrnus grimaced. Sometimes having an *ahalad-kaaslane* was like having a second conscience.

~*She made me angry.*

~*Yes.*

She had made him livid, trailing after Kaval like a love-sick kitten. He'd always known what Kaval would be. How he would use Reisil. But she didn't want to listen.

~*You were not kind to her.* There was no reproof in Esper's voice.

~*I wanted her to open her eyes.*

She had been so reserved, with everyone but Kaval, because he smiled at her and made her feel special for being allowed a sliver of his attention. And she had licked it up. Kaval had seen how little she valued herself and set out to take advantage of her.

~*She didn't have to be such a slave.*

~*You could have helped her.*

~*I was trying to. But she only wanted Kaval.*

~*You were not very kind,* Esper repeated in that slow, dry tone.

~*I wanted her to be strong,* Juhrnus insisted. And it was true, but there had been more to it than that. He had been . . . jealous. He flushed in the dimness of the entryway, and he hugged Esper against his chest like a shield.

~*She needs you now,* Esper said, his mindvoice a complex blend of sympathy, warning and affection.

~*Tell her that. She's doing the same thing she always did. Handling everything on her own. She still won't say what happened between her and Sodur.*

~*She has a difficult path to walk. Hard choices to make.*

~*She wants to go to the wizards. I can't stop her. She'll do whatever she wants, and nothing I say is going to change that.*

~*She doesn't need you to change her path,* Esper said, an impatient bite in his voice.

~*She doesn't need me for much at all.*

~*You are wrong.*

~*What do you want me to do? Tie her up? It won't work. Sooner or later she's going to go to them. She'll walk right in and hand herself to them on a trencher.*

~*Yes.*

Juhrnus made a frustrated sound. ~*So what do you want me to do about that?*

~*Nothing. She must follow her own path. You must decide what you will do.*

"Quit beating around the bush! Tell me what it is you want me to do!" Juhrnus's voice rang from the blank stone walls, and he flinched, looking about to see if anyone had heard. He heard a sudden gabbling of voices up the corridor like the sound of geese. He made his way in the other direction to a set of stairs leading back into the interior of the palace.

~*You are worse than Sodur or Reisil, I swear to the Lady. Can't get a straight answer out of any of you,* he fumed as he climbed, suddenly feeling the clinging, cold damp of his clothing, the burning ache in his knee, and the beginning of a headache.

~*Choose.*

~*Choose what? What is there for me to do? No one tells me anything. No one listens to me. Everywhere I go, I find a closed door and a blank stare.*

~*When the time comes, will you know the enemy? Will you know whose side you fight on?*

Juhrnus stumbled to a halt, his attention snagging on Esper's abrupt questions like skin on rusty nails. ~*I serve the Lady. Her enemies are my enemies.*

Esper did not reply for a long moment. ~*I don't think it will be so easy to know them.*

~*Why? What do you know?*

~*There will come a time when you must decide how you will serve the Lady. You will have to decide what is right and what is wrong.*

~*I will decide,* Juhrnus repeated.

~*Yes.* Esper waited a heartbeat. Two. *And then whose side will you fight on?*

Whose side will you *fight on.* Not *we,* but *you.* Juhrnus remembered Upsakes's weirmart, the little creature's misery at her *ahalad-kaaslane's* choices. In the end, she had freed Reisil and Juhrnus from their bonds so that Reisil could save Esper. She had known what was right, what the Lady demanded, even when her *ahalad-kaaslane* had not. Juhrnus looked down into Esper's unblinking yellow eyes.

~The right side. The Lady's side.

It wasn't enough. Esper continued to stare, curiously reserved, as though wanting Juhrnus to make up his mind alone, uninfluenced. But make his mind up to what? Juhrnus frowned, sorting through their conversation. Esper had said that Reisil needed him. That he must choose sides. Understanding broke over him like a frigid ocean wave: Esper was asking him to pledge his allegiance. Certainly Juhrnus served the Blessed Lady with all his heart, but Upsakes had committed unspeakable acts in the Lady's name. And now the Lady had withdrawn from Kodu Riik. So this wasn't just about answering Her call; it was also about figuring out what She would want and doing it. Or believing enough in someone to let that person show him the way.

Reisil. Reisil? He almost laughed. She was as confused as he was. He almost said so, but the flare of ire in Esper's gaze made him mute.

Reisil.

She was the one whom the Lady had chosen—tark and *ahalad-kaaslane*. A pairing not heard of since the legendary Talis and Galt. And then the Lady had granted Reisil power enough to destroy a hundred wizards in a single blow. How could he laugh? Reisil *was* confused, disillusioned and scared too. But she was looking for answers, even in the wrong places. And when she found them . . . what then?

Juhrnus's mind roved over myriad possibilities, spiraling around and around until he was tangled in place by the only thing he could know for certain: the Lady had bestowed such a power on Reisil with care and for a purpose. Reisil was to be the Lady's champion.

He touched Esper lightly on the head. *~Reisil. I choose Reisil. She is the Lady's beacon.*

Chapter 20

"Hmmm?" Vertina Emelovi murmured absently, her attention roving across the impatient guests. Neither the sorcerers nor her suitor from Patverseme had yet arrived. She suppressed a frown of irritation and nodded to Lord Marshal Vare, who paused to return her greeting, the bow done to just the right degree for first-tier nobility to the Iisand's eldest offspring, though not his heir. The distinction was unmistakable. He walked on, halting a moment as he encountered his son. Metyein cas Vare scanned the woman on his father's arm up and down and stood aside, his face contemptuous. The Lord Marshal said something Emelovi couldn't hear, and Metyein snapped back as if slapped. Then he spun around and walked away.

"I said, I heard they sleep all mounded together in one bed like a litter of kittens, and that they wear nothing at all beneath their robes!" The Preili's high voice cut across Emelovi's musings, sounding both scandalized and enthralled.

Emelovi flicked a glance at the middle-aged woman. "Indeed. I had not heard that."

"Oh, yes, and it's said that—"

"I think," Emelovi began, and then stopped. Aare did not like her saying what she thought. "I thought I saw the Ueles waving, Dajam Kerimal." The other woman gave a little squawk and spun around, standing on tiptoe to peer over the crowd. Seeing her husband engrossed in a conversation, she began to step away, and then turned back, her face flushing.

"Oh! Won't you please excuse me, Dazien. My husband is a most impatient man." Emelovi nodded a gracious dismissal and the Preili scurried off into the throng. Emelovi breathed out a soft sigh and retreated to the royal dais. She signaled the steward standing nearby that she did not want to be disturbed, and turned her attention back to watching the guests.

The Great Hall and its reception rooms were groaning at the seams, and it was becoming uncomfortably hot. Every single member of Koduteel's local nobility had turned out, despite the inclement weather. Many *ahalad-kaaslane* were in attendance as well. Astonishingly enough, the two groups were not engaging in open warfare—rather they clumped in startling collections, united in their vitriolic suspicion of the sorcerers. Aare presided over one group made up of a dozen of the most powerful and influential Kajes and Dajames in the three tiers, and several of the most prestigious and respected *ahalad-kaaslane*.

Emelovi blinked astonishment. Kijal Prentin, a crony of the Lord Marshal, rarely deigned to wait on her brother. But it appeared the coming of the sorcerers had given Aare the lever he needed to gain the Kijal's favor. It was no secret that Aare didn't trust the sorcerers any more than he trusted the wizards, any more than he trusted that *ahalad-kaaslane*, Reisiltark. And the rest of the court knew it. If the furious nobles thought Aare would send the sorcerers away once he was made regent, they would rally to his banner. The situation couldn't have worked better had he invited the Scallacians himself. Not that the Lord Marshal would have permitted him into those discussions. He held the reins of Kodu Riik while her father was in retirement, and he had no intention of allowing Aare any foothold into power. Though bringing the sorcerers here could do exactly that.

Watching Aare, Emelovi felt a thrill of pride for him, and beneath it, a familiar apprehension. His face flamed with charismatic energy, his gray eyes and patrician features so like their father's. *How I've missed him!* Aare's hair fell loose in crisp gold waves down to his shoulders. Emelovi shared her brother's gray eyes, but her hair was a limp, dark brown, which she rinsed in a dark mahogany henna to lend it life. They both wore the midnight blue of the royal Varakamber house, the necks and sleeves edged with tiny gold gryphons. A none-too-subtle reminder of their rank, that sooner or later, Aare *would* inherit the throne.

Emelovi felt a flutter of cold down her spine. He was her brother, and she owed him her support. She'd always known he'd inherit the throne someday. She'd never thought it could come so soon. She thought she'd be safely married and away from him. But now—

Long ago Emelovi had learned to appease Aare, obeying his demands without question. Even as a boy he had been ruthless. Her breath caught in remembered pain and fury. She had had a puppy. Her father had given it to her as a Nasadh gift when she was eleven, three years before the war had begun with Patverseme. The poor thing hadn't lived long enough for her to name it.

Aare had wanted her to dance with the nephew of Ueles Prensik—some sort of payment for a bet he'd lost. She had refused. The boy was older than she and had hot, sticky fingers and bad breath. Aare had not said anything, but had scooped up the puppy and locked her door as he left. Ten minutes later he reopened the door, his face cold and unsmiling. Footmen found the puppy at the bottom of the main stairs, his neck broken from the fall. Emelovi had not cried, and she had refused her father's offer of another animal. Instead, she had danced with the nephew of Ueles Prensik. She had even endured his hot, groping touch and the soft, slimy thrust of his tongue when he hauled her behind a curtain to kiss her. Aare had watched, his face remote and pitiless. He did not accept anything less than total submission—not then, not now.

"Your pardon, Dazien. May I offer you some chilled wine?"

Emelovi started and began an automatic smile. But her face stiffened and froze as she recognized the speaker. Like a ghost out of her nightmare.

"Kaj Prensik. Thank you." She took the glass he held out to her, casting a sidelong glance at the steward. His attention was absorbed by the man dangling from his arm. Kai Halvasti grasped the steward's liveried sleeve, speaking so quickly that flecks of spit flew from his mouth. Emelovi looked back at Ueles Prensik, and he smiled, that same smug, oily smile he had given her just before he kissed her nine years ago. Very well planned and executed, she fumed. Halvasti was a menace.

"You look well, Kaj Prensik. How is your mother?" She kept her voice cool and distant.

He gave a dismissive shrug. "Well enough, I suppose. She did not come with me to town this winter. Still decked out in her widow's weeds."

"Losing your father has been a trial for her, I am sure."

"Been almost six months."

"An eternity," Emelovi agreed sardonically, rolling the stem of her glass in her fingers. "I'm sure my father would agree."

Prensik reddened. "It's not as if they got along. Hadn't had a civil word to say to each other for years," he said. "That won't happen to me. Woman I marry is going to know her place." The smile he gave her was suggestive, and Emelovi affected not to understand.

"Really? How very fortunate for you to find such a paragon."

Unmindful of her scorn, Prensik blundered on. "Woman I want will have been raised to obey her husband, serve him properly. Mine's going to give me a passel of children. Going to have a mob of heirs, not like my uncle, passing the title to my father."

Emelovi couldn't help the flush that heated her cheeks, remembering how she had bent to Aare and let this worm rub himself against her.

Prensik's leer broadened as if he read her mind. He wetted his lips with the tip of his tongue and leaned forward, speaking in a conspiratorial whisper. "Don't need to worry about this Patverseme fellow. Your brother's not going to let the likes of him put his filthy hands on such a prize as you. He'd rather slit his own throat."

"I am sure I don't understand you," Emelovi said in a suddenly strident voice as she stepped back, bumping against a low divan within the sheltering wing curtains.

Prensik followed her, his voice low. "Aare said you were too innocent to know what was going on. But don't be frightened. It's the way marriages happen. The Patversemese boy is nothing but *skraa*," he said crudely. "Aare won't waste you on such a limp prick."

"I see," she said, and she did see. That Aare needed

Prensik's support and was dangling her like bait. Just whom did he really want to take it? Her lips pinched together. She doubted that he knew. His choice for her husband depended entirely on which direction his plans went. She was on the board, but the game was too young to commit her anywhere.

Emelovi could feel herself turning pale and clammy beneath her powder and rouge, and wanted nothing more than to find a chamber pot to retch into. Prensik noted her distress and slid a proprietary hand under her elbow to support her as she swayed. She wanted to jerk away, but was conscious of Aare's rebuking stare drilling her from across the room. She could hear him as if he'd spoken his thoughts aloud. He would not forgive her if she caused a spectacle, if she interfered with his plans. He was not above giving her to Prensik merely as a punishment.

She looked away, gulping her wine, her fingers clenching on the crystal. The chilled fluid was a balm on her thick, dry tongue. She forced a smile back onto her lips, her mind scrabbling to fend off the feeling of panic, the feeling of being buried alive with no hope for escape.

"Are you unwell, Dazien?"

The steward had escaped Havasti, and his stiff posture as he addressed her indicated that he knew very well how he'd been manipulated.

"A bit warm is all, Corven. Perhaps you might ask Prouda Verin and Preili Isel to join me? I should not like to impose any longer on Ueles Prensik." She turned to her gloating suitor, his moist hand still clutching her elbow, knowing he could read her fear and hating him for it. "Kaj Prensik—"

Whatever she was going to say was chopped off by the sudden, shrieking cry of a wild bird. At the sound, every conversation ground to an abrupt halt, and every guest turned searching gazes to the Grand Foyer from which the cry had emanated.

A long minute ticked by. And another. The assembly began to rustle and murmur, and then silence rippled from the foyer like a cold ocean wave rolling up onto a rocky shingle. Standing on the dais, Emelovi had a clear view as Reisiltark descended the last few steps of the Grand Staircase. The people about her stood back as if she were contaminated, and Emelovi felt anger hardening her expression. Her father would not have permitted this ostracization of any *ahalad-kaaslane*. He would have left Reisiltark to the Lady's justice, if she needed any. Emelovi flashed a hopeful look at Aare, who only watched Reisiltark thoughtfully. The men gathered around him wore faces of contempt, fury, suspicion and downright malice. Even the *ahalad-kaaslane*.

Reisiltark walked to the center of the Foyer and stopped at the bottom of the Blessed Lady's image, dropping to one knee and bowing her head. She stayed there for a full minute, unmindful of those staring at her, then rose and walked neatly around the Lady's figure and up into the Great Hall.

Her stride was regal and leisurely, but she radiated a wild energy like that of the storm outside. The gold vining on her face glowed in the many candles, emphasizing her difference and threat. She paused on the threshold. Her eyes raked across the silent, taut gathering. On her shoulder perched her goshawk, the bird's beak glowing a matching pattern to that on Reisiltark's face. The goshawk opened her beak in a silent scream and raised her wings. Reisiltark lifted a hand and stroked the angry bird's back.

Then she stepped into the room. As she did, the stillness around her shattered as people averted their eyes and turned their backs.

Something stirred deep inside Emelovi. She struggled against it, knowing what the consequences must be. Emelovi glanced at Aare, saw cunning malevolence flickering across his expression. Fear clutched at her heart, and she remembered the limp, broken body of her puppy. She looked back to Reisiltark. No one greeted her. Not even one of her fellow *ahalad-kaaslane*.

The thing stirring in Emelovi bucked and twisted, and she heeded it at last. She stepped forward. Deep inside she heard that child of eleven scream. Her heart pounded, her skin turning cold at what she was doing. Another step. Emelovi did not look at Aare, did not look at Prensik. She descended from the dais and walked out to welcome Reisiltark.

The silence of unwelcome was dreadful. Sodur struggled to move, to walk to Reisil. But instead he stood frozen, like a fly wrapped in spider silk waiting to die. Lume nuzzled his hand anxiously and he stroked the lynx's square head, feeling his *ahalad-kaaslane*'s pleasure at his touch like an extra sense, as if he stroked his own head. Beneath it, he felt Lume's worry, hunger and discomfort at the heat. He couldn't shut them out. The lynx's raw emotions and instincts seeped through constantly, like water through a failing dam. They overwhelmed him with smothering intensity, and he struggled to stand apart, to retain himself whole. But more and more often, he reacted with Lume's animal sensibilities rather than his own.

He rubbed his forehead with shaking fingers. What *was* this?

He could not suppress his fear. It grew like bindweed, tangling in his mind and immobilizing him. And beyond—

Beyond he could feel something gnawing at the edges of his mind, like a horde of rats, chewing and chewing. A flicker of movement caught his eye and he went still, as a lynx might when spotting prey. His nose twitched and his fingers curled into themselves.

The Vertina was moving down off her dais to meet Reisil. The rustling murmurs that had erupted as Reisil journeyed into the room hushed and silence swallowed the room again. The two women stopped opposite each other and Emelovi reached out a hand. She spoke in a clear, ringing voice. "Bright evening, Reisiltark. Be welcome in my home."

It wasn't a traditional greeting, but though Emelovi's face was white and strained, her voice was strong and steady.

"Thank you, Dazien. May the Lady's smile shine upon you," Reisil replied, taking her hand. Emelovi waved a steward to bring them fresh wine.

Sodur smiled. The Vertina's father would have been proud. He glanced at Verit Aare, and a bolt of apprehension shot through him. The Verit's face had turned black and cruel. A gush of protective fury spurted through Sodur. Sodur felt a snarl curl his lips, and he bared his teeth, a low growl rumbling in his throat. Beside him, Lume did the same. Both women were his to protect and no one, even the son of his oldest friend, would he permit to harm them.

Chapter 21

"I do not know what to say to you," the Vertina said, the silence stretching.

"You have already said more than I could have hoped for," Reisil replied gratefully.

The Vertina's breath hissed between her lips. "It should not be so. You are *ahalad-kaaslane*. You should be welcomed in every house and hovel in Kodu Riik."

The Vertina saw Reisil's surprise, the noblewoman's cheeks flaming as she looked away. Reisil took the moment to study her. The Vertina's features were softer than her brother's, though equally patrician. Her nose was straight, her cheeks high boned and her chin narrow. Her lips were wide and slightly thin, and her gray eyes were fringed by dark lashes. Above them, her brows arched elegantly along the delicate bone. Though younger than Reisil by several years, she carried herself with the assurance and aplomb of someone much older.

"My father believed that— I remember him saying that he was relieved to have you on our side. That he wouldn't have to worry about the wizards anymore."

Reisil nodded, giving the Vertina an encouraging smile that was more like a grimace. *And . . .*

"He never blamed you," the other woman said in a rush. "I know there was a lot of talk after mother died. That you could have saved her. But father knew how she was.

"Mother went frantic whenever she heard your name. She had such nightmares. . . . I don't think she truly thought you would hurt her or the baby. But she *was* afraid of the wizards. She was sure they'd come hunting you for revenge, and she feared what might happen to whoever was standing too close to you when they did."

Reisil thought of Kebonsat. If the crossbolt had struck him in the heart, she could have done nothing for him. Her expression hardened.

"I apologize. It was not your fault," the Vertina said quickly. "And you saved my baby brother. No other tark could have done that."

Reisil swallowed, remembering. She had lurked outside the Mesilasema's chambers throughout the day and night of her shrieking labor. Reisil remembered how the bustling maids became restive and tense, how the air turned turgid with the weight of fear, how the Mesilasema's voice grew fainter and fainter. And then one of her ladies-in-waiting had burst out the door and dragged Reisil back inside, where the baby still fluttered within the cocoon of his mother's dead body.

Somehow she had harnessed her power and saved the boy. Still she couldn't meet the Iisand's eyes when she handed him his son. He had taken her hand, tears rolling unashamedly down his ashen cheeks. His voice had been rough as gravel, gentle as snow.

"You must not blame yourself, Reisiltark. My wife was very troubled. But what she wouldn't do for herself, she did for our son. When she felt her life slipping away, she asked for you."

"Your father was very kind to me," Reisil said to the Vertina, her throat tightening at the memory.

"I know my father would hate the way you have been treated here," the Vertina said fervently. "If only— He took my mother's death very hard."

Reisil's stomach constricted, and she opened her mouth. Everything in her wanted to tell the Vertina about her father's true condition. She deserved to know. But somehow the words wouldn't come. What if the sorcerers really could cure the Iisand? The Vertina would have her father back, and he could tell her what he wanted. Besides, he had asked to be locked up, not telling his children what was happening to him. Reisil could respect his decision, if not Sodur's plotting. She turned her attention to the assembly, her gaze flicking from person to person, wondering which were part of Sodur's secret company.

"I hope our guests put in an appearance soon. I shouldn't

like to imagine the frenzy if the court is forced to be patient much longer."

The bite in the Vertina's voice prompted a grin from Reisil. "Terrifying," she said.

The Vertina's lips quirked. "Better they gawk at the sorcerers than you?"

"Better anyone than me."

The Vertina chuckled, raising her hand to cover it. "Every so often a school of sharks finds its way into the harbor. Everywhere you look, there will be fins skurling through the water. Always someone has the idea of throwing food into the water—the entrails of a hog or sometimes even a bit of fresh beef or goat. It's a carnival. The entire city abandons its work to gather on the bluff and watch. . . ." She looked up at Reisil, eyes glinting. "I think perhaps the sharks have nothing to teach the court."

Before Reisil could respond, the round-waisted Majordomo at the entry pounded his silver-butted staff on the floor.

"His Lordship, Kaj Kebonsat cas Vadonis of Patverseme, Knight of the Order of Ellini of the Flame, Werad of Esemlies. He is accompanied by Kaj Dumen cas Ogal, Knight of the Order of Ellini of the Flame, Evral of Ogal. Also accompanying Kaj Kebonsat is Kaj Ledus cas Eyan, Knight of the Order of Parien da pe Clure, Evral of Eyan," he intoned in a sonorous voice. He stepped aside with a stiff bow as Kebonsat entered, flanked by the two Evrals.

Reisil felt a thrill of pride at his appearance, so elegant, graceful and aristocratic. He was dressed in the colors of his house, his family crest embroidered over his heart in red: two red lions leaping at each other, a three-pronged coronet beneath, and a sword of gold thrust through the scarlet crown, indicating Kebonsat's status as heir to the House Vadonis. A single flame in orange and gold thread rose around the juncture of sword and crown. He wore his lohar on his hip. His expression was carefully neutral, and he carried himself with relaxed calm.

~He really belongs in this world, doesn't he?

~He was born to it, Saljane replied. He would have made a good mate, Saljane added, her head cocking to the side. Pain surged in Reisil. Saljane nipped her ear.

~At least she has courage. He'll like that. Reisil glanced at the Vertina, whose expression had turned bland.

~You grieve.

Reisil nodded. *~I do. I wish—* What did she wish? That she and Kebonsat could have married? Had children together? She couldn't imagine it.

~I wish we'd had more time, she said at last.

Her stomach gurgled loudly. Reisil flushed, glancing at the Vertina. Her blush deepened as the other woman smiled teasingly.

"There will be dinner soon, if it is not overcooked and spoiled," the Vertina said. "Blame the Scallacians if it is. At least my suitor has arrived." The disapproval in her voice was evident, her gaze sharpening as Kebonsat maneuvered toward the clump of men surrounding Verit Aare.

"He *is* stubborn and often rude," Reisil said.

"Not the highest recommendation. But I had forgotten you know him."

"He is what he is. On the other hand, he is also dependable, honorable and loyal, and I would trust him with my life. With Saljane's life." The Vertina's head jerked around. Reisil steadfastly refused to look at her.

The younger woman at last turned away. "Curious. I will keep your words in mind."

Reisil felt a rush of anxiety. What did she mean? Reisil hoped she had not sabotaged Kebonsat's chances.

"Forgive me, Dazien. Would you care to join us?" A stout Preili stood at the Vertina's elbow, her mouth pinched, ignoring Reisil altogether. The Vertina nodded. Reisil bowed awkwardly and backed away. As she departed, a swarm of ladies descended like vultures on the Vertina.

"Dazien, are you not well? Do you need to retire a few moments? Perhaps something to eat . . . You must be faint or feverish—"

Reisil herself was feeling faint and feverish and foolish. She slunk away from the effusive barrage of solicitations, wandering through the assembly. Yet despite her embarrassment and the frowning suspicion slewing around her, her step was unexpectedly light. The Vertina's kindness was an unexpected miracle. And if one miracle could happen, why not more?

Chapter 22

Reisil wandered up the crowded room. Someone stepped in front of her, and she stumbled against him. When she recovered her balance, she found herself staring into Metyein cas Vare's brown eyes.

"Pardon my clumsiness," he said, bowing slightly. He appeared fit and strong, though his face was haggard as if he hadn't slept in the last few days. He cast a striking figure, wearing a long coat of dark blue fabric, showing parchment-yellow silk at his cuffs and collar. He didn't wait for her to reply but spoke quickly in an undertone. "My life is yours. I am at your service. Do not hesitate to call on me at any time. Nor fear that I will reveal your secrets to my father." He stared at her, his cheeks flushed.

Reisil hesitated. She wanted to refuse him, to deny that he owed her anything. But though that was true, she also needed allies. She needed people she could trust. She nodded.

His eyes flared and he stepped aside, extending his arm, and speaking more loudly, his voice disdainful. "But do not let me detain you."

Reisil moved past Metyein and wandered toward an alcove. She needed a place to think. She ducked through the draperies, grateful to find the space unoccupied. She drew a shuddering breath, her mind racing as she paced.

"Well, you certainly created a stir."

Reisil swung around as Juhrnus slid between the curtains, Esper perched on his shoulders. His face was ruddy, his hair damp and straggly. His doublet was wrinkled and unevenly buttoned.

"Been out prowling?" she asked with a meaningful look at his clothing. He glanced down and grimaced.

"Give me a plain shirt any day. I'm wearing so many

clothes, I can hardly move. Come on, then, lend a hand. Mustn't look slovenly for our exalted guests."

Reisil helped him adjust his clothing, turning him around for a once-over. "As good as can be expected. But do stop letting Esper sleep on your clothes. You've got several tears in your doublet and shirt, and there's no fixing those now."

Juhrnus gave an unremorseful shrug. "Can't blame him for wanting a comfortable nest."

"How did you get the singe mark on your elbow?" she asked, pointing to the chocolate patch on his otherwise white sleeve. Juhrnus twisted his arm to see it and began to swear.

"White is a color only fools and ghosts should wear." He eyed the assembly through the opening of the curtain. "And we've plenty of the one in there. Seen Sodur?" he added diffidently.

"He was here a few minutes ago."

"Who with?"

Reisil shook her head. "No one but Lume."

"Where is he now?"

Reisil shrugged. Juhrnus pushed the drapes aside. Reisil looked over his shoulder.

"Not a lot of *ahalad-kaaslane* here tonight," Juhrnus observed. "Most of 'em I don't know that well." He was silent a heartbeat and then sucked his breath in sharply. "You don't think—"

Reisil hesitated. She wasn't sure there was any point in hiding the truth anymore. She rubbed her forehead. "He sent them away. Anyone who might have challenged the rumors about me, who might have told me what was really going on. He thought if the *ahalad-kaaslane* didn't accept me, then the nobles would leave me alone and give me time to learn how to use my power."

"He what?" Juhrnus's voice was strangled, and his face had begun turning a mottled red.

"He was convinced some noble, or several of them, would kill me to keep the *ahalad-kaaslane* from regaining power. But since the *ahalad-kaaslane* all hate me, I'm no threat. So I'm safe."

"That's . . . that's . . ."

"Stupid? That's what I told him when I figured it out.

He said it was for my own good and if I weren't so naïve, I'd see that."

"How long have you known? Why didn't you tell me?"

"Since last summer. And I hoped if you didn't know, you wouldn't be tarred with the same brush. I was wrong." Juhrnus had every right to be angry with her. She wasn't his mother. He was *ahalad-kaaslane,* and it wasn't her job to protect him.

Fury turned Juhrnus's face a darker shade of red. He balled a fist and struck at the wall, swearing when his knuckles came away bleeding. He shook his hand. Reisil watched and said nothing.

"So that's the way of it, then," he said finally.

"I should have told you. You have a right to know, to choose your own path."

Juhrnus looked at the wall. Reisil held herself still, waiting for his verdict.

"Is that all of it? The break between you and Sodur?" he asked, turning back to her, his gaze scorching. She nodded. He reached up and stroked Esper's head. "All right, then."

Relief rushed through Reisil, and she let out a breath she hadn't been aware she was holding.

"Saw you talking to your patient. What did he say?"

"He apologized for bumping into me." Reisil paused, then said slowly, "He thanked me for saving his life and offered his service." When Juhrnus didn't answer, she added, "Sodur would be disturbed to learn Metyein cas Vare knew I'd healed him. And likely overheard the rest of our conversation that night."

"I'll bet he would. Someone might earn his trust by telling him. But really, who wants his trust? Let him eat *skraa.*"

Reisil grinned, starting when the brassy sound of horns blasted through the Great Hall. "They're here," she said softly, and then stepped out of the alcove to see better.

The majordomo pounded his staff, and his deep, ringing tones echoed through the answering hush that fell over the assembly.

"Menegal-Hakar, Jebak of the Berjudi, Honored Pewaris of His Supreme Greatness, Tengkorak-Gadai, Kilmet and

Suzaerain of Dahre-Sniwan's chosen people in Scallas and
across the waves; Waiyhu-Waris, Oljebak of the Berjudi,
Honored Musnah of His Supreme Greatness, Tengkorak-
Gadai, Kilmet and Suzaerain of Dahre-Sniwan's chosen
people in Scallas and across the waves, and Kedisan-Mutira,
Emak of the Endul, favored *penabidan* of Jebak Menegal-
Hakar and Oljebak Waiyhu-Waris.''

Reisil barely heard the almost nonsensical introductions
as she watched the sorcerers float up the steps and through
the wide doorway of the Great Hall, two feet above the
floor. There was an audible gasp, and then Reisil felt a
wave of magic wash over her, filling her mouth and ears,
squeezing her lungs and pressing her flat. She coughed,
struggling for breath. All about her, the entire assembly
wilted beneath the onslaught, clinging together, coughing
and gasping.

The sorcerers floated along indifferently, approaching the
royal dais. Those waiting for them remained unaffected by
the Scallacians' spell.

Reisil's vision dimmed, and her chest ached. Beside her,
Juhrnus gagged, grabbing at the draperies as he sagged to
the floor. Esper made a hissing sound, and Saljane shrieked.
Fury flamed inside Reisil. She snatched at her power.

It was gone, leaving her as barren as if it had never been.
Not now! She tried again, but nothing. Her fingers curled
into claws, and black smudges dimmed her vision.

Wrath. Frenzy. Brutality. Blood-hunger.

The *presence* from the bluffs. Reisil recoiled, feeling her
bones shifting against one another as if she were being
twisted and pulled like a rag doll. Suddenly her power
roared up in answer to the ferocious assault. Raw and hot,
it burst from her like a thunderclap, shattering the sorcerers' net. She ripped at it with invisible hands, driven by
fury and pain.

Reisil's wild magic crashed against the sorcerers' shields.
The Scallacians dropped to the floor, staggering. With practiced calm, they gathered themselves, looking neither to the
left or the right as they marched toward the dais as if nothing had happened.

Reisil sobbed for air, the pressure on her lungs easing.
Her magic crackled in her hair and along her skin. She
reined it back, but dared not let go of it. *What if it failed*

to come again? She felt the pressure of it beginning to build inside her, pressing against her eyes, making her teeth and bones ache. Reisil clenched her shaking hands.

"What—?" The rest of the sentence was lost as Juhrnus began to cough. He caught his breath. "What was that?"

"That was the sorcerers telling us they are not our friends. Inviting them here was a mistake."

She pushed past Juhrnus, her attention caught by a knot of people forming near the far end of the room, far from the royal dais. Reisil strode through the nobles, brushing them aside. A woman had collapsed. Reisil could sense the old woman's heart stuttering, her life fleeing away. Reisil knelt down beside the stricken woman. Juhrnus settled beside her. Her blood roared in her ears, and her hands trembled as she set them on the woman's chest. Her power flared. With it came the *presence.* It crashed into Reisil's mind with all the force of a stampeding herd of horses.

For a moment she was helpless. Then she felt Saljane's mind surge up like a spear. The *presence* faltered in its onslaught, and it was enough for Reisil to slam shut her mental barriers.

~What was that? Saljane sounded strained.

~I don't know. Nor did she have time to consider. The woman was dying.

Before she could lose her nerve and with it her magic, Reisil settled her hands back down on the woman's chest. Magic flowed steadily, contained by their shared minds. Soon the woman's breathing deepened, her blood flowing more quickly as her damaged heart grew whole.

When Reisil stood up, the people around her parted, their faces suspicious and accusing. As she walked away, a cloud of mutterings rose in her wake.

"You can do that for her, but what about my Deintra?"

"Thought your power was all dried up. Picking and choosing, are you?"

". . . demonspawn . . ."

Reisil's steps stuttered, and then she continued, arm tensing as Juhrnus grasped her elbow with a steadying hand. Even if she knew who had spoken, nothing she could say would change their minds. Sodur had seen to that.

"Having a look at your handiwork?" she asked Sodur, who had come to meet them.

"What was that about?"

Juhrnus spoke first, his voice hard. "Your sorcerers tried to kill us all. Part of your plan?"

Sodur looked sharply at Reisil. She stared back, uncowed.

"This is necessary," he said. "They *can* help us."

"Funny sort of help," Juhrnus retorted acidly.

"They don't respect weakness. They were testing us. You put them in their place easily enough. Now let's go. I want you to meet them."

Reisil put a hand on Sodur's arm as he would have walked away. "You're wrong. It wasn't easy at all. I nearly couldn't do it. If—" She broke off. "You cannot depend on me to keep Kodu Riik safe from your sorcerers."

Something in her voice made the color bleed from Sodur's cheeks. He gripped her elbow. "You can't go. Not now, not yet. You're right. They aren't our friends, which makes your presence more vital than before. And you *did* break their spell. They'll be cautious now. Go away, and they'll certainly try again. If you stay—they aren't our friends, but they can be bought. They still might be the answer to the plague. But not if you leave." His grasp tightened, his voice dropping. "You can't go find the wizards yet. Not while the sorcerers are in Kodu Riik. You'll doom us all if you do."

Reisil yanked her arm away. How dare he invite them here and make her responsible for them! It was his fault, his choices and his secrets. Not hers.

~*But we must protect Kodu Riik.*

Saljane sounded as angry as Reisil felt, her voice sere and cold.

~*Is this the way? We can't* make *them help. We can't* make *them find a cure. All they have to do is drag their heels, and the plague does their work for them. I should find the wizards, now, while there's still time.*

~*But what if Sodur is right?*

Reisil's lips pinched together. It was an argument she couldn't gainsay. Not yet. But it wouldn't be long before the whole city was under siege by the plague, and if the Scallacians didn't help soon, she would go hunting for the wizards on her own.

She nodded and then followed after Sodur to the royal dais, Juhrnus at her side. Sodur guided them around to the back of the dais to stand behind the Lord Marshal, the Verit, the Vertina. The Castelain was introducing the sorcerers to the nobility in a stately, sonorous voice. The two male sorcerers nodded disdainfully at each introduction. The woman hardly noticed the presentations.

Reisil waited, shifting from foot to foot. The introductions concluded, and the Castelain bowed and retreated. The Verit drew a breath and opened his mouth, but before he could speak, Sodur stepped forward, bowing low.

"My apologies, Daz. But I would plead two more introductions." The Verit's eyes narrowed, but he smiled graciously.

"Of course. We would not wish to slight anyone."

Sodur waved Reisil and Juhrnus forward. They complied, though Reisil could not erase the stony expression from her face.

"These are two of our finest young *ahalad-kaaslane*, Reisiltark and Juhrnus. Juhrnus will be serving as your aide and liaison, to help you with whatever you need during your sojourn in Kodu Riik. We have given him quarters near yours for your convenience. Reisiltark will be able to assist you in understanding the plague."

As he made this introduction, Reisil studied the sorcerers. They were of a height and only an inch or so taller than she. Their dark eyes were lined with thick kohl, and their lips gleamed scarlet, giving them a sensual, exotic appearance, though Reisil felt only repugnance. Their robes were sleeveless, and their arms were bare, showing darkly tanned skin swathed in a delicate net of finely wrought chains, flashing with tiny charms in all sorts of shapes and sizes. These finely-netted chain sleeves draped across their hands and attached to carved rings circling the first knuckle on each of their fingers. Beneath their robes, the chain undergarments stretched down to the ground, visible beneath the slightly shorter length of the colorful fabric. Their feet were shod in thin-soled, strappy sandals, also decorated with a jingling array of charms. A snood matching the undergarments draped each of their pale heads, ending just above their pale eyebrows and sweeping down over their

shoulders to fasten across the chest. As on the undergarment and sandals, charms flashed and gleamed along the
crisscrossing lengths and jingled along its edges.

Sodur announced their names and titles, the alien words
rolling off his tongue as if he'd known them all his life, as
if he knew what they meant.

"May I present Menegal-Hakar, Jebak of the Berjudi,
honored Pewaris of His Supreme Greatness, Tengkorak-
Gadai, Suzaerain of Scallas."

The first sorcerer tipped his head. He was a lean man
with bony features and hard muscles roping his thin arms.
Reisil returned the bow in equal depth, taking satisfaction
in the slight flare of his nostrils.

"At his side stands Waiyhu-Waris, Oljebak of the Berjudi, honored Musnah of His Supreme Greatness, Tengkorak-
Gadai, Suzaerain of Scallas."

His bow was even more shallow than the first, and Reisil
mirrored it exactly. This sorcerer was slightly younger than
the first, though his face was wider, his features more
coarse. A ring of silver pierced his left nostril and from it
dangled more charms. The muscles of his arms were thick
and meaty, reminding Reisil of a stevedore. She wouldn't
like to encounter him in a dark alley. Not that he needed
a dark alley. Not that any of them did.

"And finally, this is Kedisan-Mutira, Emak of the Endul,
favored *penabidan* of Jebak Menegal-Hakar and Oljebak
Waiyhu-Waris."

"Abi," Menegal-Hakar added in a slow, scornful tone.

Reisil turned at last to the sorceress. As their eyes met,
Reisil's skin prickled. Whatever menace the men represented from Scallas, this woman radiated a threat that
licked Reisil's skin with a hungry tongue, standing every
hair of her body on end. *Like a wolf among the sheep.*

"It is my honor to meet you," the sorceress said in a
husky voice, bowing from the waist, never taking her eyes
from Reisil.

Reisil took Saljane onto her fist to return the bow, drawing Saljane into her mind as she summoned her magic. She
straightened slowly, examining the other woman closely.

The sorceress was dressed in similar garments to the men,
though the colors were variations on scarlet and purple. Blood
and bruises, Reisil's mind suggested, and her mouth went dry

even as sweat sprang up all over her body. The sorceress wore a similar chain undergarment, and in addition, she wore delicate silver cuffs around her wrists and neck: narrow flat bands engraved with lovely, filligree patterns.

Before Reisil's heartbeat slowed again, the dinner gong sounded, and everyone around her began lining up for the processional into the Dining Hall. Watching the Scallacians, Reisil remembered with stark vividness seeing them together on the deck of their ship. The division between the sorceress and her companions, a crevice like an inverted mountain. As she watched them now, she could see it again. And more. The two men had no sense of what hid within their companion.

~*I don't like this.*

~*She is the great lizard that hides itself in shallows and snatches its prey as it comes to drink,* Saljane replied ominously.

~*They brought their own war, and I fear Kodu Riik is going to be their battlefield. What has Sodur invited into Kodu Riik?*

Turning, she found Juhrnus waiting beside her. "What's wrong?"

Reisil shook her head. "I wish I knew. But heed what Sodur said—get close to them and soon. Especially her. There's something brewing between them. Something very dangerous. We have to know what it is. We have to know *now*."

Chapter 23

The ivy on Reisil's face had begun to glow, and a wash of red filled her eyes. The Lady's beacon.

Without a word, Juhrnus plunged away into the crowd. He reached the place where the lines had begun to take shape, the Verit at the head of one, escorting his sister, the

Lord Marshal at the head of the other, escorting a dowager crusted in jewels. Behind each came one of the sorcerers accompanied by high-ranking noblewomen, and third in the Verit's line came the sorceress accompanied by Kijal Deviik. Juhrnus paused, scowling.

"Something wrong?"

Juhrnus started, finding Metyein cas Vare beside him. "I need to sit with the sorceress," he said without explanation. Metyein didn't ask for one.

"All right. Follow me. Be ready." He strode away, and Juhrnus hurried after.

~Be ready for what? What's he up to?

~What he does well.

Juhrnus slowed, turning his head to meet Esper's yellow eyes. The sisalik sometimes seemed to have a grasp of the court that Juhrnus could hardly begin to fathom.

~Watch him, Esper warned.

Metyein had approached Kijal Deviik. He spoke quietly against the older man's ear. His expression was bland, but something in what he said made the Kijal's face darken. He turned and spoke a moment to the sorceress, then hurried away with Metyein.

Juhrnus wasted no time wondering what Metyein had said to draw the Kijal off. Instead he slid casually into the Kijal's vacated place, ignoring Sodur, who stood in the opposite line beside another *ahalad-kaaslane*.

"Your pardon, Dajam. You seem to have been abandoned. Would you allow me to escort you instead?"

The sorceress cast him a hooded glance. "If you wish." Juhrnus bowed as he lifted his elbow for her hand. He fidgeted in the silence that descended between them. It was rude to say nothing, but he didn't know what to say that wouldn't make him sound like a complete idiot.

"How do you find Kodu Riik so far?" Jurhnus asked at last, wincing at the inanity of the question. "It is not always this cold or stormy," he went on as a thundering wind rattled the windows. "We've had a delayed spring."

"I see."

"I know it's much colder here than Scallas. The palace rooms can be drafty. I hope you are not uncomfortable."

"No. It is . . . fine. Very fine."

"Good." His ears felt hot, and he was glad the procession

had begun to move. "Anyway, the spring will be here soon. It should warm up then."

"Pity."

They soon arrived at their seats beneath the baldaquin on the raised dais at the head of the room. The tables were swathed with fine white silks sparkling with gem beads and decorated with ethereal carvings of ice. Spun-sugar fairies in rainbow colors cavorted on the ice, while inside sparkled delicately wrought ornaments of silver and gold.

As everyone sat, the Surveyor of Ceremonies rose and made the traditional welcome, and then presented the salt to the Verit in an elaborate stone crock carved in the shape of a gryphon. Then the Laverer was summoned with a ringing gong to wash each guest's hands. Watching the sorceress wash her hands, Juhrnus noticed for the first time that beneath the chains and rings, her fingers were callused and scarred as if from heavy work. She caught him looking. She flexed her fingers, turning her hands over and examining them meticulously.

"One, two, three, four, five," she counted, ticking off each finger. "None extra that I can see. No warts, no growths. What do you see that puts that look on your face?" she said, fixing Juhrnus with the full force of her stare.

He felt it like a blow to his midsection, and the breath whooshed out of him in a gust. Seconds ticked past. Finally he drew a thin breath into his flattened lungs. "I see—"

"What?" She sounded curious rather than angry.

"Danger," he answered, and then instantly wished the word back.

But she only nodded. "Is that all?"

Juhrnus shook his head.

"What else?" Her voice had turned gentle, cajoling. It slid up his spine like red-polished fingernails. He felt himself harden, his loins aching with sudden lust. *Is this a spell?* He didn't know. Didn't care.

He opened his mouth to answer, but before he could speak, confess his lust, he remembered Reisil's face, the flare of gold on her face, the crimson filling her eyes. His body went cold, and his hunger for the sorceress evaporated.

"Danger and mystery," he said finally. The sorceress

eyed him, one eyebrow arching up. Then she turned away to speak to the Basham sitting on her other side.

~What did she do to me?

~Nothing. I would have felt it. But a haze of worry accompanied Esper's thoughts.

~What is it?

Esper hesitated.

~Tell me. There was more impatience in Juhrnus's mind-voice than he intended.

~She touched you. Deeply.

Juhrnus frowned. *~I don't understand.*

~It was— I don't know how to say it. The haze of apprehension thickened, and Esper squeezed his claws tight.

Juhrnus winced and stroked Esper's head with his free hand. *~Try. It's all right.*

~She—

Juhrnus had a sense of Esper drawing a deep mental breath, trying to find words for something he had no words for.

~There is something—a thread—between you, connecting you. Esper sounded frightened and forlorn.

~A thread? But you said she didn't use magic.

~She did not. This is . . . This is something else.

Juhrnus fell silent, his brows furrowed. Absently he rubbed at his chest, as if to find a fisherman's line hooking into his flesh. If not a spell, then what? His jaw hardened. If she thought to use him, to control him somehow, she would be severely disappointed. Whatever was going on, he was warned. She would not take him unawares.

"Did you hear me? Or are you unwell?"

Juhrnus stared uncomprehendingly at the sorceress.

"Are you unwell?" she repeated.

"What do you mean?" Juhrnus asked thickly.

She looked away without answering, and Juhrnus straightened in his chair. He needed to get ahold of himself. But before he could find a way to again engage her in conversation, the Surveyor of Ceremonies struck the gong again, summoning the Cupbearer to test the wine. He approached the long serving table. He drank a glass from each barrel, after which, the moonfaced young man paused for a full minute as if waiting for the fatal clench of poison around his innards. When he'd completed the wine, he

moved on to the ale and cider. Next came the liqueurs, and
before long, he'd begun to weave and stagger. The watching crowd laughed as he bumbled and lurched and was
eventually led away. Next came the Verit's blessing and
welcome, and then began the food and entertainment.

A fanfare sounded, and the first course began with the
service of a light, delicate wine, platters of various breads
and a mouthwatering array of meats, cheeses and vegetable
spreads. They were served in pastry shells shaped like
roses, orchids and tulips. Given the drought, the long winter
and the shortage of food in the city and Fringes, it was a
decadent beginning to an even more decadent feast. Juhrnus could hardly choke it down. As for the sorceress, she
ate sparingly, taking bare sips of her wine and spending
more time pushing her food around the plate than eating.

Though it was Juhrnus's turn to converse with her, the
Basham on her other side chatting animatedly with the
woman on his right, he couldn't scrape up anything to say,
his tongue clinging to the roof of his mouth.

"What do you call your *ahalad-kaaslane*?" she asked suddenly, coming to his rescue.

"Esper. He's a sisalik. From the western part of Kodu
Riik. Gets hot there, and swampy. Lots of trees."

"He dislikes the cold, then." She sounded disapproving.

Juhrnus smiled. "He does enjoy a good fire."

"I'd like to see the rest of the city," the sorceress said
abruptly.

"I can show you around," Juhrnus offered quickly. If he
could get her alone, perhaps he could discover something. . . .

"I would hate to trouble you."

"It's no trouble. I would be pleased to do it."

Once again she cast him that glittering look, and Juhrnus
squirmed on his chair.

Soon the next course began, and it was time to flirt with
the Preili on his left. Beyond he could see Menegal-Hakar,
gimlet eyes flickering over the assembly as he speared food
into his mouth. He seemed unimpressed by the parade of
servants presenting platter after platter of beautifully prepared foods—meats molded into hedgehogs and badgers,
whole roasted pigs, dozens of varieties of fish, twenty different omelets made of quail eggs, roasted partridges and

pheasants still in their feathers with gilded beaks and claws, and more. Between each course came jugglers, minstrels, balladeers, illusionists and instrumental sets.

Determined to discover more about the sorceress, with the next course and change of partners, Juhrnus began asking a barrage of questions. "Tell me about Scallas. What's it like?"

"Hot."

"Quite a change for you."

"Yes."

"Do you have family?"

"My mother."

"You must miss her."

"Yes."

"What about your father?"

"Gone."

"Where did you grow up?"

"In Keemasan. Our capital city."

"Tell me about it."

She did not answer, cutting into the golden apple that had just been placed on her plate. She took a bite, chewing slowly, then laid her fork and knife down.

"It's beautiful. The buildings are built of many-colored stones, gleaming in the sunlight like fairy sculptures. They are carved from bottom to top with celebrations of Dahre-Sniwan." Her voice dropped at the mention of the name of Scallas's patron god. "There are gardens everywhere, in every tiny corner, on rooftops, on window ledges. Even in the niches of the walls. They overflow with fragrant flowers of every color and variety, filling the air with glorious smells. The bushes and trees are extraordinary, growing in fantastical shapes and so brilliantly green. Water is precious in Scallas. Though the cloud-wardens call the rain, there is scarcely ever enough. But the gardens show our devotion to Dahre-Sniwan.

"Keemasan is an oasis for thousands of birds. Their song is the most beautiful thing I've ever heard. No matter how many walls separate you from the outside, morning or night, you can hear them."

She stopped and Juhrnus waited, hoping she'd say more. But now came the parade of pastries: pies, cakes, tarts, custards, truffles, fruit breads and compotes. Now the sorceress had turned to her other partner. The plump Preili on Juhrnus's left was busy with the mountain of sweets on her plate and in no need of Juhrnus's attention. Out of the corner of his eye he watched the sorceress.

She bent her head and lifted a bite of pastry to her mouth. Juhrnus watched her lips open, feeling once again that pull between them. He tensed against it. And just when he would have looked away, broken the connection, the pastry on her fork disappeared. Vanished. He blinked. She set her fork down and half of what had been on the plate was gone as well.

Juhrnus drew a startled breath. There was something infinitely frightening in that casual disappearance. He'd seen no evidence of sorcery, though what he'd expected, he didn't know. When Reisil used magic, her eyes generally changed color—green in healing, red in battle—and the ivy on her face began to glow. But there'd been no warning, no outward sign of magic from the sorceress. And to use such power on such a minor thing! Did she have so much to spare, then?

What had Sodur invited into Kodu Riik? For as easily as she had banished her food, the sorceress could banish a person, or the entire Banquet Hall full of people. What could all three of them do together? Was Reisil a match for the Scallacians? Juhrnus shuddered, his skin prickling. Reisil was untrained; though she bore a sharp sword, she used it like a club. The sorcerers were akin to assassins, with a hoard of weapons and infinitely greater skills. How could Reisil's brute force compete with that?

The fanfare signaling the end of the meal sounded, and everyone stood. The Verit offered a toast to the Scallacians, and then everyone began to disperse into gossiping groups.

"When would you like your tour of the city?"

The sorceress hesitated, glancing at the two sorcerers who were walking away with the Verit and Lord Marshal. She looked back at Juhrnus. "Is dawn too early?"

He raised his brows. "Not for me, Dajam. But you may not have had time to sleep by then."

"I don't doubt it," she said in an odd voice. "Dawn it is, then. Thank you for your kindness in escorting me to dine."

Juhrnus gave a short bow, scrambling for something else to say. Then something Reisil had said struck him and he straightened.

"It was my pleasure. But if I might keep you for just one more moment . . . I do not know how to address you. *Abi*, I think Menegal-Hakar called you."

The sorceress yanked her hand from his. Her face paled, and her eyes flattened over flared nostrils. She pointed a shaking finger at him, and with clenching fear, Juhrnus saw wisps of purple smoke curling from its end like smoke from a blown candle.

"Never—," she said, her upper lip curling. Then she caught herself. She drew a harsh breath, and her hand flattened in the air between them. Without another word she stalked away. For a moment Juhrnus hesitated.

~Go. She is off balance. And you learned something. Reisiltark is right. There is something dangerous brewing between her and them.

The way Esper said *them* was like an epithet, though oddly the sentiment didn't seem to extend to the sorceress. But Esper's judgment on the situation was enough for Juhrnus, who began tracking the sorceress's retreat through the throng. It was no easy task. The room was large with a great many nooks and doors.

Juhrnus peeked into the alcove where he and Reisil had taken refuge earlier. He apologized for disturbing the young nobleman with his mature lover and then moved quickly away. He searched up and down the Great Hall, but she was nowhere to be seen. He slipped out into the Grand Foyer and glanced into the other reception rooms. Would she have returned to her quarters? No. It was too strange a place. It wouldn't be any comfort to her. So where?

The wind gusted again and outside the wind howled. High above on the rotunda roof, ice clicked and clattered against the stone. Juhrnus stared up at the alabaster dome. She wouldn't. Not on such a night. But his gut told him otherwise.

~Do you want to stay here? I don't have my sling or a coat. It's going to be cold.

Esper hesitated, and Juhrnus could feel his *ahaladkaaslane's* indecision. Juhrnus reached up and lifted Esper down, setting him down beside a linen-covered cabinet. *~It should be warm enough under there. Wait for me.*

~I shouldn't let you go alone.

~I'm never alone. You are always with me. Juhrnus tapped the side of his head meaningfully. Esper licked his tongue across the back of his hand before crawling beneath the linen draperies to curl up and wait.

Juhrnus stood and rolled his shoulders, loosening the tension from carrying Esper for so long. He looked at the large front doors. No, she would have found another way out. Something less conspicuous. He dodged into one of the serving passageways. It led into another and another until he came to the bustling kitchens. She wouldn't have gone in there. Juhrnus backtracked up the corridor, testing doors until he found one unlatched, leading into the kitchen gardens.

He pushed on the door. It pushed back. He put his shoulder to it and stumbled out into the dark, winter-killed gardens. The wind pummeled him, chilling him to his skin. Ice pellets raised stinging welts on his face. Demonballs! Where was she?

He made his way down the walk, skidding and sliding on the slick stones. Giving up, Juhrnus stepped into the planter bed where the frozen furrowed dirt and leaf meal lent him better traction. He quartered the garden, finding nothing, and moved on into the next. He found her at the far wall, gazing into the violent sky.

Juhrnus paused, hunched against the wind, wondering how to approach her. As he watched, he was struck by the realization that her robes hung still and unmoving, nor did the wind tease her hair from its smooth cap.

Suddenly she thrust her hands up to the sky, and the magic shielding fell away. Her robes billowed and flapped, exposing her bare legs beneath the chain undergarment. Her hair tossed and streamed. Standing thus, she looked nothing more like a *rashani*, wild and ferocious and mad. Juhrnus didn't know whether to advance or retreat.

Then the decision was taken from him.

She turned slowly, her magical shields snapping up. She stared at him, her face white and skeletal in the violent night. Bruised purple smoke curled around her hands and up her arms. She spoke, but Juhrnus couldn't hear anything past the roaring in his ears. She moved closer, a stark, white halo erupting around her and making Juhrnus squint against its sudden brilliance. She thrust her hand, pointing, and Juhrnus flinched. But he didn't move. He couldn't. He was trapped in her spell and completely at her mercy.

Chapter 24

Metyein guided the incensed Kijal Deviik into an un-used solar.

"This is intolerable!" the Kijal exploded. "What does your father intend to do about it?"

"He has sent men to meet with Thevul Bro-heyek. But if Soka is there, they will keep him hidden. In all truth, until the Thevul crosses out of his borders, there is little to be done. Sending troops could incite retaliation, even if troops could be spared. But as my father has pointed out to me, the mystery of Soka's disappearance could equally be attributed to a woman as to his father's plotting. Bro-heyek has been content to leave his son here for more than a decade. There's nothing to suggest he'd try to liberate him now."

And indeed, those were nearly the exact words his father had used when Metyein demanded a search.

"But my lands! Bro-heyek has always coveted my eastern valley. It is the largest and most fertile valley that far north. He'll have it for the plucking. And once he's ensconced, he'll not be easily moved without taking one of his boy's ears, or his whole head!" The Kijal shook his head and paced in a zigzagged path. "I must speak to your father— the first-tier lords. They will support me. Bro-heyek must be stripped of his lands. He's nothing but a common thief and a pirate."

"Undoubtedly so, Kaj Deviik. But doing so right this moment would be a grave mistake."

The Kijal jerked around, his jaw jutting, his broad face florid. "A mistake? To defend my lands from that scum?"

"A mistake to show your hand too early, Kaj Deviik. Think about it. Soka could not make the long trip home alone. He's hardly ever been outside the gates of this city. How would he find his way? How would he deal with the terrain, with a lame horse or a *nokula*? That is, if Soka ran. I have my doubts."

The Kijal straightened, crossing his arms and staring down at Metyein with a cold look. "That's right. You and the puppy are friends."

"We still are, if I'm right. Which is why I am talking to you."

"And what do you think has happened?"

"I think that it's highly coincidental that he should disappear right at this moment, when the Scallacians have arrived and we are facing so much pressure from the plague and the *nokulas*. Bro-heyek has little to gain that I can see. Certainly a few hectares of land, but that is only temporary. He knows my father would send troops eventually, that he would lose his heir, and likely his lands. That's even supposing he'd be stupid enough not to wait until your people had tilled and planted the fields and pastured your herds. Why put himself to expense when he can take it out of your coffers? You know him. Does this sound likely?" Metyein paused. "But someone else might wish you to retire from Koduteel, to take your voice from the Arkeinik."

"This is ludicrous. You seek merely to assuage cas Raakin's guilt."

"There is a regency on the table, Kaj Deviik. Which way will you vote? No one but you knows if you'll vote Aare the regency or not. With the stakes so high, either side would play this sort of game to win the day. It need not be the Verit or my father: many others stand to win or lose by your choice, or your departure from the city. But on my honor, I swear Soka cas Raakin would not have broken the hostage pact of his own free will."

The Kijal turned away and went to the window, brooding. Finally he swung back around. "Suppose I accept for now that cas Raakin has not left willingly, but that someone plots my removal from Koduteel. What do you want of me?"

"First, that you make your own investigation. Make no secret of your ire and malice for Thevul Bro-heyek. I have no doubt that information shall be provided, too easily and too quickly. And it shall rule against Soka."

"And how will that convince me that you are right?" the Kijal demanded. "If the evidence points to cas Raakin, why should I discount it?"

Metyein nodded. "Make it known you remain undecided on the vote, nor do you intend to leave Koduteel. The longer you do, the more anxious they'll get. They'll have to make another move. Their initial feint having failed, they'll push harder, expose themselves. The rest of the first-tier lords are set in their positions. You are the only wild card."

Metyein had thought through the argument for days. If someone had wanted to influence the vote, Soka could easily have been taken by himself without harm. He often walked the streets alone and late at night, having gambled or dallied long past any polite hour. But why would someone come after the four of them in the Jarrah Gardens? And why use practice tips on the arrows, which might or might not kill? What was the point?

But if Deviik bought his argument, then whoever had taken Soka would be forced to make a move. When they did, Metyein would be ready.

"Very well. I don't relish being anyone's pawn. But mark my words, if I find Soka cas Raakin has broken the hostage pact, I'll slit his throat myself and stake his head on the battlements."

"If he's broken the pact, then it's no more than he deserves."

Metyein drained his glass as Kijal Deviik departed, wincing as the liquid flamed in his empty stomach. He'd carried it off. He tapped his fingers against his thigh. There were three or four hours before the feast ended. His father wouldn't notice his absence until then. The time was ripe to search in the seedier quarters. If Soka was alive, that was where he'd be hiding.

Metyein reached for the door and then paused, looking down at himself. He couldn't go looking like this. He'd stand out like a peacock in a cockyard. But in this weather, a man wearing a cloak and hood wouldn't raise suspicions. Metyein knew just where to find what he needed.

He hurried down the corridor and out a servants' entrance, grateful for the curiosity that had led him and Soka to explore these corridors so thoroughly as children. He sped to his father's house, where he raided Pelodra's quarters for a weathered cloak, gloves and boots. He shoved his own clothing into a pack and carried it beneath the cloak, giving him a hunched, aged appearance. He took a plain sword from his own rooms and headed down to the red quarter to begin his search.

Metyein returned later than he'd planned and was chagrined to find that the feast had already finished. He hurried up a back staircase to an upper floor, where he slipped into a lady's unoccupied boudoir. There he changed back into his own boots and gloves and removed his sword. With the aid of the anonymous lady's toiletry paraphernalia, he combed out his hair and then smoothed his clothing. There was little he could do for his cravat. It had long since wilted and flattened beyond repair.

He examined himself in the mirror. He still looked a bit unkempt. There was nothing to be done about it. But that wasn't what worried him. There was a tightness to his lips and an intensity in his gaze that betrayed the turbulence of his mind. His father was certain to notice. With effort, he forced his lips into their familiar mocking smile and slumped his body in a loose, careless way. But there was nothing he could do to temper the look in his eyes. The information he'd learned still thundered in his blood. He sighed and let his lids droop. With luck, his father would be too preoccupied to notice him.

A few minutes later Metyein sauntered down the marble staircase to the Grand Foyer. Though the Great Hall and the constellation of reception rooms remained crowded, the Foyer itself was unoccupied. Metyein nearly missed a step when there began a wild churning beneath one of the linen-covered tables against the wall. Out from beneath skittered Juhrnus's *ahalad-kaaslane,* his head and tail whipping back and forth. The agitated sisalik raced to the middle of the floor, spinning in circles, his claws clicking and scraping, the sound sending shivers down Metyein's spine.

Metyein sloughed his languid air and leaped down the remaining steps.

The sisalik whipped around, raising himself up on his hind legs and tail and preparing to strike with his formidable claws.

Metyein took a step back and knelt down. "What is it, Esper?"

The sisalik swayed in the air and then dropped to the ground. Foreboding eeled up Metyein's spine. Looking into the sisalik's staring yellow eyes, he wished fervently for his sword. All he had were two daggers hidden in his boots and his belt-knife.

"Where is Juhrnus?"

Esper flung himself onto Metyein's arm, his claws digging bloody gouges into Metyein's skin as he clambered up onto his shoulder, curling his tail tightly around Metyein's arm.

"All right," Metyein gasped, pain racing along his skin. "Where to now?" Esper made a low growling sound in his throat. A flash of memory made Metyein stiffen. "He went outside, didn't he? It was too cold to take you. Did he go out the front?" Metyein stepped in that direction. Esper tensed, digging his claws deeper, the growl turning into a yowl.

"Not the front? I didn't see any sign of him when I came in, so he didn't likely go out an east entrance. He wouldn't have left you here if he was going out the west side. That leaves just the northern entrances. So, through the kitchens or one of the solars?"

Metyein took a step toward the kitchens, and Esper didn't fight him. He sped quickly along the corridor until he reached the kitchen warren. There were only three doors leading outdoors. Two were on the opposite end of the kitchens: one leading to the well and herb garden, while the other opened into the wide chute connecting the kitchen to the stables and slaughter yard. The third was closer, near the root cellars. Metyein headed for this door first, his heart pounding as he saw the door cracked open, its bar lying on the floor.

Metyein yanked it open, gasping as the wind crashed against his chest. Ice lashed his face like a knotted whip. He ducked his head against the assault and shoved outside. Esper made a thin yowling sound like tearing metal and pressed his belly against Metyein, clasping tighter with his tail and claws. Metyein hardly felt the pain as he shuffled across the icy path. He quartered the first garden area, stomach clenched against the discovery of another bloody body. But he found nothing, the wind-driven ice making him blink and tear. He squinted, scrubbing his eyes with his knuckles.

As he passed through the gate to the next garden, he felt Esper slump against him. Metyein swiveled his head to look at his passenger. The sisalik looked pitiful, ice crusting his hide. His eyes had become mere slits. Despite Esper's sudden easing, Metyein couldn't leave off his search. Something had been very wrong with Juhrnus—he could be safe enough for the moment, but danger might still lurk. Remembering those who had hunted him and Soka through the Jarrah Gardens, Metyein trotted forward, slipping on a patch of ice and landing heavily. Shining pain burned up his thigh and into his hip.

"Skraa," he muttered through gritted teeth. He clambered to his feet, breath hooking in his lungs as he tested his weight on his injured leg. Nothing broken. Trickles of blood from Esper's claws made icy tracks down his chest and back. He shivered, finally becoming aware of the cold.

He edged against the lee of the wall and coaxed Esper off his shoulders, half pulling him into his arms so that he could press the sisalik against the warmth of his chest. It had to be warmer than sitting exposed on his shoulders.

A glow at the end at the corner of the wall caught Metyein's attention. He crept down the wall, hunching into the darker shadows. Two figures stood at the end of the garden.

Metyein crept closer, feeling for his knife. Juhrnus faced the sorceress. He held his hands out to the sides as if showing he was unarmed. Metyein was too far away to see her expression, but the glow radiated from her, sharp and bright and unforgiving. Juhrnus spoke to her. She answered, one hand sweeping through the air. Then the glow around her began to shrink and grow misty. Juhrnus stepped forward, standing just beyond the edge of her light. Slowly it faded altogether, and Metyein could no longer see them. But Esper remained calm, snuggled against his chest.

Metyein sat a moment, wondering what to do. Juhrnus seemed to have the situation in hand and remaining on the cold ground did not appeal to him. With a sigh, he made his slow, surreptitious way back along the wall, through the gate and the next garden, and back into the kitchen. The door remained unbarred. Metyein slid through and pushed it closed, dropping down the dim cross-passage and into a pantry. He nudged a pickle crock near the door so he could see down the corridor, and sat down shivering to wait.

What was going on out there? The sorceress had come close to killing. Juhrnus, sending Esper into a frenzy. Metyein had no doubts. But why? And how had Juhrnus stopped her?

Chapter 25

Juhrnus stood still as a granite plinth, waiting for the blow that must come. He hardly felt the wind or the ice melting down his collar.

~*You are my heart*, Juhrnus sent to Esper, feeling his *ahalad-kaaslane's* terror and having no way to assuage it. Tears spilled unashamedly down his cheeks. There was nothing more precious to him than Esper. He'd nearly lost the sisalik once. How could he put Esper through that agony of loss?

He found his tongue. "Allow me to apologize for offending you," he said in a carrying voice to cut across the wail of the wind. He stared into the sorceress's eyes. They were hollow, empty, as if she'd withdrawn into depths he could never hope to reach. A coldness emanated from her, colder even than the blade of the wind and the flail of the ice. Juhrnus felt its numbing grasp creeping up his legs, circling his thighs and swallowing his hips.

"I did not know that *Abi* was an insult. Menegal-Hakar used that word for you so publicly." But even as he said it, Juhrnus heard the lie in his voice and knew that she would too. For the thread that bound them together was one of kinship. *We are somehow alike.* She valued honesty.

He knew that as if she'd said it aloud. She valued honesty, and she despised deception. He thought of Sodur.

"That's a lie," he said bluntly. "I heard the way Menegal-Hakar used that word. I knew it was an insult. So I used it, hoping it would upset you so that you'd let something slip." He couldn't help the mordant grin that quirked the corners of his lips. He'd learned something, all right. More than he was likely to survive.

Cold continued to crawl upward, over his groin, circling his ribs. Pain struck him as the cold gnawed at his heart. Agony flashed down his left arm, and his knees buckled. He dropped to the cobbles, clutching his chest and gasping. From far, far away he could hear Esper, but he could not make out the words. He sobbed, feeling their bond beginning to splinter and crack. He forgot the sorceress in that moment as he grappled to hold Esper close in his mind.

But she had not forgotten him.

The wind and battering ice ceased as if a door had shut, and Juhrnus felt himself suddenly warm, as if sitting beside a roaring fire. He stood up gingerly, his mind fisted with Esper's. The sorceress stood over him, her eyes still glittering and hard, but the smoke circling her head was gone, and she did not appear so brittle. Juhrnus stood up, speaking low in the quiet sphere of the spell.

"Thank you. You saved my life." Which wouldn't have needed saving if she hadn't tried to kill him. But Juhrnus was grateful anyway.

She nodded, her marble expression unchanging. Finally she spoke. "It means 'slave.'"

How could that be? His throat went dry. If she was a slave, what kind of powers would her masters have? What had Sodur and his friends brought to Kodu Riik?

"I should thank you. I had thought I was no longer susceptible to that insult. I don't know why your repeating it should have—" She broke off, collecting herself. "You have taught me I must be more on guard. If the *pengakum* had noticed my anger, how I so easily lost control . . ." She licked her lips, her knuckles whitening as she clenched her hands together.

"If you are a slave—"

"I am not." The light around her flared brighter, and wisps of purple coiled around her knotted hands.

Juhrnus spread his own hands apart. "I don't under-stand." He spoke slowly, as if appeasing a lioness who hadn't yet decided if she was going to eat him or not.

She eyed him haughtily, and for a long moment he didn't think she was going to respond. At last she spoke. "The *pengakum* may address me as they see fit. It is not the worst thing they have done, or will do."

"Why do you let them?" he asked, sudden anger burning in his throat. His eyes dropped to the flat bands at her throat and wrists. Shackles. *"Ganyiks."* The last was ut-tered with loathing, making her eyes widen.

"You are angry. For me?" She stared at him, and he flushed, unable to look away. Whatever the thread was that bound them together was making him stupid. Still, a power-ful hatred coursed through him for the men who'd put those shackles on her, who called her slave. *It's not the worst thing they have done, or will do.* He swallowed bile.

"There is no need. I have many strengths . . . ," she mur-mured, her brow furrowing. He couldn't read her expression, but the thread connecting them tightened around his lungs until he could scarcely breathe. She rubbed the heel of her palm between the hollow of her breasts. "What is this?"

She felt it too.

Suddenly she made a sweeping gesture with her arm. The light about her turned misty and began to shrink. Juhrnus stepped forward, closing on her, his nostrils flaring. She smelled of molten metal and sharp herbs. As his toes breached the edge of the light, the glow faded until Juhrnus could see little more than her outline in the darkness.

Dimly he was aware of Esper and Metyein watching. Then the two began to retreat back inside the palace. Juhr-nus felt a wash of relief. They would be safe. He felt her eyes on him, felt the thread quivering between them like a plucked harp string.

"You should return inside. Your friends wait."

"You knew they were there?"

"I am always well warned." There was a tightness in her voice, something like fear or hate, and it pulled Juhrnus forward. He reached out, resting his hands on the edge of the silver collar. He felt her inhale sharply. Slowly he ran his fingers over the skin at her throat, sliding beneath her chain hood to caress her neck in feathery swirls.

"What are you doing?" she asked, her voice thready.

Juhrnus shook his head. "I don't know."

She flinched. "I don't like to be touched."

His hands stiffened. He lifted them away. "I apologize again," he said, curling his shaking hands into fists. "I'll leave you." He took a step back, nearly crying out as the thread tightened, slicing through him like a wire. Another agonizing step.

Abruptly she began to speak, halting him in his tracks. "In Scallas, almost everyone has some power. But only *penakidah* have rights to own land, to serve the Kilmet, or to contract the *terjebak* for children. Most important, only they are permitted to practice the larger magics. But the process is . . . difficult. It involves many trials over many years." She licked her lips, brow furrowing.

Juhrnus remained still, holding his breath that she would continue.

"The *penakidah* trials are designed to reveal the extent of a *penabidan*'s power. Scallas does not wish to become like Patverseme, gripped in the fist of a handful of too-powerful wizards. Too much or too little magic, and the candidate fails. I have achieved the stage of *penabidan,* which means I need only complete the final trials. The *pengakum* are required to offer these within the next three months, though they would begin tonight if they thought I wouldn't pass."

"They don't want you to succeed?"

"Those who are unworthy or incapable cannot be allowed to succeed." The tempo of her breathing increased.

"What happens if they do?"

She hesitated. "Your Reisiltark broke our spell tonight, didn't she?"

Juhrnus was taken off guard. "Yes," he answered finally. Who else could have done it?

"In Scallas, no one person would be permitted to hold such power. It is considered too dangerous. Such strength must be broken. The trials of *penakidah* are designed to force a candidate to reveal his true powers.

"My *pengakum* seek to be absolutely certain I am not hiding greater strength than I have shown. It is their duty. They must push me again and again in every way imaginable so that I will reveal any hidden talents. For while I wear these"—she touched the collar and wrist bands—"I am subject to their rule. Once achieving *penakidah,* these would be removed and I would be beyond their ability to contain—if I was hiding my true abilities. I could gather a faction of my own and soon become too powerful to resist. The Kilmet always favors the strong—as he must if he is to retain power—and until I was destroyed, my sect would hold ascendency over all others."

Seeing Juhrnus's repulsion, she waved her hand dismissively. "The tradition of *penakidah* has kept us from self-destruction. It limits our powers so that no mage rises up to dominate us. But it is also the root of our inability to defeat the Patversemese wizards. They are each as powerful as they can be. We are culled, like cattle and sheep, not to improve our bloodlines, but to breed out any real strength, any real power. We are forced to unite in our spellcasting, and since often the wizards do so as well, we are never enough to defeat them. And thus there are none among us who could create or break tonight's spell alone, and never as easily as your Reisiltark."

Silence fell between them again. Juhrnus didn't know what to say. He didn't know why she'd told him as much as she had. And he sensed there was more, but that she was struggling with it.

At last she began again, her voice sharp and clipped. "Sex is a common ordeal in *penakidah.* Pleasure, pain, humiliation, cruelty—these are all distractions from the magic. It is when we are most preoccupied that we are most vulnerable and begin losing control of ourselves, of our magic. Then our secrets are loosed and the *pengakum* learn what we have been hiding. Touch is *dangerous.*" The last was said almost apologetically.

"I see," Juhrnus answered, and a horde of terrible images rampaged through his mind. In all of them he saw the sorceress, her masters using her in unspeakable ways. His head spun, and a surge of revulsion hit him. He began to cough, his stomach roiling, glad that she could not see him clearly. Or could she? Reisil had the wizard-sight—the ability to see just as well at night as at noon. Why not the sorceress as well? Juhrnus spun around and retched violently. When at last he found his equilibrium, he wiped his lips with his sleeve and turned back to her, still feeling that soul-deep tie locking them together.

She stood still, as if waiting for a signal from him of how to act, what to do next.

"So," he said hoarsely. "What am I to call you?"

She hesitated. "My name is Kedisan-Mutira."

"A mouthful."

"Dual names are a *penakidah* tradition—a mark of station, a privilege of our status."

"You are not yet *penakidah*."

She sounded surprised. "True. But unless I fail, I am permitted the name."

"You will not fail." But Juhrnus wasn't thinking of her. He was remembering the first time he'd heard Esper's voice. Raised by his grandmother after his father had died in the war and his weaver mother had drunk herself into the river, he had been wild and angry and rebellious. But the Lady had seen something better in him. She'd given him Her faith and trust, and because of that, Juhrnus had become a man he could respect. And something about Kedisan-Mutira said she wanted to be *penakidah* as much as he had wanted to be *ahalad-kaaslane*, and nothing short of death was going to stand in her way. He grinned at her, feeling a sudden thrill of pride for her determination.

"You will not fail. But surely they will have begun to miss you by now. Won't that make them suspicious?"

"They will not miss me yet," she said. "They would like to think me in a nobleman's bed, seducing his secrets from him. An *ahalad-kaaslane* would work just as well. Sex is a tool for many things."

Her words were remote and impersonal.

"I can fake it if you can," he said at last. And then she chuckled, and the sound made his knees sag. It was like warm, aged whiskey running through his bones.

"Why do you want to help me?"

"I don't like your masters."

"Why?"

"I'm a good judge of character. And you don't like them any better than I do."

"It is not a question of liking them. They do as they must. As do I."

Something in the inflection in her voice caught his attention. "Why have you told me all this?"

Juhrnus felt her breath on his jaw as she bent close. He started when her fingers slid up over his cheeks, ran over his browbone and down his nose to rest against his lips. Then her mouth was against his ear, her body pressed against his as she stood on tiptoe. "It is never too soon to gather allies," she murmured.

And then she pushed past, taking with her the spell of warmth that had protected him from the wind and weather. Ice and wind flayed his face and sliced through his clothing. He stumbled after her, skittering across the icy cobbles, his head reeling with her touch, with her words.

"Allies? For what?"

Metyein sprawled on a chaise drawn close to the roaring fire, a brandy glass tilting dangerously between his fingers. Juhrnus had shoved up an overstuffed chair from the corner and sat with his bootless feet propped on the andirons. Esper stretched down the length of his *ahalad-kaaslane*'s legs, eyes closed, the end of his tail flicking slowly back and forth. On a table between the two men were the remains of their dinner.

"Scallacian politics. I think she plans to make a grab for power. To accomplish it, she wants allies, and if we can fix the plague and the *nokulas*, Kodu Riik might be in a position to help her. Or Reisil will, and the Iisand, if we can cure him. And we'll want allies too. We may have to fend off an attack from Patverseme or their banished wizards; one of them is likely to be hungry for us. They always have been. Of course, Aare will be a problem if he takes the throne. But even that can be an advantage for Kedisan-Mutira. Sooner or later you know he'll decide to go after Patverseme again. If she helps him win, she gains his gratitude and support when she sails home. And Aare won't care whom he's in bed with, so long as he wins." Juhrnus's lips twisted with the mention of *bed,* remembering the way Kedisan-Mutira had casually referred to bedding the sorcerers as part of her trials. The idea still left a bad taste in his mouth.

"Not a bad game if she can win it. Can she?"

"She didn't say it in so many words, and I can tell she's afraid she'll break and show her hand. And there was something strange about her too. Like she's in a hurry to pass her tests, but at the same time she isn't eager for it to happen tomorrow. Like she has a schedule."

"Won't be very long. Under three months, she said? Wonder how long the tests go on?"

"All she said was that her masters had to start before then. But by the sound of it, nothing they'll do to her will be short or sweet." His imagination was entirely too fertile when it came to envisioning what they would do to Kedisan-Mutira. "But neither can they afford to spend too much time away from Aare. He's not so trusting."

"I don't trust 'em out of sight for a minute, and I'm not nearly so paranoid as Aare." Metyein swigged down the rest of his brandy and poured himself another. "What do you suppose the sorcerers are up to? Why bring her along knowing they'd have to test her?"

Juhrnus stroked his fingers over Esper's back, feeling the sisalik's croon rumble against his thigh. It was echoed in his mind. He smiled. "I don't think they had a choice. This ritual has rules, and she's due for testing. They *couldn't* leave her behind."

"I hope to the Lady they don't find out the truth about the Iisand. Aare might not have brought them here, but he clearly thinks he can make lapdogs out of them: his own pet sorcerers. But he's a fool if he believes they'll heel for him." Metyein yawned and rubbed the stubble on his jaws. "Reisiltark is the only one who can hope to stop them if they decide to attack."

"He's willing to have the sorcerers as pets, but if he could, he'd drop her in a deep well and pretend she never existed."

"Don't think that he won't," Metyein said, sitting up. "I've known him a long time, and I've been hearing things in the city. Someone's stirring the pot against Reisiltark. It's like a campaign. Every tavern, every market stall, every hovel where you can buy a meal or a drink. There's always somebody whining about how she's refusing to heal the plague. How she wants to take power herself. How she heals the poor in the Fringes and ignores everybody else.

She's building herself an army, they say. She's going to march through Koduteel and turn everyone out and give their houses to the Fringefolk.

"I'm seeing less and less green, my friend. Red is the color now. And it means hate for Reisil. I don't like it. The complaints are too systematic to be coincidence. And if Aare is behind it—and it's got his stench all over it—then this is just the first step in getting rid of her. Through slander or a dark alley, he's got no intention of letting her interfere with his rule. The fewer supporters she's got and the more noise there is about her being a traitor, the easier it will be."

"Chodha," Juhrnus said.

"He's getting ready. When the plague really breaks here, it's really going to turn people against her. And Aare won't waste time. He'll take his first opportunity. And Reisiltark has got to be made to leave before it happens. I don't want to see her hurt."

"There's only one other way, and it's no safer."

"The wizards."

Juhrnus nodded.

"I hate to say it, but she might be right. They do have answers. If she can solve the plague and the *nokulas*, then we don't have any problems. We get the Iisand back, he sends the Scallacians away. The Iisand supports the *ahalad-kaaslane,* and the people will follow his lead."

"Point's moot anyhow," Juhrnus said, sounding unconvinced. "We don't know where to find them."

"Does it matter? If we can find out, then we give her a map. And if we can't, she's still out of Kodu Riik searching the hills and safer than she would be here."

"You think you can find out? No one else seems to have a clue."

"No one else wants to know, do they?" Metyein returned sardonically. "Besides, Sodur may know. He's not been particularly forthcoming with his information."

Juhrnus made a rude sound, and Metyein smiled sympathetically. "But if anyone knows where the wizards are, it's the people of the Fringes. They've been moving cross-country to get here. Someone saw something strange, heard something, found a footprint or saw smoke. I'll be able to find them. Count on it."

"All right. Do it. What about your father?"

Metyein gave a short, humorless laugh. "He's been busy. Up to his neck in this business with the sorcerers. I'd bet my life on it. He's hardly found time to climb his mistress, much less talk to me. He'd just as soon I stayed out of his way these days. He won't notice where I've gone."

He stood up, straightening his clothing, fingering the tears in his pants from Esper's claws and wincing as he grazed the scrapes in his skin. "I'm on my way, then. Good luck with your lady sorceress."

"Right," Juhrnus replied, thinking of her explosive touch on his skin. "She and I have an appointment to see the city at dawn."

Metyein opened the door.

"Better get some sleep. Sounds like you'll need it." He waggled his eyebrows suggestively and shut the door as the mug Juhrnus had thrown thudded against it. But when Juhrnus finally slept, his body moved restlessly as he dreamed of Kedisan-Mutira and her lightning touch.

Chapter 26

Reisil stared up at the carved canopy arching over her head. In the fireplace crackled the remains of the vanity table. Saljane dozed on her perch, head tucked under her wing, and outside the wind rattled the balcony doors.

Reisil sighed and shifted, pulling the heavy bedclothes over herself to ward off the chill creeping between the cracks of the doors and shutters. She hadn't bothered undressing except to shed her boots and her gauntlet. Her head throbbed, and the whirl in her mind refused to let her sleep. She had endured the intolerably long supper sitting between a self-righteous know-it-all preaching the evils of the Fringes and how to eradicate the "vermin" there, and an equally annoying second or third son of a minor house

who felt compelled to grope her under the table at every
opportunity. All the while she'd been unable to look away
from the Scallacians. Everything in her screamed *danger,*
and yet she could do nothing about it.

After the supper, she'd stalked the Great Hall. Juhrnus
and the sorceress disappeared for a time, and on their return, the Scallacians retired to a private salon with Verit
Aare and his retinue. Soon after, Reisil returned to her
rooms to find the debris from the vanity table and the crossbolt on the mantel where Kebonsat had set it. She stirred
up the fire, adding logs until it was a roaring inferno, then
tossed both the remains of the table and the poison-tipped
crossbolt into the flames and flung herself onto the bed to
await sleep. And was still waiting.

She went over her conversation with the Vertina, wondering if she'd sabotaged Kebonsat's chances. Kebonsat
and the Vertina had hardly spent a few moments together.
Mostly she'd danced attendance on the two sorcerers. How
she might have felt about that, Reisil couldn't tell. The
Vertina's expression remained unvarying in its congeniality.
And Juhrnus? Had he learned anything? She thought about
knocking on his door to find out, but dismissed the idea.
She didn't want anyone seeing her going there in the middle of the night.

She burrowed deeper into the bedclothes, wishing for
sleep. Kebonsat was expecting her at dawn, and she was
beginning to want weapons training as much as he wanted
her to have it. She was tired of being defenseless.

At first she thought it was a nightmare. A force of anger,
hatred, desire and desperate need swallowed her. It filled
her nose, her mouth, her ears, dragging her down into a
depthless mire. Reisil struggled against it, gasping, but the
more she fought, the tighter it held her.

Her mind was spinning into fragments, and she hardly
knew her own name or where she was. Suddenly Saljane
was there in her mind, a streak of cleansing white fury.
Against Saljane's brilliant presence, the other could not retain its grip on Reisil. It let her go, but Reisil could feel it
lying in wait, its hunger for her palpable.

The *presence* from the bluffs, from the Scallacians' attack
at the reception.

Reisil kicked her way out of the bedclothes and sat up. Tears rolled down her cheeks, both from fear and in strange sympathy for her agonized attacker. Saljane leaped to the bed beside Reisil, the ivy pattern on her beak glowing fiercely. Reisil hugged the goshawk against her chest. She couldn't formulate any words, couldn't gather her shattered thoughts.

At last she let go of Saljane, realizing she was drenched in sweat. Her sodden clothing clung coldly to her skin, and she shuddered at the sensation. She swung her legs over the edge of the bed, stripping off her tunic and trousers and donning fresh ones in the darkness. She poked a candle into the fire's coals to light the wick and stubbed the end into a holder on the mantel. She splashed her face before sliding into her boots and buckling on her gauntlet. Dressed and ready with no place to go, she began to pace around the room.

~What is this thing? Why is it coming after me?

Saljane did not answer, only wrapping her mind more closely around Reisil's.

Suddenly the air went out of the room. The door flew from its hinges, hitting the opposite wall with a deafening bang. The high-pitched sound of tearing metal screamed up and down the corridor. Echoing booms ricocheted down the maze of palace passages as door after door was wrenched off its hinges. Then Reisil heard a violent crash rolling up out of the entrance hall and resonating through the rest of the palace. With it came a wash of something else, something she felt like maggots in her flesh, like sunbeams on her skin. Magic.

It was here. It had come at last.

It howled with a voice that sounded like all the demons in the Demonlord's nether realm. It called to her, demanded her. Its rage was tangible. No more hiding. It wanted judgment. Revenge. For what, Reisil couldn't guess. But beneath all its roiling emotions, she felt the choking hurt it—*he*—could not hide, could not eradicate, could not escape. It drew the healer in her. She couldn't resist such agony.

"Come on," she said aloud to Saljane, lifting the goshawk up to her shoulder. "He's waiting for us." *For me.*

Reisil picked her way to the Grand Foyer, stepping over

the remains of doors and ignoring the white-faced denizens that peered out into the black corridor at her passing. She followed the sound of that howling, a long breathless note that burrowed through her head. Reisil strengthened the walls of her mind, giving herself a short-lived relief as she started down the great staircase. At her sudden distancing, the *presence* leaped against her defenses, battering at her with a blind rage unpolluted by reason. Reisil's legs buckled, and she caught herself on the railing, her vision going cloudy.

A gust of frigid air rose up the rotunda. Reisil shivered. She found her way by touch, creeping close to the wall. Ten steps, twenty, forty. The floor flattened out under her boots. She stood still, head tilted, trying to make sense of the blur in front of her, head pounding with the pressure of trying to withstand the continuing assault. If not for Saljane, Reisil would have long since collapsed and passed out.

She blinked, eyes watering. Shapes materialized. A man, taller than she, not so tall as Kebonsat. And beside him, something else.

Reisil took another step forward, her brow furrowing. Then suddenly her vision cleared as if swept away by magic, as if the being attacking her wanted her to see. Her mouth dropped open, and she stared.

Beside the man hunched a beast. Larger than a draft horse, it was matte black with fine, overlapping scales and a long sinuous neck. Barbed ridges ran down the length of its neck and faded along its tail. Its head was as long as Reisil's leg, with curved teeth meshing together along its powerful jaws. Its nostrils were ringed red, its eyes buttercup-yellow slashed with crimson. Its wings, delicate and gauzy, were slightly raised over its back. It faced her, crouching down, razor talons cutting grooves in the marble. As it stared at her, as *he* stared at her, she knew his name. *Baku.* And more. He and the man were *ahalad-kaaslane*.

Only they weren't. Pity filled Reisil in a flood. The anger, the resentment, the devastating bitterness—all of these made sense now. The man had refused Baku, had refused to be his *ahalad-kaaslane*.

~Saljane, they are us. He is you. We must help him.

She felt Saljane's answering emotions, too deep, too raw

yet, despite all their time together. They needed no words. They knew what needed to be done.

Her mind locked with Saljane's, Reisil stared into the beast's fulminating eyes and dropped the walls protecting her mind.

The world rolled over. Like a headland in a storm, wave after wave of relentless emotion washed over her. She felt Baku's endless frustration and pain at the indifference of his *ahalad-kaaslane*. And because he was no ordinary animal made sentient by the Lady, but instead was a sentient being with deeply felt and complex emotions, he felt his *ahalad-kaaslane's* rejection even more violently.

Reisil made no effort to conceal anything from him. She allowed him to ransack her mind, delve into her secrets, rifle through her fears, plunder her hopes. She let him tread those raw places that she could hardly bear to think of herself: her own sense of betrayal with Sodur, her continuing failure with the plague, her sense of unworthiness to be *ahalad-kaaslane*.

And all the while she took his pain.

How long the onslaught went on, Reisil didn't know. She clung to Saljane, needing her *ahalad-kaalsane's* strength, yet knowing their closeness would lend fuel to Baku's envy and rage.

Then she felt an arm come around her shoulders, and she was being held against a hard, broad chest.

"Baku, you must stop. We have found her. Will you kill her?"

Baku gave a scream of defiance and clutched himself deeper into Reisil's mind. For a moment she had the image of a starving wolf guarding its hard-won prey, and then her muscles went slack as her mind lost cohesion and her thoughts melted into insanity.

"Baku!"

This time it was an order, and instantly Baku obeyed. Moments ticked away. Reisil drew a breath between trembling lips. Tears ran down her cheeks. She blinked. Inches away from her face hovered Baku's muzzle.

~*Coal-drake*. The voice was deep and grating, like rocks tumbling in a slide.

She stiffened and stared. He regarded her steadily with

unnerving red-and-yellow eyes. His breath puffed over her cheeks, smelling of old stone and metal.

~*How is it I can hear you?*

~*I may speak to whomever I choose.* He sounded haughty and disdainful.

~*How?*

He did not answer, but Reisil could feel his fury rising again. She winced as her head throbbed harder and glanced up at his companion still bracing her against his chest.

He was neither handsome nor ugly. He had a wide face, heavy brows, high cheekbones, and a broad, prominent nose. His lips were wide and sensual above a strong chin. His hair was long and black and loose, but for a handful of braids decorated with beads, feathers and bits of polished wood. Heavy gold earings dangled from the lobes of his ears, and beaten hoops of the metal circled up the back of them. He wore a wrap of brilliant colors—scarlets, greens, yellows, blues and oranges. His tunic was dark green and barely long enough to cover his stomach. Heavy gold bands circled both biceps, and two more circled his wrists. Short, tight-fitting trousers covered his legs to mid-calf, and on his feet he wore boots typical of those worn by farmers in Kodu Riik. A long tube rose up over his back, attached to a leather baldric. A pouch hung at his waist and beside it hung a long knife in a scabbard, longer than a dagger, shorter than a sword.

"You've been looking for me?" she asked blearily.

He inclined his head.

"Why?"

He touched the ivy on her face. "This."

"Did the Lady send you? When She sent you Baku, did She tell you to come to me?" She straightened, her face lighting with eagerness.

He looked away, his face pained. "No. The nahuallis sent me." His words had a curious sense of being carefully chosen, carefully articulated. There was a softness to his consonants, as if he was used to speaking a much more fluid tongue. He added reluctantly, "They did not know about Baku."

"Nahuallis?" Reisil repeated, brows furrowing.

He nodded. He stood abruptly, stretching out a hand to

help her up. Baku continued to press close, only a handspan from her ear.

"I am called Yohuac Amini Achtopa Pilli," Baku's companion said, closing his right hand into a fist and laying it over his heart, thumb against his chest. He bent into a low bow, holding it for several seconds. "I have been sent to seek the foreign nahualli with gold leaves on her face. We suffer from the effects of an evil magic. It warps the weather and the beasts and the land. We have had floods and devastating storms, poor harvests, frightening beasts and great illness."

Reisil's mouth fell open. Mysane Kosk and the wizards' spell. But where had he come from that it could have such a devastating effect on his land?

"The nahuallis have done what they can to heal our land, but can do no more," he continued. "Their visions told them of you. That you could help."

Reisil swallowed, mouth dry, pressing the palm of her hand against her forehead, trying to quell the headache that throbbed there.

"I don't know who or what these nahuallis of yours are, but their visions lied. I can't stop it," she said baldly.

He blanched. Reisil could almost have laughed at his shock. Another fool thinking she could save him.

"But the nahuallis— They were sure that—"

"They're wrong."

He stood, feet braced apart. He crossed his arms, a stubborn look hardening his expression. "I cannot accept that. The gods would not send visions that lied."

"But they'd watch while their land and people were destroyed," Reisil said bitterly. "Think what you want. I don't know how to stop it. And Kodu Riik suffers because of it." His face darkened, but Reisil didn't give him a chance to retort. "If you're in that much trouble, why send you? Why didn't some of your nahuallis come?"

"There are too few nowadays. They could not be risked on such a dangerous journey."

"But you could?"

"It was thought my chances of success were better."

"And did they foresee you becoming *ahalad-kaaslane*?"

His gaze flicked to Baku and away and Reisil felt an

answering surge of anguish and rage from the coal-drake.
"No. They await my return."

The words were troubled, and Reisil softened toward
him. Who knew better than she how painful it was to refuse
to become *ahalad-kaaslane*?

"Would someone explain to me what is going on here?"
Reisil flinched. The Verit stood on the stairs flanked by
the two sorcerers and a squad of guards holding torches.
The sorceress was nowhere to be seen. Others crowded
in the doorways and hovered in the shadows farther up
the staircase.

"Who is responsible for this mess?"
Dread held Reisil frozen. Everyone already suspected
her of being a traitor. And now the palace had suffered a
magical attack, and here she stood in the middle of it. If
until now there had been a single soul who believed she
wasn't interested in taking power for herself, there wasn't
anymore.

"I am. Or rather, my companion." Yohuac stepped
forward.

"And you are?" Aare's voice dripped venom.
"I am Yohuac Amini Achtopa Pilli." Once again he gave
that fisted bow, but this time he did not bow nearly so low,
or hold it so long.

"And who are you?"
"He's *ahalad-kaaslane*," Reisil announced, startling herself. Every eye fastened on her. She lifted her chin. "He's
just arrived. He's had a long, difficult journey, and he
wishes a place to sleep." Reisil had no idea what his journey had been like or how far he'd come.

"After destroying half my palace?" Aare demanded con-
temptuously. "I'd sooner invite in the Patverseme host."
Fury kindled in Reisil at his open challenge to the Lady's
law. Never before had he so publicly dismissed the
ahalad-kaaslane.

"Fix it, Baku," Reisil ordered, never looking away from
the Verit.

~Fix it now.
The coal-drake didn't move. But suddenly the air around
him shimmered and spun with tiny white sparks. They
danced over the twisted, drunken doors of the palace. The
ruined metal slabs unbent and smoothed themselves, set-

tling into their jambs as if fastened in place by invisible hands. The gathered watchers ducked and dodged as the sparks streamed past into the palace, illuminating darkened corridors and rooms with glittering white light. In their wake, doors mended and leaped back into their frames, cracks in the walls and ceilings sealed, shattered windows gathered together and fitted themselves back into their sashes.

Reisil stared at the Verit, forcing herself to stand still, feeling her magic boiling up. She tamped it down, reining her anger in hard. Losing control at this moment wouldn't help any, much as she wanted to singe his short hairs. Right now it was important that they believe Yohuac and Baku to be *ahalad-kaaslane*. Much as it might gall, the Lady's law gave no one the authority to command the *ahalad-kaaslane,* and despite the Verit's words, he wasn't ready to put her laws to the test. Not yet. Knowing they could do magic, he'd be less inclined to send an assassin to eliminate the problem. Reisil didn't doubt he was capable of it. She thought fleetingly of the assassins hunting her. Was the Verit the hand guiding them? She brushed away the thought. Now was not the time.

A sparkling rain began to fall in the silence of the Rotunda as Baku's magic returned. The tiny embers drifted down in winding patterns, coalescing on Baku's hide in a tapestry of stars. They faded slowly, leaving the hall in the gloom of flickering torchlight.

"Your palace is repaired, Daz Varakamber," Reisil declared. "We will excuse ourselves now. It is quite late. We will disturb you no further."

With that, Reisil moved toward the stairs. Baku and Yohuac trailed after, Baku's talons clicking on the marble. Neither the Verit nor any of his companions seemed inclined to step aside until Baku brought his head close, snorting through his red-rimmed nostrils. As a body, they stepped hastily aside.

Reisil climbed the steps quickly, her head spinning. Baku remained inside her mind, a hungry, waiting presence. She felt him push against her link with Saljane as if testing its strength. She could speak to him, if she chose, and he would answer. Just like Saljane. She recoiled from the idea. That wasn't the way it was supposed to work.

Saljane crooned in her mind.

~He wants you to understand. To help. He wants Yohuac. He wants what we have.

She sounded absolutely certain, without any hint of envy or doubt. Reisil relaxed slightly. But she couldn't shake a certain feeling of tension and anger. The anger was directed primarily at the Verit, but also at Baku and Yohuac. She knew it wasn't fair. She didn't even know their story. But she hated what they represented. More demands, more secrets. As if she weren't already straining under enough of those. It reminded her too much of Sodur. How everything he asked of her was always about manipulating her, getting her to fall in with his plots. Was she to become a pawn to these two as well? Was she always to be at the mercy of others' so-called wisdom, never free to choose her own path?

With every step, her anger grew hotter. Reisil stalked back to her quarters. She reached for the handle of her door, realizing that she was not to have any privacy at all, and that Baku was not going to fit through the doorway.

Reisil spun around. "Baku isn't going to fit," she declared in an accusing tone.

Yohuac stiffened and took a half-step back. Then inexplicably he dropped to his knees, bowing down low to touch his head to the carpet, his hands spread wide to the side and pressed flat against the floor. It was an attitude of utter subjection.

Reisil stared. "What are you doing?"

He was mumbling something. She crouched down. It was a chant, and she didn't recognize the words. Except one: nahualli. He repeated the chant several times, seemingly with no intention of stopping.

Reisil shoved impatiently to her feet. "Fine. Sleep there. Or better yet, go find someone else to bother."

She slammed the door, fuming. "Couldn't someone show up wanting to help me?"

~The Lady sent them. Maybe they will help.

"Yes, unbonded *ahalad-kaaslane*. More likely She wants me to help them find their bond."

~Perhaps both.

Reisil grinned reluctantly. *~I'd just as soon have the recipe for curing the plague.*

Before Saljane could reply, a forlorn, yowling sound burrowed through the door and raised the hair on Reisil's arms. It was a soft, desperate cry and it melted Reisil's ire. She returned to the door and opened it. Outside Baku crouched over a kneeling Yohuac, who looked pained and guilt-ridden. The coal-drake stared at Reisil and then brushed his muzzle against Yohuac's hair and made the cry again.

Reisil sighed. "All right. But please get up off the floor."

She went to seat herself in an overstuffed chair by the fire. She heard a faint noise behind her, and when she turned, she found Baku inside, standing beside Yohuac.

"Neat trick," she said dryly, lifting Saljane down from her shoulders and cradling the goshawk on her lap.

Yohuac hesitated and then dropped to the floor crosslegged. Baku hunched down, wrapping his tail around himself like a cat, careful not to knock over any furniture. He rested his big head on the floor between Reisil and Yohuac. Reisil realized that Yohuac wasn't going to be the first to speak. "What was that out there?" She waved her arm at the door.

He answered slowly, as if picking his words carefully. "It is customary to apologize in such fashion when you have offended a nahualli."

Reisil rubbed her forehead. "That's an apology? You were groveling. And you did this in my doorway because—?"

His eyes flicked to the ivy on her cheek. Oh. That. Reisil sighed again. "It starts glowing when I get angry. And when I do magic. And if that bothers you, wait until you see what happens to my eyes. But please, let's have no more of that." She waved again toward the door. "If you don't want me to be angry, you can answer some questions." She lifted her brows challengingly, and he nodded.

"Why don't you start with where you came from and why you're looking for me."

~*I could pass it from his mind to yours,* Baku offered swiftly.

~*You can do that?*

~*It's how I gave him our language.*

Reisil thought about it a moment and then shook her head. It was a disturbing thought, looking at someone else's memories and thoughts. It seemed more than intrusive—a violation. Even if he allowed it. And she wasn't sure she wanted to share that much with anyone besides Saljane. She wasn't even comfortable just talking mind-to-mind with Baku.

~No.

~As you wish, Baku said, closing his eyes indifferently. But it was a façade.

Unaware of the exchange, Yohuac began his story in a careful, fluid voice. "My land is called Cemanahuatl. It is a rich, green land of tangled jungles, heavy rains, thick mists, great rivers and tall mountains. We have one great city and many villages. Ours is a tribal people, and each tribe is guided by nahuallis. Witch women. Like you.

"Nearly three years ago, something happened. It wrenched the seams of our land and soon rains increased and snow fell low on the mountain slopes—much lower than ever before, and much earlier. Tribes have been forced to move from their lands. The Citialin lost half their population to a mudslide. Their entire village and all their farmlands were wiped out. They were the most prosperous of any of the tribes. There have been terrible diseases and ravening creatures killing dozens of people. Those sent to hunt them don't come back, and no one ever finds their bodies.

"In the last year things have grown worse. Children grow stunted, and fewer and fewer women are fertile. There has been a blight on the kalmut and bean fields. Many tribes have used up the prey in their territories and have been forced to move. There has been bloodletting, and soon there will be war between many. What are the *tecuhtli* to do? The people have to eat and the *tecuhtli* must lead, though the nahuallis object. But the nahuallis have been able to do little. The have located the source of the corruption at Mococoa, a valley sacred to the Teotl, the Fifty-two Gods. But more they have not done. They do not know where it comes from. At first they thought it a curse made by one of the Teotl, to be repealed with sacrifices. But now they know it is something else. If we do not discover how to stop it, we will die."

He paused, frowning as he drew a deep breath, and Reisil heard his stomach growl.

"You are hungry," she said, bringing him a half-loaf of brown bread, a crock of fruit preserves and a pitcher of water. She returned to her seat, watching him tear into the bread. She had so many questions and hardly knew where to begin. She began with the one that confused her most.

"I've never heard of Cemanahuatl. Where is it?"

Yohuac set the bread down, rubbing his hand over his lips, his gaze troubled. "I do not know."

Reisil stared.

"The nahuallis opened a passage through—" He shook his head. "They took me to the Monequi—where the names of the gods are carved. They told me I was to seek the nahualli with the gold ivy on her face. Then they cast a great spell and opened a door into nothing. When I stepped through, I was elsewhere. High in mountains I had never seen before. Not even the plants or animals were familiar. It was cold. That's when Baku found me."

He closed his eyes, his face spasming. "And you refused the bond," she prompted softly.

"I am not of your world. Baku has been my guide and has given me your language and customs. But I cannot remain here. I cannot serve your Lady. I have . . . I have another destiny."

And what might that be? But Reisil didn't ask. His face was shuttered against further questions. "All right. So why come searching for me? What do these nahuallis of yours hope for?"

Yohuac settled his forearms on his knees, hands dangling loosely. "When it became clear that the destruction was no curse from the gods, the nahuallis from many villages gathered in one of the sacred places. Together they performed a great magic. Some died in the effort. But what they learned was this. The corruption has its roots in your world. And that someone must seek you out."

"Why?"

He shook his head. "I do not know. I do not know if they themselves know."

"What about Baku? What did he tell you?" She glanced at Baku, but his eyes remained closed as if sleeping. He did not offer any answer.

"We have not spoken much."

Reisil nodded, recalling those painful days after she'd

refused her bond with Saljane. She smiled down at the goshawk nestled in her lap and stroked her back.

~Thank the Lady you did not give up easily.

A noise rumbled in Baku's chest. She'd forgotten he still lurked in her mind and felt a pang of guilt. His anger flared suddenly, and his bitter rage swarmed her again. She collapsed in her chair, unable to move, still unwilling to sever him from her mind. The healer in her knew how much he needed the connection, how painful Yohuac's denial was. But she felt the edges of her consciousness fraying, felt herself sliding down into black nothingness.

"Baku. Baku! Stop! Stop it now!" Yohuac stood over her, his cheeks flushed, grasping her chin in a firm grip, his other hand on her shoulder to steady her.

Reisil drew a deep, ragged breath, and then another, as Baku withdrew sulkily from her mind.

"Easy. Breathe slowly." Yohuac's voice was gentle, and he moved his hands to her shoulders, where he rubbed at her knotted muscles. He smelled of wind and woodsmoke. Reisil relaxed into his touch, closing her eyes and letting her head fall back against her chair. Yohuac continued rubbing her shoulders for several minutes and then stepped away.

Reisil opened her eyes languidly. "Thank you."

Yohuac nodded and dropped back to the floor.

Exhaustion caught up with Reisil, and she fought the heavy weight dragging at her. "So why send you?"

He shrugged, looking away, lips pulling tight. "The nahuallis chose me."

"But you know why."

"Yes."

"And?" When he didn't answer, Reisil pushed again. "Secrets aren't going to help. I know that much at least."

He considered for a moment and then nodded, still looking away as he spoke. "I am the first son of the Oceotl tribe. I am the greatest hunter, and the most skilled in fighting. For this I was selected." He stopped, but Reisil waited, sensing there was more. "The nahuallis are women. My sisters and mother are nahualli, as are all the women ancestors of my line. No man has ever been known to show such abilities. Except me."

"You?" Reisil leaned forward, coming fully awake. "You can use magic?"

He shook his head. "I am not trained. But as I said, I have a destiny. If I do not return . . . It was thought that to send me was to also offer a great sacrifice and thus gain the gods' goodwill."

Reisil stared, dumbfounded.

"And now I have arrived, and you tell me that you cannot help."

Reisil lifted one shoulder. "We too are facing many problems akin to yours. A plague, drought, dangerous creatures. A few years ago our enemies attacked a town on the border between Kodu Riik and Patverseme. The wizards cast some sort of spell there. Mysane Kosk was destroyed. Or so we thought. We still aren't sure what they did. But we know now it's the cause of our troubles, and from your description, somehow it's the cause of yours."

She held out her hands, turning them over. "I have some magical ability, but like you, I am not trained."

"Do you say there is no hope?"

Reisil shook her head even as her heart quailed. She wasn't ready to give up yet. "The wizards who destroyed Mysane Kosk were banished, and no one knows where to find them. They are the only ones who know what they have done and how to reverse it."

"You think they will tell you this?"

"They don't have any reason not to." Except that she'd killed a hundred of them. "The war is over and they've no reason to want the destruction to continue." Except their hatred for Kodu Riik, except their need for a new land now that they'd been banished.

"When will you seek them?"

Reisil's lips twisted as if she'd bitten into a crab apple. "It's not that easy. I also serve, and I am told I am more valuable here."

"You do not believe it."

She shrugged. "For now. Until I can figure out the next step. Between you and the Scallacians, I'm not sure what to do." She brushed several strands of loose hair from her forehead. "For now you must pretend to be *ahalad-kaaslane*. They still might try to kill you, but you're the

first *ahalad-kaaslane* pairing since the Lady's withdrawal.
Which suggests She's not so far gone after all. That will
help keep you safe."

She turned to Baku, who was looking at her now, reinforcing her thoughts with words. "There are those who
want to kill me. They've tried twice now, and when you
overwhelm my mind, I am helpless. If you don't want me
dead, you have to control yourself."

"Who wants to kill you?" Yohuac demanded.

"At this point, I'm only certain of who doesn't. And I
can count them on one hand."

"We will guard you," Yohuac declared, and Baku
snorted agreement.

Reisil smiled. If they expected an argument, they weren't
getting one. "I'm going to bed. You two make yourselves
as comfortable as you can. There are blankets there. I have
an appointment at dawn, which," she said yawning, "is all
of a couple hours away. Good night."

And with that she settled Saljane on her perch, stripped
off her boots, and climbed into bed, not bothering to un-
dress. She fell asleep as soon as her head hit the pillow,
dreaming of tunnels of stone lit by shining jewels and colored fire.

Chapter 27

Emelovi sat hunched on her bed, knuckles pressed
against her lips. Dared she go? She couldn't wait much
longer if she didn't want Aare to catch her. Her legs
twitched, and she swallowed, mouth dry. He was angry. If
he caught her . . . Fear raced like spiders along her spine.
She scooted up onto her pillows and shoved her feet under
the bedclothes.

But she could not bring herself to relax. Aare was up to
something. He meant to have the regency. No, she cor-

rected herself, he meant to have their father's crown. And he didn't care how many bodies he left in his wake.

Emelovi kicked her legs free and slid down off her bed, determination lending her courage. She couldn't stand by and let Aare steal Kodu Riik from their father. How would he forgive her when he decided to resume his rule?

She crossed her door, glanced out at the empty drawing rooms beyond and then locked it. She went to her wardrobe and removed her dressing gown and nightdress, stuffing them out of sight. Glancing over her shoulder at the empty room, Emelovi went to the wainscotting on the left side of the hearth. She ran her fingers over the paneling about four feet from the edge of the marble mantelpiece, carved like gryphons. It was linen-fold paneling colored like dark honey. It showed no obvious signs of the secret catch that Emelovi was looking for. Two catches actually, one at the height of her knee; the other lower, three feet away, near the floor. It was an awkward position, half-lying on the floor, arms stretched wide, face pressed against the cool wood.

The hidden door made no sound as its latches released. Emelovi grasped a candle and crawled beneath the skirts of her dressing table, adjusting the cloth behind her to cover signs of her passage. She pushed open the door and crawled inside the tunnel; its stone walls were cool and dry. Inside she found the leggings and a light tunic still folded where she'd left them. She pulled these on, then picked up her candle, not giving herself time to think about what she was doing.

The passage was narrow, hardly tall enough to stand in. The walls were thick, but always she worried that someone might hear. She didn't think Aare knew of the wall passages. But if he suspected for a second that he was watched from within the walls, he'd level the palace.

The passage turned and twisted and folded back on itself. Aare's apartments were on the same level as hers, separated by a variety of private dining rooms, salons and offices, as well as linen closets, storage pantries and sleeping quarters for the ladies' maids and Aare's personal servants. The passage wound its way through and around these many rooms, offering entry to some, spyholes to others.

Emelovi moved without hesitation. She'd discovered this

maze of passageways as a child. Her father had allowed her
to play in his offices so long as she remained quiet, sometimes forgetting her presence altogether. One late evening,
she woke from her nest of pillows and blankets behind a
couch in the corner farthest from his desk.

"And you are quite sure no one else is aware of these
tunnels?" her father was asking someone.

"Not at all," answered Fresiik, her father's historian. "It
is quite possible someone else knows. Or that this information has been handed down generation to generation in
some noble house, against the hopeful eventuality of taking
power. Or that it has been noted in someone's journal
somewhere—perhaps the master mason who built the walls,
the architect, the builders . . . any number of souls. But the
odds are in our favor. If you did not know, if I found a
passing mention of them in an obscure diary by a centuries-
dead Iisand, then chances are no one else knows. But either
way, now that you know, you can make use of them as
you please."

"We must first find a room where these passages have
no access. I want a place that's absolutely safe from prying
eyes. And then I want those passages mapped. By someone
reliable. But not *ahalad-kaaslane*. I don't want this information shared with anyone."

Emelovi remembered that moment as the one and only
time her father had hinted at anything less than total trust
in the *ahalad-kaaslane*. Thinking about it now, she wondered at his caution. Upsakes had been a frequent visitor
to the palace then. Had her father already suspected him?

"As you wish, Daz Samir. Is there anyone in particular
you have in mind?"

"I don't suppose you're available?"

There was a dry laugh.

"Perhaps I should show you."

Emelovi heard footsteps and peered out from behind her
couch. Fresiik went to a glassed-in bookcase built into the
opposite wall. He stood stiffly, his tall form angular and
stooped, his gray hair thinning, though his eyebrows remained bushy and wild. He searched for a moment in the
rich carving adorning the bookcase and found a tiny lever
along the back. It was hardly noticeable, only the length of

a fingernail. Later when she went to find it herself, Emelovi had difficulty discovering it, though she had seen exactly where it was.

Between the bookcase and the fireplace, a panel swung quietly inward, and behind it gaped a passageway, this one only four feet square.

"As you can see, Daz Samir, I am not entirely suited for crawling about in the walls," Fresiik said.

"I should probably do it myself."

"Yes sir. What about the young Verit?"

The Iisand shook his head, unsmiling. "I don't think so."

Fresiik raised his brows but did not argue.

"I'll give it to Limedus. I can trust him."

"I would have suggested him," agreed Fresiik. "And he's young enough to get about with greater ease than this old carcass."

And so Emelovi had discovered the passageways and an entrance in. She was sure Limedus had completed the mapping of the passages, but whether Aare had discovered the map in her father's papers, she did not know. Fresiik was dead these last five years and would not have revealed the existence of the passages to anyone. Limedus had died in the war.

Now she turned and entered Aare's domain. A shiver streaked down her back, and she stopped, drawing several deep breaths. Then she began again, more slowly. She turned, and turned again, and when she did, she blew out the candle. The trip back would be very dark, but she never took the chance that the glow of the flame might give her away.

She crawled now. The air grew warmer, heated by the hearth in Aare's quarters. She squirmed into place, hearing the rumble of voices inside. She released the latches on the door and opened it a crack. Her father had hung a beautifully worked arras over the opening. Hidden behind the heavy weaving, Emelovi was less concerned about being seen than heard, and she forced herself to sit very still, breathing slowly and quietly, sweat dampening her brow.

"Damned *ahalad-kaaslane* tricks, that's what." Emelovi recognized the voice. Prensik. "How'd the Scallacians take it?"

"Hag knows. Faces like jasper, those two," Aare said. "The bastards eye every vase and footstool like moneylenders come to collect on a debt."

Prensik laughed and quickly cut it off as if becoming aware that Aare had not intended to be funny. Emelovi could well imagine Aare's expression. A raised eyebrow, a look of disdain colored with a bare hint of disapproval.

"They intend to support me, I'm sure of that. Suits their purposes to have me on the throne and to be rid of the plague, the *nokulas* and the *ahalad-kaaslane*."

Hearing the last, Emelovi gasped and covered her open mouth with both hands. Get rid of the *ahalad-kaaslane*? The Lady would never allow it! But everyone knew the Lady had weakened, perhaps withdrawn Her protection altogether. Emelovi shook her head. But to abandon Her . . . It was too awful a thing to contemplate, even for Aare.

"What about the Lord Marshal?"

"Ah, yes. We'll see about him in time. In the meantime, he helped bring the sorcerers here, now, didn't he? And he wants to see the plague and *nokulas* gone as much as I do. Nor has he much faith in the *ahalad-kaaslane* these days. Tonight's performance will do little to improve his opinion of that *ganyik*, Reisiltark. I'll have what I need from him. He's nothing if not predictable.

"What I want you to do is set men to watch Reisiltark and this new *ahalad-kaaslane*. I want to know everything they do. Absolutely everything, to the smallest detail."

"Yes, Daz Varakamber."

"Then you may go."

Prensik coughed. "Sir?"

"Yes?"

"What of Emelovi?"

Emelovi tensed, clutching her arms tightly around her knees.

Aare chuckled. It was a sneering sound. "Worried about your heirs, are you? Or afraid she's turned on me? Let me set your mind at ease. On both counts. My sister is mine and mine alone. Her loyalty cannot be bent. I trust her, Prensik, because her fear of me is complete. She has been well trained, like a good bitch, to sit, to heel, and to do my bidding exactly. She breathes at my will, and she knows it. What benefits me, benefits her.

"Her actions this evening were in service to me, to encourage a connection with Reisiltark so that Emelovi might gain information for me. Reisiltark is losing followers in droves amongst those who count. Not even the *ahaladkaaslane* confide in her. She is ripe for conquest, and my sister has begun that for me. If I can turn her to my hand, then Reisiltark will be a superior tool."

Hearing his words, Emelovi sagged, tears streaming down her cheeks. He'd taken her to task earlier, and she'd pleaded that she had thought to please him. But until this moment, she hadn't been sure that he'd accepted her explanation, that he wasn't planning retribution.

"She wants a friend, and if I am that friend, then you will know her mind," she had said, hands clasped together to keep them from shaking.

"And what did you talk about?"

"Kaj Vadonis. She warned me that he was difficult, rude and arrogant."

"Interesting. They are not good friends, then." Aare sounded pleased. "Anything else?"

Emelovi licked her lips. They had talked for some time. Aare would never believe that Kaj Vadonis had taken all their attention. "She seemed very alone and even frightened. She apologized for not saving Mother."

Aare shrugged and turned away to seat himself, smiling enigmatically up at Emelovi. "Did she now . . . Anything else?"

"Just . . . well, she seemed nervous and she didn't like the sorcerers at all."

"I see."

"Did I—? Did I do right?" She was disgusted with the quavering note in her voice, but she could not suppress it.

"You were irreproachable, as always, little sister. But I should certainly ask first next time."

Emelovi had nodded, fear closing like a fist around her heart. "Of course. It only occurred to me as she came in the door. I had not planned it."

"Of course not." And Emelovi couldn't tell if he believed that she wouldn't have planned it without asking, or that she was incapable of intrigue. It didn't matter. Either was better for her. Now Aare began speaking again to Prensik.

"As for heirs, you may be assured. I'd sooner let her lie

with my hounds than marry Patversemese scum. But
sniffing after her keeps Vadonis occupied, and I encouraged
my sister tonight to get closer to him. I need his attention
fixed on her and not on the sorcerers.

"You may go now, Prensik. Do establish that watch on
Reisiltark and these new *ahalad-kaaslane* before you find
your bed. And try to be discreet."

Emelovi heard the door open and close, and she waited.
Sweat dampened her tunic between her breasts and trickled
down her ribs. A knock came, almost beyond her hearing.
The door opened and closed.

"How's our guest?" Aare asked.

"Exactly as you ordered," came a lower, rougher voice.
It wasn't as cultured as Prensik's, but clearly the man had
been educated. "The wounds are healing, but he's none too
comfortable. Bad-tempered."

"And the other?"

"I sent them off. Pelodra with them. He won't be coming back."

"Good. How long before they get there?"

"Depends. I sent a solid crew. Two dozen men. Bandits
and *nokulas* are getting to be bad. But even moving slow
and fighting their way through, no more than two weeks.
They'll bring the Vadonis girl to the garrison at Gudsiil. The
men are loyal there, and no one will ask questions. Nor
will she find anyone who will want to aid her escape."

The Vadonis girl? Emelovi tensed. What could Aare
want with her? She shuddered. Nothing good. His next
words confirmed her suspicions.

"Very good. If my sister can't hold Vadonis's attention
by seduction, then I will have the means to hold it by force.
One more thing before you go. I've set Prensik to watch
Reisiltark and her new *ahalad-kaaslane* friends. You do the
same. Anything on Sodur?"

"Nothing. He's been sticking to himself, keeping up his
visits to your father. Hasn't been to the Temple for several days."

"I wonder . . . has he had a falling out with the *ahalad-
kaaslane*?" There was delighted spite in Aare's voice now,
and Emelovi frowned. Sodur was her father's best friend,
his closest adviser but for the Lord Marshal. Few *ahalad-
kaaslane* failed to heed him when he spoke. If he had lost

his status, then Aare's road to the regency, to the crown itself, was nearly clear. Only a few stubborn nobles, the Lord Marshal, and their father stood in his way. Emelovi trembled. Already he was taking steps to gain the support of the nobles and Lord Marshal. Which left their father. And Aare didn't like loose ends. It wouldn't be enough to get him to abdicate. It wouldn't be enough to have him declared incompetent. No, Aare would want to completely destroy any possibility that their father could retake the throne, and there was only one way to be certain.

Emelovi shoved her fists against her mouth, tears trickling down her cheeks. She had to stop him. But how?

She should tell someone. But who? One name popped into her head: Reisiltark. She was the only one Aare couldn't predict or control. She was the only one who could challenge the sorcerers and win. But Aare was having Reisiltark watched, both by Prensik and by this other man. There was no way to talk to her. Emelovi's mind raced. What about Kaj Vadonis? He and Reisiltark were friends, and Aare had told her to spend more time with him.

She nodded resolutely. She would not allow Aare to murder their father. If Kaj Vadonis and Reisiltark wouldn't help her on her father's behalf, they would to keep Aare from destroying the *ahalad-kaaslane* and beginning another war with Patverseme. And with Aare sending kidnappers after his sister, Kaj Vadonis would be eager to thwart Aare.

Emelovi waited to retreat until Aare went to bed. She lay awake the rest of the night, plotting her next step. She must not allow Aare to know anyone had eavesdropped on him, but she must also tell Kaj Vadonis about his sister, before it was too late to help her. He would react strongly, she knew, and so they must have privacy. And then he must act quietly. It would be best if Kaj Vadonis's men got to Ceriba. They could hide her and tell Aare's men she was dead, killed by the plague or by *nokulas*. A pang struck Emelovi. Indeed, that could well be the truth. *Lady, keep her safe. Keep us all safe.*

Chapter 28

Reisil woke just as the first light crept beneath the cracks of her windows. With a groan, she pushed back her bedclothes and clambered out of bed, stumbling to the washstand and rinsing her face in the icy water. She fumbled her boots on and buckled her gauntlet into place, lifting Saljane to her shoulder. But when she turned to leave, she found Yohuac slouching in the doorjamb. He nodded and stepped aside as she approached. Reisil paused, wondering what to say, and then walked past. He and Baku followed. Kebonsat was going to have a surprise this morning.

She stopped first in the kitchens, pilfering a fresh loaf of bread, a couple of shriveled apples and a leftover slab of roasted goat from the night's feast. She gestured to Yohuac to follow suit, the kitchen staff ducking beneath the long preparation tables and pressing against the walls, cooks brandishing knives and long-handled spoons as Baku trailed them through the room. The trio departed the kitchens, following the wide gravel walk to the slaughter yard, past the stables and out to the copse of bare-limbed trees where she and Kebonsat had arranged to meet.

~You should go out and hunt this morning while I begin my lessons, she told Saljane.

~I ate yesterday.

~I know. But go when you can. I'll be safe.

Reisil lifted Saljane onto her fist and tossed the goshawk into the air, watching fondly as Saljane beat her wings and rose like an arrow to disappear into the low-slung clouds.

~Good hunting!

Exhilaration. Eagerness. Strength.

Baku snarled in her mind. Reisil ignored his testiness, nodding a greeting to Kebonsat as he materialized out of the trees, their ice-sheathed branches shining like crystal. Kebonsat returned Reisil's nod, his attention fixed on Yohuac and Baku.

"New friends?"

"*Ahalad-kaaslane*. In a manner of speaking."

Kebonsat lifted his brows, but Reisil didn't explain, and instead introduced Yohuac and Baku. "They arrived last night," Reisil said, covering a yawn with her hand, wincing as her jaw cracked. "Late last night."

"I heard something about it."

"I imagine it was startling."

Kebonsat lifted his shoulder. "I'm getting used to that sort of thing." He studied Yohuac for a moment, but asked nothing further before turning back to Reisil. "You're late. We should get started."

Reisil followed him through the copse to a small cleared space beyond, out of sight of the main barracks and parade grounds.

"I have this for you." Kebonsat lifted a scabbarded sword from where it leaned against the bole of a smooth-skinned maple. He unbuckled the belt straps and straightened them from their careful coil.

"Might as well begin here. It isn't as simple as it looks." He then showed her how to buckle the sword around her hips. Twice around, one strap higher than the other, then adjusting the scabbard low on her left side. "The wide part should go around your back—it's more comfortable. Using the double-around lends you some balance, makes the sword easier to carry, especially when you're walking. You're going to need to wear this all day long for the next month just to get used to it. It's going to tangle your legs, catch on furniture and generally annoy the spit out of you. And that's just walking. Sitting is a whole new game of dice. Try it."

Reisil paced away, the sword an unfamiliar weight on her left hip. It rocked back and forth and in and out with every step, jouncing against her calves and tangling in her cloak, the pommel poking her side and knocking against her elbow. She walked back and forth, feeling very foolish, as if she were dressed up for a masquerade.

"All right, that's enough for now. Take it off. We're going to be working with practice swords for a while."

It took Reisil several minutes to sort out the buckles and unwind the belt from her waist. Kebonsat showed her how to loop the belt around the scabbard to keep it from tangling or dragging. Next he handed her a dull-edged practice blade, scarred from heavy use. Its wire grip was long enough to be held with two hands. Kebonsat showed her how to hold it with her thumb lengthwise along the grip for control, and he encouraged her to take several practice swings.

"It doesn't feel heavy now, but trust me, before we're through your arms will feel like porridge. Now keep your wrist stiff but flexible, like that. Same with your elbow." Kebonsat prodded at her, bending her arm into position. "The gauntlet is going to make it hot and strange for you, limit your movement some, but chances are you'll be wearing it whenever fighting becomes necessary, and no one is going to give you time to strip it off, so you may as well learn to fight with it on."

Kebonsat grabbed another practice sword and took his position opposite her.

"Keep your shoulders square to me. Narrow your stance. You'll need to keep your weight forward on the balls of your feet and keep them under you—shoulder-width apart. Now, let's jump right in. This is just to get you used to handling the sword and for me to see what you can do, so just concentrate on not getting hit. Don't try to block blows with strength alone. Winning most often comes down to who gets tired first. Raise your blade and step to the side, shoving away my blade along the line of the blow."

With that Kebonsat launched a slow series of blows that Reisil was forced to counter. Her sword vibrated in her hands as he struck, and she only just barely managed to keep from dropping it, dodging away like a scared rabbit.

"Keep your grip firm, just as if you were chopping wood with an ax. Same principle. Let your arms absorb some of the blow, and push the rest aside. There you go," he said as Reisil deflected the next strike, turning awkwardly and dropping her swordpoint nearly to the ground. "Face me directly—you can't fend off a left-sided attack if your body is turned to the right. Keep your feet under you—no, don't fall back on your heels. You'll have no power behind your sword at all."

The lesson ended more than an hour later. Reisil was drenched, and her entire body shook with strain. She could no longer hold her sword upright, and her heart pounded.

"Good," Kebonsat said, hardly winded. "It's a good beginning. You need conditioning, though. I suggest at the very least you run up the stairs to your room as quickly as you can manage every time you go up. If you can find an opportunity to chop some wood, that would benefit you as well: harden your hands and put on some muscle. Try also squatting rather than sitting, and you'll want to practice diving and rolling. Tomorrow we'll begin in earnest."

Reisil stared at him, unable even to swipe away the sweat trickling down her forehead. "In earnest?"

"Today you simply got a feel for the sword. Tomorrow you'll start learning form and technique."

"Tomorrow I won't be able to move."

"True. But give it a week or so, and you'll start feeling better."

"I need a bath. A long, hot one. And my cloak," Reisil said, shivering as the chill wind cut through her damp clothes. Yohuac leaped to his feet from the place he'd been sitting and settled her cloak over her shoulders. Reisil pulled up the hood and snuggled inside, wishing for a cup of hot kohv.

"Maybe this will help," Kebonsat said, and brought out a basket containing bread, cheese, custard tarts and a tall corked jar. Reisil reached eagerly for the cup of kohv he held out. He held the other out to Yohuac, who shook his head with a slight smile.

"You have done the work this morning. I would suggest hobbles for her feet tomorrow."

"Hobbles? Like a horse?" Reisil asked incredulously.

Kebonsat nodded. "Similar. Keeps you from putting your feet too wide. I hadn't thought about it, but it would be faster."

"There are also some exercises that may aid in strength, flexibility and reflexes," Yohuac continued. "She has a habit of dropping her left shoulder. And she wants to stand too close, probably because she trusts you."

Soon he and Kebonsat were involved in a discussion

about her training, of which Reisil understood only a bare one in four words. She sat down cross-legged and began munching on the food and sipping the kohv with half-lidded eyes. Her body was one big ache, and already she was beginning to stiffen. Reisil thought longingly of her bed.

She felt a movement behind her and found Baku curling around her. She leaned gratefully into his bulk, feeling sudden warmth radiating through her back. Reisil sighed.

~*Thank you.*

~*You are welcome.*

Reisil felt Baku relax beneath her as a long sigh shuddered down his length. There was an easing in her mind, as if he no longer needed to cling with such a desperate grip. Suddenly she became aware that Yohuac and Kebonsat had fallen silent. Kebonsat was frowning at her while Yohuac bit into a custard tart. He chewed, eyeing the pastry with a surprised, pleased expression. Kebonsat cast a sidelong glance at the other man and then looked back at Reisil.

"About last night," he said, trailing off meaningfully.

About the assassin's attack, he meant. "Go ahead. Yohuac already knows." At least that someone was trying to kill her. Probably he knew all the details that Baku had rummaged from her mind.

~*I am his* ahalad-kaaslane, Baku said acerbically.

Even if Yohuac was determined not to be. How long could Baku chase after Yohuac if the man remained steadfast in his denial?

Kebonsat's frown deepened. "All right. My man found nothing to suggest that anyone inside Koduteel is responsible for the attack. Many seem to think it would be a good idea—a quick solution to an irritating problem—but no one here seems to have taken that step yet. That said, Rocis could find no hint of who might be responsible. He may, in time, discover more, but he is very good, and for him to have found nothing at all—" Kebonsat shook his head, his expression troubled. "This is well planned and well financed. Whoever's behind it isn't using local talent. Our assassin is good enough to keep hidden, and yet he's managed to get into the palace, all the way to your quarters.

Reisil chewed her lip. She had to tell him about the first attempt on her life. He couldn't help her without knowing the truth. "They. There were more. There may still be more." Then she told him about being chased down the bluff. "I killed three," she said tonelessly. "At least one got away, maybe more. I couldn't tell. If my magic hadn't come at just that moment . . ."

Suddenly she stiffened.

~It was you! The presence in my mind, the thing that answered when I called. Your magic sparked mine somehow.

Was it possible that Baku's magic had somehow tainted hers? Had it been his rage, his brutality she had felt at killing the assassins?

~Magic is itself. I quickened yours, it is true. But how you used it—that was you. Your choice. You choose your own path. We all do.

Reisil slumped. All her. There was no escape.

~Thank you, she said finally to Baku.

~Do you wish you had not killed them?

~Yes. No. I know it was necessary. I wish it hadn't been. I just hate how much I liked it.

~Did you? Or did you like the magic answering at last?

~Isn't it the same? Reisil asked bitterly.

~Is it?

Baku fell silent, and Reisil rubbed her ear. Was he right? She thought back to the moment. The brilliant fire from her hands. The ashy outlines on the ground. That release of fierce joy and triumph. She shook her head. She couldn't separate it out. Her lips tightened, and she felt her face harden. It didn't matter. She had to stop stewing about it and get on with stopping the plague and figuring out what to do about the nokulas. About the Iisand.

Reisil set her cup down. She had no doubt that they were being watched. Dared she speak?

~No one will overhear.

And then Reisil felt something move through her and outward toward the edges of the clearing. She went cold. She looked quizzically at Yohuac.

"The na—" Yohuac broke off, correcting himself. "Reisiltark would speak. Baku has made certain no one will eavesdrop."

Reisil waited until the wary Kebonsat had seated himself. "I am told the Iisand has become a nokula. Nokulas are altered beasts and people," she declared bluntly. Kebonsat jerked upright, his dark eyes flaring.

"Altered how?"

"Whatever your wizards did at Mysane Kosk. Their magic has been spreading, twisting all it touches. Yohuac comes from a land that has been infected by it. The plague is also the result of the magic done there. And I have no ability to cure it. I have tried. It has already begun to creep into the Fringes. Soon it will spread throughout Koduteel."

Kebonsat seemed curiously unsurprised at this news. "It was spreading this way. It could not be held off for long. What are you planning?"

"I wanted to go to the wizards. They cast the spell in Mysane Kosk; they ought to know how to repair what they've done. But with the sorcerers here now . . . Sodur thinks it would be dangerous to leave. After what our guests did at the reception last night, I can't disagree. I have to stay in Koduteel. Yohuac adds another wrinkle to things. He was sent here to find me—" Reisil broke off.

Yohuac repeated what he'd told Reisil the night before. When he was through, Kebonsat glanced at Reisil, smiling ironically. "Everyone seems to think you're the key, and no one, not even you, knows how. Not a position to envy, that." He turned from Reisil back to Yohuac. "How did you come to be *ahalad-kaaslane* if you are not even of this world?" Kebonsat asked.

"I am not."

Before Kebonsat could ask anything more, Baku tensed.

~Someone comes.

"Someone comes," Yohuac echoed, climbing to his feet with Reisil and Kebonsat.

~A servant. From the Vertina Emelovi. She seeks Kebonsat.

Yohuac repeated the report to Kebonsat, who looked astounded.

"How can you know that?"

"Because Baku can speak to whomever he chooses. And pick information out of their thoughts," Reisil said before Yohuac could answer.

"Useful," Kebonsat said, looking disturbed.

Reisil understood. Were no one's thoughts safe? Would Baku know everyone's secrets? And thus Yohuac? The potential for his ability was staggering. He could spy out the plans of their enemies, of the sorcerers, of anyone at all.

Was that why the Lady had sent Baku to Yohuac? Sent them to Reisil? But no. It lacked . . . honor. Perhaps she shouldn't be concerned with honor when the safety of Kodu Riik hung in the balance. But remembering Upsakes and what he was willing to do in the name of the Lady and the good of Kodu Riik, Reisil felt queasy.

"I think we have to be careful. I don't think we can rule out asking Baku for help, but—" She gestured helplessly.

"But neither friends nor enemies will trust us if we violate their minds indiscriminately," Kebonsat said.

"I don't have very many friends. I would very much like to keep them," Reisil said wryly.

"None of us do. Not here."

"Baku," Reisil said, turning to the coal-drake where he crouched on the ground, the tip of his tail snapping back and forth, his white teeth gleaming like daggers along his jaw. For a moment Reisil didn't know what to say. He was already angry, already resentful. He had a great gift to offer, and now she was going to tell him his skills were unwanted. Just as Yohuac did not want him. But then Reisil realized it wasn't that way at all. She laid a hand on his head, meeting his hostile gaze earnestly.

"Baku, we must trust you. You are the master of our secrets. You are a great advantage to us—through you we can communicate with one another. We can ask you to pass messages more quickly and reliably than we might otherwise be able. But the trust between all of us comes from knowing that each one of us will reveal what is important when it is important. And to trust that our friends will do the same. So we must ask you *not* to share all that you hear in someone's mind. We must ask you to consider carefully before you divulge what you think we must know."

She was extending him a great trust, one that could put their lives in danger.

~I will guard well.

Reisil nodded and straightened. "It will be well," she said to the two men. "But here comes the Vertina's messenger," she said, hearing a crackle of twigs and ice beneath stolid feet.

Kebonsat frowned. "She hasn't spoken more than five words together to me. What could she want? And at this time of the morning?"

"You're about to find out." Reisil's heart twinged, watching him step to meet the liveried messenger. Baku nudged at her arm, and she turned to give him a smile and then collected up the basket and crockery.

~*We are friends*. He sounded uncertain.

~*We are friends*. She and Baku and Kebonsat and maybe even Yohuac. And don't forget Juhrnus and Metyein. You have more friends than you had a few days ago, she told herself, her heart feeling suddenly lighter.

"My presence is requested for breakfast," Kebonsat said, folding up the note and tucking it in his belt. "I must be off. Same time tomorrow. Don't forget. Take your sword with you and wear it."

He waved and disappeared through the trees, carrying with him the practice weapons.

"I want a bath," Reisil said. "And I'd like to hear more of your land, if you will."

Yohuac gave that bow he'd given her the night before. "I would like that."

"And the nahuallis. I definitely want to hear about them."

Yohuac picked up her sword and followed after her, not answering.

Chapter 29

The long winter had at long last begun to release its icy grasp on the land. The days were warming, and spring rains had begun to fall. It was a cause for celebration, as hungry people prepared garden plots for carefully hoarded seeds. The days passed swiftly and uneventfully, if one did not count the expanding numbers of plague victims in the Fringes. It had become more difficult to enter the city. No one was admitted without proper documentation and inspection. Those who departed could not be certain they would be allowed to return.

The sorcerers had done little as far as Reisil could tell, either to aid Kodu Riik or to attack. On the single occasion Reisil had cornered Sodur in the three weeks since the Scallacians' arrival, he informed her that it had been decided it was too early to trust the sorcerers with the truth about the Iisand. The Scallacians would have to prove their good intentions and abilities by first curing the plague. Then a *nokula* would be captured for them to cure. And finally, if all was well, they would be asked to aid the Iisand.

Sodur was peculiarly distracted and evasive. "They have been quite cordial, I am told. Our Lord Marshal does not trust them. Of course. But that is his job, after all." He dodged her gaze.

"You haven't asked about Yohuac and Baku," Reisil began.

Sodur waved a hand. "No time. They want you. Don't tell them anything. Don't trust anyone. Anyone!" He stared piercingly at her for a fleeting moment and then hurried away, Lume trotting at his heels. The lynx turned back once to look at Reisil.

Sodur's behavior was nothing less than Reisil had come to expect, and yet his obvious eagerness to be away from her opened her wounds afresh. All over again, Reisil felt betrayed, and angry that she should feel so. Worse was his lack of interest in Yohuac and Baku. Nor had any of the *ahalad-kaaslane* welcomed them. It was almost as if their contact with her had tainted them, made them untouchable. If only she could have news from the *ahalad-kaaslane* who were still her friends. Fehra, Reikon, Felias, Bethorn. She wouldn't feel so alone.

She continued her morning sword lessons. As agonizing as that first week had been. Reisil was proud of how far she'd progressed. Being able to swing a sword to some purpose was liberating. Not that she could hope to defeat anyone with any skill. But she was no longer an easy target, and with time and practice, she'd do better than just hold her own.

Few had noticed the addition of the weapon to her wardrobe, with the exceptions of Juhrnus and Metyein, both of whom snickered at her obvious discomfort, though they applauded her for learning. Not that she saw much of either of them. Metyein could not speak to her publicly, making his remarks under his breath as if talking to a bowl of crystal ornaments or a shelf of books, while Juhrnus was occupied by the sorceress. When he wasn't with Kedisan-Mutira, he was with Metyein, scouring Koduteel for information. And there wasn't much good news.

As she expected, Yohuac and Baku's arrival had stirred up a storm of animosity and suspicion against all three of them. Yohuac and Baku were her constant companions wherever she went. Yohuac, despite his quiet, brooding demeanor, enjoyed a good joke and would divert her with songs and tales of his land. Reisil returned the favor, her presence easing the tension between Yohuac and Baku.

They accompanied her to the Fringes, where she did her best to help the plague victims with her store of medicines, offering comfort when she could do nothing else. In the last week, the numbers of plague victims seemed to double every few days. Reisil couldn't begin to guess how many were infected or how many had already died. With the citizens of the city growing more and more frightened, blaming the Fringe population for the spread of the plague, the Fringe folk kept the sick hidden.

On those days she worked in the Fringes, Reisil could do little more in the evenings than retreat to the privacy of her room, too exhausted and hopeless to face the malicious tongues of the court. Or the oily sorcerers. Far from being condescending or spiteful, they were ingratiating and glib. They liked to brush against her, to stand too close, to watch her as a cat watches a mouse—hungry and eager. She tolerated it, knowing it was necessary. From what Kedisan-Mutira had told Juhrnus, they would eagerly cultivate a relationship with Reisil, if only to gather information.

But she could not tolerate their insinuations and invitations, not on the nights after the Fringes. Then it felt like she no longer had skin, like every nerve was exposed, every muscle raw and throbbing. She was grateful for Saljane and Baku, who nestled around her. They said nothing, but their affection and concern were palpable. To distract her, Yohuac told her stories of his village. Eventually she would

drift into a heavy, dreamless sleep. Reisil didn't doubt that
Saljane and Baku had something to do with her lack of
nightmares, but she made no complaints.

"You never speak of the nahuallis," Reisil accused Yohuac one night after listening to a lengthy story about a
young woman and her eccentric husband. Her eyes were
gritty, her head throbbing, but she didn't yet want to sleep.

"I had hoped you had not noticed."

"Did you think my ears fell off?" Reisil turned her head
back and forth, showing him that they remained attached
to her head.

He flushed, staring at her stockinged feet as she sat
against a mound of pillows on her bed. The tall doors to
the balcony were propped open a few inches, the spring
breeze chilly but welcome in rooms that had been shut up
all winter. Reisil stroked Saljane, who nestled in her lap,
sated by a meal of fresh fish. The larders in the palace had
grown sparse indeed, but there was still plenty of fish to be
had in the coastal waters. Baku too had eaten heavily, pulling an enormous fish from the ocean, chewing flesh and
bone alike and leaving nothing behind. Now he lounged
before the door, red-streaked eyes heavy.

"The nahuallis . . . We don't often speak of them."

"But aren't they the leaders of your tribe?"

"With the *tecuhtli*—the Iisand of our tribe, if you will."

Reisil turned, leaning on her elbow to look at him. "But
from what you have said, it sounds like the nahuallis are
the real leaders and the *tecuhtli* must defer to them."

"It is complicated."

Reisil waited for him to say more, and when he didn't,
she gave up and rolled onto her back with a sigh.

"The *tecuhtli* is the head of the tribe unless the nahuallis
intervene. He does not resent this. With their magic and
the favor of the Fifty-two Gods—the Teotl—they are more
wise than he.

"The nahuallis walk among tribe, eat with us, have children. The members of the tribe are careful to notice only
that which is ordinary and expected of wives and mothers
and sisters and daughters. When a nahualli wishes attention, she—" He paused, raised his hands and let them fall
back into his lap. "It is difficult to explain. We do not

normally speak of the nahuallis. They simply *are*, like the air. And like the air, they give us life. But who notices the air?"

He stopped again, gathering himself. "When a nahualli wishes the attention of the tribe, there is a change in the wind, in the earth, in the trees. A looming, as if a storm gathers in the night. Then what she speaks and what she says we will do or not do, think or not think. The Teotl speak through the nahuallis and no one, *no one*, ever disobeys. To do so is to refuse the counsel of the gods. That can only bring disaster for the entire tribe. So you can see, it is difficult for me to speak of them. I have spent my life trying to do the opposite. And what I know of them, I have been taught to forget. I will tell you what I can. Will that suffice?"

"It will. And I can learn to be patient, knowing that you are not merely avoiding my questions."

Yohuac chuckled. "You are like enough to the nahuallis to make that a dangerous proposition."

"Thank you, I think."

"You are welcome."

"Tell me something else about your people. You live in tribes scattered across your land and you move your villages from place to place within your territories following the prey. Yet you are well trained as a warrior. Kebonsat is terribly impressed at your skills. Are your tribes warriors? Do you have battles with other tribes? Do you have any cities? Who rules?"

Yohuac grinned at the barrage of questions and reached for a mug of ale. He drank it with obvious pleasure and to little ill effect. And as ale was one of the few things still plentiful in the palace, he was not forced to stint. "Answering all of those questions will take much of the night and will make me perilously dry. But I will do my best to comply, no matter how much I must suffer."

Reisil snorted. "Put water in that cup instead of ale, and I might begin to believe you."

"You would torture me, then? You are a cruel taskmaster indeed."

"Your story had better be good, or you shall have no more," Reisil said, pulling a blanket over her legs. "Go on. Don't keep me waiting all night."

"It begins with the Teotl. They are not all equal; each has strengths the others don't have. Nor are they wise and benevolent. They are greedy, suspicious and capricious. Only *Ilhuicatl* alone has strength to bind the others to his hand. He rules the sky. The sun and the moon answer to him, the clouds and the stars, the rain and the wind and the lightning and thunder. And beneath him, the earth, the oceans, the mountains, everything. He is all that's powerful, and the other gods cannot survive without his tolerance.

"Originally there were fifty-two tribes in Cemanahuatl, my homeland, each one created by the favor of one of the Teotl. Their traditions, habits and power reflected their god. But since each one of the fifty-two has strengths to dominate at least one other, or at least to withstand the power of another, the people also worshipped those others, as reflections and symbols of their primary god's powers."

Reisil shifted higher on the bed, fascinated. Yohuac paused to drink, lifting his brows at her.

"You aren't falling asleep?"

Reisil grinned. "True, you are one of the worst storytellers I have ever heard, but beggars will eat *skraa* if their bellies are empty."

"Nothing truer said, and indeed some tribes were beggars, in that they did not get to choose the gods they were to serve. This, of course, created much strife. Some tribes cared not for their new god and strove instead to prove themselves worthy to another, better god. Some wanted more prestige, better territory and wealth. Some could not stomach what was required of them by their new gods. Cannibalism, mutilation, torture, more and worse. Thus did a great many tribes shift and switch. You can imagine the chaos. No one was pleased, and the gods were bitter and angry.

"It was then *Ilhuicatl* took a hand in the bickering and wars. At first he thought to destroy all the tribes completely and put an end to the strife. But he'd grown very fond of his own tribe—the original nahuallis. And like him, his tribe answered to no other nor worshipped any other than himself. To save them, he made a great sacrifice. He released the nahuallis and sent them to the rest of the tribes to bind all to him, and yet took no tribe as his own. This only escalated the fighting, with tribes vying for the honor of becoming *Ilhuicatl*'s chosen. Then a message came. *Ilhuicatl* was tired, ready to destroy all the tribes if they could not behave. He offered one more chance, and if that failed . . ." Yohuac snapped his fingers.

"What happened?"

"He created a nation. Once every fifty-two years, a new tribe would be taken as his chosen. Once every fifty-two years, there would be a competition. Every man would compete for the honor of being named *Ilhuicatl*'s son. The winner would have riches and pleasures beyond compare, and more important, his tribe would become *Ilhuicatl*'s own until the next cycle, ruling all the others for fifty-two years."

"What kind of competition?" Reisil was sitting cross-legged, elbows on her knees, engrossed.

"It is a lengthy ordeal, and not one for the weak hearted. It tests the body in all extremes of depredation: walking over hot coals, bearing lashes of a whip, enduring poisons and much more. There is a journey over mountains, through jungle, across rivers—carrying nothing more than a knife, dressed only in a loincloth. There is physical combat—you must have been trained in all the arts and weapons if you hope to survive. And then there are feats of prowess—climbing cliffs, swimming, running, throwing, cliff-diving, hunting. Many die; others become crippled. Those who survive are taken to *Ilhuicatl*'s temple in Tizalan, our only city."

"What happens then?"

"No one knows. The final trials happen there, and only the winner emerges. He is feted. Women come from every tribe to lie with him, his seed being the seed of *Ilhuicatl*. There follows a year of rejoicing, feasts every day, his every want and wish granted. He lives in splendor, and his tribe becomes wealthy beyond compare."

"And the former ruling tribe?"

"They depart with the wealth they have gathered, returning to their homelands to prosper. They continue to be revered by all tribes. So to answer your questions, there is little war. Conflicts are taken before the elders in Tizalan, and their word is law. Every man is a warrior. The training for the *pahtia* is unceasing, though it comes only every fifty-two years. This in no small way aids in restraining wars—

there is little benefit in attacking a tribe as equally prepared
as you for war."

Reisil made to ask another question, but Yohuac interrupted. "I cannot answer all your questions tonight, and
you are in want of sleep. I have great plans for the morning." He waggled his brows warningly.

Reisil rolled her eyes. "I couldn't get enough sleep for
that if I'd gone to bed hours ago. At least I know now
where you got your ideas for torturing me."

"You said yourself. I am very good."

"And none too confident."

"A meek warrior does not win glory for his tribe."

"No danger of that."

With that she wished him good night and snuggled into
her bedclothes, falling asleep quickly and without nightmares.

~The little lizard comes.

The quiet words yanked Reisil from her dream. She sat
up. Weak light glimmered beneath the shutters on the balcony. Dawn or nearly. What brought Juhrnus at this hour?
Her stomach turned. There wasn't any good answer.

"This is a very bad sign," Yohuac said, echoing Reisil's
thoughts. They'd spent a lot of their time together dis-
cussing the political situation in Kodu Riik. Yohuac had a
sharp mind and a way of cutting through the smoke and
fog to the heart of a matter. More than that, he was detached where Reisil was not.

"Cozy," Juhrnus said when Yohuac opened the door,
flashing Reisil a grin as she adjusted her tunic around her
hips. She grinned back. Somehow she didn't mind the insin-
uation that she and Yohuac might be sharing a bed.

"Very cozy. What brings you so bright and early and
without any food?"

The smile slid from his face. "I didn't figure you'd be
very hungry after what I have to say. Went into the city
last night. Ran into our Pincushion friend." This was the
nickname Juhrnus had assigned to Metyein. Anyone eaves-
dropping would not learn his name. "He happened across
some bad news earlier in the day." He glanced over his
shoulder at the closed door and dropped his voice. "Very
bad news. Kodu Riik is cut off. The waters are blockaded.

In Patverseme there are archers strung along the length of the Sadelema. North into Gulto is the same. We're cut off completely."

"Completely? No trade? No food? How is that possible?" Reisil didn't recognize the sound of her own voice.

Juhrnus shook his head. "The Verit and the Lord Marshal had the news this morning. The list of those against us is immense: Gulto, Patverseme, Scallas, Sjeferdin, Portica . . . Every country from the Tortured Seas to the Sunless Lands. No one wants our plague."

"Patverseme? But what about Kebonsat? Why didn't he tell us?"

"I don't know. Neither did the Lord Marshal nor the Verit. But by the way our friend Pincushion tells it, the Lord Marshal is readying for war and the Verit is nothing less than gleeful. This will mean the regency. And a reason to break with Patverseme. He could hardly be happier if the Iisand turned up dead."

"Kebonsat can't know. He would have told us. His government would have pulled him out," Reisil said.

"He would not leave you," Yohuac interjected. "Knowing would have made little difference. And I doubt his country would have him back. Not until the plague has finished with Kodu Riik. He's already been counted as lost."

"Yohuac's right. Kebonsat isn't even worth anything as a hostage. Pincushion said as much. Soon as the quarantine went up, his father would have declared a new heir. He'd have to. He couldn't allow Kebonsat to be used against him."

"What will they do to him?"

"According to Pincushion, nothing. For now. There's no profit in it. He'll be put under house arrest until after the Verit becomes regent. The Verit's twisty and likely to try to find a way to profit from Kebonsat. That is, if he can find the time. He's going to have to deal with starvation, the plague and the *nokulas*. And if we survive that, war with Patverseme at the least. And sooner or later, he's going to find out about the Iisand. And then he'll take the throne. And once he does—you know how he feels about the *ahalad-kaaslane*. Kebonsat is the least of our worries."

"It's time to find the wizards." Reisil stared at Juhrnus, waiting for him to protest.

But he surprised her. "As soon as can be. There will be riots soon. It's our best hope."

"I can leave now. But I don't know where to look."

"I've been talking to Pincushion about it. We have a few ideas. But Sodur's likely to be able to narrow things down. He won't fight us now. He doesn't have a choice."

"And if he doesn't know?"

"Then we'll do it ourselves. And pray to the Lady we're in time."

Chapter 30

A constant trickling sound filled the air as the misty rain accumulated and dribbled from the rooftops. A heavy smell of brine and smoke settled into the dark crevices between buildings. A horse sneezed and scraped at the ground, its bridle jingling. Juhrnus paused, fading into a recessed doorway, ears straining. He heard hurried footsteps, and a woman trotted in the direction from which he'd come, her back bent, face contorted with effort. Water sloshed from the two buckets dangling from the bar over her shoulders. It was late to be going to the well, and a chill of foreboding rippled down his spine. The plague did not wait for a kind hour to strike.

Juhrnus swung out into the street, pulling his hood lower over his face and leaping over a puddle of fetid water. Esper clung to his shoulders beneath his cloak.

~Where do we go now? Juhrnus had looked for Sodur everywhere he could think of. But he wasn't at the Temple or palace, and no one had seen him in days.

~Go to Reisil.

~She won't know where to find him. She's glad enough not to have him dangling over her, watching her every move.

~She'll know. She always knows where he is. She does not trust him.

Juhrnus's mouth twisted.

~*Back to the palace, then. And then to get Reisil out of Koduteel as fast as we can. I hope Sodur knows more than he's told us.*

~*You have narrowed down where we should search.*

~*To better than a five-hundred-square-league patch of mountains. It's still looking for a single grain of sand at the bottom of the ocean. She'll never find them.*

~*She will. The Lady will guide her.*

Juhrnus said nothing, not bothering to try to hide his doubts.

~*We are* ahalad-kaaslane. Esper sounded tense and disapproving.

Juhrnus bared his teeth in a silent snarl, frustration burning in his throat. ~*We are* ahalad-kaaslane. *Don't worry that I'll ever forget what that means. I'll serve the Lady until I'm rotting in the ground. But it's not me you have to worry about. It's the court. Especially the Verit. Regent Aare.*

~*He is not yet Regent.*

~*He will be this time tomorrow. And he hates the idea of us. Reisil most of all. He's going to kill her as soon as he gets the chance. And the Lady won't stop him.*

~*We will. We are the Lady's eyes and hands. So long as we are here, She is here.*

Juhrnus unbent. He couldn't resist his *ahalad-kaaslane's* uncontaminated conviction.

~*Then we had best stop wasting time.*

Few lights glimmered in the drizzling darkness. Windows gaped black and empty down at the streets. Candles and oil were sparse these days, and most of the wood was going to the palace and barracks. Juhrnus walked along uneasily. Too few people were out, and the silence was oppressive. The citizens of Koduteel were suspicious of one another as the plague touched a house here, another there. Neighbors eyed each other with baleful animosity and locked their doors and garden gates, hiding inside from the disease. As if they could.

Juhrnus paused again, hearing a soft, clicking sound. When it did not repeat, he hurried on. He cut through an alley between two ramshackle residences, crossing through a tiny square centered around a decrepit statue of the Lady.

A barren flower bed circled her feet, full of bird droppings and plant bracken.

"In a hurry, are we?"

Juhrnus started and spun. The voice seemed to come from every side. His hand dropped to his sword, and he pulled it loose with a ringing sound.

"Jumpy too. And ye've a right to be, *ahalad-kaaslane*. Streets ain't so friendly of late."

There was a shuffling sound, and several figures loomed out of the shadows.

"What do you want?" His fingers flexed on his hilt.

"You, laddy. You."

Juhrnus's response was to lift the tip of his sword. A feeble gesture. He was competent enough with the weapon, but no swordsman. Still, he would sell his life dearly.

"Now, now, laddy. Doncha be that way. Someone as wants to have a word with ya, is all."

One of the men stepped forward, gesturing toward a dark archway. His face was shrouded in the deep folds of a cloak, the hand holding his sword beefy and scarred.

"I don't have time for this."

The man's voice hardened as he pointed his sword at Juhrnus's heart. "One way t'other laddy, you're comin' with us."

Juhrnus hesitated and then nodded.

"Sensible lad." The other man sheathed his sword. The others closed in around Juhrnus as he followed after. They did not go far. Three streets north and four west, down a rutted alley into the deserted backyard lot of a tall, windowless warehouse just this side of the fashionable pink district.

The door was opened before they reached it. Juhrnus hesitated on the threshold before entering. A large room opened up in front of him, musty and damp. The wood floor was uneven and flexed beneath his feet. The two oil lamps burning near the door did little to illuminate the darkness. His escorts prodded him up a set of stairs. The landing was thick with dust disturbed by the passage of a half-dozen feet. They stopped before a rough-hewn plank door with only a rope for a handle. His guide pushed it open, its hinges unexpectedly quiet, and waved for Juhrnus to enter.

"Be polite, laddy. Else you won't be leaving here upright."

The burly man touched the side of his nose and pointed at Juhrnus warningly, then put his meaty hand on Juhrnus's back and shoved him inside.

Acrid smoke filled the room from the feeble fire in the hearth. It cast the only light in the room. Juhrnus rubbed his stinging eyes, scanning the gloom, holding his sword ready.

"What has it been? A few weeks? Seems like a year."

He stiffened. The owner of the velvet voice emerged from a shadowed corner, the spindle legs of her chair scraping the floor. Her hair was the same, red and silky, her body still curvaceous and lush. But there was no longer anything soft or inviting about Karina. Her movements were abrupt and harsh, her mouth severe. Even her pale flesh seemed cold, like marble. She meant business, though what her business was, Juhrnus couldn't begin to guess.

"What's this about, Karina?" He slid back his hood and lifted his sword so that it rested ready against his shoulder.

"Right to the point. No pleasantries about how well I look or how much you've missed me. The *ahalad-kaaslane* in you, I expect. Good. I wanted to talk to him, not my frivolous lover, though I think he's found himself greener pastures."

"This must be important if you sent tilters to fetch me. You might have just sent a message."

"Too risky, and you might have dawdled. I wanted to see you tonight."

"Seems time is important to both of us. So what is it you want?"

"I sent for you because people are dying. If the plague doesn't get them, then they'll starve to death."

"If you're worried about that, then let me go."

"Oh? Have you an answer to the city's ills, then?" Juhrnus did not answer. She rolled her eyes derisively. "Such eloquence. Well, you may keep your secrets. I have a task for you."

"A task?"

She lifted one elegant shoulder. "All right. A boon if you wish, *ahalad-kaaslane*. I have the means to provide some relief for those who are starving, if I can but get the supplies here. I need transport. But I will not allow the nobles to gobble it up before the people get their share, nor can I use my family's resources. And I do not trust the *ahalad-kaaslane*. They have become ineffectual and stupid."

"Yet you want my help."

"You have never been stupid. Whether you can be of true service remains to be seen. But I know you, and I don't have many choices."

"Fair enough. Go on." She had his interest. If nothing else, she offered the lure of giving practical aid to people.

"If you will recall, my father is a merchant. He captains his own fleet of four ships. He set out for Guelt in the late fall just before the winter storms hit. He has been there since. Spring's delay has prevented his timely return, and is the reason for our meeting tonight.

"The blockade refused to allow him landfall in Kodu Riik. They want to see us starve, you see. This blockade is no mere precaution against the plague spreading. They also won't let food in," she said bitterly. "They fired on his ships. But my father has outsmarted his share of pirates and freebooters. They underestimated his speed and weaponry. Thus he made his escape, causing no little damage to the heavier naval vessels. He took refuge among the Piiton Islands. They could not follow them there.

"He then sent word. Out of luck, it was I and not my mother or uncle who was home to receive the message. My father has begun to organize a fleet whose charge will be to run the blockade, bringing food and supplies to Kodu Riik. Most are the same freebooters and pirates he's skirmished with in his trade. He says there are a series of natural harbors and coves where he may safely anchor for a time, but our shores are watched meticulously. He can only drop the goods and dash away if he is to stay ahead of the patrols. So he wishes me to get these supplies safely into the hands of our people. Which means horses and wagons, men to drive them and men to guard them. I cannot do this without your help."

Juhrnus nodded, mind clicking as he began to pace. "We'll need a base of operations outside of Koduteel. Maybe more than one. Finding men will be easy enough; wagons and horses we can get outside the city. We'll have to be careful not to make ourselves obvious, keep groups to a minimum. We'll also need a way to distribute the goods in the Fringes and the city."

"I'll take care of that. This building is one of my father's, and not the only one. My mother and uncle aren't aware of them. I've already got people I trust. When can you get the rest done?"

"I'll know better tomorrow."

She stared at him, green eyes like gimlets. "Not a promising answer."

"This is not something I can do alone."

She was silent, chewing her lips. Finally she shook her head sharply. "No. No one but you. Too many people."

"Alone I can do little."

"Ineffectual after all," she snapped accusingly.

"I can help, Karina. But I do not have the resources. Others do, and they will help if asked."

"And you are sure you can trust them?"

"With my life. With Esper's life." He did not retreat from her glare.

Finally she nodded. "I hope you're right, or we'll all find ourselves in the Verit's pleasure chambers." She shuddered, and something cold slithered into Juhrnus's stomach at the idea.

"How will I send word to you?"

"Come here. Someone will be waiting to meet you. Don't wait too long. Time is short."

"Shorter than you know. The Verit will be made Regent tomorrow."

"By the Lady's hand," Karina said, turning pale. "Not so soon."

"The *Arkeinik* met tonight. Their delegation to the Iisand was fruitless. He refused to respond. Not even the Lord Marshal could dissuade them."

"We are out of time, then. He'll lock up the city. There's no hope for us."

"Not yet. He's Regent, but the Lord Marshal equals his power yet. He's not without bite. But there's no time to waste. I must go."

Reisil's expression darkened when Juhrnus delivered the news of the regency an hour later.

He was surprised and relieved by her cool response: "I'll

need to leave Koduteel. Before the ceremony, if possible. Any more word on the wizards?"

Juhrnus shook his head. "I can't help thinking Sodur knows more than he's saying. I came to ask if you knew where to find him."

She nodded, lids hooding her eyes. The ivy along her cheek flared gold, and Juhrnus shifted his weight nervously. "I know where he is, and more important, where he will be. We'll corner him at dawn on the way. Can you fetch Metyein? I think it's time we saw the Iisand for ourselves."

"I was on my way to Metyein anyway. I'll bring him back."

Reisil cocked her head at him. "Something I should know about?"

"Not yet. It might be nothing. I'll let you know."

Reisil considered him a moment and then nodded. "Good enough. Do you know when the ceremony will happen?"

"Late afternoon."

"That's when I'll leave the city, then. It'll be our best chance."

Reisil smoothed her hands down over her thighs and gave Juhrnus a thin smile. "Wouldn't it be nice if the sorcerers really meant to help us?"

"No chance of that. Kedisan-Mutira has been clear on that if little else."

"Can they?"

"Does it matter? They aren't going to."

For the first time he noticed that Yohuac and his *ahalad-kaaslane* coal-drake were missing. It startled him. The two hadn't left Reisil's side for a moment since their arrival.

"I wanted a bath," she said in answer to his query. Now Juhrnus noticed her hair was damp and hung loose down her back. She was dressed in soft trews and a thin lawn tunic that showed off her curves, and her feet were bare. Once the sight of her like this would have stirred him. But now he wanted only Kedisan-Mutira. She was like ice and silk where Reisil was more like a warm blanket. Juhrnus's mouth curved. Not the greatest compliment. But much as he loved Reisil like a sister, he wanted to roast his soul in Kedisan-Mutira's fires.

"I'd better pack my things," she said.

Juhrnus took the hint and went to the door. "I'll find Metyein. See you at dawn."

When he opened the door, he found Yohuac leaning against the opposite wall. He wore a brooding expression, his bare arms crossed over his chest. He glowered at Juhrnus. The coal-drake was nowhere to be seen.

"Bright evening," Juhrnus said. Yohuac looked past him to Reisil, hardly waiting for Juhrnus to pass by before thrusting himself inside.

Juhrnus grinned as the door shut with a thump. That was a hungry man. Juhrnus wished him luck. He was going to need it. As lovers for Reisil went, Juhrnus liked Yohuac better than he liked most. The man had a sharp sense of honor. He wasn't quick to anger, but didn't back down from confrontation, and he knew how to fight. He wasn't going to let anyone hurt Reisil. Whether she would take to him or not, Juhrnus couldn't guess. She was easy in Yohuac's company, maybe more easy than suited the other man. Juhrnus saw nothing of the kind of nervous tension that coiled him in its fiery net whenever Kedisan-Mutira was in the room. He shrugged. Yohuac had an interesting road ahead.

Chapter 31

"Y ou are going somewhere?"

"I thought Baku would have told you. The Verit will be made Regent tomorrow. It's too dangerous to stay. It's time to look for the wizards."

"Baku is . . . hunting. His mind is elsewhere. You're leaving Koduteel?"

Reisil sat down to oil her boots. "About time for it too. I'll be glad to finally be *doing* something."

"When will we leave?"

Reisil raised her head, lowering her boot to her lap. "We? I'm going alone."

Yohuac's face darkened, and his jaw tensed. "Do you forget the assassins? They cannot have given up. Only Baku's careful watch has kept them at bay these last weeks. They will surely follow you. And you have already said the wizards will not welcome you. You cannot go alone. It is not safe."

"I'll have Saljane. She won't let anyone sneak up on me. And I need Baku here. Without him I can't know what's happening. And Juhrnus and Metyein will need to know how things fare with me, whether I have any luck finding the wizards and convincing them to help me."

Yohuac paced across the room, his back stiff, the muscles in his arms flexing. Reisil was reminded again of a hunting cat. There was a merciless strength inside him. He was a weapon primed to strike.

"I did not come here to serve you. I came so that you could help my people. I must stay with you. Baku can remain here."

"He won't without you. Saljane will see any assassins as well as you. I won't walk into an ambush, and if I do, I'm not entirely helpless." She lifted her hands, showing him the calluses and half-healed cuts on her hands from their practice sessions. "And if all else fails, I have my magic." Her mouth twisted at that last. She'd tried many times to heal the plague victims these last weeks, with no more success than the first time. Killing still seemed to be her main skill.

"You are a rank beginner at swordplay, and you've no idea how to fight otherwise," he growled back at her.

Reisil lifted one shoulder. "I'll do what I have to. And I have to go alone." What she didn't say was that she didn't want to endanger anyone else. Death was more than likely, and she didn't want to be responsible for getting Yohuac killed. At least she might be able to learn something he could take back to his nahuallis if she didn't survive.

She resumed oiling her boot, watching him from beneath her brow. He clenched his fists, then strode over to squat down before her. His eyes were black as ocean waters at night. He reached out as if to grab her shoulders, but he only touched his fingers to her cheeks and then let them fall back in his lap.

"I'm a warrior. I was born to defend my people, to keep them from harm. Please don't ask me to watch you walk into danger alone and defenseless."

Reisil swallowed hard. She hadn't expected his plea, the gentleness of his touch. But she couldn't give in to his charm or her body's sudden flare of desire. She was *ahalad-kaaslane*. She had no time for a lover. And since Kaval and Kebonsat, she wasn't sure she wanted another one.

"You can't. Your people sent you to save them. Your nahuallis think I'm the key. What if I do learn something important? Anything I learn, Baku will know too. If I don't make it back, then you'll still have the means to help your people. You must stay."

Yohuac's lips pulled into a tight grimace, his eyes flashing. But he rose to his feet, stepping back and retreating to the door.

"I'll return soon. Lock the door." And then he was gone. Reisil did as he said. She hadn't bothered to lock it since Baku had taken to guarding it.

By the time he returned, she had prepared her travel pack, oiled her gauntlet and boots and mended four pairs of socks. Last she'd dug the green cloak out of the trunk at the foot of her bed. She shook it out, making a face at the mildew growing in the creases. The soap and oil cleaned it good as new, and she hung it on a peg, ready for her departure. She no longer wanted the anonymity of the gray cloak. Not that it had worked. But she was tired of pretending to be something she wasn't. Even if she didn't know what she was. This journey would change that. She had to find out what she could or could not do, without relying on someone else's help. And she wasn't going to put anyone else at risk if she proved to be too flawed to do what was necessary.

Reisil unlocked the door, and Yohuac swept past her.

"Your world is cold and barren. There are no fires here. No passion. I cannot even speak to my gods." He caught her by the arms. "As much as I wish to, I cannot refuse to obey you. I will stay here and await your return." His face hardened, and his eyes narrowed to slits. "But if you find trouble, I will come after you. Nothing you can say will keep me here."

Reisil nodded, not trusting her voice. A prickling tingle ran over skin, but it had nothing to do with fear. She swallowed, stepping away.

"Better get some sleep. It'll be dawn soon, and tomorrow is going to be a long day."

They confronted Sodur near the Iisand's quarters.

"Bright morning," Reisil said as he and Lume rounded the corner where she, Yohuac, Juhrnus and Metyein waited. Sodur stopped, his eyes glittering as if lit from within. Then he visibly collected himself and came forward.

"Bright morning."

"We want to see the Iisand."

"Oh, I'm afraid that is impossible," he said, waving his hand. "You know he refuses all visitors but myself and the Lord Marshal."

"Don't pretend," Reisil said. "I know better, and so do they. I'm leaving Koduteel. I want to see him before I go. I want us all to see him."

"I wish you hadn't done that." His gaze lingered on Metyein.

"I wish a lot of things," Reisil retorted. "But it's about to get a lot harder in Koduteel. And we've a right to see what we are facing. Your sorcerers aren't going to help. We're on our own."

Sodur frowned and stared off at a wall. He had a befuddled look, like a harmless, mind-broken grandfather. Suddenly his head whipped around. He cocked it to the side, giving Reisil a slanting glance, sharp as a blade, like he knew what she was thinking and it amused him. His lips parted in a cunning smile. Reisil drew back, unnerved at his abrupt alteration. Masks again.

"Let's not keep him waiting, then."

They entered the Iisand's apartments with no argument from those guarding the door. Inside, the apartments were empty and chilled. Sodur set his basket on a table and set about making the place look lived in. He stirred up the remains of the previous day's fire, scooping coals into an iron lantern before adding a pile of coal. Then he set out the food from the basket, nibbling on it and crumbling pastry across the tablecloth. Most of it he fed to Lume after offering it to his silent spectators.

"Doesn't he eat at all?" Juhrnus asked.

"Nothing. Not for close to eight months now," Sodur responded airily.

"How does he survive?" Yohuac murmured.

Sodur turned around to face him. "You're the new *ahalad-kaaslane*, aren't you?" He scanned Yohuac from head to toe. "Who knows?" Sodur lifted a book from a shelf, opening it and laying it facedown on a table beside the fire. "I admit, it saves cleaning. Quite a benefit, you'll agree, when you see him." He cast another of those sly looks over his shoulder at Reisil and proceeded into the Iisand's bedchambers.

He climbed under the bedclothes, rolling back and forth, thrashing his legs and giving the impression of a restless night. Then he pulled a wadded-up set of clothes from a drawer and dropped them on the floor beside the wardrobe, choosing another set to stuff inside for the next day. The nightshirt he balled in his hands. Then he sprinkled some of the Iisand's perfume on it before dropping it in a heap on the floor of the bathing chambers. Afterwards, he splashed water on the floor around the copper tub.

"Geran was never strict in his housekeeping. Liked to make his staff feel useful. The servants may suspect something's not quite right, but they don't know anything. Good about not gossiping. Handpicked."

On a sideboard, he poured a healthy glass of brandy and swallowed most of it, wiping his lips with the back of his hand and setting the half-empty glass next to the book.

"Geran likes a glass before bed," he said, turning to examine his handiwork. He muttered and went to the chaise, where he stretched out, flattening the plumped pillows, and tossed several on the floor.

"That ought to do it for now. Follow me."

He picked up the iron lantern of coals and went to the bookshelves opposite the mantelpiece. With his foot he pressed something on the floor and stretching high, he pulled a lever hidden in the molding midway down the top shelf. Reisil gasped when the center portion of the bookcase swung open. Sodur gestured for everyone to precede him. There were two guards inside the tunnel, and like the two guarding the Iisand's door, they neither spoke nor looked at the visitors. Sodur led them away into the darkness, stooping as the way grew shorter and narrower. With her wizard-sight, Reisil was undeterred by the thick gloom, Sodur's lantern casting little light. Behind her she heard a thump and then muttered cursing as Metyein stumbled into Yohuac.

"I had no idea. Do these go everywhere in the palace?" Juhrnus wondered aloud.

"What would a palace be without secret passages?"

Reisil stopped. "Then they go to Kebonsat's quarters also?"

"In a roundabout fashion."

"Then let's go get him."

"Whatever for?"

"Because he should see this as well."

"He's Patversemese."

"I want him to see," Reisil declared flatly.

"It's too dangerous."

"It's necessary."

"Reisil, I know you think you know what you're doing. But you must see that he cannot know about the *nokulas*. He cannot know about the Iisand."

"What makes you think I haven't told him already? Besides, what I see is that your sorcerers are doing nothing, the Verit will be declared regent, and the *ahalad-kaaslane* will lose what little influence they have left. It's time to ask for help from those who will give it. Kebonsat will give it."

"And what can he offer? He is a prisoner in the palace. His country has abandoned him. He's useless."

"Maybe not."

Sodur's brows slanted up. "Do tell."

Reisil gave a slight shake of her head. "I don't think so."

"You'll have to give me more than that if I am to believe you."

Reisil stepped closer so that her right shoulder brushed his left. She bent forward to speak softly near his ear. "Your scheme has failed. I don't trust your choices. You can help me or not, but now that I know how to get to Kebonsat, you can bet I'll not let a wall or two stop me. I need him. Kodu Riik needs him. And I'm not going to give

away any chances to save this land, not now that the sorcerers sit inside our gates slavering after us, while the rest of
the world waits for us to wither on the vine. Now make up
your mind."

Reisil straightened, shocked at herself. For the first time
in a long time, she saw in Sodur the mentor and friend he
had been. Everything he'd done was for Kodu Riik. It felt
like betrayal, but was it? Was it any more so than telling
everyone that Yohuac and Baku were *ahalad-kaaslane*? Or
hiding the fact that Baku could pick their thoughts from
their minds?

She flicked a glance at Juhrnus, Metyein and Yohuac.
They trusted her. They'd chosen to follow her, to be led
by her. She did not want that responsibility. What if she
made mistakes? What if she chose wrong? How many
would die because she didn't know enough, because she
didn't see clearly enough?

~*Is it any different than being a tark, than holding another's life in your hands?* Saljane's red eye gleamed like an
ember.

~*I know what I'm doing as a tark. I've trained. I've practiced. But what do I know about any of this? Sodur knows
far more than I.*

~*But you no longer trust his choices.*

~*Who am I to say if he's right or wrong?*

~*You are* ahalad-kaaslane.

~*So is he.*

~*The Lady chooses many to serve. There are none who
are not flawed, who do not misjudge, even though they
mean well.*

~*How can I be sure I'm right?*

~*You must trust your heart.* They *trust you.*

And looking at her three companions, Reisil knew they
did. And until they decided she was making the wrong
choices, they would follow her. She took a breath. She
could trust them to tell her she was wrong, to walk away
from her. She could trust them to choose a new path without her. Just as she had with Sodur. They believed in her,
but they were not stupid, nor did they follow blindly.

"Wait here. I'll go get him. Keep your voices down."
Sodur turned and disappeared, the sounds of his feet fading quickly.

"Maybe you shouldn't have let him go without getting him to tell us what he knows about the wizards," Juhrnus said. "He's being unusually cooperative."

"He'll tell us," Reisil said, sure now that he would. "What are you two cooking up? You've had your heads together all morning."

Juhrnus winked. "A chance to keep people eating while you're gone."

"How?"

"Nothing sure yet. I'll be glad to see Kebonsat. There might be something he can do." He wasn't going to say any more.

"Be careful. The Verit's going to be watching," was all Reisil said.

Reisil had no sense of how long Sodur was gone, but she was thirsty, and the chill of the stone tunnel had begun to leach through her clothes.

"Ho, Kebonsat. It's about time. Getting soft sitting about doing nothing, have you?" Juhrnus called in a low voice when he appeared, following Sodur.

"And you, crawling in the walls like a rat. Or just peeking in at the women?"

"The women. Always the women," Juhrnus said, slapping Kebonsat on the shoulder.

Kebonsat grasped Reisil's arm in a warm grip. "It is good to see you," he said. "But what's this about?"

"You'll see," she said as Sodur called everyone to silence.

"We've a long walk. Let's not waste any more time."

There was no chance to talk as they walked, the passage narrowing so that they had to walk single file, sometimes bent almost double. They went down and down, deep into the roots of the castle. Reisil began to hear the pulse of the harbor cavern.

They burrowed down into the cliffs beneath the palace, the passage eventually growing wider and more damp, even as it grew steeper, zigzagging back and forth down steps and switchbacks. Now the thunder of the harbor cavern drowned out every other sound, and it was impossible to ask Kebonsat about the Verit or Vertina or anything else.

They came to an open space where the smell of brine

and damp was overpowering. Reisil wrinkled her nose and then gently pushed the others after Sodur, who stood inside the left-hand passage, gesturing impatiently. They pressed closely against a wall, the moss-slickened floor slipping sharply away. Carefully they edged along until they came to an opening. It proved to be a serpentine doorway leading to a flight of steep steps that dropped away abruptly from the landing. There was a sudden quiet as the pounding of the harbor cavern was suddenly muted. Light flickered below as Sodur lit a torch.

"What is this place?" Reisil asked, staring up at the arched ceilings and dangling lucernes.

"Palace was built on the ruins of another, perhaps many others. This was a dungeon for those who came before us. Come on. Geran waits."

Gargoyle heads snarled down from fluted pilasters on either side of the entryway, their expressions pitiless and harsh. The room beyond had once been a torture chamber, and Reisil could almost hear the screams of the men and women who'd suffered here. Sodur seemed oblivious and circled quickly around to the other side. There he lit two more torches, stopping at the entrance of a narrow passage.

"It's too small to fit everyone. Two, maybe three at most." He held out a torch.

"We'll wait. You go," Juhrnus said, indicating Reisil, Yohuac and Kebonsat. Reisil hesitated and then slid into the narrow corridor, turning sideways to ease through. Kebonsat followed next with Yohuac bringing up the rear. On Reisil's shoulder, Saljane mantled and clenched her talons tighter.

~What is it?

Distress. Uncertainty. Unease.

~I know, me too. I feel . . . flat . . . somehow.

She emerged into a small open space shaped like a teardrop. Kebonsat and Yohuac crowded in behind. The gargoyles' bulbous eyes glowed red, their stone tongues fleshy and malevolent. Yohuac took the torch from her and lit those in the wall sconces. Reisil examined the door. It was a solid slab of oak bound in iron. Three bars secured it closed, each etched in scrolling patterns. A grille-covered window allowed a view inside.

Reisil peered through the grille and realized there was

an interior cell door. Was he so dangerous? She thought about the *nokulas* who'd attacked her and Sodur and shivered. She took a breath, fear making her hands tremble. The walls of the cell were covered in the same scrolling patterns as those on the crossbars. The space was perhaps twelve paces deep and twelve wide. There was no furniture, only bits of wood and cloth strewn across the floor. Against the far wall was a dented chamber pot turned on its side. Otherwise, the cell appeared empty.

Then she heard a noise, a scraping, a tapping. There was a swish and the debris on the floor scattered as if blown by a stiff wind. Reisil tensed, remembering the paths in the grass made by nearly invisible bodies, the translucent *nokulas* flashing silver like moonlit water.

"What do you see?" Yohuac asked.

Reisil did not answer. Suddenly she felt a tickle across her forehead and jerked back, rubbing her skin. A painful, rough line rose beneath her fingertips.

"Reisil?"

She shook her head, holding up her shaking hand. A sound rippled over her skin, almost too high to hear. It was akin to a laugh, but high-pitched and eerie. Inhuman. Out of nowhere a form began to resolve itself, like moonflies gathering into a shapely swarm. The result froze Reisil, her mouth open in a silent *O*. She could hardly fathom that this *thing* could ever have been human.

Like the *nokulas* from Veneston, it was powerful and looming, its movements graceful and quick. It stared at her with slanted silver eyes, curved like spoons, pupilless and fathomless. Thick, translucent hairs sprang up over its head and ran down its spine and arms. They waved and undulated in deliberate motion, as if tasting the air. Its arms ended in six-jointed fingers tipped with hooking talons. As she watched, Reisil saw the beast scrape furrows in the stone floor.

Suddenly it leaped at her, and she wrenched back, stumbling against her companions, who caught her. The *nokula* peered at her through the grille. Its long, pointed snout dropped open in a slow yawn, revealing dozens of sharp teeth. Reisil gasped and stepped back, allowing Kebonsat and Yohuac to look. She leaned against the wall. Her stomach heaved. She retched, sliding down to the floor, her head

bent between her knees. Saljane pressed close against her.
A moment later hands caught her up.

"Come on. We've seen enough." Kebonsat sounded
shaken. He and Yohuac helped Reisil up the passageway,
settling her on the edge of the hearth.

"What's this?" Yohuac's fingers whispered over her brow.
She shook her head.

"You let him touch you. The tongue. He didn't break
the skin, did he?" Sodur bent over her, grasping her chin
and turning her head from side to side. "Lucky. Poison."

"You could have warned us," Kebonsat said.

"Wasn't sure he'd let you see him."

Reisil rubbed her eyes, his careless, detached tone
scraping over her skin. "Where are the wizards?" she
asked, rising to her feet.

Sodur cocked his head to the side and smiled. "Ah, now
there's a question."

"Where?" Reisil insisted.

"Near Mysane Kosk. Outside of the ring of danger. Close
enough to see their handiwork."

"Where?"

"Thirty leagues south, in a high valley between Sapriim's
Peak and the Aavrel Range. Don't know much else.
They've taken precautions against casual discovery. The
few *ahalad-kaaslane* who've gone closer have never been
heard from." His tone on the last was almost merry, and
Reisil's hand balled into a fist.

"Who?" she managed to squeeze out.

"Felias was one, as I recall. And Bethorn. Derkiin." He
shrugged. "They are missed."

Reisil lunged to her feet. "Don't you even care? Bethorn
was your friend. You taught Felias . . ." She trailed away.

Sodur's eyes narrowed to slits. He dipped his head low.
At his feet, Lume growled. "You little know my pain, Reisiltark. Do not presume to judge. I have been *ahalad-
kaaslane* far longer than you. We all do what we must. Our
purpose is to stand like reefs, meeting danger before it can
harm those we protect, so they may sleep sound at night
when demons hunt in the darkness. We are not meant to
have friends. We are meant to walk alone so that we can do
as we must when we must, unblinded by ties of the heart."

"You're wrong," Reisil retorted softly. "Ties of the heart

give us the strength to stand between those we love and the evil that would harm them. And it is our trust and faith in one another that remind us we are not alone, that we serve the Lady and Kodu Riik together."

As suddenly as he'd become menacing, Sodur's mood shifted, and he smiled again. There was a wild edge to his expression, an alien shrewdness that made the hair on Reisil's arms prickle. "Yes. True. *We are never alone.* But it is too soon to mourn. Perhaps they yet live."

Juhrnus and Metyein stumbled out of the passage to the Iisand's chambers, their faces white and clammy.

"By the Demonlord's warty horn, what happened to him?" Metyein demanded, one hand clutching the hilt of his sword.

"You know. Mysane Kosk."

"How can you be sure?" Juhrnus pressed.

"He went there shortly after the wizards destroyed it. To see for himself. Couldn't get very close. Even then there was something. . . . There wasn't much to see. The city was hidden by an unnatural mist. Changes started after that."

"But how do you know that that is what caused it? That it wasn't something else?" Reisil asked.

"He wasn't the only one, and he wasn't the first. There were the scouts. We didn't know it until it was too late. They turned into a pack and slaughtered an entire squad before disappearing into the mountains. That was the first incident. Soon the pattern became clear. It was then Geran realized it was happening to him too, and had us lock him up. He hoped we could find a cure, of course. It was more important to him that he didn't go about killing his own people, and that we would be able to see what happened to him. So we'd know."

"Back then you didn't know how close was too close to Mysane Kosk. Some men changed; others didn't. Didn't seem to be a pattern as to who got struck. But now— Now you go to Mysane Kosk, and you can see. Can't you?" He looked at Juhrnus, who nodded. "There's a growing circle of light about the place. You can see inside the edges. Grass, trees, insects, animals—it's all changed like him." He jerked his head in the direction of the Iisand's cell.

"He's gone, isn't he? There's no way to bring him back. To bring any of them back," Juhrnus said quietly.

"Who knows? It's magic."

"I'm going to find out," Reisil said.

"Yes, it's time," Sodur said, startling her. "I'll help you all I can."

"Thank you."

He smiled that queer smile again and said nothing. There was something else here, something more he wasn't saying. Did she dare trust him? Did she have any choice?

Sodur led them through the passages to an empty set of rooms in the west wing. "Don't let anyone see you leaving. The walls have eyes." He chuckled and motioned Kebonsat back into the wall passage.

"I'll come too. I'd like to know the way," Juhrnus said, following after.

Sodur turned back to Reisil. "If you will accept an old man's last words of advice, you may find that those ties of the heart may be painful indeed. Friends will die. You may even have to kill some. But whatever comes, you and your allies are all that stands between Kodu Riik and that." He waved his arm in the vague direction of the Iisand's cell. "Don't ever forget what you're meant to do."

Reisil watched the panel in the wall slide shut. She dropped onto a divan, her arms wrapped around her waist.

"Reisil?" Yohuac squatted beside her, grasping her hand. "Are you all right?"

She shook her head, unable to speak.

"You're shaking." Yohuac sat beside her, pulling her against his chest.

"Here." Metyein thrust a glass of brandy into her hand, and she gulped it down, clutching the glass with both hands, grateful for the fire that burned down her throat.

Slowly the tremors subsided, and after a few minutes she pushed herself away from Yohuac. She looked at the two men, feeling the magnitude of what must be done, and wondering how it was to be accomplished. How this tiny handful of people were to do it. They were on their own now. Sodur had given over the reins, and she didn't know if she could do any better than he. Both men returned her regard with complete trust. They believed in her. She quashed the voice inside that laughed at their foolishness.

"Mysane Kosk is the key," she said. "It all began there.

If the wizards won't reverse what they've done, we'll have
to destroy it. With luck, that will end the plague. And then
we'll hunt down every *nokula* it spawned." She stood up.
"Even the Iisand. It's the only way."

Chapter 32

Soka jogged back and forth in his cell, the rough stone
frigid beneath his bare feet. His wounds were all but
healed. His skin showed pink scars, and beneath them the
flesh ached, but he was a whole man. For now. Soka spat
at the windowless wall. He hadn't seen Aare in more than
a week. It wasn't like him. He enjoyed taunting Soka too
much. The Verit had been in every few days since Soka's
capture to mock and threaten him, bringing bits of news,
none of which Soka trusted. Even Aare's revelation that
Metyein still lived might have been a ruse, though Aare's
fury certainly seemed real. Hearing it, Soka couldn't resist
getting a bit of his own back.

"Hard to find good help these days. Course, you don't
trade in loyalty. Who'd give it to the likes of you, after all?
Did you forget to pay him? Bed his wife? Murder his
children?"

"Pelodra is a worm, and shall soon be returned to his
native home," Aare said malevolently. "As you may be.
Though I could solve much of my aggravation by simply
removing another useless part of your face. A shame for
the women though," he mused, tapping his finger against
Soka's lips and flicking out his tongue. The threat had silenced Soka. He could still hear Aare's laugh, loud and
hearty.

Then Aare had ceased to come. Soka's meager food continued to be delivered once a day, and his chamber pot had
overflowed two days ago. His cell reeked, and he could
hardly contain himself with the isolation and monotony.

In an effort to warm himself and restore his wasted muscles, he'd begun a regimen of exercise. It helped. He no longer wheezed from two minutes of jogging, nor did his muscles scream protest when he performed various exercises. But he was still weak as a kitten and found himself pounding against the walls in frustration. He slept little, the nightmares circling, waiting to pounce. He had no sense of night or day, and the moments it took to take a breath seemed interminable.

He squatted, waiting until his legs burned with the effort, then straightened with a lurch and repeated the motion. Next he lay facedown on the floor and pushed himself up until his arms screamed. Afterwards he began the warm-up motions Metyein had taught him for swordplay. His body was stiff and jerky, and he sank to the floor, propping himself up against the wall and striving to collect himself. Sooner or later Aare would be back. And sooner or later he'd finally get around to telling Soka what he had in mind. And then what? Soka knew as well as he knew his own name what Aare would demand. Betray Metyein. Spy on him. Spy on his father. Soka tipped his head back and glanced at the walls of his prison. He could take it here for months. Maybe years. But Aare wouldn't wait. Torture would come next, and soon.

The day they took his eye came back with a rush—the smell of sage sausage and stale ale on the healer's breath, the dreadful itching, Aare's cool instructions. And then afterwards, the appalling ache that bored through his head. Then Aare had been merciful, allowing Soka a measure of relief from the pain. Soka could still taste the drug: lemons and something akin to walnuts. He still couldn't abide either. But this time Aare would not be so benevolent.

Soka scrubbed his hands over his face, scratching at his filthy beard. Losing his eye would be a fond memory compared with what Aare would do next. The question was, could he take it? Could he withstand the pain and refuse Aare's demands?

Soka bounced his head against the wall, staring up at the heavy plank ceiling, tears tracking out of the corners of his eyes. He knew himself. Much as he loved Metyein, he would give in. He made an inarticulate sound. If that was the way of it, why not just cooperate? Why not just stay whole if there was nothing to be gained by fighting? He thought of Metyein, and his head fell forward onto his arms, and he sobbed in earnest.

It was another two days before Aare returned. He walked in, his face contorting at the stench. He covered his mouth and nose with a lace-edged handkerchief.

"Bring him," he ordered the two guards.

Soka struggled; he didn't know why. He'd do anything to be out of that cell. One guard cuffed him on the side of the head. Soka sagged between them as they dragged him along.

He was taken up several flights of stairs and down a long curving corridor. There were no decorations but for iron torch brackets spaced every twenty feet. At last they came to a wooden door. Aare pushed it open and motioned for Soka to enter. When he resisted, the two guards thrust him inside forcefully.

Soka's mouth went dry, and his bladder clenched. The room was wide and spacious and brightly lit, dominated on one end by a fireplace large enough to stand a horse in. Stone tables formed regimented double lines down the middle. A few were occupied, groups of two and three brown-robed men leaning over each. There was an unearthly hush, as if the snip and grind of the metal tools made no impact on the pitiful victims strapped to the stone slabs. Someone whistled a merry tune.

"You were expecting this, I should think."

Soka didn't answer, unable to tear his gaze from a sudden spurt of crimson that fountained up above the heads of one group of torturers. The man on the table neither moved nor screamed.

"They do good work. Reliable results," Aare said, following his gaze.

"Why doesn't he scream?" Soka choked out, the pressure in his bladder growing.

"I do not care much for the noise. This is my home, after all. No, there are ways to remove that annoyance, though it has its price. It is sometimes difficult for the subject to communicate his capitulation, and he suffers more than he ought. Still, a price I'm willing to pay for peace and quiet. Come, have a closer look."

Aare guided Soka around the room, walking slowly so that he could see the ready instruments in careful rows on trays, the bloodstained tables, the restraints, the forest of burning, biting and cutting devices hanging in orderly racks. And finally he came to the victims and their torturers.

There was an easy, casual pace to the torturers' movements. They spoke in muted voices, humming quiet tunes as they severed bones, dismantled feet, burned skin from flesh. In between they discussed what they were doing, how far they could push before their victims passed out, how to keep them on this side of life.

Last Aare walked him down a line of cages along the far wall, beside the hearth. Soka hadn't seen them before. The things inside were hardly to be recognized as human. Like those on the tables, they made few sounds, but their breathing was pained. They smelled of old blood, *skraa*, vomit and piss. A trickle of vile liquid wound from the cages and into a drain set in the floor nearby. Aare lifted his robes and stepped over it, peering inside a cage.

"Not yet, Kedriles? I thought we'd have broken you sooner. But not long. Not long now." Aare caught Soka's eyes. "He wanted freedom—then he pleaded for death. But those never come. Now he will choose to submit." He *tsked*. "In the end, everyone does. Imagine what a man could save himself if he just answered reason."

Soka swallowed, powerless to look away from the pulpy mass inside the cage.

"How long?" he asked before he could stop himself.

"A month."

Soka turned and retched. A month to reduce a man to *that*.

"*You* are a reasonable man, Soka. I have no doubt. And now we must talk."

Soka's mouth tasted like rotted meat and spoiled eggs. His legs were rubbery, and he swayed and weaved as he followed Aare out of the chamber. The guards on either side said nothing, merely prodding him back to the middle of the passage when he stumbled too wide. They went up a steep flight of steps into a more inhabited part of the building. Suits of armor stood at attention down the corridor, and in between, arras depicted bloody battles. Swords, axes, maces and other weapons completed the decorations.

Soka briefly thought of yanking a broadsword from its rack and thought the better of it. He wasn't ready for suicide yet. Or he would instantly find himself back in the chamber they'd just left. The bloody, pulpy mass named Kedriles filled his vision, and he held his arms close at his sides.

They stopped at another door. Again Aare opened it and motioned Soka to enter. He did so slowly, suspicion stiffening his limbs. The room was dominated by an enormous bed. The bedclothes were made of velvet and silk and hung with swathes of gauze. A fire crackled cheerily in the hearth, and before it stood a copper tub, the water inside steaming. In the opposite corner stood a table laden with all variety of breads, meats, vegetables, sauces and sweets. An array of wines and liquors crowded a sideboard. Aare poured two glasses of a dry white wine, handing one to Soka.

Soka gulped it down in one swallow, turning bemusedly in a circle.

Aare chuckled unpleasantly and sat. "And now you see your choices, my dear Soka. This, and the naked beauties waiting in the boudoir to wash and serve you. Or Kedriles. You must decide quickly. I am made Regent this afternoon, and I mean to be Iisand before long. Kodu Riik can no longer bobble idly in the waves, uncaptained. We verge on disaster, and without a strong hand at the helm, we will surely be destroyed. The Lord Marshal must be brought to heel. I had meant to use his son, but you will serve as well."

"What do you want?"

"A spy, my dear Soka. A spy. Surely you've sorted that out already. The Lord Marshal and I shall soon share equal power. We are in a governing deadlock—he has as much support in the tiers as I. But I do not wish to kill him. He is the best strategist and tactician in Kodu Riik. Once I am Iisand, he will serve me as loyally as he served my father. I know this. He knows this, which is why he will fight me every inch of the way. I want you to discover his plots, his weaknesses. It should be easy. Metyein trusts you. He's searched all of Koduteel for you since you disappeared and has not yet given up."

"And if I do not?"

He lifted a pale hand, palm up. "Kedriles." He smiled at the revulsion Soka couldn't hide. "And I shall be forced to pursue Metyein as I originally planned. He is not so pragmatic as you, however. I can't imagine he will cooperate."

Soka covered his mouth with a shaking hand. Now the vision of Kedriles's ruined body held Metyein's face.

"I shall give you time to consider," Aare said with a knowing smile. He pointed to a door next to the bed. "Your companions will perhaps ease the difficulty of your decision." And with that he departed.

The door beside the bed now swung open, and Soka stared as three voluptuous young women wiggled into view. They wore little but scarves held on by sparkling, gem-crusted chains. The thin material hid nothing. They crowded around him, wrinkling their noses at his ripe odor. Quickly they stripped away his rags and urged him into the bathtub.

After that, Soka hardly had a coherent moment. They washed him, shaved him, and fed him, kissing and fondling him all the while. Their lips were soft and hungry, their bodies warm and wet. He rolled on the bed with them, now on top, now below, now between, clutching plump, ripe flesh, ecstasy taking him over the edge again and again.

He was driven by a demanding sense of urgency. He didn't know how long it could last, how long before Aare dragged him back to his cell, or back to the torture chambers. He rose to every occasion, the women marveling at his stamina. But it wasn't stamina. It was desperation. With every passing moment, he was more sure of what he had to do.

At last the door was flung open, his idyll over. Soka was lying beneath the mound of squirming women, his mouth clamped to a breast, his manhood sheathed in silky wet flesh. He pumped his hips, unwilling to let Aare interrupt, and felt himself release. He sat up, tongue tangling in the redhead's mouth, watching Aare as he poured himself another drink, lifting it in Soka's direction.

Soka reluctantly let go and slid off the bed, panting, sweat shining on his face and chest. The three young women disappeared into the room beyond, and he fought the urge to follow, to find a place to hide.

Aare handed him a drink. When Soka had swallowed it,

Aare fixed him with a sharp stare. "Now you have had a taste of freedom. What is your choice?"

Soka's throat closed. He opened his mouth and then clamped it shut.

"I told you, I have no time to delay. I'll ask you once more. What is your choice?"

Soka licked his lips and closed his eyes. He jerked his head. "I'll do it."

"You are a sensible man." Aare's voice was thick with triumph. His next words chilled Soka. "But I would have you remember the consequences of betrayal." He motioned toward the corridor. A brown-robed figure entered, carrying a leather case. Soka made a choking sound and took a step back. Aare smiled knowingly.

They laid him faceup on the bed. The air seemed cold, and gooseflesh prickled Soka from head to toe.

"We can't leave scars or Metyein will have questions. But there are other ways to make my point. Obey Elas, or it shall go the worse for you. I shall return for you after the Regency ceremony."

Aare left then. The brown-robed man smiled disarmingly and dribbled a few drops of something on Soka's lips. It tasted sweet, and he swallowed uneasily. In only a few seconds, he found he couldn't move. He made a sound in the back of his throat, a sound that should have been a scream but was merely a creaking whuffle.

"Don't worry. You can't move, but you will feel everything I do. It will wear off in a few hours. A toxin. Comes from a tiny sea snail," Elas explained. "You ought to be able to breathe well enough, and your heart should hold up."

Soka tried to move, to struggle. His breathing sped up, and he felt himself beginning to black out.

"Easy now. Try to calm yourself. The Verit was quite specific. If you pass out, I must stop and begin again. It is in your best interests to stay awake."

And then began an ordeal like Soka had never before suffered. It would haunt him the rest of his life. The torturer applied an assortment of foul liquids and creams using brushes and sticks. Each one was worse the last. He moved from Soka's feet to his thighs, from his shoulders to his

waist, finishing with his genitals. By then the silent screams
reverberated inside Soka's skull, but he could do nothing
but lie there and allow the torturer to minister his poisons
to him. And *feel*.

The first touch on his balls was a caress, cool and sweet.
And then it began to grow hot until he thought the skin
must be blistering and peeling away. Then another and another. Then Elas spread his legs and began to probe. Lastly
Elas moved to Soka's penis. He spread something around
the tip, and an unmerciful itching began to gnaw, chewing
up into his innards. And then jagged, ripping pain. Like
steel screws twisting into his groin, to his bladder, to his
bowels. Tears streamed from his eyes, and drool pooled in
his mouth. He gagged and his stomach heaved. Elas turned
Soka's head to the side and stuck a bony finger between
his teeth to open his jaws.

"Happens. Too bad. You had a lovely meal. Shame to
lose it so."

And then Elas continued his work. Soka wanted nothing
more than to die, to slide into oblivion. But his mind
wouldn't let go of the world, of the agony.

It went on and on and on. After a while, the pain grew
so excruciating that Soka's mind fragmented, the pieces
drifting apart. He began to hallucinate, vicious monsters
tearing out his entrails, women raking needle-sharp nails
through his flesh, Aare licking him with a tongue of metal
spikes. And then he drifted further from the pain, away
and away. There was his father tossing Soka's bloody eye in
hand, up and down, up and down. And there was Metyein.
Memories rolled over Soka. A childhood of shared pranks,
of secrets and adventures. And then Metyein with his blood
dripping into the snow, arrows pricking from his thigh
and side.

And then it all melted together, and there was nothing
but glass-edged waves that rose and fell and shredded his
flesh in between.

"Ah, it begins to pass."

Soka blinked, his eyes dry and crusted. He licked his lips,
faintly surprised that he could move. He told himself to sit
up. After two or three tries, he managed to do so. He

glanced down at himself, expecting to see horrendous damage, but his flesh was whole.

"You'll want another bath. And there are some fresh clothes. You will tell Metyein that you were held captive in the city. You never saw their faces; they wore masks. They spoke rarely and never to tell you what they wanted. They healed you, but kept you drugged and locked in a basement from which you just escaped. Today has been a good day to make escapes," Aare added in a quiet, lethal tone, and Soka jerked his head up warily. But the Verit— no, the Regent, Soka remembered, seeing the chain of office around Aare's neck—was not looking at him but at the swirling glass of brandy he held in his fingers. He wondered who had slipped the Regent's leash.

"You will make Metyein believe you. If you fail, you know the consequences." He pointed to Elas's black case still open on a table with its vials and jars. "Then you will begin spying on the Lord Marshal and report his activities to me. I will not give you a schedule. You must not take chances of getting caught. But do not overtask my patience."

Soka pulled a sheet across his thighs, reaching for a half-drunk glass of wine to moisten his parched throat and clear the foul taste from his tongue.

"What is it I should be looking for?"

"I want to know everything. I'll decide what is important." Aare stood. "Clean yourself of Elas's ministrations, but I suggest you roll in a pile of manure before seeing Metyein. You wouldn't want him to become suspicious. When you're ready, a guard will show you the way out. Enjoy your freedom, Soka. Take care of yourself and your friend."

He closed the door, and Soka reached for the bottle of brandy, pouring it down his throat. His movements were stiff, ungainly. The drug had not yet worn off. He stepped into the chilled waters of the tub, still dirty from his previous bath, and scrubbed at his skin with a rough sponge. Then he dressed in clothes that were little better than rags. He checked himself in the polished metal mirror and nodded. It was time. Metyein was waiting. He went to the door.

"Lady help me," he murmured, and then walked out of his prison.

Chapter 33

The news of the Regency ceremony had gone out swiftly, and now the palace grounds swarmed with carriages and horses. The receiving rooms groaned at the seams. No one wanted to be left out, and no one wanted to be suspected of snubbing the new Regent by not attending. Even Kebonsat and his retinue had been summoned to celebrate. All the *ahalad-kaaslane* in Koduteel had turned out, though each knew the Regent would not welcome them in return. All the *ahalad-kaaslane*, that is, but for Reisil, Sodur, Juhrnus and Yohuac.

The afternoon was breezy. Puffy white clouds scudded across the sapphire sky. The group of four had assembled in Tirpalema's stable yard, where Indigo stood saddled and ready. The gelding pawed the ground and thrust his nose under Reisil's arm.

Reisil glanced at her companions, who wore their court finery beneath billowing cloaks. "You'd better get back. You'll be missed."

Juhrnus stepped forward, handing her a bulging pouch the size of her palm and pulling her into a rough hug. "Bright journey. And don't be long."

"And you be careful. Whatever you and Metyein are up to—remember, the Regent is watching."

Sodur took her hand. He still had that cunning, sideways look that reminded her of a crow. But he had given her a map to the valley where he thought the wizards' stronghold was. He squinted against the sunlight, the corners of his eyes damp.

Reisil grasped his forearm in a firm grip and then pulled him close. "Wish me luck."

"I do. I believe in you. I always have." He pulled back, giving her a long, meaningful look that Reisil could not interpret. He touched a finger to the chain holding the Lady's amulet. "Don't forget your true path." She nodded and turned to Yohuac, her throat tight. She wondered if she'd ever see any of them again. She took the arm he proferred, grasping it firmly. "When do you expect Baku?"

Yohuac frowned. "He has gone looking for magic. It sparks in your land where he did not see it before. Some very old, some new. He wonders why."

Reisil felt chill fingers stroke her heart. "That's easy enough. Another sign the Lady's withdrawn," she said. Then she shook herself and gave Yohuac a thin smile. "Take care of yourself. I'll send word when I know something."

"Remember my promise. I won't sit idly by."

"I won't forget." She tucked the pouch Juhrnus had given her into her saddlebags and swung astride Indigo. She tossed Saljane up into the air.

"Be careful," Juhrnus said.

"You be careful. The Regent will come hunting the *ahalad-kaaslane* soon," she said, and then clucked to Indigo. They trotted under the archway and into the street.

Juhrnus gazed after Reisil. "I hope this is the right thing. If I were the wizards, I wouldn't look too kindly on her."

"Too late to change your mind," Sodur said.

"Too late for a lot of things. We'd better get back. The Regent will be counting heads."

"I'll meet you there," Sodur said, and then hurried away, Lume trotting at his heels.

Juhrnus watched him go. "I hope he shows. The Regent might overlook us, but never Sodur."

"You think he won't?"

"He's not acting like himself."

"Should we follow him?"

Juhrnus shook his head as Sodur disappeared beneath the entrance to the stable yard. "Can't drag him. He's a grown man, and he knows the Verit better than any of us do. I just don't know if he cares anymore." He shrugged. "Nothing we can do. C'mon."

Yohuac fell into step beside him.

"Mind a bit of advice?" Juhrnus asked as they walked.

"What's that?"

"Next time, kiss her."

Yohuac faltered. "Reisil?"

"You didn't want to kiss the horse, did you?"

"No." Yohuac flushed, and Juhrnus smirked. Yohuac wasn't easily discomfited.

"You ought to have kissed her, then, while you had a chance."

The two fell into sober silence, striding quickly along. *You might not get another. She might not come back.*

Indigo tossed his head impatiently, but Reisil held him on a tight rein. She headed west, toward the Lady's Gate. Juhrnus had made sure a guard there would pass her through without any questions.

There were few people in the streets, though Reisil doubted it had much to do with the Regency ceremony. The plague had intruded into Koduteel. After mobs had nailed whole families up inside their homes and torched the buildings, people had begun to hide the affliction. Even those who were not infected skulked nervously, afraid that they might be suspected regardless and burned alive.

Reisil sniffed. The lingering odor of the destroyed buildings permeated the air, overriding the slighter scents of roasting meats, baking breads and the ever-present brine and fish smells from the ocean. A noise caught her attention, and seeing its cause, Reisil hastily kneed Indigo beneath an awning outside a sparsely populated kohv shop. Others ducked inside doorways up and down the street. A squad of guardsmen halted at the intersection, halberds shining in the sun. Four men marched out of the file to nail up broadsheets on each of the facing buildings. They fell back into formation, and as swiftly as they'd come, the guardsmen trotted away up the street.

Reisil hardly waited for them to turn the corner before she hurried over to read the notice.

"What's it say?" a man asked.

"Instructions from the Regent. He's locking down the city. They are going to close off the quarters. Every soul will be counted and cataloged, including names, ages and residences. Then everyone will be restrained to their homes. Head counts will be taken every morning and eve-

ning. Food and water will be provided each morning, sufficient for the day. Those refusing to be counted or who
break quarantine will be sealed inside their homes with
their families and left to starve. The same for anyone attempting to bribe a guard or sept leader."

"It can't be."

Reisil backed Indigo out of the gathering crowd. "Believe it. They are coming." The sound of booted feet and
scores of horses echoed along the streets as full regiments
of soldiers marched into the city.

People began spilling into the street beside her, running
and breathless, most carrying little else but the clothes they
wore. She threaded Indigo through the thickening flow of
humanity, hands catching at her legs and dragging at her.
Indigo tossed his head, yanking his bridle out of the grasp
of a square-faced merchant. He sped faster, boring through
the bodies, thrusting ahead in leaping jumps.

Reisil had hoped the regency ceremony would delay seal-
ing the gates, but rounding a corner, she discovered the
Lady's Gate was already closed. The gathering crowd clam-
ored and pressed to be released and were prodded back
with pikes. The tension was high, and everywhere Reisil
looked, she saw terror. A spattering of rocks flew at the
guards. Then a flurry of missiles sailed, whatever anyone
could find to throw. The guards shouted and swore, ducking
down, but there was little protection. The walls weren't
built to protect from attacks from within.

A roar burst from the throats of the massed peoples as
one guard fell to his knees, blood streaking from beneath
his hand as he clutched his head. Then like an enormous
beast, the mob bounded up the crisscrossing steps, swarming over the parapet with ravening fury. The guards stabbed
furiously with their pikes. A dozen bodies fell. But the
butchery only inflamed the mob. Townspeople rushed the
guards. More bodies fell and were churned underfoot. Just
as quickly, the guards disappeared beneath the seething
mass. Moments later the portcullis creaked upward, and the
bars holding the gates were thrown down. For a few moments it seemed as if everyone were frozen in place. A
dam of struggling bodies blocked escape. Then the dam
broke, and people went stampeding down the road and up
toward the hills.

Reisil and Indigo flowed out with the current of people. Her hands shook as she clutched the reins. Her lungs contracted so she could hardly get a breath. A sob caught in her throat. She squeezed her eyelids shut as if she could erase the memory of the massacre. Then Indigo snatched the bit in his teeth and bolted, his body low and flat against the ground, and all she could think of was not falling off.

Reisil hung on, not daring to tug at the reins, afraid she'd force a misstep. But in truth, she didn't want him to stop. The wind roared in her ears. Indigo's mane snapped against her face. She welcomed the stinging pain, the surge of his solid body beneath her, the jolting thud of each pounding stride. There was a freedom in that speed: an illicit joy in leaving Koduteel behind, in not having to be there to face the Regent's new edicts, to decide what to do, how to help. Much as she tried to quash the feeling, it continued to swell. She bent forward, pressing herself low against Indigo's neck.

He slowed of his own accord, far out along the western road. His nostrils were ringed in red, and his breath thundered in his chest. Reisil patted the gelding's drenched shoulder and turned him north away from the road, angling toward the distant mountains. She glanced back toward Koduteel.

~Saljane, dear heart. Watch carefully, she called to the circling goshawk.

Reisil wasn't worried about assassins. But those fleeing the city had done so empty-handed. She and Indigo would be an enormous temptation for those who now owned nothing. In those next hours Saljane called warnings to Reisil, who angled away from the straying people, taking a serpentine course to dodge them. They might have meant her no harm. But she dared not take chances.

When the light faded, Saljane drifted down to settle on Reisil's fist. They were climbing into the foothills, following an animal track. Reisil dismounted and led Indigo over the trail, her wizard-sight showing her the way. Near midnight, she made a cold camp in a grassy clearing. The night closed in, warmer than she expected. But she was high above the ocean now, protected by hills. She lay back with her head on her saddle.

Despite the bloody images of the fallen Koduteelians that continued to haunt the edges of her thoughts, the soothing smells of sun-warmed earth and pine cocooned her in pleasure. Indigo's soft cropping of grass, the twitter of night birds and the rustle of insect life in the bushes were a balm to her nerves, to a mind too long nurtured only by cold stone and wearying suspicion alone. She sighed, snuggling under the green cloak, stroking her fingers over its supple leather. She lay on top of the gray cloak, which served only as bedding and shelter. Saljane settled against her shoulder, stroking her beak along Reisil's chin.

The next morning's travel brought them to the banks of the swift-flowing Blan Ciiel River. They followed it north in search of a ford detailed on the map Sodur had given Reisil. She found it eight leagues up. It was little more than a widening in the snaking length of the river. In the summer months, it was belly-deep to a horse, but with the spring rains and snowmelt, the water churned muddy and deep. Reisil dismounted, tossing a stick into the current. It whipped quickly out of sight.

Indigo snorted and sidled around her so that his rump faced the water. Reisil laughed.

"I agree. But we may as well get it over with. You can rest on the other side. See? Saljane's already waiting for us." Reisil waved to the goshawk, who had alighted in a poplar on the opposite bank.

Reisil tied her cloak behind her cantle and lunged up into the saddle, biting her lips against a moan. This morning she'd had to walk a quarter of a league before her leg muscles loosened enough to ride.

Indigo shook his head and laid his ears flat as she nudged him to the edge of the water.

"No fussing," Reisil admonished, patting his shoulder. "If this is the worst of what we have to do, then we'll be lucky. Let's go."

Indigo stopped at the water's edge, dropping his nose to sniff at the ugly brown slurry. He lifted a hoof and pawed the air above the water. At last he stepped into the current, snorting and bobbing his head. They entered the river at the top of the ford, and Reisil angled Indigo against the current and away from the landing. Water closed around Indigo's legs and rose over Reisil's boots and then up over her knees. It was frigid, and in no time at all, Reisil lost sensation in her toes. She clamped her legs around the dun gelding, holding tight to her pommel with her right hand, pulling Indigo's head to the left to keep him aimed upstream.

Indigo's breathing was loud and heavy, his ribs pumping like bellows. Reisil spoke to him, urging him in a wide circle, turning him upstream. Gradually they inched closer to the shore and the current released them from its hungry grip. Indigo lunged out of the water, stopping on the shingle to shake himself, his head dangling as he panted. Reisil slid to the ground. She couldn't feel her feet, and her legs shook. She squatted, bracing her elbows on her knees until the shaking passed. Then she struggled up, pulling the cinch loose and shoving the saddle onto the ground with a thump. She grabbed the gray cloak and began rubbing Indigo's legs. By the time she was through, he had begun to breathe more evenly and the sun had done a great deal to warm them both. Reisil heaved the saddle back onto him, the saddle blanket sodden.

"Sorry about this, boy. But you're going to founder if we rest now. We'll stop a little farther on."

Reisil led him up into the trees, following a deer track. She continued on into the early afternoon, her wet boots chafing. She pushed on despite her discomfort. Every moment wasted was another moment the plague ate away at Kodu Riik.

In the late afternoon, Reisil made camp near a spring, turning Indigo loose to roll around and crop grass. She spread her saddle blanket in the sun, pulling her boots off to examine the damage to her feet. She had blisters on her heels, toes and on the balls of her feet. With a sigh, she spread salve on them and wrapped them with strips of cotton cloth from her pack, pulling a pair of fresh socks over them. Afterwards she unrolled her map.

By her best guess, she'd not made much progress. She had to cross long leagues of rolling farmland before climbing into the Aavrel mountain range. Mysane Kosk nestled in a low valley on the northern end with the wizard's stronghold somewhere in the middle near Sapriim's peak. She found it on the map with her finger. In between were two more rivers. With any luck, they would be easier to cross.

Reisil rolled up the map and tucked it back into her pack, reclining in the grass and stretching like a cat. The ground was soft and moist smelling, the scent of the grass tangy. The spring burbled, and chickadees and wrens twittered. Reisil's lids dropped.

Reisil woke blearily when Saljane returned from feeding.

~*Did you hunt well?*

~*Very well.*

Saljane radiated lambent satiety and predatory pride. She perched on the saddle and began preening herself, her stomach bulging as if she'd swallowed a small dog. A growl sounded loudly from Reisil's stomach, and she obediently dug in her pack for dinner. That night, as with the night before, she fell asleep nestled close to Saljane, boneless with exhaustion.

She awoke to a silent scream.

~*Saljane!*

Fear. Pain. Rage.

Need.

Reisil lunged to her feet. From the center of herself she wrenched up magic. It flooded her like lava, crackling around her hands, turning her vision crimson.

Then silence fell over her mind.

Irrevocable, unbearable silence.

Reisil screamed.

Chapter 34

Her scream continued until her lungs emptied and her throat was raw. Her ears were filled with a roar like an avalanche. She could hear nothing else. Reisil drew up her hands to strike. She would make them pay. She would fire the meadow. She would incinerate the entire valley. She would level the hills to the ocean. She would—

"You must control yourself. We do not wish to hurt you."

The words cut through Reisil's frenzied grief and fury like a sword of ice. She stiffened, predatory instinct settling over her. She swung her head from side to side, the crimson mist still veiling her vision. The shapes she saw were mere wraiths of red in a landscape of vermillion. It was enough. She raised her hands up above her shoulders, white energy flaming around them.

"Hold. Do not act rashly. Your bird is not dead. Merely . . . silenced." The voice was sharp and commanding and— Reisil cocked her head. Apprehensive. Her lips stretched in a smile. Good. Let them fear her.

The power wreathed around her elbows and climbed to her shoulders.

~Ahalad-kaaslane!

Panic. Killing rage. Helplessness.

~Saljane?

Reisil's hands dropped, her head whipping about, hope a firefly spark as Saljane reached into her mind with talon strength.

"Saljane!"

The connection ended abruptly as if it had never been. Reisil's head tipped back, and she wailed, an inarticulate, desperate sound.

Reisil spun, fixing on the speaker, renewed fury fueling the magic that began to scorch.

"Who are you? What do you want?"

"We are . . . emissaries. We want you to accompany us."

"From who? Where?" Her lips felt papery and tight, cracking with her words. Flames streaked along her skin. When she spoke, sparks fluttered from her tongue.

"From the wizards in exile. Our home lies in the Aavrel Mountains." The speaker's voice was urgent. "Once we are there, your bird shall be released to you, *unharmed*. An attack on any one of us will result in her death."

Reisil's body shook. She could smell burning hair. Her skin felt raw and too small. Her bones were fire. Her hands curled into claws.

"Hurt her, and I will kill you all," she whispered at last.

"Yes. I know."

The magic within burned for escape. Reisil had held it in check for too long. She could not merely disperse it. She didn't know how. She didn't want to, even if she could.

"Let me remind you."

She turned from her captors and flung the power at a tree-covered knoll two hundred paces away. The hill exploded, the trees bursting apart and sending pieces of burning wood and leaves in every direction. A hail of dirt and tree debris rained down on Reisil and her wizard captors. A sharp pain erupted beneath her right eye, and a trickle of blood rolled down her cheek. She blinked, her eyes gritty and parched. Slowly the redness cleared from her vision. She swung back around, searching for Saljane. She found her cradled in the arms of a gray stranger; the goshawk's legs were bound together, her body swaddled in a woven black material. Reisil made a howling sound and reached out, fury crackling up again.

"She is in no discomfort. Be at ease."

Reisil's chin jerked around, and she considered the speaker. Then she paced forward in slow, deliberate steps, coming to stand toe to toe with him, her head reaching to his chin. She tipped it back, locking his gaze. The glow from the ivy on her cheek reflected in his eyes and illuminated his craggy features.

"You hold a knife to my throat. I am in your trap and at your mercy. I will cooperate. But *do not* suppose me at ease. And guard Saljane as you would your own life. Because you may believe this to the bottom of your muddy soul." Reisil pressed closer, rising on tiptoe. "If anything happens to Saljane, you and yours will not survive it by more than the blink of an eye."

With that she stepped away, glancing narrowly at each of her seven captors. All seven men wore gray clothing beneath gray cloaks. Memory clicked. The assassins.

She approached the one holding Saljane. He backed away a step.

"I want to speak to her."

"She will not hear." Reisil held her ground, and the speaker nodded to the other. "Do not interfere with her bonds," he warned Reisil.

She examined the black bundle, suppressing an urge to

snatch the trussed bird from his arms. She had little doubt
that the bonds on Saljane were more magical than physical.
Trying to rescue Saljane would be more likely to get her
ahalad-kaaslane killed.

"Saljane, I am well. You must be patient. These *ganyiks*
hold you hostage for my cooperation. We will go with them
to their stronghold, and they will release you."

She paused, hoping for some sort of response, but the
goshawk didn't move. Reisil gritted her teeth, chin trembling,
fire spiraling up through her stomach. She dampened the
magic and spun away. She returned to her saddle and
grabbed her water bag. She drained it in several long swal-
lows, grateful for the cool moisture on her parched tongue.
Reisil reached for her saddle.

"We ride now."

"As you wish." The speaker motioned, and one of the
gray figures melted away, returning in moments with a
white-eyed Indigo.

Reisil saddled the horse, brushing away the dirt and
splinters that covered him. She wiped out his eyes and
stroked his head and shoulders. "Saljane needs your
strength," she murmured. "We're going to ride far and fast
with little rest. But it is the only way."

Indigo rubbed his head against her shoulder, nickering.
Reisil swung into her saddle. The wizards said nothing, collecting around Reisil like a school of gray fish. The speaker
led them out at a quick pace, evidently no less eager than
Reisil to return to his home.

Behind her, where the tree-covered knoll had been, there
was now a long furrow, as if the knoll had been entirely
scraped away to reveal a hole large enough to hold one of
Koduteel's great houses. The walls of the ravine were glassy
and smooth, as if a great fire had burned there, hot enough
to melt the dirt itself. Surrounding the great scar for half a
league was a moat of dirt, splintered wood and shredded
leaves spread inches deep over the grass.

The ride across the farmlands and into the mountains
took four days. They stopped only to sleep or fill their
water bags, eating cold rations on horseback. Reisil was
disconcerted at first when the entire group would wait on
her while relieving herself. But though she set the pace and

ordered the stops, she was their prisoner. She rarely spoke
to them, riding near the wizard who was carrying Saljane
and periodically calling encouragement to the trussed bird,
ignoring contemptuous looks from her captors.

On the fourth night as they came to a mountain stream,
the speaker, whose name she had never learned and who
was the only one who spoke to her, called a halt over her
objections. "The way is difficult. The horses do not see in
the dark as we do. We must not take chances," he explained. "We'll begin again in the morning."

It was the first hot meal she'd eaten since leaving Koduteel and Reisil was grateful for the rich venison stew and
flatbread. After dinner, the travelers sat in silence around
the fire, Reisil's eyes fixed on Saljane. They had told her
Saljane needed no food or water, that her bonds put her
into a kind of sleep.

"Why did you change your mind about killing me?"

For a few moments the speaker was silent. The other
wizards stirred restlessly. "It was never our intent to kill
you."

"Except that you tried twice."

"You are mistaken."

"I have a hole from an arrow in my cloak that says otherwise. And then there's the poisoned crossbolt one of you
left behind."

The speaker sighed, and Reisil quirked a brow at him. It
was the first indication of emotion she'd seen from him
since their first meeting. "It was thought you should be
incapacitated until we could render you harmless. We
should have healed any wounds."

"That poison on the crossbolt would have killed me before you could cure me."

He met her accusing stare, his gray eyes unabashed.
"After your vigorous response to our first attempt, one of
our more excitable members took it upon himself to exact
revenge. It was not sanctioned."

"Is that so?" Reisil said, glancing around at the stone-
faced wizards. "What did you do to him?"

"Do? I rebuked him."

Reisil frowned, giving a slow nod, realizing she was sitting in the company of a man who wanted to murder her.

It shouldn't have come as a surprise, even though in the last four days she'd become used to being a captive rather than a target of violence. She shivered. "I see."

"Do you? I wonder. However, it is not for me to explain. Good night."

And with that he left her to roll into her cloak. She thought she'd lie awake waiting for the dagger in the dark, but the four days of hard riding and short rest had taken their toll, and she fell heavily asleep. Besides, if he wanted her dead, she couldn't stay awake forever. And who knew what awaited her in the wizards' stronghold?

The mountains rose in steep, gray folds, ridge after ridge, disappearing into the clouds. The trail wound sharply upward through a heavy mist, the leaf meal dampening the sounds of the horses' hooves. Trees rose like specters around them, the forest thickening as they climbed. Soon the mist turned to chill rain, and Reisil was glad for the sheepskin lining of her green cloak.

For the first time in days she thought about her friends in Koduteel. Her cheeks flushed guiltily. How did they fare? She sent a prayer winging to the Lady that they were all right. The fact that she hadn't yet heard from Baku worried her. He'd clung to her so tightly and for so long. And her use of magic surely would have made him curious. But the idea of calling him curdled her stomach. As if he could replace Saljane. Her hands clamped around her reins. How she wanted to loose her magic on the wizards and take Saljane back! But she trusted the speaker's threat. She could take no chances on Saljane's life. And her kidnappers *were* taking her exactly where she wanted to go, after all. It was almost lucky.

But she felt Saljane's separation as if they'd lopped off her leg. It hurt in ways that were too deep for words. All that kept her moving was the hope that Saljane was not really dead, whatever her mind told her. And if they had hurt Saljane, if they lied, then Reisil would avenge her *ahalad-kaaslane*. She thought of the three attackers on the greensward outside of Koduteel, their bodies turned to ash. She thought of the wizards in Patverseme, their bodies nothing but burnt husks, the air smelling of scorched hair and flesh. Her mouth tightened as cold brutality hardened inside her. She'd spared many wizards that night. But if they'd murdered Saljane, she'd have no mercy, no—

~*Where are you?* Baku demanded suddenly, bulling into her mind and scattering her thoughts like chaff.

~*Near the wizards' stronghold,* Reisil replied, the walls in her mind snapping automatically into place for the first time since he'd come to Koduteel. She ignored Baku's recoil.

He rammed back at her with a torrent of black wrath and resentment. It slammed against her walls with no effect. Reisil felt his surprise, his confusion. But she had no room for sympathy. All she had was swelling emptiness and a chill that frosted her soul. She had nothing for Baku. He wasn't her *ahalad-kaaslane* anyhow.

For several long minutes nothing happened. Then Baku returned again, this time tentatively.

~*Reisiltark?*

~*Yes.*

~*What has happened?*

~*The wizards have Saljane. They take us to their stronghold. We will be there soon, within a few days.*

Anger bloomed in Baku and grew, expanding and spreading, ravenous and hot. It washed over Reisil, wrapped her in a conflagration. And for the first time she felt the brittle cold within her thaw slightly with her surprise. Baku loved Saljane, thirsted for the same retribution Reisil longed for.

~*They say they will release her when we arrive. If they do not . . . they will answer to me. They have been hunting me. I mistook them for assassins, but they claim they are not.* Except one. The one who wanted revenge. She could understand that.

~*Tell Yohuac. I will report more later, if I can.*

She felt Baku's reluctance to let their connection go, but she allowed him no foothold. He slipped away as if he'd never been, and the emptiness swelled up again inside her. She hunched forward in her saddle, paralyzed with the pain of it.

Three days later the small group rode through a notch and down a steep defile into a narrow, winding canyon. Snow blanketed the ground inside the tree line, giving way as they reached the floor of the canyon. At various intervals, they stopped while the speaker spoke a few words and worked his fingers in the air. Shapes like nonsensical words glowed for a moment and then disappeared. Reisil's mouth went dry. Her hands tightened on the reins, shaking. *Soon,* she told herself. Soon she'd have Saljane back.

The canyon walls rose sharply, scrub clinging in cracks and fissures. The far end was completely walled off, a mountain sitting squarely across it. Set to one side was a small, arched portal covered by a simple door. Reisil frowned at it.

"Come. The horses remain here."

Reisil glanced down and found the speaker standing at her right knee. She dismounted. The horses were led away, disappearing down a shadowy walkway lined by gnarled trees. Reisil was left alone with the speaker and the wizard carrying Saljane. She followed them to the door, her gait awkward. Her ankles ached and her joints seemed to grate together. She hadn't eaten since early that morning, and there was a hollow feeling in her stomach.

The speaker stopped, waiting for her. "You must enter here."

Reisil flicked a glance at Saljane's too-still form wrapped in the black cloth, and then reached for the latch, shoving hard. The door swung wide and thumped against the wall. She strode inside, and the other two men followed.

Reisil recognized the space for what it was immediately. A testing room, used to discover if a person had wizard-sight, and therefore was a wizard. In this case, a proving room. No one who wasn't a wizard could enter the stronghold. Except her.

There were walls set at odd angles and in zigzags. In nooks and corners were traps—pits of chittering insects, blocks of stone that slid back and forth to crush a careless body, pools of boiling chemicals, and glistening spikes protruding from the walls. To anyone without wizard-sight, it would be dark as pitch. A blundered step meant instant death. Reisil smiled.

"Do keep up, won't you?" she called over her shoulder.

And then she plunged ahead, making her way swiftly through the maze. There appeared to be no ceiling, and a fresh breeze picked at her hair and cloak, carrying on its back the scent of evergreens and cedar smoke. She wasn't inside a mountain at all, Reisil realized. It was illusion. She hurried faster. The sooner she made it through the maze, the sooner Saljane would be restored to her. Her shoulder ached for the goshawk's weight, her cheek for Saljane's affectionate caress.

On the other side was another door, and she jerked the latch up and yanked it open. Afternoon sunlight streamed down, warming her face. Beyond the door was a grassy field. She turned, waiting impatiently for her companions to catch up.

"What now?" she demanded when the speaker exited the maze.

His lips twitched, and he gave a slight bow. "Now I take you to Kvepi Kaisivas."

"And Saljane?"

"Kvepi Kaisivas will answer all your questions."

Reisil bit her tongue and followed after him without protest.

Inside the valley was a scattering of ugly buildings made of charcoal stone. Some looked incomplete; all were bare of ornamentation, their faces blank and austere. The speaker approached the largest of these. A broad walkway of crushed stone wound its way to the front steps of the somber edifice. The doors were of heavy, polished oak that swung open lightly at the speaker's touch. There were no guards outside, no servants within to meet them. The foyer was furnished sparsely with a few colorful tapestries. There was a surprising amount of light that came from nowhere Reisil could see. Magic, no doubt.

The speaker led the way up the wide central staircase. There were no carpets, and their footsteps echoed hollowly off the walls. At the top of the landing were wide corridors to the left and right and a set of doors going straight. The speaker knocked softly on these, and after a moment they swung open. The decor here was more comfortable than below. Rugs covered the stone floors, and a variety of tapestries, paintings and sculptures decorated the walls, carefully spaced to provide a sense of fullness. The furniture, though sparse, was slender and delicate, the upholstery woven of rich, butterfly hues.

The speaker ushered Reisil into a large library where at last they encountered another person. The man was sitting in a wingback chair, his feet propped on an ottoman in front of a merry fire. At the speaker's low announcement, he snapped his book shut and came around the chair, smiling broadly.

"You join us at last. I am pleased to have your company."

He bowed over hands linked loosely together. He was tall and powerfully built, with chestnut hair speckled gray. His eyes were a pale brown, his face mobile and pleasant. He wore black wizard's robes covered in arcane symbols embroidered in silver thread, and in his ears were delicate earrings fashioned from silver and amethyst.

"I didn't have much of a choice," Reisil said coldly, unmoved by his affability. "You are the Kvepi Kaisivas who can free my *ahalad-kaaslane*?"

"Ah, by the Long Night. It came to that, did it?" He sighed. "I am sorry for these measures, but I didn't think you would come without the promise of my saving your bird." He shook his head. "A shame, but no harm done, and easily remedied." He motioned for the wizard holding Saljane to set his burden on a table, and removed the cloth wrapping the goshawk.

Saljane lay stiff and unmoving, her eyes open and staring. Her talons were curled into fists. Fear quivered down Reisil's spine.

~*Saljane. Can you hear me? Come on, sweetling. Come back to me.*

The goshawk lay still. Kvepi Kaisivas glanced up at her.

"She has been under the spell for some days. Give her a few moments to regain herself. There is no need for concern."

Reisil's nostrils flared. "There is." *He* should be concerned. If Saljane did not recover— Biting her lips, Reisil reached for Saljane again, laying an unsteady hand on her feathered chest.

~*Come back to me, my darling. Don't let them take you away from me.*

A flickering began in Reisil's mind, like shadows cast by a slim flame.

~*Saljane!*

More flickering, stronger this time.

Reisil swept Saljane into her arms and peered into her staring eyes. A quiver ran through Saljane's stiff body. Then another. Then she began to move, to struggle. Reisil caught blurry thoughts from the goshawk.

Terror. Anger. Hunger.

Her talons raked the air, then caught Reisil's unprotected left arm, slicing through her sleeve and forearm. Blood welled and dripped on the carpet. Saljane shrieked.

Kek-kek-kek-kek!

She began flapping her wings as she thrashed about, dagger-sharp talons rending the air, squawking and shrieking. Reisil let her go, and Saljane landed on the floor and then launched awkwardly into the air. She careened from the library shelves and swooped across the room.

~Saljane! I'm here! Saljane! Reisil cried urgently, tears streaming down her cheeks.

But the goshawk's mind was a spinning welter of confusion, anger, and ferociousness. Reisil's voice couldn't break through the chaos.

Saljane flew near the wizard who'd been her keeper for the journey, her eyes wide and blind. The wizard put up his hands. To catch her, to block her, to cast a spell— Reisil didn't know. She didn't care. Magic flowed into her, wrapping her hands in flame.

"Don't." The word froze him in place. He glanced at her, blanching. But he didn't move. Saljane swept past him, her wing battering the side of his head, a talon scraping his forehead. She lighted on the back of the wing-back chair, wings spread wide.

Kek-kek-kek-kek!

~Saljane, I am here. I am here. I am here. Reisil continued to chant the phrase, moving to stand in front of her *ahalad-kaaslane*. Magic burned in her, but she damped it ruthlessly. It was useless for this work.

Saljane continued to make her high-pitched call, sounding much like the call of a fox in the wild. Reisil edged closer, bending to put her face close to Saljane's. A dangerous act of trust with Saljane so far out of her wits. A swift peck, and the goshawk could rob Reisil of an eye.

Minutes passed. With her mental chant, Reisil projected her love and her joy at having Saljane awake and near her.

At last the whirling tumult of Saljane's mind began to order itself. Gradually she began to quiet, her wings contracting to her sides.

~?

~*I am here. You have been under a spell. We are prisoners in the wizards' stronghold. But all is well now. We are together.*

She reached out and Saljane stepped gingerly onto her fist. Reisil pulled her close, snuggling the goshawk against her chest. She felt no pain from her *ahalad-kaaslane*, though Saljane's mind remained ragged and inarticulate. Reisil sniffed, taking a shuddering breath and turning back to her captors.

"She is well?"

This from the speaker. Reisil bit back the scalding answer. "She returns to herself."

He nodded, and Reisil was surprised to see a pleased expression settle over his sharp features.

"She hungers."

Kvepi Kaisivas nodded and pulled a cord in the corner. "Let us adjourn to the dining room."

The dining room contained a long table covered with a lace cloth. The chairs were upholstered with leather, and a perch stood near the corner of the table. Reisil took the seat beside the perch, and the Kvepi sat opposite her. He motioned for the speaker to sit. The other wizard had disappeared.

As soon as they had seated themselves, a parade of servants entered carrying trays of food, including a trencher of raw fish, rabbit and venison, chopped into chunks. This was set on the table in front of Saljane. The servant then filled the feeding tray. Saljane began bolting the food with single-minded intensity.

The Kvepi motioned for Reisil to serve herself. But as she reached for a spoon, he ejaculated and leaped to his feet. She stiffened.

"Oh, dear. I'd forgotten that. Allow me, please."

And then he came around the table, calling for a basin of warm water and bandages. Reisil followed his gaze and made a face. Blood welled from her forearm where Saljane had clawed her. With unexpected gentleness, the Kvepi peeled back her sleeve, *tsk*ing. He washed the wound and bound it. It hurt, but Reisil held still under his ministrations.

"We'll do better later," he declared. "Uldegas will have a look at it."

Reisil took her arm back as he handed the basin to a waiting servant. "It's well enough," she said, knowing she had what was needed, if her saddlebags were returned to her.

The food was delicious. Crusty white bread still hot from the oven, roasted meats and cheeses, young greens, custards, compotes, stuffed fish, thick soups and flaky pies. The Kvepi filled her glass with cool crisp white wine tasting of apricots and snow and another with red wine tasting of smoky oak.

When she was sated, she leaned back in her chair. Saljane hopped down from her perch, nestling in Reisil's lap.

~Better?

~Better.

A knot rose in Reisil's throat. It was only one word, but she'd never heard anything so wonderful in her life.

"And now we must get down to business," Kvepi Kaisivas said. "Let us retire to the library and discuss matters, shall we?"

Reisil found herself sitting opposite him in a wing-back chair, her feet propped on an ottoman at his insistence. She eyed him askance, but obeyed. The speaker stirred up the fire and then pulled around another seat as Kvepi Kaisivas settled himself comfortably.

"None of this was necessary, you know," Reisil said suddenly. "I was on my way to find you."

"Oh?" The two men exchanged startled looks.

"Mmm. The plague. You caused it. And the *nokulas*. I want to know how to stop them both."

"Ah, of course. Certainly we did, though, you understand, not intentionally. We have no cure for either."

Reisil stared. She had expected denials. And this certainly was one. But the Kvepi was so matter of fact that his words had the ring of truth. She opened her mouth, but could not find anything to say.

"I am sorry to disappoint you. However, I cannot be sorry that it brought you to us," he said. "I believe Kvepi Tapit would agree."

"Who?"

He gestured at the speaker. "Kvepi Tapit." He frowned at the other Kvepi. "You did not give her your name?"

The other man gave a slight shrug. "There was little opportunity for conversation. We rode quickly."

"Ah, my friend. Will you never learn?" He turned back to Reisil. "Please forgive Tapit. He grew up in the hinterlands of Patverseme and has never appreciated the need for manners. He does better in the company of rocks and trees, but he is one of our best. If anyone could bring you here safely, it was him."

"What do you want with me?"

"To bring you home."

"Excuse me?"

"To bring you home. You are a wizard, after all. Otherwise, you could not have come through the maze. We are your family, and it's time you came home."

Chapter 35

Metyein slouched in a chair, watching his father's valet tug his coat straight and buff a dull spot on his boots.

"I wish you'd attend. The Regent has asked about you," his father said, sipping a glass of wine and setting it back on a tray.

"Has he? And what have you told him?"

"That you've been sulking, having discovered what a spineless *ganyik* your friend Soka is. Running away. Has cost him the honor of his house. No doubt Bro-heyek has begun to invade his neighbors, just when Kodu Riik needs it least."

"When would Kodu Riik need it?" Metyein needled.

His father shook his head. "By the Lady, Metyein, have you no sense of duty in you?"

"And you, father. What about your sense of duty?"

This was too much for the Lord Marshal. He ordered his valet out, shutting the door firmly behind him. Then he whirled around, his face taut with anger.

"How dare you. I have served this land since I was a boy. I have put down revolts. I have led men into battle. I have always served this country and her Iisand with all my honor and heart. And what have you done? Sulked and caviled. Yes, I enjoy women. Yes, your mother and I have never had a close bond. But I have treated her according to her station and status as my wife. She has never wanted for anything, nor has she had to tolerate my attentions more than necessary to produce heirs.

"It's time for you to grow up. Have a look at yourself. Have a look at Kodu Riik. We're a dying land. If the plague doesn't get us, we'll starve. The *nokulas* have chased the farmers out of their fields, and we're completely cut off from outside supplies. We are on our own, and our enemies would just as soon watch us shrivel up and die. And now that stripling has taken the Regency. Still, all you do is fight petty duels with spoiled lordlings and whine about whom I take to my bed. As if that were your business. You have the balls to question my duty, but I ask you, how are you serving your country? What about your duty to this house, and if not to your father, then your Lord Marshal?"

"Oh, I know my duty well enough, father," Metyein said. "And I've time enough for duty, and to watch over my mother's honor, since her husband does not." This last was said with a sneer.

"Her husband also overlooks her lovers."

"Mother doesn't have lovers. Do you sully her name to justify your rutting?"

"I require no justification. However, since you are intent on having the truth, you shall have it. Then we shall be done with your adolescent posturings once and for all. Though she is discreet, your mother has had a variety of lovers over the years."

Metyein shook his head. "Never. There have been no men in her home. Or are you suggesting she bedded servants?"

"Oh, no. Your mother is quite blue in her blood and would never stoop so low. Nor would she ever tarnish the Vare name. She is the second Dajam of the land, after all.

But she has never appreciated the hairy, brutish nature of men. She prefers softer, more delicate companions."

Metyein could only stare. He wanted to protest, to argue. But his father's voice had the ring of truth. And his own memories corroborated them. Many visitors, mostly noblewomen without their husbands. He always thought those visits came from pity for his mother's loneliness and isolation. But now he saw them through a man's eyes. The lovers' meals with delicious wines and sumptuous foods. The long evenings spent alone, speaking of "women's things" and no children needed. Long, languorous mornings in bed. No one thought it strange that two women would choose to sleep together, to warm each other's feet in the night.

Metyein's lips pinched together. He gazed at his father belligerently. "Even if it is true, that does not excuse you."

"Boy, I require no excuses. But I am tired of your carping. If I must order your good behavior, I will do so."

Metyein came to his feet in a fluid movement. He bent in a flourishing bow. "I am at your command, Lord Marshal."

"Would that it were so," his father muttered.

Metyein straightened. "What would you have of me?"

"Your mind. Your heart. Your loyalty."

Metyein turned his head away, bitterness burning in his throat. "You don't ask much."

"I ask my due as your Lord Marshal."

"Tell me, father, what will you do when our Regent is made Iisand? Will you give him your mind, your heart, your loyalty? Knowing how much you oppose him, knowing he's in bed with the Scallacians who want nothing more than to suck our marrow dry? Or will you return to Doneviik and mother and allow him to grind Kodu Riik into dust, destroying the *ahalad-kaaslane* and abandoning the Blessed Lady?"

His father reached for his wineglass, drinking it down in one gulp, his knuckles white. "Careful how you go, son. You border on treason. The Regent would have you in chains for less."

"That is as may be, but it does not answer my question."

"I serve the crown. I have taken oaths. Now you answer my question. Will you give your due to me as Lord Marshal, if not your father?"

"Mother raised me well, father. I love this land, and I love the Blessed Amiya. In all things I serve both. So long as you do the same, I expect you may have what you wish of me."

It wasn't the answer his father wanted. "You've learned better than I thought, Metyein. You speak as obliquely as any seasoned Kijal. But you are a subject of the crown, and you do not get to choose whom or how you will serve. Agree with him or not, when Aare cas Varakamber is named Iisand, then he becomes the Lady's annointed and he speaks in Her voice. You are in no position to judge his decisions. Only the Lady may. You must obey."

"I speak as plainly as I can, father," Metyein said seriously. "I will continue to answer for my mother's honor as is necessary to oafs whose mouths are larger than their brains. But I will dun you no more. I have always respected you otherwise. Henceforth you will find me as deferential, respectful and courteous a son as a father has a right to expect." He paused, searching for words. "I dearly hope we don't end up on opposite sides of what is to come. That would be painful to me. But in plain terms, I have grave doubts that our Regent still serves the Blessed Amiya, and I believe we shall soon see proof enough of this. And then our paths will likely diverge. There is no choice. I am my father's son. I must do as honor and duty require."

His father closed his eyes, a pained look on his face. And for the first time since he could remember, Metyein saw in his father the man, torn between loyalties and uncertainties. A man who stood alone, his family far away and estranged, his son and heir little more than a viper in the nest. He had no friends anymore, not since the Iisand's transformation. No wonder he sought solace in the arms of women. But never just one, and never for very long. He couldn't afford that kind of trust. A rush of feeling swept Metyein.

Impulsively Metyein reached out and grasped his father's shoulder. "You are a great man indeed, and I shall ever hold you in high esteem. I hope that I will earn your regard in the days to come. But no matter what, father, I will always be proud to be your son."

His father stood a moment, walnut eyes boring into Metyein. Then he pulled him close, hugging him tightly.

Kebonsat gazed out the window at nothing. He still could hardly credit what he'd seen. The Iisand had become a demonspawned beast. He shuddered and dragged his fingers through his hair. Patverseme had sent men to Mysane Kosk, spies to discern the situation. Whether they'd been tainted, he didn't know. And worse, he had no way to warn anyone!

His fist thumped the desk, and he shoved away, striding to the window. It was a bleak view. The Verit—the Regent, Kebonsat corrected himself sardonically—had taken a firm grip on the city. A pall of smoke hung over everything from the new plague pyres outside the walls. Soldiers patrolled the city in innumerable squads. The city itself had been broken into manageable sections called bureaus, and within those, smaller precincts. Business still limped on as workers were shuffled into housing within their employer's precinct. Every morning and every night they were examined for symptoms of the plague, then they were checked off on lists and escorted to and from work.

Thus far the system was working. At least there had not yet been riots beyond those initial hours when the Regent had sealed the city. The Jarrah Gardens had been converted into a prison camp and a garrison. Many of the new Regent's conscripts were thieves and thugs and had little compunction in using force to keep the peace.

Kebonsat tapped his finger against the windowpane. He couldn't disagree with any of the Regent's decisions, though his methods were a bit too bloody for Kebonsat's tastes. The speed and efficiency of implementation were breathtaking and ruthless. If he hadn't already known how dangerous an enemy the Verit was, Kebonsat certainly knew it now.

So what does he have in store for me? The Regent certainly didn't intend for Emelovi to marry a Patverseme *ganyik*. And Kebonsat wasn't worth much as a hostage. But then the Regent was the kind to hedge his bets and plan for contingencies. Maybe he thought the son of the Dure Vadonis would be useful down the line.

Kebonsat swung around, pacing across the room and back. He worried about Emelovi. She was terrified of her brother. But despite her fear, she'd resisted his machinations, particularly against the *ahalad-kaaslane*. What would she do if she knew the truth about her father? A pang of guilt thrust through his chest. Everything she did was against the assumption that sooner or later her father would wake from his grief and resume the throne. She loved him dearly and hated her brother's plots to usurp the crown. If she knew what had really happened to her father, would she cede those loyalties to her brother? Did he dare tell her the truth about her father?

But no. She wouldn't be able to conceal her grief. The Regent would insist on knowing, and even if she resisted, he'd get it out of her. One way or another. And once he discovered her secret, he'd want to know how she knew. Her spying, her confidences to Kebonsat, everything would come out. What Aare would do to her then, Kebonsat feared to guess. But it would release a dam. He and all his people would be taken in for questioning. Given the young Regent's hatred of anything Patversemese, Kebonsat doubted any would come out whole, if they survived at all. And Juhrnus, Metyein, Sodur, even the Lord Marshal— none would be safe. Worse, Aare would have the excuse he needed to assume the throne and destroy the *ahalad-kaaslane* once and for all.

Kebonsat sighed, rubbing his eyes. He couldn't tell Emelovi. It was too dangerous. And when she did finally find out, she'd never forgive him for his silence.

"Better than dying," he muttered. But in the short time he'd been allowed to court her, he'd discovered a woman he could love. A woman he'd begun to love. And she had just as quickly sped as far out of his reach as Reisil.

"Am I a masochist? To fall in love with women I can never have?"

At first he'd thought Emelovi fragile and weak, a tool for her brother's hand. But she soon disabused him of such notions. During that first morning's breakfast, she'd baldly confided her brother's scheme to kidnap Ceriba. He'd sent Rocis after her as soon as Emelovi had revealed her brother's plan. He prayed Rocis had made it in time, but even if he had, there was no way for Rocis to inform him of that.

How was it that he could do so little to protect the women he held most dear? Aare could be doing anything to Emelovi, Ceriba might already be captured, and Reisil— There was no knowing if she'd escaped Koduteel or not, or if she'd been killed in one of the gate riots. Juhrnus didn't know, though it had been four days since the city had been sealed and he'd been to consult with Kebonsat. He might know something more now.

Helplessness ate at Kebonsat's gut, and he continued pacing, formulating plans and discarding them. He had to get Emelovi away; he had to get them both away. And then he had to find Ceriba—

He started at the knock at the door.

"Yes?"

"Sir, will you be wishing your supper now?" It was Quillers. Imprisonment seemed to have steadied the steward. He had kept his composure, reassuring the other servants and allowing Kebonsat his privacy, only occasionally intruding, mostly to subtly remind Kebonsat to maintain appearances for the other members of his party. Both Dumen and Ledus had lost their titles and holdings as soon as Patverseme had severed diplomatic ties. Though both men remained stoic, imprisonment grated on their nerves. Both had wives and families. Or at least, they had. Their children would have swiftly been adopted by the heirs of their titles, their wives encouraged to remarry within days. If they thought Kebonsat had fallen apart, holing up in his study and bewailing fate, they would soon follow suit.

"I'll be there shortly," he replied, glancing toward the paneling behind his desk. The entrance to the passageway was hidden behind a narrow wall cabinet and a painting of some ancient Iisand in battle. It remained steadfastly closed. He scowled. If Juhrnus did not come by the end of supper, Kebonsat would go in search of him.

Soka crouched between a newly leafed hedge and a wall. Beyond it soldiers paraded by, dragging the struggling body of a middle-aged man. They'd tied ropes around his ankles and were hauling him across the cobbles. The man held his arms around his head, begging and crying, but to no avail. The soldiers marched on without taking the slightest notice of him.

Soka pressed himself deeper into the hedge. Four days. Aare had to have known how hard it would be to get to Metyein. Without money, without food, without a weapon. Soka's hand dropped to the scarred sword he wore belted on his hip. Illegal. And not only for a hostage to the court, but for any citizen. No one save soldiers and *ahalad-kaaslane* were permitted to go armed in the city anymore. But after the weapon's former owner had thought to rob him, Soka had simply taken it.

Not far now. He'd been forced in the wrong direction, carried by the riots. It had taken him four days to work his way back. He'd crossed six bureaus, and the Vare manor lay only two streets away in yet another precinct. The soldiers passed and Soka scurried across the boulevard. The sun had fallen past the walls, and he was nothing more than shadow inside shadow. He easily avoided the patrols. Harder were the barriers with soldiers checking licenses for each person crossing precinct lines. Still these were not impossible. But on the doorstep of the palace and noble district, the soldiers were no longer slovenly, and there were more of them. Soka ducked into an alley.

There was one way through, and that was possible only with the proper documentation. He now had to wait for his opportunity and take it. It came more quickly than he hoped, shortly after moonrise. The courier trotted quickly along, a satchel over his chest. Soka slid his sword free. He waited until the courier was opposite the alley opening and then leaped out. The flat of his sword crashed into the back of the man's head, dropping him like a stone. Soka sheathed his sword and grabbed the limp man's legs, dragging him into the alley. It was a matter of moments to switch clothing.

He approached the checkpoint at a trot, pulling up the hood of the cloak to hide his telltale ruined eye. "Message for the Lord Marshal," he announced, opening his cloak to show his satchel and uniform. The guards gave him a cursory glance and waved him through. No one impeded couriers. Interfering guards paid the price for late messages. Soka sped up, forcing himself to run, though his legs screamed and his lungs spasmed. Turning onto the avenue containing the Lord Marshal's residence, he saw the Lord Marshal's gilded coach rattling away. He smiled and flung himself toward the gates, pounding against the wood with his fist. The spy panel snapped back.

"Message for Basham Arceres," he declared breathlessly.

The panel slid shut, and he heard the bars on the pedestrian door slide back. The guard motioned him inside, pointing up the drive toward the house.

"Can't leave m'post," he mumbled. "Go to the front. Butler will let you in."

Soka almost groaned, but he knew that a courier would be expected to run the remaining distance, and so he did, up the long driveway and scrolling steps to the portico. He hammered the knocker, panting heavily and pulling his hood closely around his face. The butler guided him to a salon and left him, pointedly staring at his dirt-stained clothing and then at the furniture. Metyein smiled sourly. He was in no mood to sit anyhow. He poured himself a glass of red wine sitting on the sideboard. He gulped it down and poured another, just as the door opened.

"Basham Arceres," the butler announced. Soka didn't turn, hearing the doors close behind him.

"Making a bit free, aren't you?" came Metyein's sardonic drawl. Soka closed his eyes. The moment had come at last. He drank the rest of the wine and turned around.

"You've never complained before."

The two men stared at one another.

"By the Lady . . ." Metyein leaped across the room, grasping Soka by the shoulders. "What in the three hells happened to you? Where have you been? Demonballs, I thought you were dead!" And then he pulled Soka against him, hugging him tightly and pounding his back. Soka closed his eyes. Until this moment he hadn't been quite sure that Metyein *had* survived, that it hadn't all been one of Aare's cruel jokes.

At last he pushed away. "Peace, Metyein. I cannot take too much manhandling."

Instantly Metyein let him go, remorse darkening his expression. "I have looked for you, my friend. Every day. But there was never even a clue. Pelodra vanished, the horses gone, everything."

"Ah well, I can explain that," Soka said. "And you have healed well?" He scanned Metyein, but there was no sign that he'd ever been hurt. Metyein grinned.

"Seems we both have a tale to tell. But not here. Let us find somewhere more comfortable."

Two hours later, Soka and Metyein sat in the latter's

rooms. Soka wore a suit of fresh clothing, though it hung loosely on his too-thin frame. His feet were bare, and his long hair wet from a hot bath. He wore a blue silk scarf tied rakishly across his ruined eye. The remains of a hearty meal sat before them.

"I have been patient, you must agree. But now you must tell me what happened to you," Metyein declared, pushing away from the table and retreating to the fire. He motioned for Soka to join him, pouring them each a glass of port.

Soka stood, his feet apart, hands laced together, forefingers pressed to his lips. Here it was. The precipice. He thought of Kedriles and jeered at himself. He'd already decided. Standing in front of Aare, he'd made his choice. The dice were thrown. Now was no time to falter. He dropped his hands.

"You know you are my only friend? Brother of my heart. I have never understood why you should have taken to me so. I dare say no one else did either."

"I have good taste," Metyein replied.

"I think your taste is questionable," Soka said with a crooked grin. "But your friendship is the one thing I value. I don't think even you know how much. It is the only thing for which I would willingly give my life. It is the only thing for which I would give more than my life. I would suffer for it." He said it matter of factly and did not allow Metyein a chance to respond.

"Pelodra was in the employ of Aare, and directly after we left you in the Gardens, he turned me over to our Verit."

"Regent," Metyein corrected reflexively, his eyes wide.

"Ah, yes. He did tell me that before letting me go."

"He let you go? Just . . . let you go? Just like that?"

"For a price. He does nothing for free. But let me go back to the beginning. It seems the ambush was intended to capture you and use you against your father. But thanks to your annoying heroics, he ended up with me instead. Pelodra, I understand, has fallen on sharp times." His lips pulled into the semblance of a grin. "Aare brought me to the accomodations he keeps beneath his residence for people he holds in low esteem. There I was healed. Four days ago, on the day of his Regency ceremony, he came to me. He offered me a chance at freedom if I would use you to spy on your father. He demonstrated both the touch of his favor and disfavor. In the end I agreed. And thus I was freed."

Metyein stared at him, head shaking stupidly.

"You agreed to spy. You do realize that telling me that makes your mission difficult."

Now Soka's grin turned feral. "Doesn't it? Still it was the only way out that didn't involve a coffin, and Aare found it less difficult to believe I would betray you than he would ever have believed that I could no more betray you than I could cure the plague."

Metyein dropped down onto a chair. "I'll see him dead."

"One day. But it's the meantime I worry about."

"And you should. I've had some adventures of my own since the ambush."

At Soka's questioning look, Metyein shook his head. "Think whether you really want to know. Our friendship has already put you in grave danger. I could still get you out of the city. You could do as everyone believes. You could run to your father."

"Aare would come after me sooner or later. And I'm not running from the likes of him. I owe him."

"Be sure, Soka. Once I tell you, you're in it with me."

"I'm in it with you already. I told you. You are my heart's brother."

Metyein gripped Soka's hand. "I have missed you." He refilled their glasses. "My tale also begins with the ambush. Seems that last arrow caused a fatal wound."

Soka's brows lifted. "Yet you sit here, hale as ever."

"Have you heard of Reisiltark?" And Metyein plunged into his story, leaving nothing out. Afterwards it was Soka's turn to stare glazedly.

"If Aare catches you . . ." He thought again of Kedriles and shuddered.

"I told my father tonight, I have a duty to the Lady. I never felt it before. Father is right. I was petty and sulking. But Reisiltark is Kodu Riik's only hope. The Iisand is . . . gone. There's nothing left of him. Aare will be Iisand, sooner or later. And when he is, he will wipe out the *ahalad-kaaslane*. He believes the sorcerers are his pets, but they have come for their own purposes, and they smell blood. They merely wait until we are helpless and then will take us at their leisure. And if they don't, the wizards will. Kodu Riik will become a magical battleground. I have to do this. I have to help her."

"Because you owe her your life?"

"I do owe her my life. But that isn't why. It's because she's the Lady's chosen. And she's all that stands between us and our enemies."

Metyein sat for a moment and then jumped to his feet. "I have to go. I'm late for a meeting. I know this is a lot for you. It's more than I can ask of you. I'll still get you out of Koduteel to safety. You don't have to be a part of this."

Soka grinned, one of his familiar flashing grins. "I don't think so. You see, I don't know your Reisiltark, and I have no real cause to be loyal to Kodu Riik. But I do owe Aare, and I mean to pay him in full." He stood, stretching, wincing as his muscles protested. "You need someone to look after you. Otherwise you'll be all work and no play. Very dull, Metyein. When was the last time you had yourself a woman?"

Metyein rolled his eyes, chuckling as he slapped Soka on the back. "You are impossible. But let's find you some boots. I've got some people for you to meet."

Chapter 36

"Y ou are late."

Juhrnus slid through the panel in Kebonsat's study followed closely by Yohuac, Metyein, and Soka. Kebonsat waited opposite his desk, feet propped on the corner, a sheaf of papers on his lap. Outside the window a streak of blue glowed above the incoming fog. Juhrnus yawned. It had been a long night, first with Karina and then with a pair of edgy *ahalad-kaaslane* he'd recruited to help. The soldiers still allowed the *ahalad-kaaslane* to travel freely in the city, but more than once he'd found himself followed or delayed by a round of questions. Worst of all, he hadn't spoken to Kedisan-Mutira in two days, and the separation was starting to wear.

"Did you have somewhere else to be?"

Kebonsat looked edgy. His face was pulled into an austere mask. For such a man, inaction was the worst kind of torture.

Kebonsat tossed the papers onto the desk. "I have many other places to be."

"Then we will be brief."

Kebonsat glared at him. "*Sharmuta*."

Juhrnus grinned, lifting his brows. "I didn't think a man of your blue bloodlines knew such language."

"Just at the moment it may be the only language I know." Kebonsat scanned the gathered faces. "What news?"

"Nothing good." Juhrnus perched on the edge of the desk. He lifted Esper down from his shoulders and set him on the chestnut wood. "Seems the Regent decided he *would* see his father and *would not* be denied, never mind the old man's wishes. Went to his apartments and forced the doors. Found things quite empty, as of course he would."

"And what conclusion did your wise Regent draw?"

"That's what's making us nervous. He made his invasion last night and has been closeted behind closed doors since. The guards stationed outside the doors were taken for questioning, and those hidden in the inner passage came to me in a panic. They could not find Sodur and"—he paused, looking at each man in turn—"they said Sodur hadn't been for a visit since the night he showed us the Iisand. The night of the Regency ceremony. That must have been when they left Koduteel." He shook his head. "I wish I knew what he was thinking."

"Maybe he was afraid of what would happen when the news came out," Kebonsat suggested.

"But how did Sodur get him out?" Metyein shuddered. "That beast wasn't going to go tamely."

"The prison was near the harbor cavern. Likely they went by boat, though I can't imagine how Sodur kept it from killing him," Kebonsat said.

"The good news is that with the Iisand gone, the Regent

isn't yet going to find out his father's turned *nokula*," Juhrnus said. "The bad news is that the explanation he comes
up with for why his father is missing is likely to be very
unpleasant. And it brings him a whole lot closer to the
throne."

"Lucky for Aare," Soka said sardonically. Juhrnus
frowned at him. Metyein's friend was thin, almost emaci-
ated. He burned inside with fever intensity and his blue
eye glittered. The eye patch over his left eye was the same
brilliant azure of his remaining eye, and it was embroidered
with a map pattern. He rarely seemed to stop moving and
nearly crackled with energy. Juhrnus remembered him from
before his disappearance: a swaggering blade with a cutting
mouth and a penchant for loose women. But he'd become
something else now. Metyein trusted him with his life, with
all their lives, but Juhrnus wondered. It was said the Regent's torturers could make a man do anything, be anything. Any man that survived their ministrations belonged
body and soul to the Regent.

"Those guards are going to tell everything they know,"
Soka said into the silence.

"They know we were there with Sodur. Except you, Kebonsat," Juhrnus said.

"This is the excuse he's been waiting for. He'll tear the
Temple apart hunting the *ahalad-kaaslane*. He'll say they
were working with Sodur and Reisiltark, that they've kidnapped the Iisand. Or killed him," Metyein said.

"I agree," said Kebonsat. "It isn't safe to be *ahalad-
kaaslane* in Koduteel anymore. You have to leave."

"We can't just run—the people here still need us. The
ahalad-kaaslane aren't supposed to cower in hiding." Juhrnus stood, his jaw jutting angrily.

"And what good will you be dead? There's much that
can be done outside these walls that cannot be done within.
You need an army. You have the means. You have food
and supplies coming in from ships runnning the blockade.
You've got wagons, horses, and more than enough people
in the Fringes alone. How long do you think your Regent
is going to wait before eradicating them like so much vermin? You can save them. Or at least give them a chance.
The plague may kill them, but Aare is a sure bet. What
else—?"

Suddenly Yohuac let out a groaning wail and clutched his head between his hands. He flung his head against the wall with a terrible *crack!* and then slid down the wall to the floor, his eyes rolled up in his head, his legs and arms twitching.

Juhrnus scrambled to his side.

"What is it? What's happening to him?" Metyein demanded over his shoulder.

Spittle ran over Yohuac's chin, and he wrenched at his hair. Juhrnus grabbed his arms and wrestled his hands to his sides.

"Yohuac! What's wrong?"

The other man's head turned from side to side, his mouth opened wide as if he were screaming, but all that came out was a gurgle.

"Is it magic? The sorcerers? Did they attack him?" asked Kebonsat, coming to kneel on the other side of the stricken man.

"I don't know."

Yohuac went rigid and his body arched up off the floor, his weight supported by only his head and heels. Then he collapsed like a discarded rag. His breath came thick and harsh between his lips, and when Juhrnus shook him, he did not move.

The other three men stared at him.

Juhrnus began to panic. *Was it magic? Were the sorcerers behind this? Kedisan-Mutira?* He knew he shouldn't . . . couldn't . . . trust her. She had plans of her own. Still everything in him wanted to believe her.

~*Can you tell?*

~*It is and it is not.* Esper's answer was slow in coming.

~*What does that mean?* He sensed deep and uneasy concentration from Esper.

~*I feel magic. Akin to Baku. But Baku would not do this.* Esper didn't sound all that certain.

~*Not on purpose. Not to his* ahalad-kaaslane, Juhrnus agreed. *What's wrong?*

~*They are not.*

~*They are not what?*

~*They are not* ahalad-kaaslane.

"What?" Juhrnus demanded aloud, jerking to his feet. The sisalik dipped his nose, abashed.

~*They are not* ahalad-kaaslane, he repeated.

~Of course they are, Juhrnus said very slowly.

~No. Yohuac does not accept the bond.

~But Reisil said—

~Baku may speak to anyone he chooses. He speaks to Reisiltark.

"He can what?" Juhrnus said, his voice turning hard. He bit his tongue, feeling a black hole opening up in his chest. More lies. More deceit.

"What's going on?" Kebonsat asked with concern.

Juhrnus drew a breath. "Seems Yohuac isn't really *ahalad-kaaslane.* Seems Baku can talk to Reisil and anyone else he pleases. It's all been a masquerade."

Kebonsat nodded. "Yes."

Juhrnus drew back. He clenched his teeth, feeling the muscles in his jaws jumping. "You know this?"

"Yes."

"You know but she didn't see fit to tell me?"

Kebonsat shook his head. "We thought it too dangerous. People needed to believe Yohuac was *ahalad-kaaslane* or he would have been at the mercy of the Verit or the Lord Marshal." He glanced at Metyein. "I'm sorry."

"My father hates Reisiltark and distrusts anything she touches. No need to apologize."

Kebonsat turned back to Juhrnus. "There's more."

"Are you sure it's safe to tell me?" he returned bitterly.

Kebonsat stared back at him, and Juhrnus shifted uneasily. The look said, *Grow up, boy. There is no time for bellyaching over hurt feelings. There isn't time, and too much is at stake.*

Juhrnus took a tight rein on himself, rolling his shoulders to ease the muscles. "Tell me."

"She believed that telling you or anyone else would endanger Yohuac. She wanted your reactions to be authentic. And she did not want to become dependent on Baku. He can pick thoughts from most minds."

"He reads minds? Oh, this is getting better and better."

"It caused Reisil grave concern. She asked Baku to watch for trouble, but not to violate the minds of her friends and allies. She thought it best that each be trusted to confide in her when—and if—they so chose. Her only request was that he listen for trouble, so that if someone was in peril, help could be sent."

Juhrnus wiped his hand over his mouth and jaw. "Is that it?"

Kebonsat shook his head. "She was attacked by an assassin at her quarters some weeks ago, the night of the reception for the Scallacians." He quickly sketched the story. "Since Baku's arrival, none have tried to attack her, undoubtedly because he kept watch."

"They have her now," grated Yohuac from the floor. He sat up, arms clasped around his ribs, the whites of his eyes blotched with spots of red where veins had burst. "They've got her."

"Tell us," Kebonsat ordered, dropping down beside Yohuac.

"Wizards after all. Never wanted to kill her. They've cut her ties to Saljane. Magic. They are taking her to the stronghold. Baku—" He broke off, coughing. Metyein handed him a glass of wine, helping him to sit up.

"She has put up walls. Baku is afraid. Reisil is very, very angry. They say they will free Saljane, but Reisil is—" He paused, searching for words. "She is *dochezatl*." He circled his fingers near his head. Out of her mind. "And *nahualli*. A dangerous combination. She forgets herself. She thinks only of death. Baku found a place where she made a great magic. He fears for her, for what she will do. It is difficult to track her. He says the land has come alive with magic, and where she travels it grows thick and dense like an ocean fog. He cannot reach her. She will not answer."

He struggled to his feet with Metyein's help, knees buckling. "I must go find her. Baku will seek for her and show me the way."

"I think we need to think and make a plan first," Kebonsat said.

"I must go now!" Yohuac thrashed himself free only to fall against the desk. Soka and Metyein caught him before he hit the floor and helped him to a chair.

Kebonsat looked at Juhrnus. "We are in trouble."

"True. But at least she's going where she wants. With guides." He sounded sullen and could have bit his tongue. "She'll get there faster now. Worse things could happen."

"And she's gone out of her mind."

"Losing your *ahalad-kaaslane* is . . . unbearable." Juhrnus reached out to Esper, shying away from the memory of his sisalik's broken, dying body. "Still we must trust she will remember what she's gone to do, whether she gets Saljane back or not. We don't have any choice. It is our only hope. And she needs time. Getting what she wants from the wizards won't happen overnight. She'll not abandon us," he said stubbornly. "Even without Saljane. She won't forget us."

"Demonballs, what in the three hells is that?"

Juhrnus turned at Soka's strained whisper, slapping a hand to his sword. The others followed suit, following Soka's pointing finger to the floor. As they watched, a small green snake wound across the floor toward the desk. It was tiny, no bigger around than a woman's smallest finger and perhaps six inches long. Its eyes glittered like golden topaz as it came to the foot of the desk. Unperturbed, it slid upward along the silver-edged wood.

"How is that possible?" muttered Kebonsat.

"Don't touch it!" Yohuac said urgently, struggling out of his chair.

"You know what it is?"

Yohuac gave a jerky nod of his head, watching the emerald green body undulate up onto the top of the desk. The snake coiled itself into a neat knot, raising its head in the air and gazing about. It had a triangular head with needle fangs protruding down over its jaws. Its belly was the color of fresh blood.

"It's a *copicatl*. But I never thought to see one here."

"Where does it come from?"

"My land. It can only mean—"

"It can only mean that there are nahuallis about," came a gruff, feminine voice from the entrance to the hidden passage. "Run and hide if you can."

The men spun around, staring as a gray-haired woman stepped into the room.

"Nurema?" Juhrnus asked incredulously. "How—? What are you doing here?"

"Ah, well, that is a story for a long winter's night by the fire, boy, and I don't imagine I want to cuddle up with a bare-faced child like you."

The men chuckled, all but Yohuac, whose face had turned to flint, his dark gaze watchful. Nurema looked the same and yet different, not that Juhrnus had ever paid that much attention to her. She was sharp tongued and difficult, and everyone in Kallas breathed a sigh of relief whenever she passed them by unmolested. She'd been a fixture of the town since he could remember, and to see her here, in Kebonsat's quarters, having used the secret passage—it made no sense.

"I don't understand how you can be here, Nurema. In the palace. In Koduteel. In *here*."

Nurema smiled, her teeth brilliant against her tanned skin. "Ah, now that is a story you *do* need to know." She turned to Yohuac. "This one knows already. Or thinks he does. He and I come from another land, another world, you might say. On the other end of that hole the wizards poked at Mysane Kosk. It's a hot, wet, green place, where there are many gods and many magics. The nahualli are witches, and I am one.

"I came here, many years ago, searching for someone. But not without cost. I lost all my powers but one. And that one proved to be slight indeed. But I was young and foolish, and I got what was coming to me. I have served the Blessed Amiya ever since, knowing that to do so was to serve my gods as well.

"Since the Lady has retreated from Kodu Riik and the taint of Mysane Kosk has spread, my powers have begun to flourish again, and indeed the murkiness of my foresight—my only ability for years—has decreased. And so I knew to come here, now, and give you warning. The *copicatl* showed me the way."

"Warning? What warning?" Juhrnus asked, feeling as if the floor was tilting. Nurema a witch. How could there be so much magic when months ago there had been almost none at all? And what could any of them do against such forces?

"Mysane Kosk must not be destroyed. You must protect it."

"But it's the source of our problems. It's a stain on the land. The *nokulas*, the plague—they wouldn't exist without Mysane Kosk."

"Yes. All of that is true. But it changes nothing. You must not permit it to be destroyed. Worse will come if you do."

Juhrnus ran his fingers through his hair, hardly knowing

what to think. "Worse? What could be worse? Kodu Riik
is falling apart. People are dying. If not from the plague,
then they are starving. With the blockade, we have very
little time. Our only hope is Reisil and the destruction of
Mysane Kosk."

"Don't be a fool, boy!" Nurema snapped. "You don't
have any idea what you're saying."

Anger flared, and Juhrnus flushed. "Don't I? I've
watched people die, old woman. Horrible, painful deaths.
I've seen a *nokula*, and I fear him. I fear all of them. I've
seen the hunger, the desperation, the riots. Our Regent
wants war and he means to have it. He doesn't care how
many have to die or who he has to get in bed with to get
his way. He means to destroy the *ahalad-kaaslane*. Then
who will protect Kodu Riik?"

Nurema bent close, waving her finger at him. "Mysane
Kosk is a source of great power. The sorcerers and the
wizards will fight for it. And not just those wizards who
were banished from Patverseme. Wizard magic has
changed. The Demonlord has seen to that. Now they will
have difficulty defending Patverseme if the Scallacians attack. Should the Scallacians take Mysane Kosk, then Patverseme *will* fall, and the wizards still in good order can't
allow it. Among the three of them—Scallacians, good wizards and bad—the battle for control will raze Kodu Riik.

"But that is nothing compared with what will happen if
Reisil or anyone else tries to destroy it." She paused, tapping her fingers against her jaw. "You want plain words,
but explanations of magic don't bend well to plain speaking. So listen carefully. What the wizards did at Mysane
Kosk opened a well between two worlds. The spell went
wrong, and now both suffer. The purpose of the spell was
to lend the wizards more power so that they could make
a decisive attack on Kodu Riik and overcome the Lady's
prohibition of magic. But it was flawed somehow. I don't
know how. I don't know if the wizards know. But they are
like cats with a bowl of cream. They have what they
wanted.

"The obvious solution is to destroy Mysane Kosk. But
what I've seen, what is true of all the possibilities in my
visions, is that to do so would remake both this world and
my homeworld on the other side of the well."

There was silence. Juhrnus blinked, trying to get his mind around her explanation, trying to choose from the questions swirling in his skull.

Kebonsat spoke first. "Remake? What does that mean?"

Nurema's eyes glittered. "I can't say. There is a cloud that I cannot see beyond. Too much depends on what comes next to know."

"Why should we believe you? Have you proof?" Soka had circled around behind her and lounged on the window seat, picking at his nails with his dagger.

"Ah, proof. I hope you accept that I am nahualli, though I can prove that as well, if you like," she said caustically.

Soka smiled, flipping a hand out. "By all means. You are a witch. I shall take that as given. But are you really on our side? Seems to me that in your battle between the wizards and the sorcerers, you forgot to mention whether the nahuallis would be eager to carve themselves a bit of the power."

"The nahuallis will seek to close the well, and because of this they are an equal danger, though they will not grasp at the power for themselves. As for me . . ."

She reached her right hand out, palm down. The emerald snake on the table sprang up into the air and circled around her wrist. The men watched in fascinated horror as the tiny beast raised its body and then plunged down, burrowing into her flesh. Juhrnus felt his stomach turn as the creature's tail disappeared, the shape of its body wriggling beneath the skin of Nurema's forearm to disappear beneath her sleeve.

"What does that prove?" Soka challenged, swinging his legs down.

"That was for him," she turned to face Yohuac. "That I come with the blessing of the Teotl. A *copicatl* may be offered as a blessing by any one of the Teotl, but the snake, this snake, belongs to one in particular." She stared at Yohuac, brows raised, demanding, impatient.

He jerked forward in a deferential bow. "*Ilhuicatl*, the father of all."

She nodded. "Exactly. And if I have his snake, what does that mean?"

"That you have the approval of the entire Teotl."

"Right. Do not forget it. And now for the Blessed Amiya." She turned her attention back to the other men. "I don't expect a snake to mean much to you, but this ought to." She turned her hand over and opened her palm. It was grimy, her fingernails dark with dirt. But as they watched, her hand flared, and on her skin appeared a golden image: a gryphon inside a ring of ivy.

"Convinced?"

Juhrnus looked up, his tongue sliding across his teeth. A niggling voice in his mind said she could fake such a sign. She was a witch. But he knew in the marrow of his bones that it was real. The others were watching him, waiting for his judgment. "It's real."

"So what do we do now?" Metyein asked heavily.

"We do what Kebonsat proposed. We pull together an army, such as we can get, and we go to Mysane Kosk and pray we can stop what's coming." His words rang hollow. How were they going to stop the sorcerers and wizards with an army of ragtag refugees, many of whom were already dying of the plague? And Kedisan-Mutira—would he have to stand on the opposite side of the wall from her and try to kill her? The thought tore at him, and he bent, feeling suddenly as if he'd been punched in the balls.

Nurema nodded. "You won't be alone. More help will come. And Mysane Kosk will defend itself."

Juhrnus sucked in his breath, and she gave him a somber look.

"You're seeing it now, aren't you? About time. Mysane Kosk is not an empty shell. And those within will not wish to be killed or conquered. What they'll do I can't begin to guess. But I have nightmares about it. You will too."

Chapter 37

Reisil yawned and stretched luxuriously. They'd given her an entire suite of rooms, decorated as lavishly as any quarters in the building. Her sheets were silk, her blankets the softest wool, the mattress plump with eiderdown.

The rugs on her floor were thick and deep, the furnishings made of warm, honey-colored wood. A fire, lit by a discreet servant, crackled in the hearth, and the sun glowed through rose-colored curtains. The scent of dried flowers mixed with spices wafted through the room.

Reisil sat up.

~Did you sleep well, dear heart?

It was a question she already knew the answer to. Reisil had woken often in the night, reaching out to Saljane and finding the goshawk sleeping contentedly. It had not been so the first few days after her captivity, but more than a week had passed, and Saljane had put the dark memories behind her. Something Reisil had not yet been able to do. She didn't know if she would ever be free of that unbearable loss. She stroked Saljane's crisp gray feathers, laughing when Saljane nipped her fingers happily. Saljane raised herself from the nest of pillows Reisil had made on the bed and shook herself like a dog before leaping to her perch to preen.

~I am well. I would hunt.

Reisil grinned at her. Saljane had dined well in the past days, but on meat brought by the wizards. She had not wanted to leave Reisil's side, any more than Reisil wanted to be separated from her. It was a good sign that she was now at ease enough to hunt.

Reisil slid off the bed and padded to the window, pushing the casement wide. The room flooded with brisk, mountain air. Reisil breathed deeply, shivering with the chill. "C'mon, you. Out you go. And remember the illusion. If you fly too high, you won't find your way back in. If that happens, come to me in the valley outside."

Kvepi Kaisivas had explained about the stronghold's covering illusion and warned that if Saljane left the valley, Reisil wouldn't be able to hear her, nor would Saljane be able to find her way back on her own. Reisil shuddered at the chance that their bond might vanish again, but Saljane must have her freedom. Just in case Saljane might accidentally go too far, Kvepi Tapit had returned them both through the maze to the mountain valley beyond, allowing Saljane to orient herself.

"The maze, of course, is not the only way out of the valley. However it is the quickest for someone on foot," he explained. "Kvepi Kaisivas has asked that I serve as your guide until you are comfortable finding your way. I will show you the other entrances."

"So I am not a prisoner any more?"

"You are one of us, and to be treated as such. You have long hated us, and we believe it is because you do not know us. It is our hope you will find friends here, a family, a home."

"Even after what I did on the Vorshtar Plain."

"Even so," was his noncommital answer, and he would not be pressed into saying anything more.

It was too absurd to think that the wizards did not resent her attack on them in Patverseme. She'd killed a hundred of them and been largely responsible for their banishment. But they didn't mention it, and when she made an oblique reference, they seemed not even to remember. Instead they had given her extravagant quarters and welcomed her with congenial warmth. Tapit had been as good as his word, showing her all the entrances to the valley as well as the buildings, gardens, stables, and the workshop caves along the northern and western walls of the valley. There was a small village in the southeastern end in which lived a variety of servants and retainers. It was separated from the main buildings by sweeping fields of newly turned earth, orchard groves and a swift-running creek.

"Few are allowed to leave the valley, and those who do are most loyal. Still, we do not care to be discovered by outsiders, and we set a minor spell on them to prevent them from speaking of the valley," Tapit explained when Reisil asked about them. "We treat them well, try to assist them in any way we can. Their duties are not arduous, and most have plenty of time to practice an art or craft of some kind. We are not severe in our demands, and they are content enough under such a light yoke. Many were treated ill in Patverseme after our banishment, and they had little choice but to join us. We try to make the burden of exile and our need for secrecy as comfortable as possible."

His explanation, like every other kindness and courtesy exhibited by the wizards, startled Reisil. The previous evening she'd been invited to attend the monthly gathering.

"We get so caught up in our work that we tend to forget to eat. We reserve one evening a month for everyone to

congregate and enjoy each other's company," Kvepi Kaisivas explained over kohv. "It is very informal, and I know
that the others would like the opportunity to know you."

"Why?" Reisil asked, surprised.

"I told you. You are one of us."

And indeed they had been very welcoming. They often
had her laughing at jokes and pranks amongst themselves,
stories of mistakes in their laboratories, social blunders, and
general foolishness. They were so varied, so . . . ordinary.
Like the people she had grown up with in Kallas.

By the end of the evening Reisil's ribs hurt from laughing, and her throat was raspy from all the talk. Afterwards
she sank into bed exhausted, more content and at peace
than she could remember since becoming *ahalad-kaaslane*.
Her ease of mind communicated itself to Saljane, and the
goshawk had begun to recapture the playfulness Reisil had
missed so much since arriving in Koduteel.

A knock sounded at the door, and Reisil started from
her reverie. ~*Come on. Out you go.* She crooked a finger
at Saljane.

Saljane fluttered to the sill and then leaped out, sinking
in a long glide and then flapping her wings strongly to climb
the wind. Reisil shivered and pulled the window closed,
wrapping herself in a red velvet robe before opening her
door.

"Sorry to disturb you, Kvepi," the maid said. Reisil
flinched at the title. But they all had begun calling her
Kvepi, and nothing she could say would change their minds.
She was a wizard after all, they said, politely obdurate.
"I've come to fill your tub before breakfast."

Reisil swung the door wide, and the woman went quietly
into the boudoir. There was a sound of running water.
More magic. The wizards had all contributed equally to the
comforts of the building. Hot and cold running water, lights
without candles or oil, dinner knives that never needed
sharpening, wineglasses that would not break.

When the maid departed, Reisil peeled off her robe and
shift and padded into the boudoir, loosening her braid and
letting her hair flow down her back. The tub was made of
moss-green stone, four feet deep with a wide seat running
along two sides. She eased into the warmth. Content with

the temperature, she touched a pink beryl inset into the stone along the top edge of the tub. It would maintain the water's temperature until she was done. Never before had she enjoyed such luxury. It was like having a private hot spring inside her bedroom.

An hour passed before Reisil could convince herself to leave the tub. She dried herself and combed her hair, then went to her wardrobe. Inside hung several black robes, plain except for the silvery embroidery around the cuffs. The pattern was intricate and artful, showing a goshawk in dancing flight, diving, swooping, gliding. Leaves and stars whirled on an invisible wind in between. They were so beautiful, Reisil couldn't resist them, ignoring her old clothes piled at the bottom of the cabinet. Besides, wearing the robes would make them believe she was succumbing to their blandishments. Her own clothes would still be waiting when it was time to leave.

She dressed quickly and went to the window, leaning out to peer up into the sky.

~Where are you?

~Here.

And high up Reisil could see a speck of black. Saljane plummeted toward the window, catching herself above the level of the sill with a pop as she flung her wings wide. Reisil reached out her fist, and Saljane settled onto it.

Smugness. Satiety. Mischief.

She flung herself off Reisil's hand and winged through the suite, twisting sharply around the furniture and pouncing in the middle of the bed.

Reisil laughed.

~Full of yourself, aren't you?

~Hare ran very fast. I flew faster.

Now she began to preen herself, ignoring Reisil, who laughed again.

~Well, it's time for my breakfast. Are you coming?

There was a flash of exuberance, and Saljane waddled to the edge of the bed, wings raised high, waiting for Reisil to lift her up.

"Of course, Your High and Mightiness," Reisil said with a grin as Saljane gripped her fist. She transferred the goshawk to her shoulder, wincing as Saljane's talons grasped the cloth of the robe. But the robe was impervious, and despite Saljane's fidgeting into place, not a single hole appeared in the material.

"Handy, that," Reisil said.

Kvepi Kaisivas met them for breakfast, ushering them into a solar. Reisil set Saljane on a waiting perch and sat down.

The Kvepi watched her a moment, a smile turning his lips. "You look lovely."

Reisil flushed. "Thank you."

"I waited for you this morning because I wanted to discuss something with you," he began.

Reisil set her cup down, her heart beating faster.

"You want us to teach you how to use your magic, and we are pleased to do so. But I must make you aware of a problem before you can begin. When Kvepi Mastone and the others summoned Pahe Kurjus—the Demonlord—to the mortal plane, what He discovered distressed Him. He ordered that the Guild should be cleansed. Chollai took this to mean the banishment of those of the Nethieche branch of the guild. In particular, those of us who had participated in the plot against the Karalis.

"It was a fair decision, and I cannot object to it." He lifted his hands in the air. "I would have done the same in his position. One simply does not disobey Pahe Kurjus. But the Demonlord was not done. Banishment was not enough. He changed our magic. You know what we were. You *are* what we were. But no longer.

"Now our magic is greatly diminished. Only the spilling of our own heart's blood unlocks it. Any sacrifice we make not of our own bodies is useless. Greater spells may be accomplished if many wizards contribute blood to a spell, but this is exhausting and difficult to balance correctly. We have been able to store magic in vessels and artifacts. Over the course of time, you understand." He pulled back his sleeve and Reisil saw the hashmarks of old and new scars. "And we may draw on each other's stored magics, which enables us to make this building comfortable, for example. Additionally, with the retirement of your Lady from Kodu Riik, we have discovered many sources of ancient magic that in time we will learn to harness."

At this last, Reisil felt a wash of fear. "Why do you tell me all this?"

"Because it will make teaching you difficult. We won't be able to show you what to do as we would have before. We will instruct you, but it is not the same, and you may find it frustrating. I would not have you think we withold our knowledge from you. I know you find it difficult to believe that we would include you so freely. I have asked Kvepi Debess to be your teacher. I think he will suit you well." He paused, a pained look on his face.

"What?" Reisil asked.

"Please be certain that this is merely a recommendation and you may, of course, decide otherwise. But the workshops in the caves are unlit. Wizards have no need of light, and it serves as an added protection against intruders. But it would make your goshawk quite uncomfortable. I think she may prefer not to accompany you inside."

Reisil nodded. It didn't matter. Saljane could watch through her eyes and never enter the caves. She noted too that he never referred to either her or Saljane as *ahalad-kaaslane*. No one in the stronghold did. They perceived Saljane as her companion, even a pet, but never conceded that either of them were anything else. If she was, then she couldn't be a wizard.

Kvepi Debess proved to be a gruff man in his fifties. He had gray hair streaked with white and a thick beard brushed silky smooth. His cheeks were ruddy, his gray eyes quick and sharp. He was shorter than Reisil by several inches and built like a barrel. His fingers were stained with ink, and there was a red rime circling his fingernails. A glimpse of his arms revealed a broad slice across his left wrist.

"Come along, then. Don't dawdle. I haven't so much time as that, young miss."

He hurried up the gravel path ahead of Reisil, his robe swinging around bare ankles, his feet clad in sandals. He dived into a cave. Reisil paused long enough to toss Saljane into the air before following him inside. She ran to catch up, matching his quick pace.

"So, tell me about yourself. What have you done? What can you do? Don't want to go through the basic nonsense if you don't need it, but I expect you have gaping holes in your understanding of magic, and you can't just ignore them. They'll rise up against you the first thing you turn your back, and you'll find yourself visiting Pahe Kurjus in His own dark pits."

"I—" Reisil began and then stopped, searching for words.

"Come, come. Out with it." His words echoed in the cave.

"I've killed with it. Burned really. Several times. And I have healed with it—fevers, bones, but not the plague."

"Killing's easy enough. Blast of power, though you've got to find the power to make the blast, which can be tough enough. I heard about what happened back in Patverseme. A good blast that. Healing, though, that takes some control. Have any accidents in that direction? Healings that got out of hand?"

"No." The thought made her cringe. She'd never thought about what should happen if she lost control during a healing.

"That's good news. Unusual too. Surprised you didn't leave a tangle of bones and muscle once or twice. This way." He directed her into a side shaft that led gently upward.

"But that's the problem," Reisil explained. "I don't control it really. When I heal, it just sort of happens, and I mostly can't call up my power unless I'm angry."

"Perfectly normal. Need some principles. Come now, in here."

And he directed her through an archway and into a large room full of a jumble of tables with odd materials stacked on top and underneath, as well as in corners and on shelves. Several doors led out of the room on the other side. Kvepi Debess went to one of these and pushed it open. Inside was a plain room containing a small, square table and a single chair.

"We'll start in here. Grab that chair there and bring it."

Reisil picked up the indicated chair and carried it inside. The Kvepi had set a chunk of milky quartz the size of her two fists in the center of the table.

"Right. Now I'll just set the wards. Don't want to blow up the mountain if we can help it." He shut the door and ran his hands over it, chanting softly. There was a brilliant flare of green light, and for a moment the walls came alive with symbols and patterns. After a moment, they faded into dull rock again. "That should do the trick." He lowered bristly brows at her. "Hope it's enough. The rest of 'em spent the last week reinforcing the wards, but what we can do is limited these days, and you're powerful."

Reisil glanced quickly at him, wondering if there was a double meaning to his last words. But he merely sat down, motioning for her to do the same.

"We're going to start with this." He touched the chunk of quartz. "You're going to learn to channel your power into the quartz. That way when you lose control later, you'll know what to do with the excess. One word of warning: I know what that bird is, and I'm telling you right now, she's got no part in the learning. You must do this yourself, without help. Later she will add to what you can do, but for now, you don't borrow strength from her. Do you understand?"

Reisil nodded. So the Kvepis couldn't entirely forget she was *ahalad-kaaslane*.

"But before we involve your magic, we're going to review how magic works and where it comes from. Listen carefully. I will quiz you as we go. You cannot go further until you understand this perfectly."

The hours reeled away, and Reisil hardly noticed. Kvepi Debess spoke quickly, but clearly and methodically. He never lost patience with her, and by the end of that day, she'd learned to find her power without the crutch of anger.

"It's like a river flowing through your deepest center. The calmer you are, the deeper. And even though it rises higher when you are angry, it loses potency. In many ways you are lucky you have not been able to reach it with calm deliberation, or you might have incinerated yourself. To peform to your highest ability, you must be able to summon the power without fear or anger or frustration, or whatever else happens to be driving you."

What proved most difficult was summoning only what she wanted.

"That's too big a hammer for the nail," Kvepi Debess said for the fifth time. "You don't want to divert your river out of its bed, you want to borrow a little stream. Enough but not too much."

At the end of the day, Reisil was exhausted but exuberant. She'd managed at last to summon her power, drawing only what she wanted.

"Tomorrow we'll actually do a bit of work with it. Small things. Basic skills work. You're quick, though, and it won't be long until you can do much more. Now get on with you. I've a thing or two to get done. Supper's waiting. Take your time in the morning. I won't want you too early."

That night Reisil ate ravenously, pattering enthusiastically to Kvepi Kaisivas. Hope and pride danced in her blood.

The rest of the week passed in similar sessions. Each day Kvepi Debess closed the wards, and Reisil learned to move objects, to light candles with a thread of power, to burn designs on a slab of wood. The power of the quartz stone continued to grow as she channeled excess energy into it. The stone itself had begun to glitter with an inner core of energy, its pink and yellow seams like dark veins against the milky flesh of the rock.

By the end of the second week, her third in the stronghold, Reisil had become proficient enough to begin creating her own spells.

"You understand that ordinary apprentice work lasts years?" Kvepi Debess said sourly one morning, drinking from a pot of kohv. His eyes were bloodshot, and there were fresh wounds on his arms. Dark circles framed his gray eyes. "Well, nothing for it. You're further along than that, and you have already performed larger works of magic. You have an instinct for it, and with principles, you shouldn't do more than light your hair on fire or burn your clothes off."

Reisil smiled uncertainly, not sure he was joking.

"You're ready for the apprentice test. May as well start there and move you through journeyman levels as seems fitting. For your first part of the test, take this iron bar. I want you to remake it into a filigree like this." He produced an intricate drawing, the pattern fine as a thread in some places, the surface etched with still smaller designs. "You use too much magic, and the bar will melt and you have to begin again. The entire work must be done with utmost control."

And then he left her in the warded workroom. Reisil

began slowly, resting herself every time fatigue started to fog her control. Still, the delicate work took her far into the night. By the time she was through, her underclothing was drenched and her hair was matted to her head. Kvepi Debess examined her work with a critical eye, nodding finally. "Not the most artistic representation, but it'll do. Now off to bed with you. Be here at first light." At Reisil's pained look, he grinned remorselessly. "Part of the testing. Lucky you finished before light or there'd be no sleep for you at all."

Reisil began the next day bleary-eyed and tense. Her heart raced, and she could hardly hold down her breakfast.

"All right, then. Today it gets a bit harder. You've shown you can maintain fine control; now you're going to show how you do with varied controls and distractions."

Kvepi Debess led her away from his laboratory, through a maze of tunnels until they arrived at a spacious room cut into the rock. A group of twenty or thirty Kvepis were gathered, their robes sparkling in the lights. As he closed the doors, Kvepi Debess activated the wards. The room flared with rainbow light, and then it subsided.

"Fairly simple. We're going to throw things at you, and you're going to catch them and put them in bins over there." He pointed to rows of boxes, some large enough to hold three horses, against the far wall. "Points off for dropping anything, or worse, for destroying it."

With that, Reisil was thrust into the middle of the room. She didn't know how long she remained there. The first objects were small. Mugs and glasses, plates and jars. Then came stones ranging from pebbles to boulders. There were dressers and wardrobes, a horse trough, an anvil, a flurry of eggs, a tree trunk. More than she could remember. At first they came one at a time, then as she caught these easily, two and three and four until she could hardly breathe. Her magic fought her. She grew more tired and tense, the objects coming faster and more of them. She hardly dared blink lest she miss something. Desperately she whipped out tendrils of power, no longer able to see *what* was coming. Grayness closed around her vision, and her legs trembled. She could smell her fear, acrid and sour. Sweat rolled down her skin, and her clothing clung clammily. Still she fought to keep her controls. The room was warded, but only against escaping power. What would happen to the Kvepis inside if she let her power erupt? Ash. She remembered the bodies on the bluff. The burnt-out husks in Patverseme. The deep scar on the land where they'd taken Saljane. She felt her fingers blister, the heat crawling up her arms. She began to smell smoke, burning hair. Her own.

"Enough."

It was Kvepi Debess. He came forward, examining her from head to foot.

"Refused to give in, did you? And would have let yourself burn up too. It's a lesson well learned. You can only swim in that river for so long before it eats you alive. What say you?" he said to the gathered Kvepi. "Need we the final test, or has she done both in one?" There was a murmuring, not unfriendly. Reisil blinked, seeing only a mass of blurry movement. "So be it. You passed the second test superbly. I don't believe I've ever seen any other last so long. And the final test would have been to see how much power you could restrain and for how long. But again, you've outdone our expectations. Most apprentices fold far before they begin to burn." He lifted her arm at the elbow to examine her hands. They were red and raw and covered with weeping, white blisters.

"I didn't know what would happen to you if I let go. We left the quartz," she mumbled through dry, swollen lips. Kvepi Debess stared at her a long moment and then threw back his head in a long, ringing laugh. It went on and Reisil swayed, baffled. Finally he caught himself, gasping and sniffing.

"Ah, my young friend. Sometimes I forget what you do not know—you seem so far advanced. We have the power to shield ourselves, and each and every one of us has become adept at capturing loose magic and storing it away." He patted her shoulder. "Still, I expect you would have lasted equally as long with such knowledge. Your power would not have gotten the best of you without such worries and fears. Congratulations. The day after tomorrow we begin again with the next stage of your training. Go, get some rest. Eat. We'll send Uldegas along to treat your burns."

Reisil turned away, stumbling as she went to the door. Then Kvepi Debess's voice called her back.

"Be proud of what you've accomplished today, Reisil. I am certainly proud of you. Would that I could claim more responsibility."

At his words, a flower of pleasure bloomed in her chest, and neither the pain of her burns nor her exhaustion could smother it. She smiled wide.

Chapter 38

"**Y**ou aren't really a healer," Kvepi Debess said abruptly, chewing on a meat pie, a napkin tucked in his collar. Reisil shot him a startled look, washing down a mouthful of buttered bread with a cup of milk. It was the morning following the apprentice test.

There had been a grand celebration in her honor the night before. Most every Kvepi had attended, offering toasts and praise. She couldn't remember ever having felt so happy. In the midst of it, she had caught herself. What was she doing? The wizards had done so many horrible things—the list of their crimes seemed endless. But that all seemed so far away. She found herself reveling in their compliments, wanting them to think well of her. They were such a change from the *ahalad-kaaslane*. The wizards had every reason to be suspicious of her, every reason to despise her for killing so many of their own, and yet they welcomed her. And the *ahalad-kaaslane*, who had had every reason to welcome her, to trust her, had chosen instead to ostracize her.

"Did you hear me?" Kvepi Debess asked gruffly.

Reisil pulled herself back to the present. "What do you mean?"

"It's not really your talent. Oh, you are reasonably good

at it. I expect that has a lot to do with your tark training. You know the bits of the body and how they work, and so you make the proper repairs. Still, you don't have the same kind of instinct for it that I've seen in other healers."

Reisil stared at him. Not a healer? But of course she was. She'd trained to be since she was ten; even after becoming *ahalad-kaaslane* she had thought of herself as a healer. The Lady had said it too: *Heal my land. Heal my children—human and animal.*

"Now Uldegas, he's a proper healer. Quick as a thought, he is. What did you think of the way he healed your burns?"

Reisil stared down at her pale hands and wrists. The tan was gone from them, but so were the burns. And Kvepi Uldegas had done it with hardly a glance, then retreated back to his workshop with little more than a grunt in response to her thank-you. *She* couldn't have done it that easily.

"A battle mage maybe. Or weatherworker. Earthworking is a possibility too. Larger magics. The difference is that healing takes fine, small magics, and you've proved you can do that, but the larger magics take the talent to withstand, to hold, to channel it to a purpose. Uldegas never could, even before the banishment. You've demonstrated a talent for that. Of course, some depends on whether you can create the proper spells—"

"Why are there no women Kvepis?" Reisil interrupted suddenly, wanting nothing more than to shift the subject. And it was a question that had been gnawing at her for weeks.

"Eh? Women Kvepis? Don't have 'em," Kvepi Debess replied.

"Why?"

He shrugged a broad shoulder. "They exist. Fewer than men. Don't know why. Whieche side of the guild mostly. Haven't had one in the Nethieche since I can remember."

"You destroyed most of the Whieche, didn't you? And anyone else who wouldn't follow you. The Karaliene said that, the night Kvepi Mastone summoned the Demonlord."

His gray eyes fastened on her. When he answered, his voice was unchanged, conversational, congenial. "We did.

Women are unpredictable. They do all right for a while, and then they start getting ideas. Start paying more attention to wanting children and such instead of concentrating on the magic. Get soft. Too bad, too. A lot of decent women with power."

Reisil swallowed, setting her fork back on her plate. "So why bring me here?"

"You're one of us. Proved it with that killing on the Vorshtar Plain, and then again with the men we sent after you. Impressive. Most women don't have the heart. Always arguing against necessity. But not you. You think things through, see what's what, and you don't hide from it. Always got to remember your purpose and stick to it. Sometimes it means hard choices. But you know that."

As he spoke, Reisil felt as if a hand were squeezing her throat. Her food sat in her stomach like cold lead, and her hands shook. She wanted to protest, to defend herself from his praise, but all she could remember was killing the assassins—wizards. The predatory anticipation, the thrill of power, the terrible joy.

She looked down at her plate, no longer hungry. Was he right? Was she really one of them? All these weeks she'd been content to pretend so: wearing the robes, learning how to use her magic, delighting in the warmth of their welcome. They all seemed so kind and generous, so . . . *benign*.

But they weren't. These were the same people who'd destroyed Mysane Kosk. They'd kidnapped and raped Ceriba. They'd created the plague. Here in the stronghold, they practiced and perfected their magic. But to what end? Regaining power. Harvesting Kodu Riik. And they didn't care who had to die in the process.

Reisil wondered for the first time what the wizards did in their laboratories and workshops.

"Ahem. Kvepi Debess?"

Kvepi Kaisivas stood in the doorway. His hair was damp from the steady rain falling over the valley stronghold. He rocked back and forth from his heels to his toes, an air of suppressed excitement surrounding him.

"Kaisivas, what brings you to my workshop this fine day?"

"Good news. There's been a sighting. Tapit's just gone out. Took two teams, the source is so powerful. At least two of them. I thought you'd like to know."

Kvepi Debess slapped the table with a pleased bellow. "Wonderful! How long did he think?"

"You never can tell. But Tapit's getting to be very good. By tomorrow or the next day, I should think. They've not shown a lot of movement since discovery, and they are not too far away. You'll want to prepare."

"Indeed I will, indeed I will. Well, this is good news," he said when Kvepi Kaisivas had departed. His thick, blunt fingers tapped the table. "Just about ready. Been waiting, don't you know, just not sure exactly when. You can help, of course. Be good for you to see the design of it." He glanced at her, brows raised.

"I don't know what you're talking about," Reisil said.

"Ah, well then, I'll show you. Finish your lunch."

The cold lead continued to sit heavily in her stomach, and she shook her head. "I've had enough."

"Then follow me." He shoved his chair from the table, picking up a fruit tart to carry with him. He led her past the door to the little square room where she trained and through the maze of clutter in the workshop to an oversize door at the far end. It stood eight feet tall and six feet wide with neither handle nor hinges visible. Kvepi Debess paused, turning around and frowning at the room as he brushed the crumbs from his beard. "Going to have to clear a path," he muttered.

He opened the door, placing a hand on the center and whispering several words. Light flickered around his hand and then ignited a flurry of symbols. They spun outward to the edges of the door in a scrolling spiral, fading as quickly as they flared. As the last illumination died, the door popped open. Kvepi Debess pushed it wide. Ahead was a short corridor that opened into a large workspace.

She followed him into the oval chamber, equal in size to the room they'd just left. The threshhold consisted of a band of silver etched with arcane symbols. The band extended upward around the entire entry. A path of yellow jasper inset into the gray rock floor circled the room. A cross-path in the middle led to a wide yellow puddle in the center, where stood a group of tables piled with a variety of materials. Along the left-hand wall were three cages, perhaps nine feet tall by twelve feet wide. "Get used to staying on the path," Kvepi Debess ordered. "Haven't closed the seals yet, but once I do, stepping off will be quite dangerous. You'll also not be able to cross back over the threshold without the proper incantation."

Reisil nodded, her stomach churning. There was something all too familiar about the room. Reisil stopped to stare at the three cages. The bars were close set and appeared to be made of silver. There were symbols etched into the bars, wrapping them in a lovely scrollwork.

"Beautiful, aren't they?" Kvepi Debess called from inside the central work area as he shifted items around on a table.

"What—?" Reisil swallowed. "What are they for?" But she already knew. These bars were kin to those holding the Iisand beneath the palace in Koduteel.

"Nokulas."

"What do you do with them?" She flinched when Kvepi Debess came to stand beside her, admiring his handiwork.

"Each bar contains forty-three spells. Then the floor has another twelve. I've been working on this for more than a year, with the help of some apprentices." He sighed. "What I wouldn't do to have my old reservoir of power back. Things went so much faster then. But Pahe Kurjus isn't to be gainsaid. Lucky we discovered the *nokulas*. Once contained, they are immense sources of power. Stronger than any artifact any of us have created since the banishment. And their power renews constantly. Never need to be fed. Not one of those we've taken has died so far." He shook his head in wonder. "They are perfect. They are the answer to our every need."

The words struck Reisil like hammer blows. She remembered her disgust and horror at the sight of the Iisand, at his palpable malignance. But now she felt something different. Pity. And guilt.

"You know they used to be people and animals," she heard herself saying, her lips barely moving.

"Of course. One of several good things to come out of Mysane Kosk. We believe that some were our people, which accounts for their discrepancies in power. With luck, there will be more benefits."

Reisil's hands turned so that her fingernails cut into her palms. She felt as if she stood on the deck of a storm-tossed ship, the world spinning around her. And when it stopped . . . The blood drained from her face. She didn't want to look at what she'd see. She didn't want to think about how complacent she'd become, ignoring the wizards' evil because they complimented her and made her feel good.

"Here is what we need to do," Kvepi Debess said, retreating back to the work area, oblivious of her distress. Reisil followed with jerky steps.

~*What have I done?*

~*You are here where you are supposed to be,* came Saljane's swift answer, as if she'd been waiting for the question.

~*But . . . I am the same as they. I left the Iisand caged. I wanted to kill them all.*

~*And now?*

"She said heal Her land, heal Her children—human and animal. She said there was more to do than I knew," Reisil whispered.

"Eh? What's that?" asked Kvepi Debess absently, pulling out a roll of parchments and flattening them on a table.

~*She meant the* nokulas. *I'm supposed to find a way to save them. Heal them.*

~*You are a healer.*

~*Kvepi Debess says not. He says my magic is better suited for battle.*

~*Your magic is what you make it. In one hand a flower is poison. In another, it is life. You came to learn. You have learned.*

More than she expected, Reisil thought, cold purpose settling over her. More than the wizards expected. And not enough. She still didn't know how to cure the plague or the *nokulas.*

"Look here. The threshold and surrounding floor isn't quite complete. Left some blocks undone. With your help, I can finish it quickly. Where's that quartz of yours?" He looked around as if expecting to see it underneath a stack of pens and parchment. "The training room, of course. Off you get, then. No, confound it. Better I go. You won't be able to get back through the door."

Off he bustled, muttering and ticking off items on his fingers. Reisil returned to the jasper path to look at the cages.

~There must be fifty or sixty workshops in the mountain.

Did they all keep *nokulas* inside? How was she to find them all? And what about Bethorn and Felias? Sodur had said they'd disappeared here. Had the wizards taken them? Were they even now prisoners?

~We must leave. We must go to Mysane Kosk. You cannot free them. Not now. There was a decisive, imperative note to Saljane's voice.

~We can't just walk away and leave them here. And what can we do at Mysane Kosk? I still don't know how to stop what's happening, and I can't destroy it. I've got to find another way. Maybe Sodur was right. Maybe the sorcerers are the answer after all.

~You cannot release the nokulas *here before the wizards stop you. The sorcerers are not the answer. You are. It's time to trust yourself. You must go to Mysane Kosk.*

Reisil's attention sharpened on Saljane. *~Why? What do you know?*

Saljane was quiet a moment. *~You are stronger than you were. You have seen what the wizards are. You are not one of them. They seek only power. Now you must go to Mysane Kosk and see what it is.*

Reisil stared at the cages. The spells on them were more complex than she understood. Much as she didn't want to agree with Saljane, faced with such magic, she knew she couldn't free all the *nokulas*. Maybe not even one. But neither could she stay here anymore. Not now that she'd seen past the wizards' kindly veneer to the indifferent brutality beneath. Returning to Koduteel would serve no purpose. Perhaps at Mysane Kosk she might learn something. *And if not, then where?* She smothered the thought.

"Here we go," Kvepi Debess called as he returned, his face pink and shiny with sweat. "Now let me show you."

The stack of parchments provided careful detail on the layers of spells on floor and cages. Kvepi Debess explained how each were connected, overlapping and cascading together to increase their strength. "Like weaving a basket," he said. "Not all are active at once, of course. We have holding spells, then several for pain—they do feel pain you know. Not entirely as we do, but they can be trained. Then here"—he flipped pages—"we've got several for suppressing their magic. This is the masterpiece, though," he said with pride, turning another page. "Had a hand in this myself. Disable the suppression spells and activate these, and their magic is channeled here." He motioned to a small pedestal inset into the floor, obscured by the larger tables surrounding it. It was a slender finger of black stone. All along its trunk and crown were symbols of inlaid silver. In the center of the crown was a palm-sized round clear stone.

"What is it?" Reisil asked, not wanting to know.

"A focus. The *nokulas'* power is channeled here—keeping in mind that they constantly radiate magic. They *are* magic. Whoever puts his hand here"—he set his thick hand over the clear stone—"receives the energy. It can be overwhelming. Even before the banishment, many of us never enjoyed such power."

"And then what?"

"It can be used immediately in a burst, though most often we store it in an artifact to be used later. The spells in the floor catch an excess—once you remove your hand, there is an overflow before the suppression spells can be reset. Ingenious, eh?"

"Very." Reisil swallowed the bile that rose on her tongue, her face rigid. And he was going to use her magic to finish this malignant masterpiece.

"Now, the threshold and the unfinished blocks are for security. An added gate for anyone trying to enter, and should the *nokulas* escape, they will be struck by paralyzing pain. They won't be able to move until someone comes and retrieves them. Let me show you what I want you to do."

Reisil spent the next hours studying the parchments and helping to lay the final spells. Everything in her revolted at what she was doing, but she forced herself to continue, to try to understand the patterning of the spells, how they worked, where they showed weakness. But the symbols and figures made little sense. More than once Kvepi Debess corrected her.

"No, no, no," he said, standing over her. "See there? You've not closed that loop on the *evlees* and there, you've reversed the *pahne*."

Reisil sat back on her heels, staring at the floor. As soon

as she copied the symbols from the parchment onto the floor, they faded from her sight and all she could see was the smooth, gray expanse. "How can you tell?"

"You look. Can't you *see*?"

Reisil rubbed grimy fingers over her face and shook her head. And what was she doing if not looking? "I *am* looking. I see ugly gray stone," she snapped.

"Use your inner eye."

Reisil stared up at him, her teeth gritted. "I have an *inner* eye?"

He blinked and scratched his head. "Ah, dear. That's another of those gaps of yours, isn't it? I get so used to you being ahead of such things. All right, stand up then. Now, close your eyes. It's easy enough, though it takes some practice. You've got to concentrate on the magic. You can feel it, I know. You've been swimming in it for weeks, so it's going to be a bit harder to separate what's here from what's all around. You might see a kaleidoscope of light before you can refine it into the specific symbols and figures. What do you see?"

Reisil saw the backs of her eyelids. She groped, sensing the magic around, a prickling in the air, a slow current near her feet, a breath across her neck. She shook her head. "I don't see anything."

"Well there is a knack to it. Can't concentrate too much or it won't come. Imagine going slightly cross-eyed."

"Cross-eyed with my eyes closed," Reisil said. "Right."

Kvepi Debess chuckled, patting her shoulder. "You keep trying, and I'll finish up. Think about what you feel when you channel energy into the quartz stone. You can visualize that, no? It's easy enough to see a flare of power when you expel it, but if you can't see the spells as you build them, you'll end up with a mess. Melt the flesh off your bones. Seen it happen. Spells are more subtle and difficult because they use little magic until they are activated. Think about the wards on the doors. You see the symbols brighten when I activate them, no doubt." Reisil nodded. "With spellsight you'd have seen them all the time. Lucky you didn't poke around too much. Might have lost a hand."

Reisil sat cross-legged on the jasper path, her eyes closed. She ruthlessly suppressed all other thoughts but that of *seeing* the spells. It was going to be a crucial skill, especially when she made her stand. Knowing exactly what the wizards were doing and how could give her an advantage.

The minutes ticked away, and her head began to ache. Here and there she thought she caught a flicker of something, a ghostly glow at the edge of her concentration. But otherwise all remained black, and she was reminded how tired she was, how much her back hurt, how stiff her hips and knees had become from crawling on the floor and now sitting on the cold stone.

"Any luck?" Kvepi Debess stood at the threshold, dusting his hands off with a satisfied air. Reisil shook her head. "Try again tomorrow. Good rest will help. Try it in your rooms. Plenty to see there. All over the valley, really. That's a good idea actually. Don't bother coming here. Going to borrow some apprentices to clear out some of that clutter, anyhow. Your time is better spent on the spellsight, and you won't get distracted. Can't move to creating spells unless you can see what you're doing."

He motioned her to the door and murmured the incantation to release the new guard spells. Reisil strained to hear, catching a few of the words. They sounded like nonsense.

"What is that you said?" she asked boldly as she stepped past him and into the passage.

"That's not for you to know," he admonished. Reisil nodded. She wasn't so stupid as to think he'd give away the key to the door, though she *had* hoped.

"That's not what I meant. It wasn't in any language I know. In fact all that"—she waved her hand in the direction of the prison room—"all that is sheer nonsense as far as I can tell."

"It's an ancient language of the gods, one that is entirely devoted to magic. Called *rinda*. It will be the next thing for you to learn so that you can construct your own spells."

Reisil rubbed her aching eyes and groaned. "Why can't I just think of what I want to do and do it? The way I made the filigree in the iron or caught all those things you threw at me in the test?"

"You can. It's exhausting to maintain, however, and severely compromises what you can do. With careful spells you can maximize the impact of limited exertions of power. You can set a cascading network of spells so that you can trigger the spell from afar or at another time. You can overlap and reinforce them so that they work together to increase what strength you bring to them. There is a reason, Reisil, that the work of the journeyman lasts years, why full mages continue to experiment and refine their designs, why difficult spells take so very long to develop and perfect. And no matter how you plan, the spell sometimes goes awry. Take Mysane Kosk. We still don't know what went wrong there. We have been fortunate that we can make use of the results anyway.

"Now go, clean up and eat. Don't return until you have conquered spellsight."

It was just dusk and instead of returning to her rooms, Reisil wandered along the edge of the valley. The grass was damp from the earlier rain, and the wind made a soughing sound in the trees. She drew a deep breath of the pungent air, calling Saljane and settling the goshawk on her shoulder. She reached up and stroked Saljane's gray feathers as she walked, turning to follow the chuckling brook toward the village.

~I never expected there would be so much more to learn. The apprentice test was nothing compared with this. But I have to learn some of that language before I leave. It's the only way to understand what they do.

Saljane dipped her head and nibbled Reisil's fingers. Reisil cupped her fingers around Saljane's head and scratched her neck.

~What do you suppose is happening outside? In Koduteel? She had avoided thinking about it. Had the Regent attacked the *ahalad-kaaslane*? Had the plague decimated the city?

~They have to take care of themselves. You are only one weapon, and you cannot keep everyone safe. They would not forgive you for trying.

Reisil halted with a jerk, twisting her head to stare up at Saljane. *~What do you mean?*

~You want to keep them safe. But you cannot keep them from danger. You must do what you must and let them do as they will.

~What if I can't do this? What if I'm too late?

~Then they will die. But that will be their choice, not yours. You cannot claim that responsibility. That belongs to the Lady. You can only do what you can do.

A hard knot bobbed in Reisil's thoat. Saljane had a raptor's sense of reality and truth. Things were or were not. You acted or did not act. You ate or you starved. You killed or you were killed. You hid from the truth or you faced it.

All the next day Reisil tried to *see* the spells around her. She began in bed, then in her bathtub, then at breakfast, then walking the length of the valley. To no avail. The rain returned, a gray drizzle, and Reisil retreated back to the main building in the middle of the afternoon. Saljane shook herself like a dog, sending droplets running down Reisil's neck.

"Stop it! You're a menace," Reisil admonished. "Besides, you needed a bath."

Saljane snapped her beak and glided to a perch on the back of a chair, proceeding to preen herself and thoroughly ignore Reisil, who pulled off her dripping cloak and turned it over to the servant hovering nearby. She took a towel from the stack on the entry table and did her best to soak up the dampness from her hair and feet.

"Are you ready?"

Saljane flipped her tail and raised her head regally as if waiting, and Reisil lifted her onto her shoulder.

"You're getting fat."

~I hunt well, was Saljane's haughty reply.

~You eat well, you mean. I'm surprised you can fly with that belly.

Reisil poked at Saljane's breast, the gesture turning into a caress as she scratched. Saljane lifted herself up, stretching, so that Reisil could reach under her soft stomach.

"You have no pride," she told the blissful goshawk. "And neither do I. I think I'm ready to go have a soak and then bask by the fire with a bucket of wine and a whole roast pig. Perhaps I'll see spells then."

~Perhaps you need someone to scratch your feathers, Saljane suggested.

~And maybe I'll have roast goshawk instead of roast pig.

A few hours later found Reisil lying on a quilt on the floor wrapped in a soft flannel robe, eyes closed, her head propped on a stack of feather pillows. Beside her on a table was a half-finished glass of mulled wine. Saljane drowsed on her perch by the bed. The fire crackled and popped, providing the only light in the room. Suddenly Reisil sat bolt upright, her robe gaping open.

"I did it! I can see them! I can see the patterns of the spells!"

Saljane blinked groggily. ~*Good.*

Reisil leaped to her feet. "They are beautiful, like tapestries woven of light. Come, look with me."

She snared Saljane's muzzy mind and together they surveyed the room. The spells glowed softly in jewel colors. Some were written in tiny flowing script, others bold and sharp edged. Some were layered over each other, white on amethyst, on emerald, on sunstone. Reisil wandered through the entire suite, intrigued. She recognized some of the symbols from the parchments in Kvepi Debess's cage room, but mostly they were beautiful but incomprehensible pictures.

Peering outside she saw trails of scrolling symbols flowing around the valley walls and up the mountain. They glowed brightly in the village, here and there flaring with brilliant light as they were activated. Reisil turned back to her room, activating the lights, the tub, the water, everything she could think of in turn. Various parts of each pattern flamed in response, and she began to understand how the layers worked, though she could not have repeated any of them.

At last she stopped, a headache growing in the back of her head. "Tomorrow I'll start to learn the language," she told herself. "I'm going to be the fastest learner Kvepi Debess has ever seen."

With that, she pulled on her nightshift and slid into bed, falling into a heavy sleep, Saljane a contented presence in her mind. She was roused only a few hours later by clamoring bells, shouting voices and a long, haunting cry of fury. It coiled around her, scraping over her skin like teeth.

"Baku!"

She scrambled out of bed, tripping and falling heavily to her hands and knees. She jumped up and ran to the window, shoving the casements wide. There was nothing. Her window faced the southern side of the valley, and several of the smaller buildings where most of the Kvepis made

their homes. She leaned out, trying futilely to see around
the edges of the building. The cry came again. Fear dug
sharp talons into Reisil and she yanked on her clothes.

~Baku? Baku!

There was no response. More than that. There was emptiness. Her mouth tightened, remembering the *ilgas* used
on Saljane to restrain her. What had they done to Baku?
And why?

But the answer struck her almost as soon as the question.

"By the Lady," she whispered. "He's like the *nokulas*. He's
a creature of magic. That's who they sent Tapit to hunt."

And if they've caught Baku, where is Yohuac?

She dragged on her boots and gauntlet, not bothering to
fasten her robe as she lifted her fist to catch Saljane and
settle her on her shoulder. The goshawk clamped her talons
tight. They plunged out of the room, the bells still ringing
a tocsin over the valley. Reisil pelted down the halls and
out onto the gravel path, where a stream of others collected
and flowed toward the workshops in answer to the bells.
Reisil jumped off the path and raced across the tall grass,
her breath whistling between her lips.

She topped a low rise and jerked to a halt.

"Oh, Lady, no."

Baku was tangled head to foot in an enormous *ilgas*
woven thick with spells. Reisil squinted against their brilliance. They dragged him along the ground with a team of
draft horses. Every now and then he struggled, and when
he did, the net flared brighter and again came that long,
bellowing howl. A sound of red pain and black fury. And
desperation. Reisil dropped to her knees, the thick grass
stalks tickling her cheeks.

"Where's Yohuac?" she whispered.

But she soon caught sight of another horse. It was Tapit's. A body was slung over the saddle. It too was wrapped
in an *ilgas*, though this one was much dimmer, as though
the spells weren't active. Reisil pressed her hand to her
mouth, her lips trembling. *~Do we leave them too?*

Saljane's response was immediate and scorching. *~No.*

*~Good. Because I may have to let my friends fight their
own battles, but I'm sure as the Demonlord's horn not going
to leave them to be tortured.*

Chapter 39

A heavy gale rattled the windows, rain falling in thick, battering sheets. Kebonsat settled a pile of papers in the cold fireplace and touched a candle to them. Things would be lax, as lax as they ever got under the new Regent's strict regime. A perfect day to make their escape. They'd been waiting for just such an opportunity.

He added more papers to the fire, watching the stiff pieces of parchment blacken and curl. All was as ready as could be except for these last bits of housekeeping. His household was packed, though he'd told them nothing of the plan. The fewer people who knew, the better, though Dumen and Ledus resented his silence. But the less anyone knew, the safer for everyone, should anybody get caught.

He waited until the fire died, leaving only the candle to light the room. He stared at the flickering flame, considering his plan again. Finally he shook his head. He wasn't leaving without at least making the attempt. And he'd better get to it. He had only a couple of hours left.

Kebonsat exited his office. There was a crease of light beneath Dumen's door. Kebonsat knocked gently. The door swung open almost immediately. Dumen scowled at him, his lantern jaw twitching.

"Get Ledus, and come to my office."

The two men came swiftly and silently. They were both dressed akin to Kebonsat in nondescript travel leathers. They halted just inside the closed door, arms crossed and legs wide. Ledus shared Dumen's scowl, his fleshy lips pulled back to reveal square, yellow-stained teeth within a thick black beard.

"Is it time to tell us what's going on?" asked Dumen, the twitch in his jaw growing more pronounced.

Kebonsat ignored the question. "I've got some business to tend to. I may not be back in time. If not, I want you to go on without me."

"Go where? How?" Ledus demanded.

"Someone is going to come get you and show you the way."

"Who?"

Kebonsat shook his head. "I can't say. But they'll have a password. *Copicatl.*"

"*Copicatl?*" The two men exchanged confused looks and then glared again at Kebonsat.

"Whoever gives you that word, I want you to follow their orders exactly and without question. Do you understand?" His voice hardened, and they nodded unwillingly. "Good. With any luck, we'll be far from Koduteel by nightfall. And now I must take care of one thing more." He reached out his hand and grasped each man's forearm in turn. "Remember what I said. If I don't get back in time, you're not to wait. Bright Light shine on your journey."

With that, he lit a second candle and opened the panel in the wall. Ledus and Dumen swore as he eased inside the tunnel.

"Keep in mind that our hides won't be worth much if your father finds out we let you wander off to get killed," growled Dumen.

"If you survive to see him again, you can tell him I risked my own fool neck."

"All the same, watch yourself," said Ledus gruffly.

"Don't wait," Kebonsat reminded them again, smiling grimly as he pushed the panel closed and trotted away down the tunnel, hand cupped around the candle.

Emelovi lay in bed, rigid and shaking. She'd sent her officious ladies' maids away hours ago, but she couldn't so easily banish the feel of Prensik's hands on her, his moist lips and his probing tongue on her neck, in her mouth. Aare had loosened his leash. She shuddered, wanting another bath. It was punishment. Aare really wasn't ready to turn her over to Prensik. Unless she refused what he asked.

Her hand crept to her shoulder where Prensik had bitten her in his eager lovemaking. She'd fought him, only increasing his lust. He'd held her breast and bit her and ordered her to open her mouth or he'd tear her dress and show everyone whom she'd belonged to. Aare had been just beyond the curtains, flirting with the sorceress. He wouldn't have forgiven her calling for help. She could hardly imagine a punishment worse than Prensik.

She turned over, clutching a pillow over her face and screaming into it.

She didn't have to imagine what Aare wanted her to do with Waiyhu-Waris. The sorcerer had for weeks been officious in his attentions, growing more and more bold as Aare turned a blind eye. When they danced, his hands strayed too low. In corners, he had begun to whisper of his want and need, describing the pleasure he could give her in bed.

In the dark she flushed hot, remembering the feather touches across her breasts and between her legs during supper two nights ago as he watched her over the rim of his glass, his lips shiny, his gaze knowing. All through the supper, course after course, the magic touches persisted. She could not escape them, forced to sit calmly and enter into the toasts and gossip. In the end, she wasn't strong enough to resist them. She remembered the shivering power of the tide that swept over her. Pleasure so intense it was almost pain. And he did not stop there. He kept his distance, never even asking her to dance. But the touches never ceased, and twice more she succumbed to them before she could escape her duties and flee to the safety of her room.

"He's expressed an interest in you, and I want you to spend time with him. Discover his secrets," Aare had said just this night, before he sent Prensik to teach her a lesson.

"I can't," she'd said before she could stop the words. It was a mistake. The kind she couldn't afford to make with him.

"What?" That quiet, colorless voice, the raised brow. She'd seen that expression and heard that voice too often not to know the danger.

"He—" She faltered, mouth dry, scrabbling for something to say. Finally she resolved on the truth. Aare wouldn't want her soiled for marriage. "He has said things, things he wants to do. . . ." She trailed off, blushing, and Aare had laughed. *Laughed!*

He scanned her up and down appraisingly, pausing on her décolletage. "Good. Then you won't have to work hard getting him into your bed. Men talk in bed. I want to know everything he has to say. It's a pity you're not more skilled in those arts, but perhaps your innocence appeals."

Emelovi had stared at him openmouthed. "But, the gossip," she said weakly.

"This is *my* court now," he said with a dismissive flick of his fingers. "Should anyone think to make a gossip of you, they shall soon be taught better."

She'd refused again, too shaken and appalled to be afraid. And with Aare, that was often a fatal mistake. He'd not hesitated long to teach her the error in her thinking. Prensik had caught her in the curtained antechamber and forcefully pressed his suit. She was not a slow learner. But what to do?

A scraping noise made her stiffen. She wiped her tears away, listening hard, the hairs on the back of her neck prickling. There it was again. In her room. Someone was coming in through the secret panel. Emelovi froze. She forced herself to breathe slowly and quietly as she sat up, pushing back the bedclothes and inching toward the nightstand.

Footsteps, soft and careful. There was a slight thump and a sharp indrawn breath. Emelovi snatched at the candlestick, catching its heavy length in her fingers. There was another scrape, a rattle of bric-a-brac on a table. The intruder moved closer, and now Emelovi smelled the scent of a blown candle. Her heart pounded so loud, she could hardly hear. A step on the pedestal, low ragged breaths. The mattress sank slightly. Still Emelovi could see nothing in the stygian darkness. A hand touched her knee. She yelped and swung the candlestick with all her might. There was a dull thud and the hand jerked away, the intruder collapsing onto the bed with a *whuff* and an agonized groan.

She scrabbled backwards, still clutching the candlestick.

"Emelovi—it's me."

"Kebonsat?"

There was an inarticulate sound of agreement.

"By the Lady, how?" Swiftly she felt for the second candlestick on her nightstand. She clicked the striker and at last was rewarded by a flickering flame. Turning back to Kebonsat, she found him lying on his side, right hand holding his left arm, his contorted face frighteningly pale, even in the ghostly light.

"Oh, my Lady! Are you all right?"

"What did you hit me with?"

"A candlestick," she answered, helping him sit up. He cradled his left arm. "I didn't know—"

"My fault. I was afraid you might have one of your maids here."

"No." Her voice turned brittle, and he frowned.

"What's happened?"

"Nothing." Yet. But she couldn't tell him any of that. "How are you here?" She glanced at the panel.

"Now that is a story. And one I have no time to tell." He paused, staring at her. She shivered, suddenly aware of her light nightshift. She raised a hand to cover the spot where Prensik had bitten her. "I've worried about you," he said abruptly.

She nodded. "Me too."

The silence stretched between them, and Emelovi shifted, curling her toes into the piled rug.

"I am leaving Koduteel," he said at last. "I want you to come with me."

Emelovi just stared.

He reached for her hand, his fingers warm and firm. "Please. I can't leave you here. I know I have nothing to offer. I don't even have my name anymore. But at least let me get you free of the city, from Aare. There must be someplace safe you can go until this is over."

Emelovi's mind clicked on the last. Over? Nothing was going to be over. "My brother is planning to take the crown. But he's been hunting the *ahalad-kaaslane*. He says they kidnapped my father."

But Kebonsat was nodding. "I know. I know more than that. The *ahalad-kaaslane* did not kidnap him, Emelovi. That much is a fact."

"Then he is safe?" She clutched his hand.

He shook his head. "I don't know where he is. I know he did leave with Sodur, and I believe he went freely."

Emelovi closed her eyes as a sudden wave of dizziness swept over her. "Thank the Lady."

Kebonsat tugged on her hand, pulling her down onto the bed, grunting as he jerked his injured arm. "Emelovi, surely you see how dangerous your brother is? Hunting the *ahalad-kaaslane*? I'm Patversemese, and even I know how deranged that is."

Emelovi thrust herself to her feet, an odd sense of protectiveness driving her. "Aare is a strong hand and intelligent."

"You're a good sister, Emelovi. Loyal. But you can't tell me you really agree with what he's been doing. You know what he's capable of. You can't defend him."

His voice had turned hoarse. Emelovi stared at him, her mind whirling. Everything in her craved escape. But she was the Vertina and a Varakamber. To run would be a coward's act. And who would speak for her father? Kebonsat read the answer in her face. He swung to his feet, sliding his hand around to cup her neck, his lips inches from hers. She splayed her hands on his chest. He could persuade her. So easily.

"Please listen," he said. "If you leave, you will have a chance to find your father, to stop your brother from destroying everything your father built."

Emelovi licked her lips. *Find Father.* Hope blazed within her—he would know what to do. He could stop Aare with a word. Hope joined inclination and fear. "Yes, I'll go with you."

Kebonsat let out a gusty sigh, like he'd been holding his breath for days. "Gather some traveling clothes. The sturdier the better. Any jewels or money you have. You might need them."

Emelovi turned to obey. He watched as she packed, then dressed behind her screen.

"Here," she said, dropping her bag at his feet. She held up a silk scarf and threaded it around his neck and arm, tying it firmly. "Shall we?"

As they stepped into the passage, pulling the panel closed, Kebonsat laid a hand on her arm, his face haggard in the candlelight. "Emelovi—" He broke off and glanced away at the wall and then back. "Emelovi, I want you to know how much I've come to care about you. I want nothing more than to see you safe. I could never forgive myself if I left here without you."

His words made her eyes burn with sudden tears. She took his hand, brushing his cheek with her lips, delighting in his musky scent, like tobacco, mint and bryony.

"Let's go find my father."

Juhrnus skulked in a shadowed doorway, his skin clammy. At the end of the corridor was the entrance to Kedisan-Mutira's room. He'd watched long enough to know she was alone. Still he dithered. Since the Regent had begun purging the *ahalad-kaaslane* these last weeks, it wasn't safe to walk along the streets, much less come here. Standing in the palace now was the most supremely stupid thing he'd ever done. He stroked Esper's head. Not content to risk his own fool neck, he'd brought Esper too.

~I wouldn't be left behind.

Juhrnus twitched. He should turn right around and leave. Forget about her. Instead he pushed himself out of the shadows. He tapped lightly on her door with his fingertips, glancing back up the corridor, his spine prickling. He tapped again. Finally the door swung open. His tongue clung to the roof of his mouth. She wore a silken wrap tied loosely at the waist and nothing else. The skin arrowing down to her navel was white and splotched with red, yellow and purple. Bruises. He didn't want to imagine where they came from.

She said nothing as he slid into the room. Her face was remote, and it was all he could do to keep his hands at his sides.

"What brings you here?" she asked, her voice husky and low as if she'd had a cold.

In the five weeks since the Regent had begun his campaign to be rid of the *ahalad-kaaslane*, Juhrnus had kept hidden, helping Karina to move people out of the Fringes and out of the city when possible. Following his warning to the Temple, many of the *ahalad-kaaslane* who escaped had joined the effort. Too many others had been caught. What had become of them, Juhrnus hated to think about. The way Soka went silent and all expression bled from his face told Juhrnus more than he wanted to know.

Juhrnus had been grateful for the labor, for the danger, for the worry—anything to take his mind off *her*. Still he had not slept for more than a few hours at a time. And now he was here, where he shouldn't be, and he couldn't think of a thing he wanted to say.

"You're a mess."

Juhrnus reached up to touch his hair. It was tangled and matted, and the gale outside had done little to improve it. He hadn't shaved in weeks; his eyes were deepsunk and bloodshot. He looked more than halfway to being a corpse. Kedisan-Mutira wasn't the first to say so.

"I thought he might have taken you," she said.

"Had some warning. Got away."

"So I see."

An awkward silence fell. She continued to look at him with that remote, inscrutable expression, as if she watched him from a great height.

He smoothed the nap of his cloak with uneasy fingers.

"I wasn't sure I'd find you alone."

"No?"

He glared. "No."

"Well, you have."

She ceded not an inch, everything about her armored and forbidding. What was he doing here? What did he expect? She drew him like a moth to flame, but there was nothing here for him. Nothing at all.

"I should go. I'm going to be late." He reached for the door.

"You're leaving."

He stopped. "Yes."

"Koduteel," she added.

He hesitated. He *couldn't* trust her. Even if he wanted to. But he couldn't help himself. He nodded. "Yes."

"Why did you come here?"

He turned helplessly. "On my life, I do not know."

As he watched, the mask slipped from her face. She frowned, her dark eyes tired and troubled. "You shouldn't have. It's very dangerous."

The more so if she decided to sound the alarm. He fingered the wax-covered pellet of tanghin poison in his pocket, a gift from Soka with the helpful advice, "Don't get caught."

"I had to see you. And now that I'm here . . ." He spread his hands out helplessly. "You are the enemy."

"Do you think I'll betray you?"

"If necessary." Her flinch at his forthright response startled him. "Don't think I wouldn't do the same," he added softly.

"What do you need?" she asked, folding her arms across her stomach.

Juhrnus drew back. "I can't—"

"I'm not asking for your plans. I ask only what you need. If I can afford to give it to you, if it's in my power— tell me."

He licked his lips. "Time. We need time." Time to get away, time to organize.

"How much?"

"All we can get."

She nodded. "You should go. I never know when the *pengakum* will come."

Juhrnus scowled at the mention of the two sorcerers. His eyes slid to the bruises on her pale skin. There wasn't anything he could do. She didn't want rescuing, even if he had the means.

"Don't take chances. Keep yourself safe. I'd like to know you were safe," he said.

She smiled and shook her head, reaching out to stroke his cheek. Her touch jolted him to his boots, and he closed his eyes against the force of it.

"There is no such thing as safety. Only chance."

He caught her fingers and held them. "May your Dahre-Sniwan guard you well. I won't forget you."

His throat closed and he dropped her hand, yanking the door open. Juhrnus slipped into the corridor, returning to the hidden passage. His face contorted. What had he told Yohuac? *You should have kissed her while you had a chance.* He wiped roughly at the corners of his eyes. He doubted he'd have another chance. Next time he saw her, she'd be in the midst of Aare's army.

"I don't care what you say. We aren't going with you."

Metyein took a breath to argue, but Soka jumped in first. "Suit yourself. Give our regards to the Regent when you see him." Soka winked at Metyein with a knife-edged grin.

Metyein frowned. There was a growing wildness about him; one might even say madness. Soka hardly seemed to value his own life anymore, though he'd become almost fanatical about improving his sword skills. If he was going to die, he wasn't going to sell his life cheaply. He carried quick-acting poisons secreted all over his body. He wasn't going to let Aare take him again. Not for the first time did Metyein wonder what had happened in Aare's underground torture chambers. But Soka wasn't telling.

"Come, gentlemen. We have given you the password. Do not be foolish. Surely Kebonsat said to trust whoever gave it to you, no matter how unlikely?"

"I did." Kebonsat stepped through the panel. He looked at his men, and they blanched. Kebonsat turned back to Metyein. "Perhaps I was not entirely clear. We shall, I hope, have time to sort it out later. But now I think it best we leave, as we are now late and we no longer have the option of staying."

He extended his hand toward the panel, and for the first time Metyein noticed that Kebonsat's left arm was caught in a makeshift sling and that there was someone else in the passage. He drew a short breath. "Dazien." He pursed his lips. "I think Aare's going to be a very unhappy Regent. We'd better go now."

Kebonsat ordered his household into the passage. All told, there were nine of them. Metyein fell in behind the Vertina.

"I must warn you, Dazien, the means of our leaving will not be pleasant."

"I did not expect it," she replied. "Nor did I expect you. Your father has ardently defended you against the charges of kidnapping my father."

"My father is correct," Metyein said. He thought of the message he'd left in his father's study. A scrap of paper tossed on his desk. Just five words and no signature: *What honor and duty require.* Would he find it? Would he understand? He dropped back beside Soka.

They reached the ground floor and left the palace. The wind howled and the rain fell like ax blades, soaking them to the skin. Metyein couldn't remember experiencing such a storm and thanked the Lady, hoping it would last long enough to mask their escape.

The guards at a sally port on the west side were friendly to a pouchful of gold and motioned the group through with little care for who they were, wanting only to return to the warmth and protection of their guardhouse.

Metyein led them down along the curtain wall parallel to the road, the path ankle-deep in mud and rainwater, dawn just beginning to glimmer through the thick pewter clouds. Eventually he led them across the road and down a narrow thoroughfare, turning at last into the courtyard of a dilapidated mansion.

He waved the small group into the stables. The wide entry doors were hanging drunkenly, and grass was springing up around the cobbles. Inside, the sound of the wind and rain seemed even louder as it rattled on the loose roof tiles.

"Nice day for a walk," Juhrnus observed, moving out of the shadows.

"We had a delay," Metyein said, nodding toward Dazien Emelovi.

Juhrnus's eyes widened. "I guess you did. Soka has to be over the moon."

"It will be a lovely surprise for Aare," Soka said. "I should almost like to be there to see it."

"I think you've seen quite enough of Aare these last weeks. Enough to make my hair fall out."

"All of it?" Soka scanned down Metyein's body. "The ladies will be so disappointed."

Metyein shook his head, unable to suppress a grin. "I'm just relieved you'll be out of Aare's reach. Why you've insisted on reporting to him instead of lying low, I'll never understand."

"Couldn't disappoint him now, could I?"

There was that wildness again, brittle and dangerous. And Juhrnus's face was bleak and unrelenting.

"Someone break your favorite doll?" Soka asked.

Juhrnus made a rude gesture at Soka and strode away. Metyein followed.

"Nothing's wrong?"

"Only if Karina doesn't get the wagons."

Metyein didn't push further. Taking this step was wrenching for all of them. Abandoning friends, leaving them to the mercy of Aare, was bad enough. But after that— Treason. For the right reasons and the right cause. They hoped. But it was a difficult, dreadful decision all the same, and until now, one that they could always back away from.

They settled uneasily into the stables to wait. The first wagon rolled in less than an hour later. The driver sat hunched against the wind and rain. He wore a floppy-brimmed hat pulled low over his face and an oilskin cloak. A large red *X* was painted across the back. The high, slatted sides of the wagon rose behind him as if meant to carry hay. Water sluiced off the wagon boards, and the mules shook themselves like dogs. The driver pushed his hat up with a thick, scarred hand. He had a broad face and gray, curly hair.

"Stevaal! I didn't expect you," Juhrnus said, reaching up to grasp the other man's arm in greeting.

"Orders, laddy. Given the cargo," he replied. His gaze snagged on the Dazien, and he pursed his lips in a silent whistle. "Good thing, too. Everyone up for this?"

"They will be. Or they'll not live long enough to learn better."

Juhrnus turned to the assembled group, capturing each gaze in turn. "What you're looking at is a plague wagon," he announced. "No one stops them, no one checks them. The bodies are tossed inside and taken out of the city to be burned. There's a false bottom box inside. Three of you will be loaded inside, and then Stevaal will make the rounds. When the wagon's full, he'll drive it out to the pyres, and more of our people will unload you. You'll then make for the trees, where supplies and horses await. But here's the promise we made. Anyone who doesn't go, doesn't get left behind to talk about it."

"But— Won't we catch the plague?" This from a loose-jowled man, his watery eyes wide.

Metyein nodded. "It's a chance."

"Better than staying," Soka added. "The Regent would make you a guest of his pleasure chambers. Wouldn't matter if you knew anything or not." He touched his covered eye. "I'd rather have the plague and die easy."

Metyein swallowed. If Soka called that easy . . .

"It is the only way out," Kebonsat said. "And the walls of the palace will not protect us from the plague, even if that were the worst of our worries. Do you agree to come?"

They each nodded, faces pale.

"Good on us all, then," Stevaal said. "Load up and on our way."

The first to go were Kebonsat, the Vertina and Juhrnus. The Vertina's face was pale. Metyein smiled reassuringly as he dropped the door back into place.

"Be careful, Stevaal. And give our thanks to Karina. Warn her about the Vertina. The Regent is going to screw things down."

"I will. And no thanks needed. Just don't forget us. Oh, and this." Stevaal reached gloved fingers inside his cloak and pulled out a small packet wrapped in oiled canvas. "For Dannen Relvi. If you can get it to him."

Metyein took the packet and slid it into his cloak pocket. "I'll get it to him."

Stevaal yanked his hat back down and flicked the whip. The mules jogged to the side, unwilling to return to the tempest outside, but Stevaal spoke sharply and pulled them around, and soon the wagon was moving down the barn rows and back out into the courtyard.

"He brought the Vertina along." Soka came to stand next to Metyein. "And you tell *me* not to antagonize Aare."

"I tell you not to do it when you're standing within arm's reach," Metyein corrected. "But you're right. Aare's not going to take this well. If it wasn't personal before, it is now. He'll likely raze the city looking for her. I hope my father can keep a leash on him."

"I'd rather your father put chains on him."

Metyein shook his head. "He'd never do it. And when Aare takes the throne, my father will serve him as loyally as he served Aare's father. And when that happens, we'd better be ready."

"You think it will be soon."

Metyein met Soka's shrewd look, his heart sitting like a stone in his chest. "Maybe even before the end of the summer."

"That doesn't leave us much time."

"And we don't even know if Reisiltark is still alive. And sane."

Chapter 40

Reisil rubbed her eyes. Her stomach growled, and her shoulder itched just out of reach of her fingers. Sighing, she shoved back the book and slumped down in her chair.

~*What time is it?*

~*Near dawn.*

~*That late? I've been here for hours. And so has Kvepi Debess. What is he doing in there?*

Since Baku and Yohuac's capture, Reisil had not been allowed into Kvepi Debess's laboratory. Instead he'd set her to studying the *rinda*. He never mentioned his two prisoners. Reisil didn't ask about them, not wanting to give the impression she cared. She never pretended not to know them. Tapit would quickly have exposed her lie, having seen them together in Koduteel. She had instead maintained a manner of professional interest. When Kvepi Debess asked her about her relationship with the two, she shrugged.

"I spent a great deal of time with them. I hoped they could help me with the plague and the *nokulas*. But they couldn't give me what I needed." She smiled, her jaw tight. "You gave me that."

"Do you think they came looking for you?"

"They probably thought I needed rescuing. Most people thought you wouldn't welcome me."

She didn't know whether he believed her, but she still was not allowed into the laboratory, nor did he discuss his work with her. Unable to do anything else, she submerged herself in the study of the *rinda*. If she was going to free Baku and Yohuac, she would have to know how to read the spells.

Behind her, she heard shuffling footsteps. She swung around as Kvepi Debess wandered into her study room.

He yawned, scratching his stomach. "You're still here, Reisil?" He smiled approval. "I'm feeling a bit hungry myself. Join me in the kitchens?"

Reisil nodded, shutting the book and following after him. "I have been meaning to ask you something," she said as they stepped out into the brisk night air.

"Oh?"

"I wondered if it would be possible for me to observe Kvepi Uldegas in his work."

"Uldegas? Whatever for?" There was a thin line of suspicion in his voice. Uldegas had Yohuac.

"He's a healer-mage. And while you say that my major talents aren't in healing, nevertheless, I know at least a bit about it. I thought if I watched him, watched his spells, I could learn something about how the *rinda* work. I've tried sorting out the spells on my lights and my bathtub, but it's like looking at an already painted picture. I've no idea where one would start. If I understood how things connected, it would help me remember better."

She held her breath, waiting. All night she'd practiced the speech, trying to sound logical.

Kvepi Debess turned into the main building and trundled down the stairs to the kitchens, Reisil trailing behind. Inside the kitchens, the baking crew was hard at work. A boy was dispatched to serve Reisil and Kvepi Debess, and he swiftly supplied a tray of cold meats and cheeses, bread, pickles and steaming kohv sprinkled with nussa. Kvepi Debess piled together a hearty sandwich. Reisil sipped her kohv, watching him over the rim of her cup.

"It's a good idea," he said finally around a mouthful of sandwich. "But you know Uldegas. He's crotchety even when he's in a good mood. Still, you're a journeyman and have healing experience. I expect you'd be far more helpful than that brace of apprentices he's always nattering on about. I'll speak to him—but mind you, only for a week at the most. I'll have need of you soon myself."

Reisil nodded, hope soaring. "Does that mean I'll get to help you with the coal-drake?"

He shot her a look from beneath his grizzled brows. "Could use you. But mind, I don't want any foolishness!"

Female foolishness. Hysterics. Reisil smiled. "You won't get any of that from me." And he wouldn't. She bit hard

into her sandwich, enjoying the feeling of her jaws grinding the food. Hysterics weren't going to help Baku and
Yohuac. She was going to have to watch their suffering.
She was going to have to make it worse. She was going
to have to torture them herself. It was the only way to
free them.

Though a part of her cringed at the thought, she refused
to let herself be overpowered by guilt. This was war. Kodu
Riik was at stake. What sacrifices were required, she'd
make. Even if it meant sacrificing the blood of her friends.

She felt a warm sense of approval radiating from Saljane.
Reisil went very still. Her mind fled back to the moment
when Tapit had put the *ilgas* on Saljane. At that moment
Reisil had forgotten herself. She'd been insane with grief
and rage. She'd forgotten who she was. What she was. The
relief at getting Saljane back hadn't diminished the fear of
losing her again. It gnawed at Reisil like a pack of starving
rats. Only now she feared something more.

A shaft of ice drove down inside Reisil and for a moment
she couldn't breathe. It had never occurred to her before
that she might have to do this without Saljane. But it could
come to that, couldn't it? And she could either destroy
hillsides in wild grief and fury, or she could do what she
was called to do. She swallowed, coughing, and reached for
her kohv.

~*It can't happen again. We aren't more important than
Kodu Riik. We're* ahalad-kaaslane, *whether we have each
other or not. Baku's the same. That's why he can't give up
on Yohuac. We can't just surrender to our emotions and
give up. We have to keep fighting.*

Easier said than done. But if it came to it . . .

~*Yes. Whatever comes, we will continue on.* Despite the
undercurrent of apprehension underlying Saljane's mindvoice, she spoke proudly and defiantly.

Black-robed bodies sprawled across couches and floors
and slumped over the arms of chairs. Some of the Kvepis
had fallen asleep facedown on the table, drooling. Snores
resonated through the dining hall, intermingled with moans.
A few men had turned gray and clammy; others twitched
and muttered.

Reisil picked her way through the bodies. She wore the

clothing she'd arrived in, her sword in her right hand, Saljane on her shoulder.

There was Uldegas. He slept upright in a chair, his mouth gaping open. His breathing was high and light, and Reisil wondered how much of the henbane tincture he'd ingested. Not taking any chances, she'd put some in the wine and more in the platters of herb-roasted salmon. The feast had been in honor of the Patverseme new year, when the sun began to wane and the Dark Lord waxed in strength. Ironically, it was also Lady Day. Reisil took that as an omen. Today the Kvepis abandoned their laboratories and spells for a few hours of wine and food and merriment. Today she could drug them all in one sitting.

Reisil swung her sword around, poking Uldegas's throat with the tip. Blood beaded on his skin. ~*This one I wouldn't have minded seeing dead. Or better yet, thrown into one of his cages, where he could rot forever.*

~*Kill him now.* Saljane's voice offered no judgment.

Reisil hesitated and then slowly lifted her sword away. ~*He's helpless. I won't be like them. Not today of all days.*

It had been four weeks since Yohuac and Baku had been captured. In all that time Reisil had wrestled with a plan to get them out. She'd been overjoyed when she learned of the new year's celebration. With all the Kvepis incapacitated, she had time to free her friends. If she could figure out how.

Satisfied the henbane would not soon wear off, Reisil retreated outside.

She paused to check on the two horses she'd cached in the trees near the entrance to Uldegas's workshops. They remained where she'd left them, saddles and packs intact. Indigo greeted her with a nicker. The other was Tapit's leggy gelding. She scratched the bay's starred forehead and fed them each a handful of grain before setting off.

Uldegas had been as jealous as Kvepi Debess of his wards. But Reisil had listened vigilantly and finally discovered the keys to the spells. She entered easily. Inside was a long, oblong room with a row of tables down the middle. They were separated by fifteen feet. Each was set on a pedestal carved with *rinda*. More *rinda* etched the floors, the tables, and the straps dangling from their sides. Chunks of quartz and amethyst crystals dangled down over each table, serving as reservoirs for collected energy. Along the left wall were a series of workbenches and storage cabinets. Here Uldegas performed dissections of flesh. Here he stored his instruments in all their grisly array. Here he mixed potions and poisons. Here were jar after jar containing bits and pieces from *nokulas*, from humans, from Lady knew what else.

Cells lined the opposite wall. Their outer doors were made of heavy planks without openings. The cells contained cages much like those in Kvepi Debess's workshop. Inside, Uldegas stored his victims like potatoes in a cellar. Reisil had never seen any other but Yohuac, and wondered who else suffered in these walls.

She shunted the thought aside, feeling Saljane's steel resolve winding around hers.

~*Let's get him out of here.*

Yohuac lay on a table midway down the room. His eyes were open and fixed on the ceiling above. He was naked, his head shaved smooth, as was the rest of his body. Straps inscribed with complicated *rinda* lay across his forehead, chest, waist, thighs and ankles. They weren't fastened down, and they glowed with a faint green light. There was a patchwork of bandages all over his body and a bucket of bloody rags on the floor. His skin wrapped his protruding ribs and bones shockingly tightly.

"Yohuac? Can you hear me?"

He didn't move.

~*We've got to get him off the table.*

But how? Reisil bent to examine the straps. These *rinda* were more complex than she understood. She stood up, scrubbing her hands over her face. They were meant to hold him paralyzed and senseless. Perhaps that's all they did. They shouldn't be dangerous to the wizard working over him. That would be foolish. She licked her lips. If she was wrong— But he was going to die if he stayed here, and she didn't doubt he'd rather have her try than leave him here for Uldegas.

Reisil drew her sword, and the sound of it rang in the silence. She edged the tip beneath the strap across Yohuac's ankles and then twisted sharply upward, flinging the offending strip into the air. Nothing happened. She repeated the process. His thighs, his waist, his chest, his head.

When she'd flung the last one away, she sheathed the sword and bent over him again.

"Yohuac?"

He blinked. He drew a long rattling breath and then began to cough, deep racking coughs. She slid her arm around him and helped him sit up. He clung to her, his fingers shaking. She continued to hold him for long minutes. At last Yohuac regained control of himself and began to breathe more easily. He couldn't stop trembling, and Reisil hugged him against her firmly, careful to stay away from the bandaged patches.

"Who are you? What's happened?" he rasped.

"I'm Reisil," she said, realizing suddenly that he couldn't see in the darkness. "The wizards captured you," Reisil said. "I still have to get Baku. Can you walk?"

"Whatever I have to do," he said haltingly.

"I'll find clothes."

She eased out from under him and began rummaging through the storage bins where she knew Uldegas stored what he called *artifacts*. In one she found Yohuac's clothing neatly folded. His weapons lay beneath the clothing in the bottom of the bin. Everything had been cleaned and mended. Even his armbands, earrings, and hair beads were there. As if Uldegas ever meant him to wear any of it again. What made her stomach clench were the four other bins full of clothing. She stared at them a long moment and then returned to Yohuac. She helped him dress, wondering how he'd ever get out of the valley, much less make it all the way to Mysane Kosk. He touched his head as she pulled on his tunic.

"What have they done? I don't remember—"

"I don't know," she said.

She helped him with the rest of the clothing. More than once he moaned or flinched as she brushed the bandaged places. When he was dressed, he sagged back onto the table, his head dangling low, his entire body wilting boneless to the side.

"Let me see if I can find some food or drink."

"A light," he whispered. "I want to see."

Reisil retreated to the outer room, rummaging until she found a drawer full of candles. She grabbed one, unwilling to think what Uldegas might use them for. Certainly not light. Next she found a jug of water and a quarter loaf of stale bread. She took them back to Yohuac. She lit the candle with a tendril of power and poured him some water.

"Not too much. You've not had any food for a while." Then she dipped the bread into the other mug and let him have a bite.

He took the bread from her, chewing slowly.

"Will you be all right a moment? I want to look in the cells."

Yohuac nodded, his eyes bleary.

~You must not tarry long.

~I won't.

Reisil went to the first plank door and opened it. There was no one inside, and she inspected two more before she found anyone. A woman sat inside the cage on the floor facing Reisil. She was naked, her head and body shaved. There were no marks of torture or experimentation on her. She sat still and upright.

Reisil knelt beside the cage. "Are you all right?"

The woman lifted her head. Reisil scuttled backwards in shock.

Her eyes were just like those of the *nokulas*: silver and opaque, like the curved bottom of a spoon. The bones of her skull had widened, and her cheeks ridged upward. The skin covering the rest of her very human body was pale as milk. She was beautiful in a terrifying, alien way.

She tipped her head at Reisil, fixing one eye on her like a crow. "You're not him," she said in a voice that reminded Reisil of rain.

"No."

"Can you free me?"

"I don't know."

"Will you try?"

Reisil hesitated. "I don't know how."

"Ah." The woman bent her head down, dismissing Reisil.

Reisil examined the cage. The *rinda* glowed in rainbow light, layered one on top of the other, much like those holding Baku. She felt like spitting. She knew many of the symbols, but not the configurations, and she didn't have the slightest idea how to unravel them. But everything in her rebelled at leaving this woman—or whatever she was—inside. She examined the cage again. There was no lock, only a latch. But clearly the latch was warded, and there was no way to turn it without dangerous repercussions.

"Do you have magic? Is that why you're in here?" Reisil asked, wondering exactly how the spells on the cage were focused.

"Some. I'm a plague-healer."

Reisil froze. "A what?"

"A plague-healer," she repeated.

Reisil had sunk to her knees. "How? I can't even touch it."

The woman tipped her head again in that birdlike way. "The plague has no harmony. I sing it back to joy."

Reisil stared uncomprehendingly. "Sing it?"

"I would like to leave here. It calls, but I cannot answer."

A cure for the plague. Was it possible? Reisil's stomach churned. Given that the woman was locked up in a wizard's cage, Reisil was inclined to believe the notion. Though she could be lying just to trick Reisel into letting her out. Reisil swallowed. But what if her story was true? Reisil snarled. She should have killed Uldegas. She levered to her feet. She had to free the woman; there was no longer a choice, not if there was a remote chance of stopping the plague. But how? Again Reisil examined the *rinda* on the cage.

The cage was undoubtedly designed to suppress the magic of those within and make it impossible for them to free themselves manually. But the wizards never expected to have to counter an attack from without. She just needed an object. . . .

Reisil turned around, her hand falling on her sword hilt. No. She didn't want a magic sword. She needed something else. She retreated out of the cell, alighting finally on Yohuac and the gold armbands sitting beside him. She snatched one up and returned to the cell.

"You did not leave."

"With any luck, we'll leave together." Reisil set the armband on the floor and stepped back.

~*Stay apart, Saljane. If this doesn't work, leave Yohuac. Get to Juhrnus, and tell him what we've learned here.*

She waited for Saljane's reluctant agreement, felt her withdraw. Ruthlessly Reisil suppressed the pang that shot through her. Then carefully she extended a tendril of magic to the armband, anchoring it firmly. Next she turned her attention to the cage. The *rinda* were brilliantly active. She should be able to siphon off their power much as she had sent her own excess magic to store in the hunk of quartz. She stretched out another careful tendril. It touched the cage.

Magic flashed, incandescent as the afternoon sun. Reisil closed her eyes against the painful brilliance. Power sluiced through her. She staggered and dropped heavily to the floor. She couldn't let go. She had no strength to do anything but hold on. Hotter and hotter, spurting and spitting, gushing through her like a torrent of lava. Reisil felt the patterns of the *rinda* softening, dissolving in the flush of raw magic. As they broke apart, Reisil at last understood their patterns and purpose. One after the other they lost cohesion. As each unraveled, the deluge surged and then dropped, dribbling away to nothing.

Reisil opened her eyes, feeling the hard stone of the floor against her back. She blinked. Spots of white and yellow danced across her vision.

"Cage is opened. Free others, yes?"

Reisil drew a shallow breath, all she could manage. Her lungs ached as if they'd been seared black. The rest of her body felt battered as though she'd fallen over a cliff. She sat up with a gasping groan. Between the spots on her vision, she saw that the cage was twisted and black. Unusable. She smiled in grim triumph. She clambered to her feet, leaning against the doorjamb, her head spinning.

"Free others, yes? Yes?"

"I'll try," Reisil answered hoarsely. She couldn't leave any of them here. Plague-healers. She almost sobbed. *Please let it be true!*

"Come. Before he returns."

The woman gestured toward the door, uncaring or unaware of Reisil's pain. Reisil bent and picked up Yohuac's armband. It glowed softly in her spellsight, and she tucked it in her hip pouch.

There was a man in the next cell. He might have been the woman's twin. This time as Reisil examined the cage, she understood the scrolling *rinda*. This one for pain, that one for stealing magic, that for sleep, that for locking the cage, the other for dampening magic. And more. The *rinda* were stacked together like overlapping bricks, repeated on every surface. Removing one, the right one, undermined the rest.

Reisil paced around the cage, the man and the woman watching her with the same unnerving avian expression. At last she found what she was looking for. The spell for dampening magic on the fourth bar from the bottom. It was unfinished. There had been no room left on the bar. A small gap. It was enough.

She pulled the armband out again and set it on the floor. The flood came more slowly, more bearably, as the spells caved slowly in on each other. Even so, the freed power gushed powerfully. But this time she was more prepared and did not collapse. When she was through, the cage was equally as useless as the last.

By the time she freed the fourth plague-healer, she could hardly stand. Her eyelids drooped, and her body shook. She pointed the freed prisoners to their clothing and stumbled back to Yohuac and Saljane. There was a spatter of water and bread on the floor where he'd vomited, but he continued to eat and drink, holding more food down.

"Let's go. We still have to get Baku. I don't know when the wizards will start waking up. But we have to be far out of the valley." She spoke in a rough whisper. She was surprised when the four plague-healers—three men and the woman—offered to help. She leaned on their strength gratefully, barely able to raise her feet off the floor to walk.

They took Yohuac to the horses and sat him down next to a tree. Reisil offered him an apple. "Don't eat too fast. Your stomach is going to take some time to adjust. Rest now. We'll have to ride soon."

She drank deeply from a water bag and bolted down a slab of cheese and a handful of nuts for strength. From her medicine pack she drew a handful of millesti seeds and chewed them. They were bitter, but their juices restored her vigor within minutes. The exhaustion dropped away like a discarded cloak. She'd pay for using the seeds later, she knew, but by then she hoped to be far out of the valley.

The four plague-healers watched her as if waiting for direction.

"There are horses down that way. And a tunnel out of the valley. Shouldn't be anyone to stop you. You should get out of here. Go as far as you can."

"You open more cages?" This was the woman.

"One more. A friend."

She nodded and turned away without another word. The others followed, disappearing into the trees. Reisil watched them go, rubbing her jaw. "Let's hope they make it. And that no one kills them before finding out what they can do. Lady hold them in Her hands."

After a moment she turned to Saljane, who perched in a low branch above. Reisil wished she could send Yohuac to safety, but she doubted he could manage a horse alone.

~*If anything happens, you leave. Go to Juhrnus,* Reisil reminded Saljane. *Don't interfere, whatever Baku does.*

~*He'll be insane.*

~*You came around. Maybe he will too. I'd better get to work.*

Unlike Yohuac, Baku had been aware of Reisil's part in these weeks of experiments, of torture. And she'd had no way to reassure him. What must he think? The last time she'd spoken to him was before arriving at the stronghold, and then she'd ruthlessly banished him from her mind. Since then, everything about her—from her clothes to her actions—said she was no longer *ahalad-kaaslane.* That she'd betrayed the Lady.

"Maybe he'll be reasonable and listen," she muttered as she jogged up the path to the mountain laboratories. "And maybe fat pigeons will pluck themselves and fly into the cook pot."

Chapter 41

She found Baku exactly as she had left him earlier in the day. He hunched at the bottom of his cage, his eyes sunken and staring. His hide was dull like pewter. If she hadn't known better, she might have thought he was a statue. She came down the walkway, stopping opposite the cage. She gave the commands to neutralize the *rinda* on the floor. In the last weeks, Kvepi Debess had trusted her with several commands. Others she'd overheard. She approached the cage and knelt down, dropping her head so she was nearly eye to eye with the coal-drake.

"I've come to get you out, Baku. But before I do, I want you to listen. I've freed Yohuac. He's weak and hurt. He won't be able to survive much of what you can throw at him. I'm not sure he's even going to survive our escape. You're going to have to be careful until he regains his strength. I've drugged the wizards. I don't know how much longer that will last. We have to get out of the valley and into hiding quickly. They can track magic. Remember that."

If she hoped for a response, she was to be disappointed. Baku remained still as death. Reisil's throat ached. She'd played a good part in his suffering, and she couldn't blame him for hating her. She'd better have her say now. He might not give her the chance to do so later.

"I wouldn't have done any of this if I could think of another way." Reisil paused. What else was there to say? It all sounded like excuses. She stood.

Reisil circled the cage, examining the *rinda*. Kvepi Debess had been far more meticulous than Uldegas. His script was small and tight, and he repeated the *rinda* far more frequently. He built a good trap. But not good enough, Reisil thought. If she didn't find a mistake, she'd destroy the cage in the same manner she'd destroyed the woman's cage.

Reisil found an error in the *rinda* at last. In layering the bars, it appeared that Kvepi Debess had become confused in his patterns and switched from one spell to the other in the middle of inscribing. It wasn't much. The rest of the spells were so imbricated that this tiny flaw made little difference to the strength of the cage. But for Reisil, it was the loose thread she needed to unravel the tapestry.

"Here we go," she said, and then set the armband on the floor and began her work.

She woke on the floor. She became aware first of the acrid smell of burning hair. She coughed, and her body spasmed. She tasted blood. Then she felt a weight on her lower limbs and a pressure constricting her head. She opened her eyes, struggling against the crusted tears that glued them shut. She tried to lift her hand to rub at her eyes, but found herself trapped. She whimpered and arched her back, but to no avail.

At last her eyes came open, and she went still, her heart in her mouth. Baku crouched over her, his taloned claws clutching her head, his back legs holding her arms and legs immobile. She stared up into his yellow eyes.

There was a tickle in her mind. Like the wriggling of a worm. And then two. And then her skull was a roiling mass of worms. Reisil jerked against Baku's unrelenting grip. Her moaning wails echoed from the walls, sounding like the cries of a wounded cat. Blackness washed the edges of her vision. Her throat closed and she choked on bile.

At last the onslaught ended. Reisil collapsed in on herself, her heart thumping, her clothes soaked with sweat. Blood trickled over her forehead and down her scalp where his talons had pierced her skin as she struggled. Still Baku did not speak.

Long moments ticked past. Slowly Reisil's breathing eased, and she began to think again. How long had she been lying on the floor? How long before the wizards woke and blocked their escape? She licked her cracked lips.

"Baku. Whatever you're going to do, do it. The wizards will come soon, and Yohuac is helpless."

He remained still. She watched him, wondering what else she could say. Suddenly he dropped his muzzle to her chest. Reisil grunted at the sharp pressure. He let out a snort and stood. He swayed and Reisil realized he'd also gone without food and water for weeks.

"I should have killed them," she muttered.

~*Yes.*

It was the first, the only word Baku had spoken. Dry and splintered as a lightning-struck tree.

"One of these days, I promise," she said, climbing to her feet. She picked up the armband and put it back in her pouch. "Let's go."

Outside, the sky was beginning to lighten. Reisil heaved Yohuac onto Tapit's horse, using the saddle straps to tie him down. She mounted Indigo, catching Saljane on her fist and lifting the goshawk to a perch on the shoulder. She turned Indigo down the valley toward the horse pens. She felt the redness of Baku's hunger as he scented the beasts.

~Drive them through the tunnel and out. Scatter them as best you can, and feed before you collapse.

He lurched into the air, swerving awkwardly from side to side, his wing beats slow and clumsy. He bellowed and the terrified horses ran before him. They fled to the tunnel, breaking through the gates, stampeding to safety beyond the valley. Baku landed, chasing them on foot. He caught one near the entrance. Reisil heard the crunch of bones. Baku tore away a haunch and bolted meat and bone together. Three more gulps and he roared again, plunging through the tunnel after the rest of the fleeing animals.

Reisil urged Indigo forward, leading Tapit's bay behind her. Both horses snorted and shied from the bloody carcass on the ground. Reisil shortened her reins and clamped her legs around Indigo, urging him past. Tapit's horse followed, pulling away to the length of the leading rein, head thrown high, eyes edged in white.

They entered the tunnel, and Reisil activated the light wards for the animals. She nudged Indigo into a trot. Tapit's horse settled in close at her knee. She glanced at Yohuac. His eyes were barely open. His head jolted and bobbed with every stride the horses took. He listed to the side, though his hands gripped the pommel as best he could. He wasn't going to make it very far. She had to find a place to hide him. But where? The wizards could track magic. The armband in her pouch was a beacon for them, even if Baku wasn't.

The millesti seeds were wearing off, and exhaustion pulled on her. She sagged in her saddle as Indigo jogged along the winding curve of the tunnel. Saljane weighed heavily on her shoulder, and the physical aches of channeling so much magic began to throb. It was a relief to see the circle of ghostly gray light open ahead.

"Almost there," Reisil whispered.

Indigo tossed his head, pushing at the bit. She let him break into a canter, keeping a careful eye on Yohuac. The hoofbeats echoed along the tunnel like a hail of rocks, and Reisil winced at the noise. But she doubted it would make any difference. Baku's departure had been anything but subdued. If the henbane had worn off, the waking wizards wouldn't have missed it.

They broke out into an alleyway lined by gnarled trees,

their leaves rustling in the cool morning breeze. The alleyway emptied into the narrow canyon just below the maze door. The steep sides of the canyon rose like iron walls. They were still trapped. The only escape was through the notch at the far end. And the canyon was warded against intruders. Was it warded against departure? But there was no sign of the plague-healers, which meant they had surely passed the wards safely.

Reisil guided Indigo up the canyon, wondering how far Baku had gone. The ground was rutted and torn in places where the stampeding horses had churned the soft dirt in their frenzied escape. She could feel the coal-drake at the edges of her awareness, a red-rimmed black maw. She didn't reach out to him. She wasn't sure he was entirely sane, though he'd not come out of the cage with the same disorientation and panic as Saljane had experienced.

A bolt of energy sizzled into the ground beside her, churning up a gout of dirt that pelted Reisil in clumps and clods as it fell. Saljane leaped into the air. Indigo reared and skittered away, spinning around and sinking down on his back legs as if to bolt. Tapit's horse lunged. Reisil's shoulder popped as the gelding hit the limit of the rein and jerked around. Pain ripped through her chest. Instantly she wrapped Indigo's reins around her pommel, freeing her left hand to snatch the leading rein from where it tangled around her useless right hand. She anchored the rein securely around her pommel and then dropped to the ground, smacking Indigo on the rump. He gave a snorting whinny and galloped up the canyon.

~Baku, there's trouble. Come get Yohuac to safety.

With that she slammed up her mental walls, not wanting to be distracted, leaving only a narrow opening for Saljane. *~I think we're going to have to fight our way out.*

~Yes. The eagerness in Saljane's voice made Reisil smile harshly.

She'd never meant to fight. It wasn't the smartest choice. Better to run and hide. But there was no choice now. And everything in her hungered for retribution: for her friends, for Mysane Kosk and the damage to Kodu Riik, and most especially for the wizards' absolute indifference to the suffering of those still imprisoned in their cages.

"You didn't think we'd let you walk away from us?"

Tapit stood near the open maze door. A semicircle of a dozen Kvepis ranged behind him with several more straggling through. Most of them looked pale and pinched. Only Tapit stood straight and firm. Reisil cocked her head.

"You think to stop me, then?"

"We are stronger here than we were at Vorshtar. And you don't have surprise on your side this time. You shall not win so easily."

She felt it more than she saw it. It dropped from above like a great black bat. An *ilgas*. But she had expected a surprise attack and burned it out of the air. It took more effort than she liked. Destroying the cages had dangerously weakened her, and while her magic came easily to hand, she could hardly contain it. It filled her like a river of glass. She couldn't afford a battle of feints and parries.

"You are stronger here because of Mysane Kosk. Because of the magic you steal from the *nokulas*. They were people. Even wizards." Reisil slipped her hand into her belt pouch, gripping Yohuac's armband. Stolen magic to fight stolen magic.

"If any we keep were wizards, then they understand our need. They would not begrudge what we do."

"No? I do."

And with that, Reisil struck. She did not aim at the wizards, but at the ground beneath them. She drove deep into the roots of the mountain. She released her full might, uncaring of the heat searing her from the inside out. Her eyes bulged, and her blood boiled in her veins.

~Saljane!

Suddenly there was a shield around her and an endless well of cool strength. Reisil drew on it eagerly, releasing the full power of the armband, emptying it into the ground.

Rocks, dirt and grass erupted into the air. Distantly she heard shouts and a cracking, like the echoing booms of river ice fracturing apart in the spring. Then there was a grinding and the ground began to tremble. Roaring filled the air, and rocks began to fall, clattering all around them. Something thumped Reisil on her damaged shoulder, and she shrieked. Still the power flowed down out of her. She had no strength to stop it. The air around her clotted with dust and debris, and still she stood, the ground starting to roll like an ocean wave.

~Saljane!

The strength was there. Reisil let go of her power, and
it drained away. She lurched sideways, falling to her knees.
In her right hand was a glob of hot metal—the remains of
Yohuac's armband. All around her was a thick fog of dirt.
The sides of the canyon shivered and rumbled. There was
a great black hole where the wizards had stood. Smoke
issued from the hole, billowing as if something deep underground had caught fire and now blazed out of control.
Boulders dropped off the canyon walls in long, slow arcs.
Reisil caught sight of a pair of feet jutting from beneath a
stony pile.

Suddenly the ground beneath her heaved up. A crack
appeared just beyond her boot and widened as she
watched, stretching apart with a groaning, tearing sound.
The smell of rotten eggs wafted up from the gap, and she
gasped, her throat and nose burning.

"Run, Saljane! Run!"

And she fled up the rippling path. All around her, the
canyon walls continued to sigh and shiver, and it seemed
as if the tops had begun to lean inward. Reisil held her
useless left arm against herself as she lumbered along,
coughing and sneezing. Saljane winged ahead, hopping
from branch to branch.

Reisil's lungs hurt, and she could hardly catch her breath
as she began the ascent to the notch. The ground heaved
and then dropped. Just ahead, a portion slipped away. It
looked as if a giant had taken a great bite from the stone.
Reisil eased out onto the remaining ledge and inched along,
clutching the scrub springing from the cracks in the canyon
wall for balance. She had to leap over the last two feet and
then sprawled on her stomach, her left arm banging the
ground like a sack of meal. Black clouds swirled over her
vision. Reisil struggled to her feet, seeing the lip of the
canyon ahead of her.

At last she pulled herself over, the ground trembling so
violently that she could not keep her feet. She rolled onto
her back, gasping. But there was no time to rest, not so
close to the edge. She struggled up and dragged herself
down the path. The mountain continued to tremble, but
with less force. Here the trees were thicker, and she went
from one to the next, bracing herself upright, coughing and

wheezing. Saljane called encouragement, urging Reisil along.

Dawn came, and soon the sun rose above the trees. Reisil stopped at a stream, cupping icy water in her good hand. She drank all she could and fell back against a sugar pine to rest. Her shoulder throbbed with an ache that pulsed through her bones. She panted shallowly, her lungs too raw to allow a proper breath.

What had she done?

Suddenly she heard a booming roar. The tree she leaned against shivered, and the ground jolted, pine needles spritering into the air as if a great hand had slapped the earth and made them jump. The roar went on for a long minute, and then there was silence. Not even a bird chirped. The wind fell still, and even the stream seemed hushed. Reisil struggled to her feet, turning back the way she'd come.

~No. You must not go back.

~What has happened? What did I do?

~What was necessary. Now they will not soon follow. We must find Baku and Yohuac.

Reisil hesitated. Finally she nodded and lurched across the stream, soaking her boots.

They found Baku with the horses and Yohuac in a hollow a quarter of a league away. Baku had regained some of his color, and his hide no longer appeared so desiccated. When Reisil came over the rise, he stood, sniffing. Then he hunched back down onto the grass, watching as she stumbled down the path.

Yohuac had untied himself and managed to dismount. He now slept beside Baku, his scalp and brows pale against his dark skin. Reisil built a small camp, unwilling to go farther that night. Her shoulder flamed in agony, and she knew she could do nothing until she shoved her arm back into place. She wandered back into the trees, finding what she was looking for in a moss-covered juniper. There was a branch sticking out on the side, and she grabbed it with her good hand. Taking a breath, she used the branch to heave herself around, smashing her shoulder against the tree trunk.

She screamed.

She woke on the ground, Baku staring at her, his head

resting on the ground inches away from her face. As she opened her eyes, he rose and walked away. Fair enough. She'd watched him suffer. She'd made him suffer. He ought to get a bit of his own back.

She staked out the horses and built a small fire, heating a pot of water. She made a broth for Yohuac, mixing into it several restorative medicines, floating bits of bread on top. He woke and drank it and soon fell asleep again.

She watched him sleep with gritty, burning eyes. There was no way she could heal him. In unleashing the power of the armband, she'd overloaded herself. The invisible part of herself that channeled magic was raw and bleeding. She looked down at her hands. She and Yohuac would have to heal naturally.

Despite Reisil's misgivings about being so close to the wizards' stronghold, if indeed it still existed, they remained in the hollow for three more days. Yohuac slept for most of that time, waking only to eat. Baku hunted and remained unrelentingly silent. Reisil made little effort to speak to him. She gathered wood and dug roots for their meals. Saljane brought back squirrels and rabbits for roasting. Reisil's arm improved, and the stiffness in her body wore away, her lungs gradually allowing her to breathe more deeply. But she could still not draw on her power. Those wounds remained throbbing and exposed.

~I think we need to find somewhere more secure to camp. Until Yohuac is better. Until I can use my magic again. Then we go to Mysane Kosk, Reisil said to Saljane on the morning of the third day. She was cleaning the saddles. Across the hollow, Baku lay with his head between his front claws, Yohuac sleeping in the curve of his tail.

~They come to Mysane Kosk. It was Baku.

Reisil started at his unexpected intrusion, bewildered. *~Who?*

A fleeting pastiche of faces flittered through Reisil's mind: Juhrnus, Metyein, Kebonsat, others—many, many others.

Reisil clenched the rag in her hand. What had happened? Then she smiled. They were alive. She hadn't been sure. She'd been afraid even to think about it.

~Then we'll have to hurry. But where can we go? We need shelter. And I want to get farther from the stronghold.

*~There's a cave. Near a river. Good hunting there. I will
show you.*

~Thank you. Relief swept Reisil. She felt too exposed
here. If the wizards hadn't been killed, if Tapit hadn't died
in the rockslide, then he'd be coming soon. Unable to draw
on her magic, she would be helpless against them.

Baku stood and yawned hugely. He bent into a long,
groaning stretch. Reisil smiled. He looked like a cat. A big,
scaly, ferocious cat. He looked nearly back to normal. She
wished the same could be said of Yohuac. He still had not
spoken much. She wasn't even sure he really recognized
her. What if Uldegas had hurt him irreparably? Among all
the other wounds, she'd discovered a seam along the back
of his head and down his neck. The wizard had not bothered to seal the wound magically. Which meant that he
didn't want to waste energy on someone he figured would
die soon—or he meant to open it again. Reisil scowled. She
hoped he had died. Painfully.

They departed the next day, traveling slowly so as not to
tire Yohuac more than necessary. He hardly woke enough
to stay on his horse and slept whenever they stopped. It
took four days to reach the cave, which was located high
on a ridge above a lush river valley.

Reisil settled Yohuac on a pallet of grass and pine limbs
before leading the horses down to the valley to graze. Baku
agreed to keep watch on them, well content to sun himself
on the rocky bank. Saljane brought back two fat rabbits.
As the sun dropped lower and the mouthwatering scent of
roasting rabbit drifted through the cave, Reisil knelt beside Yohuac.

His eyes were open.

"How do you feel?"

"Better." He coughed, and she poured a cup of water,
putting her arm around his thin shoulders to help him up.
He drank, and she poured him more. "What happened?"

Reisil hesitated.

He smoothed his fingers over the bristles springing from
his head. With horror he looked at his hands. "What did
they do to me?"

"What do you remember?"

"We were looking for you. We knew where the stronghold
must be—Baku could sense the magic. But we couldn't find

any sort of entrance. We ran into a trap." He shook his head. "So obvious. We should have known. I couldn't hear Baku at all." His face contorted, and he sat up.

"Baku!" He closed his eyes and slumped, his face crumpling. "He is here. I can hear his voice."

Reisil put her arms around him, holding him as he wept. "It wasn't supposed to— I can't."

"Sh-sh. You're both all right. You're both free."

"No. I can't do it. I can't be *ahalad-kaaslane*."

"Then you cannot," Reisil answered, but wondered how he'd survive losing Baku when at last Baku gave up on him. She thrust the thought away. It was his choice, and he must bear it. "But now you must eat and regain your strength."

"Wait. There's something I have to tell you. What I should have told you before."

Reisil squatted back down on the ground. "What?"

"I told you about the competition to be *Ilhuicatl*'s son, do you remember?" Reisil nodded. "What I didn't tell you is that the nahualli blood is failing in Cemanahuatl. Every year fewer and fewer are born. But the nahuallis arrived at a solution. If a nahualli was made the son of *Ilhuicatl*, then his seed would be spread throughout the tribes. Not only that. They believe that a nahualli winning the competition would have greatly enhanced powers. They hope these would be passed along as well."

Reisil's brows furrowed. Where was he going with this? Why was it important to tell her this now? "There are more men like you—who have magic?"

"A few others. The nahuallis did not want to put all their wishes in one basket. But I have been thinking." He struggled up on his elbows. "If I did win the *pahtia*, I might have the power to help you." He dropped back with a sigh, arms trembling from the strain of holding himself up. "I told you I was untrained. But I am not without skills."

Reisil stared down at him, her mind spinning. "You *can* use your magic," she breathed. "Why didn't you tell me this before?"

He opened his eyes, his dark gaze earnest. "It is a secret I have kept my whole life. I was never supposed to practice magic."

"And now?"

"Nothing matters if Cemanahuatl is destroyed. And if I do not help you, I fear it will be."

Reisil nodded, her head beginning to ache. She looked away, needing to get out into the night, where she could think. "Dinner is almost ready. I'd better get the horses." She started to get up and was halted by his hand curving around her neck.

Reisil met his dark gaze again, her voice sharper than she meant it to be. "What else?"

Suddenly Yohuac leaned close and kissed her, his lips warm and soft. His tongue slipped inside her mouth. Reisil froze for an instant and then pressed close, opening her mouth against his. The kiss went on, and then finally he pulled away, his breath coming in short gasps.

Reisil swallowed, touching her tongue to her lips, tasting him. "What was that for?"

"Juhrnus . . ."

"Juhrnus? What does he have to do with it?"

"He said I should have kissed you when I had the chance." He stretched back out on his pallet with a deep sigh.

Reisil smiled bemusedly, pulling the blanket up around his shoulders. She went outside, pausing on the ledge outside the cave. The sky overhead sparkled with stars. Below, the river glimmered like a silver ribbon in the moonlight. Crickets chirped and night birds twittered. The smell of woodsmoke and roasting rabbit mixed with the scents of the evergreen forest blanketing the surrounding hills. She drew a deep breath, pulling her cloak close against the night's chill. In the west, clouds bundled on the horizon— thick, black thunderheads. Flashes of lightning flickered across the massed cloud bank like bolts of magic.

A fist of foreboding closed around Reisil's heart. Time was running out. And how she was going to protect Mysane Kosk *and* save Kodu Riik from its destructive magic, she couldn't begin to guess.

~But we'll not do it alone, will we? Kebonsat, Metyein, Juhrnus—they're coming to help us.

She touched her fingers to her lips, still feeling Yohuac's kiss. She smiled, somehow her heart lightened. With a sigh, she swung down the path, her step springy.

Tapit wasn't dead.

Reisil drove her sweat-drenched gelding across the scree. She felt a sickening lurch as the rocky slope began to roll away. Ahead, Yohuac's horse—formerly Tapit's—bounded onto the firm slope and disappeared into the trees.

Indigo twisted and stumbled, his haunches sliding as he scrabbled on the tumbling rocks. He neighed: a fearful, braying sound. Reisil leaned forward, catching at the rolling scree with a net of magic. She gasped at the pain, the magic flowing through her like a river of broken glass. It wasn't as bad as it had been after she'd freed Yohuac and Baku and destroyed the wizards' stronghold. Then she couldn't even *think* of her magic, must less use it. Her lips pulled into a triumphant grin as the rocks firmed into a stony carpet. Indigo lunged to safety with a groan. Reisil reined him in and swung around.

Tapit appeared from behind an outcropping. He wore gray robes, as he had when he'd taken Saljane hostage. Reisil tensed and let the magical net unravel. The freed rocks thundered down the escarpment between them. In the same heartbeat, Reisil reached out to Saljane.

~*Where are you?*

The image of a glittering snow-covered peak whirled across Reisil's mind's eye, followed by a pastiche of blue sky, trees, and Baku's reptilian shape.

~*With Baku. Mysane Kosk is not far.* Saljane paused. *He comes?*

There was an unfamiliar thread of fear stitching through Saljane's mindvoice. Reisil's teeth ground together. It was the only thing Saljane feared: Tapit and his *ilgas* and losing her tie to Reisil.

Reisil glared across the churning stones. The wizard wore his hood down around his shoulders. His features were sharp and austere beneath his bristle of dark hair. She felt his dour gaze on her like a coal-hot brand. What did she read there? Hate? Greed? Revenge?

Her hands tightened on her reins. Indigo snorted and took a step back.

~*He's here.*

Saljane clutched at Reisil's mind with iron talons.

~*Watch well*, she urged, her voice sounding thin as a frayed wire.

~*I will, beloved.*

Reisil held her magic ready. She couldn't let him drop an *ilgas* on her. If he did, she would be helpless, like meat on a golden platter. Infinitely worse, she'd lose her tie to Saljane. The prospect was unbearable. Never again would she let Tapit separate her from Saljane. Her fist knotted. How much she would love to drive it down his throat! But she didn't dare. Not now. Too much was at stake and she couldn't afford to lose it.

She eyed the scree. It wouldn't hold him long. Tapit was relentless. He'd driven the fugitives from their river valley haven a week ago, and it seemed he never needed to rest. But his horse was as tired as Indigo, and it appeared the wizard had outstripped his companions. He was alone now. That might give Reisil the advantage she needed.

"Don't stop running now. I was looking forward to a better fight than this," Tapit called through the dusty haze left behind by the slide.

"You haven't caught me yet. And don't forget I destroyed your stronghold," Reisil retorted.

"The stronghold still stands, with only a handful of us lost. But you shall see for yourself soon. The others are eager for your return."

His words sent a tremor through Reisil. The stronghold still stood? It wasn't possible. She'd seen . . .

She'd seen the valley cave in when she'd driven a spear of pure power deep into the mountain's core. She'd seen rubble falling over the small group of defenders as the ground leaped and buckled. She'd assumed the stronghold had been crushed. But then again, she'd thought she'd killed Tapit, too. Fear slithered like a snake in her gut. What if he was telling the truth?

"You mistake me for a moon-eyed child," she called back, refusing to let him see her doubt. "I am not foolish enough to believe you."

"But foolish enough to run away from us, and taking such prizes with you."

"Again you mistake me. It was the wisest thing I've ever done. Second only to becoming *ahalad-kaaslane*."

Saljane's fierce trill of pleasure rippled through Reisil.

"Your pet. Yes, that was a mistake. To be one of us, you must be rid of it."

"To be one of you?" Reisil repeated incredulously. "How can you still think I would be? I killed a hundred of you at Vorshtar. I destroyed your stronghold."

"You *tried* to destroy the stronghold," Tapit corrected. "But your actions only affirm what you are. A true wizard. Soon you will know that."

Reisil shook her head. "You're mad."

"We shall see soon enough."

Anger flamed in Reisil and power crackled around her fingers. She caught herself. She wondered how far Yohuac had managed to get. The longer she drew this out, the safer he was. "How do you think you'll catch me? I know about the *ilgas*. I won't walk into that trap again."

Tapit smiled. It was the first time Reisil could ever remember seeing such an expression cross his basalt features. Fear screwed through the marrow of her bones.

"Not *that* trap, no."

Reisil recoiled, then a small smile stretched her lips. Tapit had revealed his weakness. He loved the hunt, the struggle. *Don't stop running now. . . .* He wanted her to sweat, to fear, to fight against him. He relished it. And that meant he wasn't going to even try to use his power against her in a head-on battle. That wasn't sporting. He wanted to match wits, to finesse her, to play at strategy and tactics. And she was happy to oblige. It gained time until she could squash him like a mosquito.

And she'd begin right now.

~Baku?

The coal-drake's awareness bubbled in her mind. His presence was muted, as if he had to push through a dense, fibrous mist to reach her. The effects of the magic leeching from Mysane Kosk. It was the reason he hadn't been able to speak with their friends who camped near the destroyed city. He couldn't tell Juhrnus they were coming, or ask for help. But it also meant that Tapit would have a harder time tracking them. He sniffed out their magic footprint somehow, and soon it would be smothered by the tide of magic rolling out of Mysane Kosk.

~I have an idea, but I need your help. Can you do it? she asked Baku, picturing for him what she wanted him to do.

The coal-drake did not respond immediately. Reisil got the impression he was considering whether he *wanted* to help her. She held her breath. He had every right to resent her. If only she had learned faster; if only she could have saved him from the wizards sooner. But she hadn't known what to do and instead she'd been forced to watch silently as Kvepi Debess tortured Baku, slowly draining his power. Sometimes she had even helped. It was the only way to discover the key to unlocking Kevepi Debess's spells. It wasn't until later that she could tell Baku, and by then their delicate trust was ruined.

~Can you do it? she repeated gently.

~It will be difficult. The magic thickens here . . . I will try. ~Hurry.

Reisil waited, staring not at Tapit, but his leggy roan mare. The animal tossed her head, her ears twitching. Then suddenly she leaped into the air, twisting and bucking. Tapit gave a startled yell and fell onto the scree. The hillside began to roll again. The mare came down and exploded into a gallop, disappearing over the ridge in seconds. Reisil smiled, watching Tapit, who was rolling down the slope like a bundle of rags.

~She won't soon trust him again, came Baku's smug voice.

~Well done, Reisil said, clicking to Indigo and turning the dun gelding into the trees after Yohuac. The trick had worked better than she hoped. Tapit was too distracted with failing to bespell the mare to stop. By the time he did, he'd have a good walk to retrieve her, and then he'd have to catch her. Reisil doubted the mare would come willingly. It gave them a little breathing room.

"A very little," Reisil murmured.

Yohuac was waiting just inside the trees. He smiled crookedly at her scowl. His scalp gleamed white through the stubble of his hair. Scars showed livid on his head and neck. There were plenty more hidden by his clothing.

"You shouldn't have waited."

"He means to have you," he said darkly, his smile fading.

"Tapit means to have all of us. We'd better get going before he catches his horse."

Reisil took the lead, angling down a steep ravine and following it up across a ridge. Clouds thickened above and as evening approached, a heavy, solid rain began to fall. She looked back at Yohuac. He had begun to list to the right, his hands clamped around the pommel, his shoulders bowed. He couldn't go on much longer. Reisil scanned the wood slope, angling up along the ridge. They would have to stop and rest, and hope Tapit didn't overtake them in the night.

As darkness fell, the two found a traveler's pine and took shelter under its sweeping boughs, staking the horses out in a nearby clearing.

Reisil dug a hole and built a tiny fire. She set a pot over it and made a hearty soup of roots and dried meat, crumbling into it stale acorn cakes. "I can't wait to eat some real bread," Reisil said to Yohuac, who sat shivering beneath both their blankets. "And hot kohv. With nussa spice."

"The bread I would like. But you may keep your kohv," he said, accepting the cup of soup and wrapping both his hands around it.

"That's right. You like that other stuff—what do you call it?"

"Xochil. It has . . . character."

"Mmm. I don't much care if my kohv has character."

"Your kohv is like—it's like the sun without heat, with fire. Xochil lights fire to the soul."

"Sounds unsettling."

"Someday you will try it and see."

Reisil finished eating and scooted over next to him, curling close against his side. He put an arm around her shoulders and snuggled the blankets around her. Soon their shared warmth permeated them both. Yohuac's hands began to slide over her. Reisil caught them.

"You're too tired. This week of running has undone much of your healing."

Yohuac's dark eyes were like polished onyx. "I am well enough for this." He bent and kissed her. Reisil kissed him back. She pushed aside his clothing, grappling him close against her, his heart beating rapidly beneath her fingers. There was an urgency to their lovemaking. They hadn't lain together since Tapit had sent them fleeing; neither knew when they would have the chance again.

Time was running out.

Reisil nestled against Yohuac's side, their legs tangled together. His chest rose and fell in a slow rhythm. She stared up at the branches overhead. Time was running out, and she still had no solution to Mysane Kosk. She hadn't even thought about it since escaping the wizards.

She sighed and sat up, tucking the blankets around Yohuac and pulling her clothes on. She crawled out from under the drooping branches of the great pine, needing to be out under the sky. The rain had settled into a soft drizzle. Mist wound through the trees. The pungent scent of pine, spruce and cedar filled her nose as she drew a cleansing breath. She closed her eyes, listening to the patter of the rain on the trees, the rush of the wind through the treetops, and the trickle of water across the ground.

She wondered if Tapit had caught his mare yet, and if he'd chosen to take shelter. Was he already pursuing them again? Her stomach tightened and she scanned the woods around her. Nothing. She turned and climbed up the slope to the top of the ridge. There was nothing to see. The mist filled the hollows and valleys in softly glowing gauze. Gray hid the stars. She sat down on a boulder, unmindful of the rain soaking her clothes.

What good is thinking about it if I can't figure out what to do? she thought to herself, and then flushed. *So do nothing? That's the stupidest thing you've ever come up with. You know better. Ignoring it won't make it go away. Things will only get worse. That's one of the first rules of healing.*

She rubbed her aching forehead and thought of her predicament. *The biggest problem is Mysane Kosk. Its magic is still fueling the plague and killing Yohuac's land. The* nokulas *inside used to be people and animals and so I can't kill them, even though they are killing the rest of the people I'm supposed to protect. The wizards want to draw power from it, as no doubt do the Scallacian sorcerers, which hurts the* nokulas. *The Regent Aare wants to start a war with Patverseme again and he hates the* ahalad-kaaslane, *and they all hate me. I somehow have to stop the plague without killing the* nokulas *or destroying Mysane Kosk, or else the world will be unmade. Plus I have to figure out how to fix Yohuac's world—oh, and also stop the war.* She sighed. "And do it all without the help of the *ahalad-kaaslane,* who will probably be fighting against me."

"Sounds easy enough. When do we start?"

Reisil jumped, magic sparking from her fingers. She glared at Yohuac, who had stepped out of the mist to perch beside her. "Scaring me to death isn't going to help." She frowned. "You shouldn't be out in the rain. You need rest. Why aren't you asleep?"

He reached out and gently curled a long, damp tendril of her hair around his fingers. Reisil leaned into his touch. "You need rest as well. And I do not sleep well apart from you."

"I don't think I'm going to sleep well for a long time to come," Reisil said. She stood. "Come on. You need to get dry."

Under the traveler's pine, she rekindled the fire and made more soup. While it cooked, she and Yohuac stripped and dressed in dry clothing from their packs. This time Reisil sat opposite Yohuac to avoid temptation. She wrapped her arms around her legs, fixing her gaze on him.

Her heart ached at the weariness that made his shoulders droop and dulled the fire in his eyes. Worse were the scars that marked him from head to foot. She hardened herself.

Throughout the five weeks since their escape from the wizards, she'd been content to drift from moment to moment, speaking little, thinking even less. It had been a time of healing, a chance to rebuild their strength. But Tapit's arrival had shattered their idyll and it was time to get back to work.

"Tell me about your magic. What you can do."

Yohuac's head jerked up, his expression shuttering. The soup bubbled and sizzled as drops spattered into the fire. Reisil rescued the pot and served them both. When each had scraped the bottom of the bowl, Reisil turned her attention back to Yohuac. He sat up straight, crossing his legs and lacing his fingers together. His mouth was pinched and his eyes looked haunted.

"Understand that I was never supposed to use my magic. I was meant to be a vessel—to win the *pahtia* and become *Ilhuicatl*'s son-in-the-flesh. In the year of celebration that would follow, every woman in Cemanahuatl would come to my bed. On each I would get a child. Even barren women. In this way, the nahuallis thought to revive the magic in the blood of our people."

"You were to be their stud?" Reisil asked, smiling.

He shook his head. "Not *were*. I *am* to be their stud." He flushed, avoiding her disbelieving gaze. "For many hundreds of years, magic has been dwindling amongst the nahuallis. There have been fewer and fewer of them, and each generation commands less power. It's been a slow, gradual diminishing. The nahuallis could find no cause and no way to stop the decline or rejuvenate their power. They feared what would happen to our people when we no longer had magic to guide and guard us."

"So they decided to breed power into a man and cross their fingers that he win the *pahtia* and impregnate the entire female population," Reisil said sardonically. "Your nahuallis are gamblers."

"It is highly unlikely we'll succeed. More so now that I am here and the *pahtia* will begin in less than a year. I have been severely drained by my stay with the wizards, while my competitors continue to develop their skills and strength. Still it is our only hope, and—" He broke off, his cheeks blushing hotter. "The need to renew the magic of Cemanahuatl has only become greater with the terrible destruction caused by your Mysane Kosk," he added finally.

"You're telling me you use your magic to gain an advantage in the *pahtia*," Reisil said, understanding clicking like a key in a lock. "That's why you're willing to use it, even though it's forbidden."

"That is so. I . . . cheat."

Reisil snorted. "Hardly."

Yohuac looked askance, his eyes widening. "How can you say that? No other man can claim magical powers. I have an unfair advantage."

"Over some, maybe. You said yourself, you aren't the only man bred to have magic. But even if there weren't others, what difference does it make? Would you hesitate to use your advantage if it was bigger muscles or greater intelligence or sharper weapons? No, you're using what the gods gave you—sure, the nahuallis helped, but they can't do anything the gods don't really want them to, now can they?" Reisil thought of the wizards and the way they tortured their prisoners. What gods wanted them to do that?

For a fleeting moment she remembered that day in Veneston, the first time she'd seen plague victims. Sodur had lectured her about the old gods. All were vicious, bloodthirsty monsters, full of rage. When the Demonlord had restricted the wizards's magic, had they turned elsewhere? To a less fastidious god? She shuddered. Of course they had. She thrust away the thought.

"And even if it is cheating, you'd have to do it anyway. Because this isn't a game anymore to decide who is going to rule for a few decades. This is the survival of your land, of mine. And if it takes cheating, lying, stealing and murder, that's what you—what we—have to do."

Yohuac stared at her, poleaxed. His throat worked and his mouth opened, but he made no sounds.

Reisil waved her hand dismissively. "All right. Leave that aside for now. So in a nutshell, only women are permitted to use magic, but no women are allowed to compete in the *pahtia*, so no woman could become *Ilhuicatl*'s son-in-the-flesh. And besides, a woman couldn't very well impregnate the rest of the female population. They needed a man with magic. You, or someone like you. But why in the Lady's name risk it all to send you here?"

"If I do not return, then they have given their greatest possession, the fruit of years of planning and sacrifice. The Teotl will know what they have given up and will smile favorably on them." He paused, his brow creasing. "I have long been the strongest competitor. But it is possible another with magic will succeed in my place Especially if he . . . cheats." He brightened, startling Reisil. "I hope so, for if I cannot return, or if I am in no shape to compete—it would be well to believe the nahuallis had good options.

"The silver lining," Reisil drawled. "This is all interesting to know, but it doesn't answer the question—what can you do?"

Yohuac stared into the fire a long moment and then sighed unhappily. He lifted his hand and held it out over the ground, palm down. After a moment, bits of dirt rose in the air and began to rotate slowly. Their speed increased and more dirt rose. Soon a small tornado whirled beneath Yohuac's hand. Reisil could feel the pull of the funnel. The fire flamed higher and then guttered as the spinning dirt pulled the air into itself. Reisil felt the pressure on her lungs and began to breathe in short, sharp gasps. Dark spots clouded her vision as pine needles, grit and pebbles stung her face and hands.

"Yohuac, stop!" she cried.

He looked up at her, his eyes shocked and fearful. Blood trickled down his cheeks and forehead where he'd been struck by flying debris. He *couldn't* stop. *By the Lady, he couldn't stop!*

Reisil rolled up onto her knees, hearing her heart pounding in her ears. Her throat was raw and her nose was choked with dirt. She reached for her magic. It filled her raw channels in a flood of pain. She ignored it, feeling the ground beneath her knees beginning to undulate as the great pine that housed them began to uproot itself.

She loosed her magic. It surrounded Yohuac and the maelstrom, wrapping them in a ball like silk and white diamonds. She could have just siphoned off his renegade magic; it was the first skill Kvepi Debess had taught her. But to do so would devastate Yohuac, if not kill him altogether.

Reisil bore down carefully, pushing his magic back inside him. She felt his panic as he grappled for control. His magic was stronger than she expected. *He is what he was bred to be,* she reminded herself. *The seed of the nahualli magic. Of course he's powerful. And they didn't bother training him. Idiots. Being this close to Mysane Kosk doesn't help either.*

Yohuac strained against his power. Reisil felt him hauling it back as she shoved. Debris rained down on the ground as he closed himself off from his magic. Yohuac keeled over on his side, panting. Reisil sucked in a deep breath and then another, feeling her spinning head beginning to steady. She crawled over to Yohuac, wrapping the blanket around his clammy length.

"So you can move the earth. I thought that was just in bed," she said hoarsely.

He grinned weakly and coughed, then slid his arms around her. "You should see what I can do with wind."

"Well it's something to work with anyway. The two of us against the *nokulas,* the wizards and the sorcerers. Should be interesting. Seems we both have a knack for destruction."

"Don't forget the nahualli—Nurema. And your friends. They are very resourceful."

"They'll have to be. They're going to stop the Regent's army."

Reisil clambered to her feet, banking the fire. "I'll keep first watch."

"Don't forget to wake me. You need to rest as much as I." Yohuac waited until she sighed and nodded before closing his eyes. Reisil donned her cloak and crawled out from under the tree. She took up a position a short distance away beneath a narrow ledge.

The mist grew thicker, even as the rain pelted harder. Soon it was difficult to see more than a few yards. Nor could she hear anything but the rushing wind and the rattling water.

Her eyes grew heavy and she knuckled them, watching the mist slide in and out of the trees. She stiffened and blinked the rain from her lashes as a shape shivered into being before her.

Its eyes were silver and curved like a bowl and face was

heavy-boned with jutting jaws and dagger teeth. Its body was muscular, fluid and sleek—like a lion. Its fingers moved like tentacles and were tipped with thick, tearing claws. Its feet were bony and long, with talons that curved like scythes and bit gouges in the dirt. A long tail twitched slowly back and forth behind it.

Reisil stared up at it in horror, too stunned even to reach for her magic.

Nothing remained of the man he'd been. His expression was alien, his body monstrous. Still she recognized him.

"Sodur," she whispered past the hard lump lodged in her throat. "By the Lady, it's you."